GRASS WIDOW

by

NANCI LITTLE

BELLA
BOOKS
2010

Bella Books, Inc.
P.O. Box 10543
Tallahassee, FL 32302

Printed in the United States of America on acid-free paper
Originally published by Madwoman Press 1996
First Bella Books Edition 2010

Editor: Diane Benison and Catherine S. Stamps
Cover Designer: Judy Fellows

ISBN 13: 978-1-59493-189-5

Acknowledgments

To my parents,who raised me not as the girl they had or the boy they didn't have, but as a person: a tough, tenacious human being, able to do what needs doing.

And to Nana, for reading *The Grapes of Wrath* to me when I was nine years old and giving me the fever for the words.

Thanks also to Uncle Bill, for living simply, and for giving me his copy of the *Old Fashioned Recipe Book;* k.d. lang, for two of her songs that were important to me in the writing of this book; and Diane Benison, for checking my homework.

And to the people who have written to tell me what *Thin Fire* meant to them: many, many thanks. You help keep me going.

In Memory
Evelyn Randall Lamoreaux

May 24, 1905 - June 20, 1995

a pioneer woman

About the Author

Nanci Little lives in Aroostook County, Maine with Sawyer, her Miniature Pinscher.

They tried
to persuade me
not to cross
the curious hills:
finally, shrugging
called me foolish, stubborn.
That's how it is,
I said;
I'm going where
my pig is headed.

—*anonymous*

(ergo. probably a woman)

Dramatis Personae

Aidan Blackstone
the Daughter of a Physician from Portland, Maine

Adrian Blackstone
her Father

Mrs. Blackstone
her Mother

Three Rude Soldiers

Captain Argus Slade
an Officer of the United States Cavalry

Two Agreeable Soldiers

A Dusty Man a
Gambler or Gunfighter

Joss Bodett
Aidan's Cousin twice removed, of Washburn Station, Kansas

Ephrenia Richland
a Merchant

Hank Richland
a Son of Ephrenia and Thom

R.J. Pickett
a Physician

Ottis Clark Junior
a local Lad

Jack Bull
a Saloon-keeper

Ottis Clark Senior
a Farmer

Marcus Jackson
a Farmer and Farrier

**Gideon Jackson, Ezekiel Clark, Will Grant, Daniel
Washburn, Nathaniel Day, and their Younger Brothers**

Flora Washburn
a Founder of the Village

The Ghost of Ethan Bodett

Jacob Hart
a Lumberman

Levi
an indigent Man of Colour

Captain Malin Leonard
an Officer of the United States Cavalry

Earlene Jackson
Wife of Marcus

Three Guards
Jesus

A Pawnee Warrior

An Infant

April, 1876

Two are better than one; because they have a good reward for their labour.

For if they fall, the one will lift up *her* fellow: but woe to *her* that is alone when *she* falleth; for *she* hath not another to help *her* up.

Again, if two lie together, then they have heat: but how can one be warm alone?

And if one prevail against *her*, two shall withstand him, and a threefold cord is not quickly broken.

Ecclesiastes 4:9-12

CHAPTER ONE

There had still been gray and dirty snow in Portland when the train puffed from the station on the second day of April, but as it rumbled south and west the dreary end of winter and fresh burst of spring blurred by its windows; the landscape freshened through buds and lilacs and at last their fading, and Aidan Blackstone mourned that this spring she would not know the brief fragrance of those fragile blossoms. More sweetness than lilacs would be missed in this spring; more pleasures than her mother's garden would be lost to the clear New England summer that would pass in her absence, for the coming year was to be given to Kansas, and as the train sped across alien countrysides, she argued with tears and lost to them often.

A week ago her tears had softened her mother into almost-acquiescence, but there was no breaking the Christian will of Dr. Adrian Blackstone. "You know the condition by which I'd allow you to stay," he said flatly. "You made your bed, daughter."

"But Kansas!" she wailed. "Papa, it isn't civilized, there are savages—"

He slapped her with careless irritation, as if she were a fly buzzing at his ear. "There is Fort Leavenworth," he growled from the sideboard where he kept his liquors; her mother looked at her in grave pity, and didn't offer her hand. "Cousin Jocelyn has a husband and sons—cousins distant enough to you to be marriageable, might I add. You'll be well enough protected. Now pack your cases! I'll hear no more of your mewling."

And now it was Missouri the train chuffed across, the great Mississippi River behind her; the bruise the back of his hand had left was coming green on her cheekbone. In her last visit to her grandmother, the frail old gentlewoman had pressed a daguerreotype into her hand; she studied it now, trying to sense the hearts beating behind silvery images.

There was a thick-shouldered, heavy-chested man with a droopy gray mustache, an indelible good humor lurking behind a severity assumed for the camera; his mouth was stern, but his eyes were kind. Leaning into his right side was a willowy girl of perhaps fourteen years, a black braid draped over the shoulder of a faded dress, her dark eyes expressively wary of the photographer. She would be a lovely young woman by now, Aidan supposed, the one with whom she would share a room—if she wasn't long wed and gone, with babies of her own; the photograph was ten years old.

Jocelyn Blackstone Bodett, obviously once beautiful, now as wearily faded as her daughter's Sunday dress, stood at her husband's left side, her arms corralling her sons: the younger fair and handsome face glinted with the inherent mischief of six-year-old boys, but the older of the lads, dark-haired as his elder sister, seemed to share her suspicion of the itinerant photographer and his contraption, or perhaps he resented having been coerced into a collar and tie on a day not Sunday; whatever it was, something unhappy simmered in his eyes.

She slipped the photograph from its frame and read the delicately-drawn ink on the back of the plate.

2

Jocelyn (Blackstone) Bodett & husband Harmon with children
Jocelyn (14), Ethan (11), & Seth (7),
August 1866

Ethan, then, was the unhappy one. She studied him, trying to add ten years to his darkly handsome face. "Ethan," she murmured. "Will you let me know you?"

She looked again at her father's cousin.

For all Grandmother spoke lovingly of her, Aidan had heard little at home of her elder Cousin Jocelyn. In the rare times when her father mentioned his uncle's daughter, his voice dripped with distaste. "Why a woman of her fine looks and breeding," he always said, ever an unfinished hint of insult; recalling it now, Aidan smiled acidly. *The same could be said of me, if we threw open the closets to dance with the skeletons. Fine looks and breeding—*

Aidan Blackstone wished she had been born poor and grown up homely. Perhaps then she wouldn't have won this exile in disgrace, an exile now speeding her ever farther from Portland.

"There is Fort Leavenworth." So her father had said, and so there was. The rutted street looked as if it had recently been a quagmire. Boardwalks in front of false-fronted buildings teemed with hard-looking soldiers and coarse-looking women; shouts and curses and laughter rang in the air. Tumbleweeds and dust blew willy-nilly in the gusting wind, and horses danced at hitching-rails, shaking their manes and rolling their great soft eyes.

Her stomach took a queasy lurch as the porter handed her from the train. Three soldiers, smelling strongly of drink and long days in hard heat, crowded around her: Buy you some dinner? "No, I—" Need help acrost the street, dearie? "Thank you, no, I—" Buy you a drink, li'l lady? "Most certainly not! If you might but kindly direct me to—"

She almost screamed when a hand closed around her arm. "Be off, you ill-bred cretins! There's no decency in the lot of you!"

Muttering darkly over their shoulders, the soldiers obeyed,

and Aidan dared look up to find pale blue eyes and a flowing white mustache under the gold-braided hat of a United States Cavalry officer. "Captain Argus Slade, madam, humbly your servant in this disgrace that presumes to call itself a village." With the sharpness of command removed from it, his voice was smoothly sonorous, and his face, while weather-beaten, seemed much younger than his silver hair and mustache would suggest. "May I assist you in the comfortable termination of your journey, or perhaps in its expedient continuation?"

Gratefully, she gave herself to his assistance. She identified her trunk and traveling case, and he ordered a chevron-sleeved soldier to guard them; the fellow gave her a brilliant smile. The captain escorted her to the Wells Fargo office, and rousted a soldier from a bench that she might have a seat while he inquired of the station-master. Her wait would be brief, he assured her, checking his watch; might he wait with her, if for no better reason than to ward off the riffraff?

She murmured her agreement, for the riffraff still loitered about the station, eyeing her and the captain and grinning at one another.

"A long train ride's best moment seems always to be its end," he smiled; she managed a smile in return. The bench he had secured for her seemed almost to sway. "Odd how the sensation of motion continues when the fact of it has long ended." He smoothed his mustache. His hands seemed too big for his body, graceful despite their size. "I've heard sailors speak of it as well. Sea legs, in the vulgar—begging your pardon, ma'am."

She was too weary to manage a blush. "How far is it to Washburn Station, Captain?"

"Two hours by stage, on a road rougher than the one to the devil's back door." He drew a slim silver flask from his boot, unscrewing the cap to pour it full and offer it. "Perhaps a taste of this would ease you. This must seem so heathen to a woman of your refinement—it's not whiskey," he assured her, when she eyed the cup. "Very old, and very French—a fine libation, if not a proper vessel in which to serve it."

4

He made her think of the men who gathered in her father's study to talk of politics in low, intense voices on nights when the fog lay heavy in the streets of Portland. "I've interest in the Station myself," he said, "it being under the protection of my troop—and there's a fine farm there that's caught my eye, only recently and tragically come available. Please, have just a taste of this. It will calm you, ma'am."

Not without misgivings, she accepted the cap to his flask. "So you shan't be a soldier all your life?"

His smile was fleeting, tolerant. "Most men are soldiers all their lives only by the circumstance of misfortune, my dear."

"Yes...yes, I suppose you're right." Embarrassed, she dared a sip of his brandy. It was warm from his leg, as good as anything her father served, or better; she tasted again and let her eyes convey her thanks.

In his returned smile she realized that the gentleness of that smile was only on his lips; his pale blue eyes considered her the way a man considers a horse he thinks he might buy. She shied her glance away, and regretted accepting his drink. "Thank you," she murmured, returning his tiny silver cup. He looked into it and knocked back what was left.

He tucked the flask back into his boot and straightened up, cocking his head to the north. "The stage is coming." He hailed a soldier to help the guardian of her cases with their loading to the roof of the coach when it was time. "Will you be long in Kansas, Miss...? Teaching school, perhaps? Lord knows a ration of civilized education would behoove the youth of Washburn Station."

She heard his hinted request for her name. "I'm sure I don't know how long I might stay, Captain Slade. The climate seems, so far, to be most disagreeable."

"It'll seem farther that way if you're still here in July." Her omission of introduction hadn't escaped him; the near-curtness of his reply made her glad of the stage as it rattled down the street.

His soldiers made room on the roof for her cases and secured them there, and the captain handed her into the coach. "Enjoy your stay in Kansas, my dear lady." His smile might have made him very handsome, had it strayed to his eyes. "Mayhap we'll meet again."

"Perhaps. I thank you for your gracious assistance, Captain."

"I am ever your servant."

The man already in the stage was unshaven, unwashed, unscrupulous looking; he wore a thin mustache and a gold watch chain and enormous pistols in scuffed leather holsters, and she knew he must be a gunfighter (for since the subject of Kansas had first arisen she had read every dime novel of Western theme she could find, no matter how forbidden they were by her mother, and they had told her that gunfighters wore two pistols, and cowboys only one). She settled to the seat across from him with a look that suggested if he said a word more than hello she'd burst into tears or screams.

He returned a polite smile and touched the brim of his dusty brown hat. "Lady," he said, more compliment than greeting, and tipped his hat over his eyes and crossed his arms over his vest and slouched in his seat to sleep through the trip.

Rougher than the road to the devil's back door, Captain Slade had said of the track; by the time the stage made Washburn Station, Aidan was sure he had woefully understated its condition. She had all she could do to stay on the seat—and marvel at the dusty man, who snored through the ordeal. He roused enough to hand her from the stage, blearily ensuring that the driver and his shotgun rider unloaded her cases; he tipped his road-weary hat and slammed the door and the coach departed in a whirlwind of dust, leaving her alone on the platform of a village so small it defied the idea of township as she knew it.

"A year . . . ?" It slipped aloud from her as she looked down the hardpan track that was Washburn Station's only street. "There must be lifetimes I could spend that would seem shorter!"

Besides the coach station (which doubled as the telegraph

station), there was Richland's General Mercantile, the Red Dog Saloon, Mrs. Schrum's Eatery, and an unnamed tonsorial on one side; across was the Station House Hotel, the Bull and Whistle Saloon, a financial institution as creatively-named as the barber shop (BANK, said its window), and Jackson Bros. Livery and Forge. At the end of the street was a small, squat church with an afterthought of a steeple. Two wagons stood in front of the store; outside the saloons, saddled horses twitched their tails at flies. A whip-slim young cowboy—at least, she surmised by hat and spurs and single pistol that he was a cowboy—emerged from the livery to approach the station at a determined clip, dust clouds puffing from his boot heels with each step. His two-step jump to the platform barely broke his fluid, feline stride.

"Aidan Blackstone?" His fingertips touched the brim of his hat, not quite a tip but manners enough to be called such. "Like you could be anyone else."

He was clean-shaven, handsome in that smooth, fine-featured way of certain lean, long-legged, black-haired men, but his dark eyes held no welcome, and brusqueness negated the silken tenor of his voice. *The unhappy one? Is this Ethan, then?*

"See you got here in one piece. Stage ran early just 'cause I ran late, I suppose." His look flickered to the bruise on her cheekbone; his eyes narrowed. "Yuh. Come on to the store with me. I got some things to pick up, an' we'll bring the wagon back for your cases. None'll bother 'em here."

She drew herself up, managing composure where none had existed. "You have the advantage over me, sir."

Something—it couldn't possibly have been called a smile—twitched at a corner of the cowboy's mouth. "I reckon I do, Miss Cousin. I'm Joss Bodett."

Joss—Jocelyn?? She choked it back before she choked it aloud. *This is Jocelyn—? But—but—*Her mind seemed to stall there, babbling buts at her. A cryptic smile flickered to Joss Bodett's lips, there and gone. Aidan recovered her voice. "I've so looked forward to meeting you, Cousin—is it Joss? Forgive me, I...I didn't expect...I didn't expect it to be so lovely here!"

7

"I'll wager somethin' else surprised your expectations. The last damned thing I'd name this place is lovely."

Aidan flushed, shying her eyes away. That voice had been as hard as a Portland winter, and Joss had sworn easily, as if she were the man she'd looked to be in dusty Levi's, a faded cotton shirt and work-worn boots, her hair hidden by a sweat-stained hat pulled low over unwelcoming dark eyes—and most incredibly, the gunbelt around her narrow hips, its holster tied by a thong to her thigh, the grips of the pistol glossy from the wear of years of rough hands. "Let's get these chores done," said the extraordinary Joss Bodett. "I've things to say to you—an' ask of you—that want for more privacy than this here." And she turned and headed down the boardwalk, not looking back to see if her cousin followed.

I want to go home! Aidan's mind screamed, but her feet hurried after her long-legged cousin as scuffed boots rang down the boardwalk from the station to the store. She focused on the pistol; the gun was as terrifying as the idea of being trapped in this hot, lifeless place in the company of such a cold, flinty woman, but it was tangible; she could compare it to something known. Her father kept a derringer in a desk drawer in his study, but it seemed a toy compared to the dark tool worn as close to Joss Bodett's lithe body as blankets to a bed, as frivolous as a debutante compared to the hard-worked being pausing at the door of the store so she might catch up. She didn't want to catch up with this bizarre cousin. She wanted a room with a door to slam, a featherbed to catch her, a soft pillow where she could bury her face. She wanted to cry.

"Y'all right?" Joss held open the door.

A glimmer of warmth might have softened her; she felt no warmth from her cousin. She felt only impatience, and it spiked something coldly resistant into her. "Quite so, thank you," she snapped, and swept into the store, careful of the hem of her skirts against the fresh proximity to horses odoriferously suggested by Joss Bodett's boots; the noise Joss made sounded suspiciously like a stablehand's term for the very smell of those boots.

"Joss Bodett!" The woman behind the counter was plump and sharp-eyed; she spoke to Joss, but she probed at Aidan with her glance. Aidan looked away, disliking her as reflexively as she'd disliked everyone she'd met so far in Kansas—*except a gunfighter on a stagecoach? Oh, I hate this place! I hate it!*

"Hain't seen you t'see how you been holdin' up," the storekeeper said. "Hard times f 'you, girl; awful hard times. How come y'ain't been to town?"

"I been too joe-fired busy diggin' graves to be sociable."

Graves? Cautiously, Aidan looked up from her perusal of a slim selection of buttons.

"An' we so sorry, Joss. Thom wants talkin' at you. Let me go get—"

"I know what Thom wants an' the answer's no."

"Joss, you got to think reason now! Things ain't like they was, you—"

Joss barked a laugh. "Like I need you to tell me that! Save your breath, Effie, an' let Thom save his—an' save me a trip to Leavenworth an' tell me you got seed, 'cause I know you do. Ours mouldered in that dank spell back March."

"You ain't thinkin' of plantin'! Joss, you got no men left! You cain't—"

"The horses didn't die an' the plow didn't rust, an' I didn't disremember how to pull a straight furrow. Can't eat dirt come winter."

"Cain't stay there come winter neither." Effie's voice bordered on cold. "Takes men to run a place, an' ain't none chasin' you lately that I seen."

What a cruel, hateful woman! Amazed by the meanness, Aidan forgot her own resentment. *But what does she mean, no men left? What's—*

"You hear my heart breakin' over that? I plow like I do 'cause Seth's crippled an' Ethan, God rest'm, never turned a lick an' someone had to, like you never knew that, Effie Richland. God rest Pa too, but him gone means I ain't got to fill his hollow leg with whiskey nor do his work, like you never knew that neither.

Doc looks after me, an' 'sides"—she jerked her head at the handsomely-dressed, if road-weary, young woman by the notions counter— "I got help now. 'S my cousin there."

"Not much, y'ain't," Effie muttered. Blackstone women were all built puny as far as she could tell, and this new one took puny to extremes. Jocelyn had been right scrawny and passed it on to her daughter; even if Joss had got some height from her pa, she still wasn't but a shadow and a half. This new Blackstone female was oh-too delicate for western words: high-cheekboned handsome—pretty was too strong of a word (one of those high cheekbones sported a mouse, she noted)—rich by the cut of her clothes, pampered by the look of her hands...

And pregnant. She wondered if Joss knew that, or if that secret had died two weeks ago with her mother.

For Jocelyn Bodett was dead, her husband and sons with her, along with ten others of Washburn Station. Some called it the grippe; Doc called it infernooza or whatever he'd said, but it was a pure plague right out of Revelations to Ephrenia Richland, and she knew her true faith in the Lord Jesus was all that had spared her family. The Bodetts had been godless free-staters and were nigh gone, only Joss left—and why Joss (disgraceful anyway, let alone the display she made, swearing like a hayslayer and dressing like one, too, in Ethan's clothes and Harmon's gunbelt) had been spared was past Effie.

"'Sides, where'd I go? East? East be sendin' theirs here." Aidan almost flinched from the derision in her cousin's voice. "I need that seed—twenty acres o' each—an' sugar an' salt, an' soda, an' a box o' .44/40s." Joss turned to bury a sneeze in a gloved hand, and sniffed and wiped her nose on the back of her glove. "Damn dust!"

Effie's look, and the one Joss returned, made Aidan wonder what question and answer crackled between these women whom she didn't know (past knowing neither of them cared a whit for her existence on the face of the earth). They liked each other as little as they cared for her; that much was blatantly evident.

10

"I ain't askin' for credit," Joss said. "I ain't ever goin' to be that far up to the hubs."

Effie gathered the small parts of her order, and Joss rang a double-eagle to the counter to square the bill. Effie tendered her change at long distance. "Hank'll load you."

As Effie turned to fetch her strong-backed son, Joss sneezed again. "Bless you," Effie muttered. Every soul dead in the Station in the last weeks had started their dying with a sneeze, and if ever a soul needed blessing it was Joss Bodett—and that fair-haired, blue-eyed (pregnant) cousin of hers, looking for all the world like no one had yet broke the news to her that all her Kansas kin save Joss Bodett had been buried in the past two weeks.

"Fool girl's sneezin' an' wants seed," Effie snorted. "Load her, but stand fair away from her. She won't last out the week."

Hank Richland studied the speculation in his mother's eyes. "How you so sure you'll get that place? Lots others want it."

"That piece o' Yankee work out there'll take the money an' run, an' who save Flora Washburn can overbid us? Flora don't want it."

"Neither do I, an' I ain't goin' to oversee no tenant farmer you suck in on a promise o' credit here paid for by sweat there an' blood interest. Th' whole idea's wrongful. It ain't but slavery by some other name."

"I heared enough free-stater talk out'n you, boy," Effie snapped.

Hank turned. 'The War's done an' over. An' now you take her money for seed, hopin' she'll live long enough to plant so you can harvest the crop? That's a right good Christian ethic, Ma."

"You watch that mouth. I'll wear you out, boy."

He bucked a sack of bean seed onto one shoulder and took another under his arm. "Ma, you wore me out a long time ago."

"Everyone? But—" Aidan sat stunned on the seat of a wagon lightly loaded with her cases and the day's purchases as her cousin handled the reins to a pair of enormous bay horses. They were barely away from town, and Effie Richland had been rankly

11

damned: "That miserable old sow can't shut up long enough for her brain to cast a vote, let alone run the show. I work a week to figure how to say all this to you, an' then I'm stupid as she is mean to think she wouldn't flap that God-damned mouth o' hers an' takin' you in there to hear it so cold! So how else to say it now? I'm all the kin you got left here, Cousin."

"But they—but—how—" Aidan drew an unsteady breath. "How, Cousin Joss?"

"Doc said influenza; I called it the grippe. Whatever you want to name it, it came on quick an' took 'em. In a week it was over, four gone." She adjusted her hat against the lowering sun. "An' they're buried." The words sounded like the airless whump of a Baptist preacher's Bible being closed in damning finality. "But I ain't, an' I got a farm to tend to. You can stay if you care to, long as you want, or go home. If it please you to lend a hand, I could surely use one."

Aidan didn't—couldn't—reply. She wondered how the deaths of four people she had never met could drive such a breathless ache into her. She wondered how this impenetrable woman could be so coldly stoic in the wake of such a bitter loss. She wondered how love and warmth could reside in such a heart—

Joss glanced at her. She averted her face, not wanting that last thought to show in her eyes.

The hand that touched hers was surprisingly gentle. "Don't think I don't miss them," Joss said quietly. "I don't mean to sound hard, or cruel. It's just ... sometimes a hurt's too big to get too close to it. I wish it was different, but it ain't, an' you need to know the truth of it. All I got to offer you is a fair bed under a tight roof an' a long season o' hard work. The whole county'll call me a fool for tryin' to keep it up, an' it's my choosin' to be so stubborn as to try, but you needn't be tarred with the same brush."

"You assume the luxury of choice is mine."

Joss's glance touched the bruise under her eye; Aidan flushed and looked away. "Your daddy's the Blackstone, ain't he," Joss murmured. "An' prob'ly not a dime in your pocket. I got enough money to get you home an' you're welc—"

"I have enough money!" She turned from her cousin, hating her. "They won't have me there! And you don't want me here—"

"Don't think that. I'd've wired you not to come had I not wanted you to."

Of course you did; you need a cook and washer-woman. "Then I'll try to be of help," she said stiffly. "I'm able to learn whether you think so or not."

"I didn't figure you for stupid." Joss's voice was low. "An' I surely didn't mean to hurt your feelin's. I'm a right smart o' sorry if I have."

Miserably, she knew that her cousin had only spoken the truth, and she had lashed back in return. But offense was easier than apology; it was too long before she could think of an appeasing word. When finally she turned, the hardness was back in Joss Bodett's eyes, her lips thinned in the tailing end of a look sliding coldly away. The apology died in Aidan's throat. "God bless you," she whispered when Joss sneezed, but there was no more conversation; Joss clucked the horses up to a trot that took them home.

"This is it." Joss jumped lightly from the buckboard, leaving her full-skirted cousin unsure of how to dismount the unfamiliar wagon without assistance. Aidan heard her sigh as she spilled a lean gray cat from her arms to the ground and came back. "Hold your skirts—put your foot here. I've got you. Just step off." Strong hands closed around Aidan's waist; it seemed the only effort needed for Joss to bear her to the ground was one of diminishing patience. Aidan stepped away from her with a curt thanks, and regretted the curtness when a flicker of bewilderment showed in dark, hat-shaded eyes, but the tone of Joss's "Y'welcome" made the apology that leaped to her heart retreat unsaid; her throat felt full of the corpses of unspoken regrets.

Joss refused her tentative offer of help in unloading her trunk from the wagon, working up a sweat as she swore it into the kitchen. "That's my room." Joss aimed her chin at a close door. "Savin' events we'd've shared, but events came to pa

Have either other one now; no mind to me." She rattled open the stove and raked down the ashes, coaxing coals to life with sticks of fatwood, adding hardwood, checking the kettle and tank. "Got warm water here if you want a wash whilst I tend the horses, or you can wait on hot an' a bath. We've got a real bathtub." Aidan knew by the way she said it that bathtubs were an oddity or a luxury in this spare, strange place. "Necessary out the side door, if an' when."

Aidan watched the weary set of her elder cousin's shoulders as she led the horses away. "Oh, Joss," she whispered. "I'm sorry, but how could I have expected you? How could I have expected any of this?"

Woman and beasts passed into the darkness of the barn, leaving no answers in the dusty gray yard.

She turned to inspect the house in unobserved dismay. From the outside it had looked to be a bastard mix of a log cabin and a board shack; the log part was the half she stood in now. She had grown up with wallpaper, cabinetry, pegged oak; dirt floors hadn't occurred to her, but here was dirt under her feet, its commonest traffic evident in the patterns worn smoothly into it, its hard surface scarred by her trunk. Where she would have expected cabinets with countertops were benches skirted with faded gingham; shelves were braced on walls where cupboards might have hung. Near the central stove was a rustic table with six chairs. In a far corner, a clawfoot bathtub nosed past the edge of a folding privacy screen. The space beyond the stove could have made a dining room and parlor as well; a paucity of chairs save at the table suggested that sitting had been done there, had sitting after supper been done at all.

She let her eyes roam the perimeters of the room. Far past its rusticity, something bothered her, and finally, looking at a mantel shelf with a clock and a Bible and a few photographs, it occurred to her: but for the Bible, there were no books. "Dear Lord," she murmured. "What rank poverty have I fallen into?"

Dust motes danced in the afternoon sun slanting through unchinked gaps between logs; brittle beams of light trailed

slenderly onto the dark dirt floor.

She traced a finger along the edge of a china cabinet that had once been a fine piece of furniture. Now it was as chipped and worn as the hard-used dishes it held. Almost unconsciously, she noted things in it: a porcelain soup tureen, a few cups and saucers that matched—all with nicks taken from their edges—and tucked into a corner, a book. She opened the glass-paneled door.

Baptist Hymnal.

Softly, she sighed. "Baptists, no less." She slipped the book back to its place.

Reluctantly, she opened the doors of the rooms her cousin had offered. The rooms were Spartan, meant but for sleeping and the storage of a few clothes; daylight glittered between each unbattened board. The beds were militarily made up, corners sharply angled, sheets tightly cuffed over quilts. One room had a bedstead wide enough for two; the other, two narrow cots with thin ticks. Peeking into Joss's room, finding the scant tick that had apparently been the lot of the Bodett offspring, she smiled in weary lack of surprise that the lesser mattress hadn't been abandoned. Joss Bodett didn't seem the sort to fall sway to creature comforts.

But it relieved her to see the case by Joss's bed; it bulged with books, its top stacked with volumes the shelves were too full to accept. She would have perused titles, but she didn't know how long Joss would be about the barn, and she had no desire to be caught snooping; her cousin's patience seemed too tightly reined already.

She chose the double bed. It had obviously been Jocelyn and Harmon's, and she felt more kinship with the cousin she had never met than she did with the one she had.

A half-hearted tug to her trunk didn't budge it. She carried its contents by the armful into the room she had chosen, hanging what she could in a shabby armoire, stacking the rest on the bed. She dragged the empty trunk into the room, stashing it in a corner, and reloaded it with what hadn't fit in the cupboard.

She opened the valise she had hand-carried from Portland.

15

Wrapped in the soft folds of a woolen cloak she found the bone china teapot and tin of tea she had intended for Cousin Jocelyn the Elder, and a shaving mug with brush and soap that she would have presented, at the right moment, to Harmon. Seeing them, she battled back tears for what felt like the thousandth time in the last week.

When she could, she lifted another fold of the cloak. "How hard it was to think what to bring you," she murmured, "and for naught! Mayhap you'd have cared for these trinkets" —there was a folding knife with a scrimshaw handle for Seth, a silver watch and chain with an ivory fob for Ethan— "but how will I know?"

Gently, she turned the next fold of her winter wrap, and she sighed in resignation at the Spode teacup and saucer, delicately painted with a winding pattern of violets, that she had chosen for her female cousin. "This will mean nothing to you! My stars, you wear a gun!"

She forced back tears, wiping away the few that had escaped. By the bed was a rude stand with tree-branch legs, its top sawn from the bole of a large tree. Because she had them, she put two framed photographs there: one of her parents, and the one her grandmother had given her. She lingered at the feminine image of the pretty girl who had been Joss Bodett ten years ago. "Where are you?" she whispered. "Whatever became of you, Jocelyn Bodett?"

Cousin Jocelyn the Younger had no answers.

In the kitchen, the kettle billowed steam. Aidan closed down the stove and made tea in the pot that would have been her elder Cousin Jocelyn's. She filled the Spode cup with hot water, and found a lesser cup and saucer in the china cabinet. She opened the icebox to get milk and blinked at its contents: frying pans, a dutch oven, pie plates; the ice tray held wooden spoons and spatulas, and the drip tray had been converted into a knife drawer. Slowly, she closed the door. "No ice? But how..." Wearily, she leaned against the sink—a sink that didn't include the amenity of a pump. "Oh, my. Oh, this is going to be so terribly difficult!"

"Would you care for tea?" she asked when Joss came in; her

16

cousin looked up warily. "I brought it with me," she snapped, to the look. "I troubled you for the water."

Joss hung her hat on a nail by the door; she came to the table undoing her gunbelt, and set it in a black sprawl across the oilclothed surface. Aidan regretted her sharpness, for her cousin's face held a weariness far past a hard day's work as she sat and pulled off her gloves. "You trouble me for nothin'." Joss's voice was softly raspy. "It's been weeks since I tasted tea. I thank you for the bringin' an' the sharin'."

Self-consciously, Aidan saved the hot water from the cups into the tank at the end of the stove and put them on the table; she got the pot from the warming shelf and turned to find Joss with her head on her arms on the table, a study of exhaustion. "Cousin Joss?" Uneasily, she asked. "Do you not feel well?"

A sleeve caught a deep sneeze before Joss dragged herself up. "This dust in my throat! I'm but a bit weary." She offered the nearest thing to a smile Aidan had seen from her. "Like you ain't, crossin' half a continent by train an' met by such news as I had for you—an' it must be days since you've had a decent meal. I'll have my tea an' make up some supper." She wiped a hand across her cheek; Aidan saw the gloss left by the spread of a sheen of sweat. "Be a pleasure to cook for more than one. Lord, tea will taste good."

Too aware of her cousin's dark eyes following her hands, Aidan poured. "Do you take sugar? Milk?"

"No. Thank you. This is—but do you? Pourin' in a kitchen you've never seen; my manners! Please, let me get you a bit of lemon—"

"Oh, no, please! I drink it this way. Mother says I'm simply uncivi—" She bit the rest of it back. Announcing that her mother thought black tea was uncivilized hardly seemed appropriate, given Joss's preference.

"Lemons are rare here," Joss said softly. "A fellow came up from Texas with a sack full. Lit here lookin' for work. Rebel soldier, you know. Had a thin horse an' a poke o' lemons. Pa worked him an' we drank lemonade. His name—I think—we's

17

free-staters all right enough, but a hungry man's a hungry man. He done good work—ate good an' shared that fruit. Johnson? Ma could tell you. Some son. Jameson? Cousin, you've gave me your cup. No cup o' ours got such violets on it, nor no nick to watch your lip on. God love Ma, she lets us drink off 'em anyways, what of 'em we've left her. Lord, but that's a pretty cup. All fine an' thin—never saw one so thin, like ice on the trough in November. Fritz cut his lip once on ice like that. Ma, you see this cup?"

It came on quick and took them. She laid a palm against her cousin's forehead, her stomach queasing at the heat there. "You've just a touch of fever." She forced calmness to her voice. "Better an ounce of prevention; let's get you into bed. I'll bring your tea there."

Joss struggled to stand, clinging to the table for balance; it struck Aidan with precarious clarity that this extraordinary, impenetrable cousin wasn't either of those things; she was just a girl, hollowed by loss, vulnerable in sickness, needing someone's help—

"There's a spot o' loose dirt under my bed." Joss's voice was hoarse; her balance threatened desertion. Aidan reached to steady her, feeling her fever even through her shirt. "A tin—money—buried there." A hard shiver sucked the strength from her legs. "If I—if you're my kin," she whispered. "By the Kansas Constitution, this goes to you as it came to me. Let no man tell you different. Sell it—go home, Aidan. They can't turn you away. Tell Doc—" Her hands sought Aidan's shoulders; her face had gone dead pale. "He'll sell—tell him—the horses—"

Aidan caught her as she crumpled. "Cousin, I'm sorry," Joss whispered with the last of her consciousness. "Doc can—Doc—"

CHAPTER TWO

R.J. Pickett drew up his mare, frowning at the Bodett homestead. Something had been nagging at him since he'd first crested the hill to see the sad, gray house tucked into a stand of sad, gray elms. Since that first sight he had been wondering about his old friend Joss, hardest hit in the Station by the influenza. Effie'd said she'd bought seed anyway, paid cash for it—like she'd give credit to the last Bodett and Joss at that, she had sniffed; Seth, maybe, but—

Doc Pickett's lip curled. On her best days, Effie Richland could invest him with the dyspepsia. He leaned on the saddle horn, gazing narrow-eyed at the farm. Smoke meandered from the chimney. Chickens scratched in the yard. The wind drifted the voice of an unhappy milk cow to him...

The cow. She wasn't unhappy; she was in full-uddered agony. Doc touched a heel to his mare's side. What had bothered him wasn't the cow, but that Joss had bought seed and her fields were untouched late the next day; he knew her better than that. No Eastern cousin could have kept her from the serious business of planting this late in the spring; no cousin could long have filled the void she seemed able to satisfy only by driving herself at the farm with a fury unreleased in any other way. He dismounted, tossing a rein over the porch rail. "Joss! Joss, it's Doc! You here?"

He pushed open the door to a kitchen muggy with steam, pungent with the scent of eucalyptus; four pots and the teakettle on the stove boiled clouds into the air. "What the hell—?" He went cautiously in, his eyes probing the dimness of the kitchen. "Josie?"

He found them in the room the Bodett boys had shared, Joss fighting for the labored breaths he had heard too often in this house in the last weeks, a golden-haired young woman collapsed in exhaustion on the other bed. He gave her a cursory glance before he touched the backs of his fingers to Joss's face.

The fever was hard and dry. Wearily, he turned the damp cloth on her forehead and turned away. He knew he could do more for the suffering cow than he could for her.

With his face against the cow's warm flank, unashamed, he cried; he loved Joss Bodett with the fierce protectiveness men usually reserve for daughters and little sisters, and watching her die would be the hardest vigil he had drawn since the influenza had struck a month ago. Not for the first time in the past sixteen years, he wondered bitterly why God had chosen him to do His healing work.

He dumped grain into the trough for the pigs and slopped most of the milk over it, lingering to watch their greedy appreciation; he whistled the horses in from the pasture to rub their big soft noses and treat them to a scoop of oats apiece, and scattered grain for the chickens, and took the pail with its scant gallon of milk and trudged through the glare of afternoon sun to the porch to push open the kitchen door.

A gasp and a crash of crockery met him, and the frantic hiss of liquid sizzling a steaming dance across the surface of the cookstove (tea; he could smell it even through the eucalyptus),

20

and his eyes adjusted to the darkness to show him the blonde girl looking at him like a deer on the verge of panicked flight, tea still hissing and spitting on the stove behind her. "Please," she whispered. "Enough ill has happened here. Whoever you are, if you've a shred of human decency, go away and let me let her die in peace."

Cautiously—for she was young and supple and Joss's gunbelt on the table was much closer to her than to him, and he was forty and his left leg as much wood as flesh—he set the pail on the floor beside him. "I mean no harm, Miss. I'm a friend of the Bodetts—just Joss, now—and a doctor." He took off his hat, holding it in both hands. "You're Joss's cousin from Maine? Miss Blackstone?"

"She spoke of Doc." She was wary, admitting nothing; she was quite lovely, he thought, and still mostly terrified. "She said no name."

"Doctors have no name to our townsfolk. We're just Doc." And something in her eased, as if in some comprehension he didn't understand, but it gave him leave to go on. "When did she take sick? I know she was in town yesterday."

"Yesterday afternoon, before dark." She glanced at the stove and bit her lip, as if the teapot shattered across its surface had meant much more to her than someone else's china. "I'm terribly afraid for her," she said softly.

He ventured a step into the room. "I don't mean to question you," he said gently, "but all of this steam—"

"My father is a physician" —a faint smile twitched to her, there and gone— "Doc to his townsfolk. His specialty is ailments of respiration. Have you heard of hydrotherapy? It has enjoyed some success in cases of pneumonia and bronchial influenza. I knew nothing else to do to try to save her." She sank to a chair at the table, resting her head in her hands for a moment before she looked up. "But I've forgotten my manners," she said wearily. "Please sit down, Doctor. I fear I can't offer you tea."

"I'm terribly sorry I frightened you. I'll replace the teapot at soonest."

"You mustn't even think to. My clumsiness isn't your obligation."

"It is when I caused it, and no matter. Please tell me about your hydrotherapy. I've heard of it, of course, but not for this."

"Autopsy of such patients shows that their lungs are stagnated with blood, and so congested with mucus that—in effect—they drown. The steam is lighter than the mucus, and helps separate it when inhaled so all may be expectorated. Thrice daily, woolen pads are boiled, wrapped in a dry cloth, and applied to a chest protected by a towel. When the fomentation cools, the chest is wiped with a cold cloth, and another pad applied, until three applications, which creates reflexive increase of circulation, relieving stagnation. Oil of eucalyptus stimulates expectoration of bodily poisons—clove will work as well—and I beg of you, Doctor, don't approach her with leeches."

"I'm no Philadelphia doctor." He saw the dry flicker of her smile before he applied himself to thinking through what she had said. It was so simple he wondered why he hadn't thought of it himself—but, he supposed, discoveries sat under all noses, patiently awaiting the one that might sniff them out. "Damn! Begging your pardon, Miss, but this town has buried fourteen we might have saved, all loved and lost for want of naught but more modern medicine. It makes sense, your hydrotherapy."

"Save the fifteenth." Her voice was gentle, her utter weariness showing. "My Cousin Joss means more to me than you could possibly imagine."

He could imagine. Effie had said the girl was with child, and Effie had a gossip's vicious eye for such things; it was a common enough reason for Eastern girls making sudden visits to distant kinfolk in the west. *And her father a physician? Why not a simple abortion and be done with it? If needs be and she allows, I'll send her home relieved of this burden.* She hadn't even had time for a proper toilette, he knew: her clothes had been but lightly brushed, her hair hastily re-pinned; she wore that pinched, contained look of gritty efficiency women got about their mouths when their lives went to hell all at once.

"As she does to me, Miss, so help me more. What of food? Liquids?"

"All you can force, but only when the patient is lucid; there's danger of choking. Good fat chicken stock, spiced with oregano and sage, garlic if you have it, onion if not. The steam and spices help break up fluid in the lungs, and the fat gives strength if the patient can't accept meat. Food is fuel; fever burns it. If the stove goes out, you've lost your patient."

"But you've no chicken on to stock."

He meant no offense, but her response held a privileged chill: "I've experience in neither catching nor killing chickens, sir."

"I've plenty of experience in both. Do please allow me to deplete the Bodett brood."

And they both had the same uneasy thought as he went out the door: his dearth of knowledge had already grievously depleted the Bodett brood. He wondered how much of her father's expertise she would be able to recall without a specific example before her to jog her memory—and if this jog of her memory would be enough to save Joss Bodett.

The smell of frying chicken brought Aidan awake. She sat up in the chair by the bed, scrubbing her hands over her face and hair; how good a bath would feel! A steaming tub of water, the soothing scent of lilac soap...

Joss's face was hot and dry. She rinsed a cloth in the pail by the bed and smoothed it across her cousin's skin, pushing her hair back from her forehead. Joss moaned under her touch, shivering with the fever. "The horses," she rasped. "They have to take you in. Ma, don't they have to? Ma? Wouldn't they—?"

"Yes, Joss," Aidan said softly. "They would. They have to. Rest, now. Rest."

"Would you care for tea, Dr. Pickett?" He had waked her from her doze by Joss's bed, and when she was awake enough to teach him he watched while she applied steaming fomentations to her cousin; he held Joss while she coughed, racking the fever from her lungs; he held her while she fought weak protest of her helplessness, soothing her while Aidan, nearly unknown to Joss and more accepted for that anonymity, did baser nursing things involving nightclothes and bed linens. Now Joss slept; Doc washed his hands, and Aidan, as good a nurse as any he had known in all his years of medicine, offered him tea, for she had found Jocelyn's battered old pot in the china closet.

"Tea would be glorious. I've not tasted it for a week." He hung his towel on the wire over the stove and limped to the table. When he was weary—and he was, desperately—his stump ached and itched, and the leg he had left at Manassas ached and itched with it. "Thom and Effie Richland see tea-drinkers as free-staters; they won't stock it. That leaves Leavenworth, and the post road isn't one in which Stationers take pleasure, as you may imagine from your recent experience."

"I daresay calling it a road is giving it a bit of a compliment. Please, Doctor, sit down." She lifted the lid of the teapot, checking the progress of the brew. "Might you tell the ice man to put this household on his route? I'm afraid I don't know how to keep food without an icebox."

He sat, stretching his wooden leg under the table out of the way. "Our ice man met an untimely end a few years back, and none has taken up the job. Others miss him more than the Bodetts, I imagine; they have a spring that serves as well as an icebox, if not as conveniently. I'll show you where it is." He accepted the tea she offered, adding sugar as he wondered how to make his suggestion; it felt strange to be hesitant in this house he had known so well for so long. "May I keep the night watch, Miss Blackstone? It seems sleep might ease some edges from your life."

She looked at him across the rim of her cup; it seemed to him that the mistrust in her eyes was more instinctive than immediate. "I lost more than a leg in Virginia," he said quietly. "You're most lovely, but I couldn't harm you if I cared to." The lie served him well in the Station, where his devout lack of interest in women would have been noticed and cruelly commented upon without its protection; he took his urges to the waterfronts of Kansas City, where a one-legged man could be anonymous in his search for physical companionship. "Not to mention that mistreating a guest in Joss's home would betray our friendship. She'd not take such betrayal lightly, and her temper has a lighter trigger than her daddy's Peacemaker." *And no threat; she's likely dead by morning. Oh, Josie—*

Reluctantly, she returned his strained smile. "I'll admit I'd feel her better cared for if you stayed. When it comes down to the night, sir, you are the physician."

"And a better one today for having met you. Now my prescription for you, my dear, is a long hot bath. Make your preparations, and I'll make your tub. Heaven knows there's no dearth of hot water."

"Miss Blackstone?"

Drowsily, Aidan stirred. Her dream was undefinable: essences of warmth and closeness, of suspension, of precious nurture…

"Miss Blackstone."

But a man's voice didn't belong where the world was warm and wet and safe, even a voice as gentle as the one penetrating that womb of semiconsciousness, and when a hand touched her shoulder she started awake to the realization of her nakedness in a cooling tub of water and the apologetic, mustached smile of the handsome (and harmless) Doc Pickett. "I didn't mean to frighten you, but you mustn't take the risk of a chill."

She struggled to sit up, trying to cover herself with her hands; he turned his back. "Joss? Is she—"

"She's breathing well enough." He offered a flannel towel behind him. "You must feel better. Ofttimes a bath is as close to God's heaven as we'll know on this earth."

"This one was." Acutely aware of him—and feeling as much safety in his presence as she had felt in the dream—she wrapped herself in the towel. "I don't think I've ever wanted one so badly." She slipped into a silk nightdress and matching wrapper. "Is there any change?"

He glanced back to see her dressed, and sent her a half-guilty, half-worried smile. "Have I been hasty with the fomentation? They seem to improve her so, I applied them again."

"The danger is over-stimulation of the blood. What behooves the lungs may be of detriment to the heart. If—" She hesitated. Her father was a talker when it came to his calling; she had heard progressions of research that included things later proven erroneous. Now, she had to separate the wheat of memory from the chaff. "If the lungs labor too soon after fomentation for reapplication," she said slowly, "hot water may be offered to the feet, or a cloth with pungent oils to the face. Dr. Pickett, I'm playing with fire—"

"I trust you," he said simply, and made her trust herself. "Seth was dead by now—poor Seth never stood a chance—and this far into it I knew we'd lose Harmon. Ethan fought to the end—" Wearily, he sat. "I thought he'd pull it out," he whispered. "'I'll beat this son of a snake, Doc,' he said, so surely I had naught but to believe he could, and then he—" tight-lipped, he shook his head. "Forgive me. You're too young for all of—"

"Do you think God cares how old I am? He simply thrusts life upon you."

His laugh was strangled: it was the laugh of a brand-new doctor turned onto the fields of war without even the grace of a cause in which he could believe, so torn had his home state of Kansas been in that conflict. "He does that, Miss Blackstone; yes. God does do that."

She made tea, and lifted the lid of a Dutch oven he had set back on the stove to simmer; he had fried the legs and breasts of the chicken and put the rest to stock with onion and spices. "Have you tasted your soup?"

"I've not had the stomach."

She knew by the look of him how much he loved Joss Bodett. "Her last lucid word was for you," she said gently. "Can she take some of this, do you think?"

He pushed at a bowl on the table. "She wouldn't for me."

"Have your tea," she murmured. "I'll try." She ladled a cupful

26

into a new bowl. "What did her mother call her, Doctor?"

He knew what she meant: the sweet names mothers use when their love beats strongest out of fear. "I—" He himself called her Josie, but was the only one who did; he had treated the ills of this house for ten years, and displays of affection had been rare, but at the end, when Jocelyn had known she would die, her fever delirium calmed for that last hour... 'My best son,' she had whispered, her only daughter at her side. 'My most precious son.' It had startled him, and mortified Joss; now, he looked away, reaching to scratch at the knee over his wooden leg. "She called her Joss," he murmured, and felt the examination of forget-me-not blue eyes before Aidan turned.

He heard the murmur of her voice, and watched as she cooled the fever with a wet cloth, her hands gentle as a mother's; she coaxed half the broth into her cousin, and eased her back to the pillows and smoothed the covers before emerging with that look around her mouth, that mask of women's gritty stoicism. "Go to bed," he said roughly, and she leveled a look at him and took her cooling tea to her room and gently, she closed the door.

"The horses," Joss muttered. "They have to take you in."

"There, there, Josie," he said, helpless at her side. "There, there."

By the time the cow was milked in the morning Aidan thought she knew how, and she waved to Doc as he rode reluctantly up the hill to see to a neighbor-woman on the verge of birth. He had promised to be back for the night if he could, but by night...

She fled to the house to sit with Joss.

She held a cloth dosed with oil of clove to her cousin's face until Joss turned in weak protest from the pungency. She boiled pads until they were too hot to handle and wrapped them in scraps of blanket, and put them to Joss's chest until she gasped and coughed under the heat; when she coughed, Aidan held her up to spit out the poison.

She read aloud from books she had brought: Cervantes, Dickens, the Brownings. She forced her to sip at broth or milk. She covered her when she shivered, and cooled her when the sweats of fever broke on her; she changed nightshirts and bedclothes, when that was necessary, with a nurse's grim efficiency, and that laundry fluttered on the clothesline in the ever-present wind.

When it was time she milked the cow, resting her forehead on that warm, patient flank, her hands aching; the lean gray cat watched her intently, but she didn't know to aim a squirt of milk at him, and gave him some in an old tin saucer instead. She fed the pigs and chickens, keeping an ear open for Doc.

A young boy arrived on a horse. "I'm Ott Clark Junior. We's next up the road t'ard town. Doc's birthin' me a brother an' sent me to aks after Joss."

"She's alive," she said quietly, and the lad flapped off, all knees and elbows on a horse too big.

There was a brief, neat fence under a weeping willow between two fallow fields. She went to it, and read what was carved on the planted boards:

Harmon, Jr. Jan 21 - Feb 27, 1854.
Joshua B. Oct 16, 1857.
Hannah M. Nov 24 - Dec 2, 1858.
Ruth S. Sept 24, 1863 - Aug 16, 1864.
Abraham L. July 4, 1864.
Harmon William Bodett. Sept 27, 1815 - March 20, 1876.
Jocelyn Ruth (Blackstone). May 12, 1833 - March 21, 1876.
Seth Aaron. June 15, 1860 - March 23, 1876.
Ethan Allen. Feb 28, 1855 - March 25, 1876.

She sank to her knees and wept, and prayed for those she had never known, or known of, and she prayed for Joss Bodett, living daily with that fence and the memories it might surround but could never contain.

She gathered eggs, hard-boiled half a dozen, and ate two; she coaxed Joss to swallow warm, slippery pieces of one. "Go home," Joss rasped. "Get away from me."

"Shhh," she soothed. "We'll worry about that later."

She dozed.

She slept.

She awoke to the feel of a hand on her shoulder, not knowing where she was or who might be touching her, and found herself half in the chair, half on the bed, her head cradled on Joss's hot belly and Doc's hand gentle against her. She let him lead her to her bed, not questioning how long it might have been since he had slept, and when sometime later he spoke to her she sat bolt upright in the dark, dread spiking into her. "Doc, no. Don't say she—?"

"Asking for you." The lamp lit his smile of weary triumph. "The fever's broke. God bless you, my nurse; one Bodett's going to make it."

She raced barefoot across the dirt floor. "Joss—!"

"Aidan." Her voice was just a breath, her hand barely strong enough to feel its squeeze. "I'm sorry I was so hard with you." She shivered, as if in residue from the fever. "Knew I was sick," she whispered. "I didn't want you carin' about me at all, if all I was fixin' to do was die on you."

"Shhh," Aidan soothed. "You need to rest, Joss."

"You took good care o' me. More'n I did them. Wish you'd been here." Her eyes closed. "One thing left in this life to do an' I figured I'd die 'fore I could get at it. I was...I was—afraid—" She drew a soft, deep breath. "For you...maybe of you. I don't know what, but how fear feels."

She sat on the edge of the bed, smoothing the damp hair back from Joss's face. "I know that, too," she said quietly. "How fear feels." Joss looked a cautious question at her; Aidan traced the backs of her fingers across her cheek. "Of you. For you. Of here. Of. . . nothing." Joss closed her eyes, and Aidan knew how closely she had understood that. "We had a hard beginning," she said softly, "but I know we'll be friends."

Weak fingers tightened around hers. "You might stay?"

"Of course I'll stay." She leaned to press her cheek to her cousin's face, to brush her lips across mercifully cool skin. "As long as you want me to."

"I hesitate to intimate that Joss Bodett can't accomplish anything she's set on," Doc said on the porch, inhaling the musky fragrances of his tea and the sweet, damp morning. "I've seen her have varying degrees of success, but I've never seen her fail. But a farm's a blamed hard row for two men with a woman in the kitchen. I know Joss; she'll go where her pig is headed, but if you try to keep up with her—" He shook his head. "In the time I've known her she's done the work of two men because it was required of her. Her brother Ethan was—may I say, less than reliable? Seth fell from the haymow when he was eight; he broke his left hip, and contracted pneumonia in his convalescence. He made a fair enough recovery to allow him to get around with a crutch, but he had no stamina. Joss took up the slack. So did her mother, and my dear, she probably expects you to pick up where Jocelyn left off, not understanding that such a load of work would kill most women."

"And of course I'm but a poor little rich girl, raised with servants to attend my every need," Aidan said dryly, "ergo not only not half the woman my elder cousin Jocelyn was, but barely a quarter. Don't bury me yet, Doctor. I may surprise you."

"I meant no such implication. I know you're strong, for I've seen it. I meant but to imply how much work you're liable for if you stay, and how likely it is to be for naught."

"I'm as short of options as she is, Dr. Pickett." Doc waited when she hesitated, sure she would tell him now of her condition, but she only shook her head, looking at the split-rail fence and the markers under the willow tree. "But I think I might stay were the world open before me. I've never met a soul so critically lonely as is my cousin Joss."

Doc's eyes followed hers to the little cemetery. "Critically lonely." It was a soft echo. He finished his tea in a swallow and stood, cautious of his balance on his wooden leg. "I'll help with the hardest labor when and where I'm able," he said, looking down at her, "but I doubt that a year of my help could ever equal a day of yours."

CHAPTER THREE

"Why, Doc, what's this?" Aidan asked the next Monday, when the broad-shouldered fellow appeared in time to join them for breakfast, for he handed her a paperboard box and held her chair that she might sit to open it. "But I can't, I've ham on—"

"I'll worry about the ham." He didn't worry about it much; he slid the skillet to a cooler place on the stove and sat. "It's a thought you told me not to think that I couldn't help thinking when I saw it. Open it."

Carefully, she lifted the cover. "Oh, Doc!" Tears stung her eyes as she took the china teapot from its nest of excelsior. It was delicately curvaceous, with a scalloped neck and handsomely finialed lid, painted with violets and winding leaves, almost a match to the cup she had given Joss. "Doc, it's lovely! But you shouldn't have—"

"I swept up the shards of our disaster a week ago, to know

the quality lost to my thoughtless intrusion. This was the least I could do. And Miss Josie—" He offered a tin of tea and grinned at the way her eyes lit up when she saw the label. "This vile brew you favor, direct from China via Kansas City. Did Miss Aidan get you to church yesterday?" He aimed the question more at Aidan than at Joss; Aidan shook her head.

"I'm still feelin' pretty peaked." Joss dug in her front pocket for her folding knife. "Hitchin' up the horses seemed an awful lot of work." She opened the knife to pry the lid from the can so she could smell of it. "I love this tea. Ma says it smells like a ol' anchor rope rottin' on a clam flat. Not knowin' from a clam flat, that's by me."

Aidan raised a dubious eyebrow, reaching for the can. She sniffed and gasped, "Oh, my stars!" and shoved it back at Joss, her fingers pressed to her lips. "She's right! Joss, surely you don't drink that!"

"It don't taste like it smells. It's good."

"I'll never know. Don't you dare brew that horrid leaf in my new pot."

Dolefully, Joss sighed. "Back to strainin' it through my teeth. Ma never lets me use her pot, neither." She lidded the can and set it on the table. "Thank you, Doc. Where's your watch, sir? You leave that with some Cowtown card shark?"

His hand went to the place on his vest where the chain had rested. "That's more story than I can tell in mixed company, but in a nutshell it involved a Baltimore drummer selling toothbrushes—I ended up with a lot of them—and a Mexican who didn't know any English except, 'Señor, you got to eat the worm,' and a game named Red Dog."

"Red Dog! Hell's bells, Doc, even Ethan knew better!"

"He never ate the worm," Doc said ruefully. "I did."

"Don't sound good to me. What about these toothbrushes? You got to show me one o' them. Ma said a hundred strokes on my hair; do I need to do as many on my teeth?"

"My father doesn't believe in them," Aidan supplied. "He says they abrade the gums and cause premature aging."

Doc tried not to let his reaction to the last part of Dr. Blackstone's opinion show. "Well, invested of fifty of them as I am, I tried one. I'd seen them, of course, but they'd never impressed me until" —he stifled a laugh— "until I'd eaten a Mexican worm. It got the taste out of my mouth, anyway. You all right, Aidan?" he asked, for she'd gotten up from the table; she sent him back a reassuring smile and went into her bedroom.

"Sounds like that worm was a powerful feller, impressin' you into buyin' fifty of a thing you'd got along without all this time— an' losin' your watch to boot. Hope it wasn't your daddy's." Joss got up to move the ham back to the hotter part of the stove, turning the pieces with a fork.

He dismissed the watch with a wave of his hand. "I won it in a poker game while I was going to medical school."

"Get any schoolin' losin' it?" Joss asked dryly. "Ethan told me all about them Kay Cee poker parlors."

He could imagine that Ethan had, including the fact that most poker parlors were also whorehouses of one description or another; Joss had never felt like mixed company to Doc, either. "The name of the drink is tequila. The first one tastes like kerosene, but after that it's like drinking silk. After the worm..." He shook his head, which still ached vaguely; there had been a lot of tequila between the first taste and the worm, and he'd had more witnesses than assistance in its disposal. "It's like puking burlap. Stay away from it, Josie. I know you like a taste of the corn now and again."

"I don't expect they'd let me into a poker parlor in Kay Cee or any other place to get a taste o' anythin', 'less I was painted up an' showin' tits I ain't got," she grumbled, but she grumbled quietly, for Aidan had come back to the kitchen.

Aidan offered her hands cupped around something; Doc held out his hands to receive a heavy, ornately-carved silver watch and chain. "I—" Sure of her thought but not of her timing, she shied a glance at Joss, who had come to look. "I brought it for Ethan," she said softly, and saw her cousin's hand close hard around the handle of the fork. "I hope it's all right to give it to you. I hope it's not—I—I—It's Swiss," she stammered. "You need a watch. A doctor needs a watch."

Doc looked at it, and at her; he looked at Joss (she had turned from them, and he knew the raw wound in her heart that was Ethan had just been ripped open anew); he looked at the watch again, and finally found his voice. "I couldn't ask for one with more meaning than one meant for a man who was like a brother to me," he said softly. "Thank you, Aidan."

He examined the scrimshawed ivory fob, and tucked it and the watch into his vest pockets, then took the watch out and opened it; he set it to the clock on the mantel and wound it, and listened to hear it tick and slipped it into its pocket again. "Thank you," he said huskily. "I've never had a watch I felt was mine the way a watch becomes a part of a man by its passing down to him. Now I do, and no worm will ever make it poker stakes." He stood. "I need to check my horse."

Aidan turned, feeling the ache radiating from Joss like heat from the stove. "Joss, have I—"

Joss drove her fork into a piece of ham in the skillet. "He'd've liked it." Her voice was hoarse; she didn't look up. "Ethan. He'd've liked that watch. I'm glad you give it to Doc."

Aidan slipped her fingers down Joss's wrist and took the fork from her. "I'll cook the ham. We need a few more eggs if Doc's staying for breakfast."

She found him sitting on the porch step with his elbows on his knees and his forehead on his wrists, the silver watch clenched in his fist; she laid a hand on his shoulder and felt the quiver of what he was keeping pent. "He'd like you havin' it, Doc," she said roughly. "Wish he'd got to carry it first." He swiped a knuckle under his eyes. "The crazy son of a bitch—no disrespect to your mother, Joss, but Jesus, I miss him!"

Her fingers closed hard around a handful of the fabric of his coat. "Ain't much you can tell me about missin' Ethan. I got to go find some eggs."

Glad to be out of sickrooms and into sweet air, Doc planted

the Bodett fields, good-natured in Joss's jibes about his pegleg making seed holes too far apart; when she got too fresh he tossed clods of soft black dirt at her. She batted them away before they hit her, reflexive as a cat even in the lingering frailty of her recovery. When he rested, Aidan brought him tea chilled in the well.

Ottis Clark, who had the next place toward town on the post road, came to call. He was a ropy-muscled, big-eared man with teeth stained by the wad of tobacco he kept in his cheek; he shot brown streams of juice to the ground with as little thought as Aidan gave to breathing, and his grin made her vaguely uncomfortable. Doc came from the field in time to hear his offer.

"That's a right smart o' neighborly, Ott," Joss said, coaxing something out from under a fingernail with the point of her pocketknife, "but I ain't considered sellin'."

"Y'cain't keep it up." Ott's voice was flat. "Ain't a way in the world."

"There's a will," Joss said curtly. "Means there's a way. Give the missus my best."

Ott looked at Doc; Doc shook his head in silent warning. Dismissed, Mr. Clark grumbled away, and Joss sat glowering at the scarred heel of the boot resting on her knee.

"It was a fair offer, Joss," Doc said quietly. "Allowed for crops in."

She huffed a chilly laugh. "Ever'body but me knows what my claim's worth? Maybe I need to go talk to Mister Carpenter over t'the bank. Get his idea on it."

"You won't hear much different than what Ott said."

"You see everyone in town in a week." She gave him the glare she had been aiming at her boot. "Tell the whole damned lot of 'em the Bodett place ain't for sale!"

"Well," Aidan mused, when Joss had let the kitchen door slam behind her, "if she does sell, she'll have driven the price up."

Doc snorted a humorless laugh. "She'll die before she sells." He went back to his labor, and in a while Joss came grumpily back to her chair.

Aidan requested Doc teach her to plow. She didn't have the

brute strength the job required, but she walked with him, and it was there behind the patient horse Charley that he asked his medical question of her. Joss studied them from her rocker at the edge of the field as Doc rested in the traces. Even from her distance she could see the shiver that took Aidan, and how her arms hugged herself against that internal chill as she stared at the ground and spoke words Joss couldn't hear.

When Doc was fed and gone Joss helped Aidan with the dishes, and they sat at the table to read in the last of the daylight: Aidan a days-old newspaper Doc had brought, Joss *Don Quixote*, but the Spaniard couldn't capture her and at last, quietly, she asked. "Is there something I should know, Aidan?"

Aidan looked up as if the words had reached across the table to slap her, and silence hung long between them before finally, softly, she said, "You've not wondered why I was sent here?"

Joss scratched her lower lip. "I wondered what sort o' folk would send you off to a hard place an' people you didn't know, an' feelin' you had no home to go back to."

"You're not stuck with me forever. Just—" She drew a shaky breath. "Just until the baby's old enough that I may return with a story of a dead husband. No one will believe it, but the glaze of propriety will be spread."

Joss drew the place-ribbon across her page and closed her book; she stared at the cover. Tight-lipped, Aidan waited.

It was long before Joss spoke. "Do you miss him?"

She looked away, unable to answer.

"Aidan..." Her voice was soft and cautious. "Do you—did you—love him?"

"I—" She jerked loose the bow of her apron, and wadded the cloth and flung it to the table. "Why haven't you even a floor in the kitchen? A real floor, with boards, not dirt?" The tears that had been dammed up since Doc's gentle question tried to flood over; she jammed them back and fled for the privacy of her room, slamming the door so hard the iron latch bounced back open. "A floor?" She gave the door a vicious kick, hurting her toe; the

36

latch caught and she threw herself onto the bed. "A *floor?* Have you lost your mind?" She drove her face into her pillow. "A floor! She'll think you're insane!"

A hand touched her shoulder and she recoiled, barely choking back a scream.

"Aidan, I'll make you a floor in the kitchen. I'll make floors all through the house if you want them, but don't turn from—"

"You know perfectly well a floor has nothing to do with it!"

"I know." Again, her hand found Aidan's shoulder; again, Aidan flinched. Joss stood and paced the room a helpless turn. "Aidan, you don't have to go back until—or unless—you want to. I thought we'd long since settled that."

"I don't need your pity! I'll not—"

"The day I pity you I'll *send* you back to God-damned Maine!" The roar of temper drove Aidan cringing into her pillow. "Send you back? To what fresh hell? People who discard you like a book whose endin' they didn't like? I'd treat a stray mutt with the mange better than they've done you!"

Shivering, her breath suspended in her, Aidan waited. She knew that sooner or later a hard hand would come; one always did when such anger powered words. It didn't matter whether the crime and the punishment fit one another; the crime was awakening the rage, and punishment would be served. Such random service was a quirk of Blackstone character, and Joss was of Blackstone blood.

"I wager they call 'emselves good Christians, too," Joss growled. "That sort always does, them an' Effie Richland—always ready to take whatever they think they can steal, right down to your pride an' your dreams. God damn 'em all to hell!"

Just be done with it and get out and let me— "Oh, no—" It was a moan drawn by a hand at her back; she didn't feel the gentleness of the touch. She didn't expect gentleness after such a snarl of words. She only knew Joss Bodett was as strong and hard as tarred rope and could hurt her, and was a Blackstone so probably would. Joss said something, but the roar of blood in her ears blocked all but the buzz of her voice. She didn't know if she would faint before she vomited, or after. She felt the mattress shift under the weight of her cousin and she fought not to cry, or cry out.

"Listen to me?" It was a low almost-plea, and a hesitant touch at her back. "Do you fear I'd strike you? I'm not Blackstone enough. Aidan—" Joss's hand slipped softly across her shoulders. "Please, Aidan. I'd never—"

Curled around her pillow in instinctive protection of her face and her belly, she managed to breathe.

"Oh, Lord—" Joss's forehead rested briefly on her shoulder. "Damn my temper." The warmth and weight of her went away, but not far; she was still there, touching-close. "I meant but to ease the weight of this, if I could. I didn't mean to intrude, or frighten you. I'm so sorry if I've made it worse for you." Her finger drew a few errant strands of hair away from Aidan's mouth, tucking them behind her ear. "How can I leave you alone with such hurt? But it seems I add to it with every word. Should I just leave you be?"

She didn't want Joss there to see her weakness; she didn't want to be alone; wordless wants clashed in her, none of them winning her voice. She heard that soft sigh again, sounding much more like resignation as Joss's hand lifted from her shoulder. "If I can get you anythin'—" That trailed off, as if Joss knew she wouldn't ask. "I'll knock in a little while. I'll just be out at the table."

Aidan heard the clink of the latch as Joss closed the door. She drove her face into her pillow, trying to cry, but the tears wouldn't come. The ache was huge and hollow, an ache of missing the warmth and nearness of the oddly gentle side of Joss, an ache of residual terror of the coarseness of her cousin's anger—and an ache of fear that Joss would send her away now that she knew. "No," she whispered. "Oh, Joss, please, no. No. No—"

The last glow of sunset had almost faded from the window when she heard the soft knock at her door. Dazed by the sodden ache of tears that still refused to be cried, she couldn't find words; still curled around her pillow, she could only wait until the door opened. "Aidan? Can I come in?"

She managed a nod, not knowing if it could be seen in the fading light, and heard the scrape of Joss's boots against the hard dirt floor before the bed creaked under her weight as she sat at the edge of the mattress. "I ain't much good at comfortin'," Joss said at last. "Brothers don't want it, an' the only sisters I had died when all the comfort they knowed about was dry clothes an' a tit when they was hungry. What I asked you was none o' my affair an' I'm sorry for makin' you feel so bad. I ain't here to pester you if you want to be alone, but I know sometimes bein' alone makes the hurtin' worse." She cleared her throat, a nervous, almost shy sound, before Aidan felt a hesitant touch at her shoulder. "Aidan, I know I got the talk an' the ways of a man. I reckon that's 'cause I got raised up with 'em an' like 'em, an' I expect I must be a oddity to you, but it means I learnt about raisin' a hand to a woman, too. I'd ask God to strike me dead before ever I'd hurt you. If you're holdin' away from me for fearin' that—"

"I don't know how not to." The words felt as dully familiar as a week-old toothache. "I don't know how to believe you. I'm sorry."

"How the hell have they treated you, then? Didn't they ever even love you? You still got color from where he hit you last! I can't take the place of your mother, but Lord, girl, I can at least hold you an' let you—"

"Then do it!" She forced the words past a need to cry so immediate her throat ached with it. "Beat me or hold me or something—do something! Do something—"

And even when Joss took her into her arms, she still fought the tears; she had no memory of such gentleness of touch as the hands that held her close to a warm, dusty shoulder to be able to trust it now. "Aidan—oh, little cousin." Joss's voice was a low intensity under her ear. "It's all right, Aidan. Let it go. Let it go. Damn them—damn their hard hearts an' what they've done to you that you can't trust love! I'll love you if you let me, Aidan—or even if you don't. I'll just love you, so you'll always know there's someone who does."

She was warm; she smelled of dust and sunshine, of fresh easy sweat and the nearness of horses, and Aidan remembered the day she had first come here: Joss had jumped lightly from the wagon, and from under the porch had come the lean gray cat to wind around her ankles. Joss had scooped it into her arms to bump heads with it, her hands giving it quick, ear-scratching affection. It had wallowed in her arms, trusting her completely, and Aidan had known that no matter what their differences, this odd and unexpected woman would never hurt her. She had forgotten that, this hard night.

She shuddered a sigh into Joss's shoulder. "Don't send me away," she whispered. "Please let me stay—"

"Let you stay? Good Lord, Aidan, why would you think I wouldn't?"

"My own folk had no use for the shame of me—"

"The shame of *you?* Their own should take them straight to hell!" Again, that flare of temper, a rupture of tolerance that roughened the arms around her and tightened the fingers in her hair; she shrank from it, ducking into herself in self-defense.

"Oh, damn—" It was a shivering breath into her hair. "Aidan, I'm sorry, I've frightened you again—it's just so hard for me to understand them! Who's to love someone right or wrong, if not family? Family's supposed to allow error an' love in spite of it, an' damn those Blackstones—"

"There's a difference between error and sin."

"An' such difference is for the Lord to decide. No one else has right nor power to judge you. What was your sin? Love?"

Do you—did you—love him?

Her voice, when she found it, felt harsh and brittle. "There was no love." And she waited for Joss to retreat, to have finally heard enough.

Joss drew a jittery breath, and seemed about to speak but didn't; she seemed frozen, unable to move or speak or, for a moment, even to breathe again, and Aidan's head went light in the thickness of her cousin's silence, knowing it would only be a moment before Joss put her away from her, disgusted, repulsed—

"Aidan, was it—" Joss swallowed; Aidan felt that, and the hard breath she drew before she asked softly, "Aidan, was it against your will?"

Miserably, she nodded, not daring to think Joss would believe her.

"Oh, no—" Joss's arms tightened around her. "How could they do this to you?"

She held Aidan hard against her, and the ache finally broke; she sobbed like a child in arms giving her the only sympathy she had known for the horror of that January afternoon.

Jared Hayward had invited her skating. She went without a chaperone because he was the banker's son, because she had known him all her life, because she trusted him. He pinned her against a wall in the boathouse, forcing his kiss to her. He choked her when she tried to scream, and wrestled her to the floor. He tore open his buttons, laughing at her terror when she saw what he had, and what he intended. He took no pause with her virginity the first time, and no care with her pain the next.

Five weeks later, her bleeding hadn't come and the morning sickness had. Only then did her father call young Mr. Hayward into his study and demand that he make an honest woman of her. Jared agreed readily; Aidan was a handsome woman, and Dr. Blackstone was a wealthy man.

Aidan refused. Her father bellowed and she refused; he beat her and she refused. More gently, her mother tried to talk sense into her. She put her hands over her ears and turned her back.

And so she was sentenced to Kansas.

At least it had seemed a sentence then. Now, with her cousin holding her, rocking with her, whispering assurances into her hair and sketching consoling kisses against her face, it felt more like salvation.

CHAPTER FOUR

She stiffened awake in the gray before dawn, panicking in the alien warmth of arms around her, breath against her neck, legs entwined with her own, before she remembered: *Don't leave me, I'm so afraid of the dark, please stay with me*—and then she was embarrassed, and confused by her near-nakedness in only a silk chemise. She struggled through hazy memory to recall the solicitude of hands that had undressed her in the wake of torrential tears, the quietness of Joss's voice, the consoling length of her cousin's body against her as Joss held her until, at last, the thick sleep of exhaustion took her.

Shakily, she sighed; she supposed she hadn't expected Joss might stay through the night, but was glad she had. She drowsed back into her cousin's warmth, soothed by the protective spread of Joss's right hand against her belly.

And she blushed; gently, she moved Joss's other hand, for it had been cupping her breast in an unconscious embrace—and then wished she hadn't when her nipple, missing that cradling palm, hardened painfully in the cool morning. Joss muttered a sleeping protest, her hand seeking that fullness again; finding it, she buried her face into the curve of Aidan's shoulder, shivering a deep sigh before her breath went softly even again.

Aidan let her hand stay. Her breast appreciated the warmth, and she could imagine no sin in the touch of a sleeping woman. She listened to the rhythm of their breaths, and finally, the mourning doves cooed her back to sleep.

When next she awoke it was a glorious day, the sky a dazzling blue, sun blaring through the east window. Voices came from the kitchen: Joss's, deeper than most women's, and a sonorous, vaguely-familiar male voice. Sleepily, she imagined Doc's drooping mustache and gentle eyes, and she dozed a little longer, smelling woodsmoke and coffee and finally the eye-opening scent of bacon, a smell she couldn't doze through. She waited for her stomach to tell her if she would be able to eat. It obliged her with a hungry growl. She sat up, stretching hugely, and sank lazily back to the pillows; she hadn't slept so well in weeks. "God love you, Joss Bodett," she murmured. "If I could have a sister, I'd want her to be you."

She got up, finally, to find her ewer filled with hot water, a washcloth and towel folded beside her basin, and she had to blink back tears of warm surprise at the small kindness. She had a leisurely wash, humming some song she didn't remember the words to, and because she felt good she chose her prettiest chemise to replace the plain one she was retiring, and put lilac water behind her ears and inside her wrists, and picked her favorite blue dress from the armoire after she had pinned up her hair. She had been saving the dress for church, but there would be time enough to wash it before Sunday.

She wondered what Joss would wear to church; so far, she had worn only Levi's and her father's old shirts. The very thought of wearing dungarees was alien to Aidan, though she admired their pockets and the small treasures that spilled from

43

them in the evenings: coins and pretty stones and bits of string, Harmon's watch, a folding knife, the whisker of a horse. Even with Joss yet weak from her sickness, Aidan knew their domains were established: hers was the house and yard, Joss's the barn and beyond. She didn't mind; she liked to cook, and didn't object to cleaning—but that floor was a trial; sweeping it didn't ever make her believe it was clean. (And recalling her outburst of the night before, she blushed; why had that, of all things, come in answer to an honest question?) She shrugged off the memory, buttoning her dress, and went to investigate the good smells coming from the kitchen.

"Well, Sleepin' Beauty. Finally decide to try on the day?"

She smiled back at the grin in her cousin's eyes, loving Joss Bodett and Kansas and life in this fresh morning. "Thank you for the water. That was sweet of you, Joss."

"I reckon I owe you some sweetness yet, for the care you took o' me an' no reason to believe I was worth savin'." She stirred the bacon. "You look nice," she offered, shyly gruff. "That's a pretty dress."

Aidan blushed, shy too; she wasn't used to compliments. "Thank you." She stole a bit of bacon from the plate, evading the unmeant swat Joss aimed at her wrist. "Did I hear Doc?"

"It's—damn!" Joss jumped back from a spit of bacon fat, rattling the spider to a cooler place on the stove as boots sounded on the porch. Still expecting Doc, Aidan looked up...and into the pale, faintly-smiling eyes of Captain Argus Slade.

"You have company, Miss Bodett." A lazy smile quirked under his mustache, but his eyes were untouched by whatever humor his mouth had found; they made her feel as she had felt with him a week ago in Leavenworth: like merchandise under consideration. "Please don't allow me to intrude any further."

"When've I ever took back a offer of a meal to a cavalryman?" Her tone suggested that the occasional feeding of soldiers was her civilian duty, but no pleasure. "Cap'n Slade, my cousin Miz Blackstone. Cap'n commands a cavalry troop at Fort Leavenworth. He pays a call now an' again." Her mother would have added

44

that it was always a pleasure; Joss didn't. She had slim use for the Cavalry in general or Captain Argus Slade in the specific, but to be blatantly impolite was to risk a possibility of reprisal she could ill afford.

"Delighted to see you again, Miss Blackstone." He offered a small bow. "Please, don't allow me to interrupt your morning."

"Given your permission, sir, I shan't." She tied on an apron, and on her way to the well and woodshed she muttered that a gentleman might have filled the bucket and brought in an armload of wood in an attempt to earn the breakfast he obviously expected to be fed. She simmered over his presence, knowing that without it she and Joss might have lingered over breakfast and coffee, perhaps talking more calmly of the baby...a pretense of Sunday in the middle of the week.

"—Montana," he was saying, when she returned to the kitchen to bang the wood into the box by the stove; he paused for her noise. She poured a cup of coffee, refilling Joss's and then the Captain's; she could feel his eyes following her, and it made her skin crawl. "Crazy Horse and Sitting Bull are raising Cain in the Black Hills, disdaining the reservation order in the Dakotas." He tilted back in his chair, its legs digging holes in the dirt floor; Aidan raised an eyebrow at them, and at him. He raised an eyebrow back at her and brought the chair to all fours again, his hand going to smooth his mustache; she saw in his eyes the smirk his hand was hiding on his lips and knew as certainly as if his mouth had said the words "white trash" what the Captain thought of the Bodetts—or what remained of them. "But I'm sure the Cavalry will be well able to convince even such brutes as they of the wisdom of honoring their treaty with the U.S. Government."

Joss dropped an egg. "Shit," she said, with a flatness so unlike her usual flare of temper when she swore that Aidan could only suspect that the egg had been dropped purposely, to open the door for some sideways observation. "Now ain't that just a careless mess."

Slade eyed her. "Eggs are a beast to clean up, aren't they, Miss Bodett."

"A body might think to find enough grip on a thing that cleanin' up a mess ain't necessary."

"So true!" Slade's laugh was cold, liquid. "Best never to lose it at all, but a grip lost must be immediately regained, Miss Bodett, or a mess most certainly ensues, as you can see."

Aidan wasn't sure what they were saying, but the last topic of conversation had been Indians; she'd read enough in the newspapers Doc brought to know that in Kansas, opinions about Indians were almost as wildly divided as they had been about slavery. She kept her eyes on her coffee, uneasy with the possibility of veiled politics being spoken. As if trousers and guns and fluent profanity weren't enough, did Joss think to express political opinion as well?

"Mayhap hands too clumsy for eggs ought leave them be," Joss suggested.

"An egg left be becomes a rooster or a hen, begetting ever more eggs. If you break that one under your boot, it'll soak into the dirt and be gone before you can remember it."

Joss moved the front burner plate of the stove and bent to scoop the egg into her palms; she dropped it into the fire. "I've no desire for a stinkin' reminder of my ineptitude."

Land sakes, Joss, he'll have you tarred and feathered if you don't stop! "Tell me, Captain..." Aidan made her smile part forward, part fawning, over the rim of her cup when his eyes came to hers. "Do tell me why you've honored us with your visit. Such a busy man as yourself must surely have motive past home cooking for a call."

She wasn't sure where her biggest trouble loomed: with Joss, her anger sizzling as hot as the bacon on the stove and just as likely to spit and burn, or with Slade, eyeing her as if she were half chocolate, half whipped cream, and all his. He leaned onto his elbows on the table, his voice lowering to exclude Joss. "Had I known this was where I'd find you, Miss Blackstone, I'd have called much sooner. I've spent the time since last we met with the memory of your smile."

She managed to hold her smile. Her stomach was queasing horribly.

"But I had a much less fortunate errand when I departed the garrison this morning." He offered the words like a breath of regret.

"Aware as I am of your cousin's uniquely precarious circumstances, I felt it my duty to warn her that given the possibly prolonged absence of much of the Cavalry, there is the not-unlikely possibility of savages making sorties into the more remote areas of the county. This section of the post road is unquestionably remote."

I've interest in the Station myself...a farm that's caught my eye, only recently and tragically come available, she remembered, and knew with repulsed certainty that he was sitting at that farm's kitchen table. "Then I shall certainly have Miss Bodett teach me to shoot," she said tightly. "It becomes ever more obvious that a woman need be capable of defending herself against the various evils that may descend upon her doorstep when least she expects them."

An unpleasant smile twitched at his mustache as he eyed her; she let her own smile suggest a sudden and offensive odor. "It would be my pleasure to provide that instruction," he said at last. "It's unquestionably a skill you should have and hone."

"How many eggs, an' how d'you want 'em?" Joss thrust the words between the Captain and her cousin. "I know how to do 'em fried." *Or scrambled, poached, boiled hard or soft, shirred or made into an omelet, but you, Slade, get them how I make them or you can go hungry. And you—* She shot a look at Aidan. *You don't know the rules of this game, nor the stakes, so fold your hand, girl.*

"Four fried would be excellent, if you'd flip them once in the fat of the bacon—and mind your biscuits. They smell hot."

Joss potholdered those out of the oven, skittering the tin onto the table. "I ain't so sure Miz Blackstone's feelin' up to lessons today," she said coldly. "Long train ride left her a mite puny." She had suggested Aidan learn to shoot, applying gentle pressure until Aidan reluctantly conceded the wisdom that women in such harsh country should have certain skills, and Joss had looked forward to the lessons. "I'll give her some teachin'."

"I'm sure you're most capable of providing excellent tutelage at your leisure, but I suspect leisure is such a precious commodity for you of late." The mockery of sympathy in his tone made Aidan think of Effie Richland. "And given your precarious circumstances, you may appreciate the Army buying the bullets." Deliberately, he tilted his chair onto its hind legs. "Miss Bodett, surely you're not thinking of wintering here alone? If you are for lack of options, I've an offer that may leave you room for consideration."

Aidan saw the slim, throbbing cord of anger in her cousin's neck; she wondered if Slade had ever considered how it might feel to catch a ten-pound cast iron skillet full of sizzling grease with his face. He was apparently unaware of, or unimpressed by, Joss Bodett's hair-triggered temper. "She isn't alone," she said flatly. "And her options, given the resources of the Blackstones, are wondrously varied; ergo, there's naught to consider. But you may teach me to shoot, Captain. I'm sure I should find it most amusing."

Slade regarded the rigid, angry back of Joss; he slid his look back to Aidan, letting it linger at her breasts. "If you're wintering here, it's past my pleasure." He didn't bother to try to hide the smirk. "It's my duty."

Joss delivered his plate: four flipped, a rasher of precious bacon, a gob of grits. "Go well fed to your duty, then. Have a biscuit."

He had five, with a quarter-pound of butter. His table manners were casually and maddeningly impeccable.

Harmon Bodett had been a drinker, and their dump was liberally scattered with bottles. Slade lined up twelve on the fence and unholstered his Colt. "Mightn't it serve better if I learned to shoot the one I may be required to?" Aidan asked; the captain raised a faintly approving eyebrow and strolled back to the house for Joss's revolver, the rowels of his spurs clanking musically.

Wearily, Aidan rubbed the nose of the big bay gelding who had come to the fence to visit with her. "I may have won small battles of words, but I lost the war, Charley, and now I'm stuck with this. What might he do if I vomit on the toes of his boots?"

In the house, Joss handed over her Colt. "Mind it's got a hair trigger."

Slade's look suggested he hardly believed she might know a hair trigger from a hair brush.

She shrugged. "Just thought I'd mention it." She leaned against a post on the porch, the dishes neglected in the sink. She didn't trust Slade any deeper than she could have buried him today. He had her Peacemaker, but Ethan's was handy, and the Winchester (also hair-triggered; her father had come up arthritic, and had taught his steady-handed daughter how to hone the inner workings of his guns) hung just inside the door. She supposed she could kill him with it if she had to, or talk him out of enough shells for Aidan's instruction with that more deadly weapon.

Slade cocked the revolver and handed it to Aidan, and took off his coat and hat. Joss bit her lip, wishing she'd told him to go to hell with his condescending offer to buy the bullets. He slipped his arms around Aidan from behind; Joss jammed her hands into her pockets. "You oily son of a—"

The revolver roared interruption. Dirt sprayed from the ground at their feet. Slade backpedaled an ungainly dance. Joss vaulted the porch rail and landed running, praying that Aidan hadn't just relieved herself of part of her own right foot.

"You idiot!" Slade bellowed; Aidan, who had only flinched at his touch and was more surprised than he was that the gun had gone off, looked up in amazement as he raised his hand. "Stupid woman! I'll teach you—"

"It's the last thing you'll ever do, Slade!" Joss was still ten steps away; her throat would be sore for a week from the force of her roar. He wheeled as she skidded to a stop between them, shielding Aidan, blazing her rage at him: "You're the God-damned idiot! I told you it had a hair trigger! Did you hear me? Did you even listen? If your brains was bullets you couldn't hit a bull's ass with a bagful o' banjos! Aidan, are you hurt?"

Something feral burned in those dark eyes; Aidan would have looked away had she been able. "No," she whispered. "No, Joss. He just—startled me."

"That you're unhurt is this imbecile's extreme good fortune." Joss took the revolver from her. Slade's hand hovered near his pistol. "Hang your fright, sir; I'd've killed you from the porch had I cared to," she snapped, and yanked a black hair from her head to thread through the trigger guard. She looped the single strand across the trigger and drew back the hammer; she aimed at a bottle on the fence and tightened the fragile loop of hair.

The Colt roared. The bottle exploded. She cocked it and pulled again; another bottle blew glittering shards into the sunlight, and another; on the next one the hair broke and Joss squeezed off the round with her finger. "That, you skirt-chasin' son of a bitch, is a hair trigger by definition. Startle her again an' I'll define it a right smart o' closer to you."

"Are you threatening an officer of the Cavalry?"

"I'm tellin' you how it is."

"The round remaining in your weapon makes it sound a threat, Miss Bodett."

She opened the loading gate to eject five spent casings and show the tip of the ejector rod through a sixth, empty chamber, the one she always left clear under the hammer. She offered the Colt. "Your turn to buy the bullets."

He shook his head, and deliberately dropped six rounds into the revolver. He dangled it at Aidan by its trigger guard from his longest finger. "Does perchawnce" —it was a smirking drawl; Aidan was heartily weary of his damnable smirk— "the lady so desire?"

Her look made him seem like a neophyte in the unpleasant-smile business. *"Mais oui,"* she purred, accepting the Peacemaker. "But my dear Captain Slade" —her voice was like honey, her meaning clear as the morning sky as she held the revolver casually aimed at his belly— "do please remember how easily I'm startled."

Joss turned, barely stifling a laugh. Slade watched her stroll to the house; she settled into a rocker on the porch, her feet on the rail, her hat on her knee, a picture of arrogant disrespect for him and his position. He didn't know she sat because she couldn't stand, cold sweat prickling hard over her; she was but a week on the well side of death's door, and between the run and the run-in, her legs had deserted her.

"You tell her—" he started.

"If you want her told, Captain, you tell her. You teach me to shoot. It is, if you'll recall, your duty?"

"This is a harsh country teeming with savages with four legs or two, not some suburb of Philadelphia with constables you may call on," he gritted. "God knows she's crazy as a backhouse rat, but surely you have sense enough to see that two women alone stand no chance here. You'll die here, probably horribly."

And it dawned on her that Argus Slade was himself afraid of the West, of its harshness and its teeming savages, and that he swaggered and postured in a piteous attempt to hide that fear; she had heard his voice rise an octave when he had felt the threat of Joss's rage. "That's possible," she said gently. "I merely doubt that our exflunctication will happen as soon as so many people seem to think. May we begin, sir?" Joss watched from the porch. Aidan's first attempt went high, wide and handsome of any target; Slade talked, gesturing desultorily. Aidan raised the Colt. Smoke puffed and dirt kicked up in front of the fence—but purely under the post she had been aiming for, Joss noted; her aim was good even if her elevation wasn't. She had to shake her head in grudging understanding for Slade's predicament as a teacher when he started to touch her and remembered in time not to get shot. "Good boy," she murmured, as he folded his arms. "You learn a right smart o' quick, ol' son."

The Colt came up in Aidan's two-handed grip.

A bottle exploded.

Joss scratched her jaw, wondering if luck or inherent ability should be credited, and was answered when the next three bullets blew three bottles to shards. The captain's hands implied that anyone might enjoy a moment of good fortune; he reloaded and offered the revolver. Joss didn't hear what Aidan said; she only knew she said something before riveting her attention to bottles and fenceposts and the pride of Samuel Colt.

Four of six bottles disintegrated. The sixth wobbled, its fencepost newly-plugged; finally it toppled. A breath of breeze carried Aidan's words back to the porch: "I think a man shot there might tip over as well." Joss laughed out loud; a look like the one her cousin was giving the captain, Brother Ethan would have said, was enough to leave a man pissing straight out for not being able to find enough pecker to hang over the edge of his buttons.

Slade whistled to his horse. The mare trotted up agreeably, and from his advantage of height on her back he stabbed a finger at Aidan, obviously for some last, rancorous word before he gave the reins a jerk toward the Newtonville trail. Surprised, the mare reared, and got a rake of the spurs for her protest. "Take him under the sweeper at a dead run," Joss muttered at the bolting horse. "Knock some sense into the damn fool."

She stood as Aidan came up the step. "So what was the parting shot?"

Aidan turned to aim the pistol at Slade's departing back. Before Joss knew she would do it, she pulled the trigger. The impotent click of the hammer on a spent shell was, to Joss, almost as loud as an explosion of powder would have been. "His prophecy for our mutual and untimely demise," Aidan spat, and slapped the empty gun into Joss's belly. "Here. Now I know how to shoot."

Joss managed to hang onto the pistol. "Aidan—" She caught her cousin's arm. "Aidan, wait! Why are you steamed up at me?"

"Because you—" She turned, looking as angry as her beginning words, and Joss braced herself, but the flare didn't come; Aidan sagged against the side of the house. "Because I—" She put her face into her hands. "Because I wanted you to teach me," she whispered. "And he just—he just—he just thrust himself between us. And you didn't stop him."

52

"You didn't leave me much room," Joss said softly. "I opened every door I could think of, Aidan."

"And I didn't take them." She crossed her arms over her breasts, hiding them from the memory of Slade's eyes. "I know. I'm not angry at you. I'm just—"

Joss put the pistol on her chair; hesitantly, she touched Aidan's arm. "Why'd you keep on with it? A few bullets wasn't worth you goin' through that."

"It had nothing to do with bullets. I had to know I could stand up to him. I felt—"

Joss didn't know what it was that flickered in her cousin's eyes; she only knew that it was deep and cold. She touched her fingertips in bare suggestion to Aidan's shoulder, but Aidan turned from her, refusing the solace of her arms. Joss stuck her hands into her hip pockets. "Well, I'm real proud of you," she said roughly. "Took a parcel more'n twelve rounds 'fore I shot that good."

"I had to get away from him."

Joss snorted a humorless laugh. "You could rake out Hell with a fine-tooth comb an' not find his likes in the lot." She followed Aidan into the kitchen, hating Slade for his disruption of a morning that might have been so sweet, angry at herself for knowing no way to comfort her cousin now that her embrace had been rejected. "I won't cry to see him off to Montana nor cry if he don't come back. Pa hates him. Says if that's what the Cavalry's comin' to we're in for a hard go."

She got the kettle from the stove to heat up her dishwater. "Sit. I'll do them," she said, when Aidan reached for a dish towel; it sounded so abruptly like an order that meekly, Aidan sat. "They got no God-damned business in the Black Hills anyway. They gave the Sioux that land, like it was ever theirs to give. Now they find gold an' want it back. They act like that Roman god with two faces, an' talkin' out o' both mouths at the same time." She banged the kettle back to the stove. "I got no damn use for soldiers. They're for the most part young an' drunken louts from the cities who can't ride or shoot, but I never met a Indian I didn't respect."

She sniffed the dishcloth, rejected it, got a fresh one. "The way folks keep comin' round here tryin' to get this place, I got a feelin' for the natives. I'm a better farmer by a damn sight than ary o' what's offerin' to buy me out, but the sons o' bitches act like they're God over me 'cause I'm a woman, same's they act like they're God over the Indian. I'm white so they prob'ly won't just up an' kill me for it, but they'll try every other damn thing they can scheme up to get it." She rattled dishes into the washwater. "I might win. But Crazy Horse is dead. So's Sittin' Bull. So are all their people. They just don't know it yet."

Aidan had known Joss was angry beyond the unpredictable flares of her temper; she hadn't known how deeply ... and it had never occurred to her that Indians might be more than the savages she'd been taught they were, or that Joss might know and respect them. "You're not afraid of them? The Indians?"

"They're a clean, spare people. We've cornered 'em like cats in a stall, an' that's worth bein' afraid of. Most cats got sense enough to back off from a fat-tailed tom in his own barn." She jerked the rinsing kettle from the stove and thumped it beside the sink, and put the plates she had washed into the steaming water. "But a soldier'll just shoot every cat he sees for knowin' they all got claws." Her words were part rage, part resignation. "The only land the red man'll have left when the government's done is the two-by-six he's buried in, an' the white man won't respect that, just like if I took Ott Clark's or Thom Richland's money an' lit out for California—hell, they'd have beans growin' up top the Bodetts buried out there an' them headboards burnt in the stove. White men don't respect nothin' but their own wants." She snapped a cup towel from the wire over the stove and banged dishes to their places as she dried them. "They don't understand home, or give a damn for just havin' enough. They only ever want more, an' don't care how they get it."

She dumped the dishwater, poured the rinsewater into the pan, and jammed cup towels and dishcloths into the still-steaming water. She grated in soap and sloshed the small laundry around, leaving it to soak while she took the bucket to the well. Back with it, she slopped the rinse-kettle full; water hissed and danced over the surface of the stove. She dumped the laundry water and poured the rest of the fresh water into the dishpan to rinse the soap from the linens, and dumped that and wrung the cloths and hung them over the stove, all in a dark fury words hadn't dissipated. "I'd burn this house an' salt the fields ere I'd see that son of a bitch Slade own a speck of it." She banged around in the china closet, finding a small, soft leather bag, and slammed out to the porch.

Aidan sat at the table, her eyes closed, her breath shallow in her throat; Joss might be a Bodett by name, but there was no denying her Blackstone blood. She sighed, finally, and stood. There was something she'd neglected to say, and if that oversight was part of Joss's ill humor, it was a part she could try to appease.

Joss was leaning on the porch rail, trying with fingers not quite steady enough to roll a cigarette. "I owe you an apology," Aidan said quietly, and Joss looked up. "I was dreadfully rude to you. You didn't deserve it, and I'm sorry. And thank you for defending me. I'm sure he meant to strike me."

"I'd be diggin' a hole in the beans by now if he had. You've been struck often enough." She abandoned the cigarette she'd been trying to make, jamming the little bag inside her shirt and her hands into her jeans pockets. "There'd be a measure o' satisfaction in plantin' that jackanapes."

"He's hardly worth the risk to your soul. Are you all right?"

"I'm angry. It's nothin' you did. It's over principle, an' it don't go away. It only rises an' ebbs, an' it needs to ebb." She picked the Colt from the rocker and took it inside; she cleaned it meticulously, and loaded it, and snugged it into its holster, and by the time she was done, the anger had receded.

On the porch, Aidan sat wearily in one of the rockers; she didn't look up until Joss spoke.

"It seems since you've been here we've had so much turmoil, an' so little chance to just sit an' talk," Joss said quietly. "If I made a pot o' tea, could we try an' start fresh?"

"English tea, please. That Chinese brew of yours—"

Joss grinned. "I know. The vile concoction. Good pekoe it shall be."

She managed a smile, holding it until Joss turned, then went back to her silent battle with her digestion. For weeks, waking up had been enough to distress her; any disruption of her morning routine queased her breakfast in her. The Kansas battles with her father had reduced her to a cold-sweating misery huddled over a basin or the back porch rail; halfway across the continent by train was an experience she wanted only to forget. Argus Slade—

"I forget if you take milk or—Aidan? You're white as butter! What—"

"I'm sorry, Joss, I'm going to be—"

Joss got her to the edge of the porch, and held her head; *strange*, Aidan thought, gagging, *how a cool palm at your forehead helps you know you'll live through the indignity.* "I'm—oh, Joss, I'm sorry—"

"Shh. Just let it come."

She had no choice. When it was over her legs deserted her; Joss supported her in her collapse to the porch floor. She hated needing the support, but had no choice in that, either, and she leaned, swallowing and shivering, into Joss's worried embrace.

"Aidan, what is it? Are you—please, are you all right? What's the—"

"It's just the baby," she managed. "I'm fine, I just feel like hell—oh, Joss." It was part sob, part laugh. "Now you've taught me to cuss."

"There's naught wrong with a cuss if you feel better for the sayin'." Her hand was cool, holding her head to her shoulder. "Should I go for Doc?"

"No," she whispered. "No. Just stay with me. Just for a minute—"

Joss held her. For a moment, that was all she wanted. She hated the raw taste in her throat, the tears, the stuffy nose; she felt like a child ill with something, wishing for a mother to hold her as gently as Joss did now, and that want shivered through her like a leftover from the night before. After Jared, all she had wanted was to huddle in her mother's arms, to know the elemental bond of women wounded by a common enemy, but that day she had learned what it meant to be alone.

"It's all right—" Joss was all arms and legs and comfort around her, keeping her close to the hard curves of her body. "It's all right, little cousin. I'm here."

I'm here.

I'll just love you, so you'll always know there's someone who does.

She drove her face hard into Joss's chest, clenching her jaw against the tears that wanted to come, against the words that wanted to come: I love you too. She didn't want to say them; she didn't dare say them. She was afraid she didn't know what they really meant. "I need some water," she whispered, and felt Joss's lips brush the top of her head before she untangled herself enough to stand and offer her hand to help Aidan up.

She sank into a rocker, wondering when she had ever felt so awful, or so pampered, and while Joss got her water she missed her with a low, lonely ache; her last conversation with Doc turned over in her mind the way her breakfast had turned over in her stomach. She wished she could so easily get rid of the words.

Joss brought a glass of water for her, and a cup of tea for herself, but she didn't sit; she tapped a booted toe against a rocker of the chair, and finally, hesitantly, she said, "You said it was the baby. Aidan, should I go for Doc? If you're—"

"It's just morning sickness, Joss. The baby's all right. Didn't your mother go through this?"

"No. Did it happen while I was sick?"

Wearily, she smiled. "I didn't have time to be sick while you were sick. It's simply self-indulgence now that you're well."

Appeased, Joss sat at the edge of the porch with her cup. "Indulge yourself, then. I owe you an' welcome the debt."

She snorted a laugh. "Some self-indulgence, puking off the porch."

Joss laughed, too, a burst of spontaneous amusement at her crudity. "There's those who'd choke ere they'd suffer the indulgence! Lord, I've no use for them who'd falute so high the porch rail's past their possibility." She had started earlier to roll a cigarette, and found her makings now to complete the job; Aidan watched in bemusement. "Seems to me" —Joss paused to lick the seam of her smoke, then sealed and shaped it— "as like too many got their noses too high up in the air to scent the difference between commonness an' common humanness. We all puke, an' we all call it that to ourselves. The difference is what we call it in polite company" —she scratched a match on the sole of her boot— "which I ain't."

"My stars," Aidan said faintly. "You're going to smoke that."

A smile twitched at a corner of Joss's mouth; she lit up and blew out the match with a smoky breath. "I've been known to take the occasional an' not entirely medicinal dose of whiskey, too. I'll warn you now to save surprisin' you later." She slid a sidelong glance at Aidan, seeing her shock; she sighed and used the matchstick to coax a bit of something hard and brown out of the crease between her boot and sole. "Cousin, I've spent my life cheek by jaw with men, puttin' out the same sweat an' blisters for no more reward than the wings o' the chicken whilst the menfolk get the breasts an' thighs an' drumsticks—an' Ma gets the pope's nose an' the bones to give a pickin' once the boys is out smokin' on the porch." She broke the stick of the match between her fingers and tossed the pieces into the yard. "Seems if Ethan earns a drink drivin' the hay-wagon, I've surely earned one spendin' the day forkin' hay into it an' waitin' while he gets first water in the bath. But if it offends you—the smokin' or the liquor, either or both—I'll keep it out of the house."

Aidan ticked a nervous fingernail against her glass. "I can't make such a demand of you in your own home."

"You don't sleep under that roof? It's your home as well."

"Not to the point of denying you your pleasures."

Joss watched the smoke drift from her cigarette. "I take more pleasure in your company than anything else," she said softly. "I wish you'd feel enough at ease to say if things I do distress you, so I'd know to stop."

Aidan hid behind a sip of her water, confused by the warmth

her cousin's words had stirred in her; Joss seemed discomposed, too, scratching at her jaw, flicking a forefinger at a spot of dirt on the knee of her jeans, finally staring out across freshly-turned fields, searching them as if for a hint of burgeoning life in soil planted but a day before. "I've never known anyone like you." Shyness softened Aidan's voice. "You do puzzle me sometimes, Cousin Joss."

"I expect you ain't the first one I've puzzled."

It wasn't the first time she had seen the set of weary disquiet in her elder cousin's shoulders, but it was the first time Joss had allowed it there if she thought Aidan could see. A breeze wandered across the porch, ruffling Joss's shirt and taking the smoke of her cigarette away, and Aidan leaned back in her rocker, letting the cool air and the dry, comfortable creak of cane calm her. Almost reluctantly—for in their silence there seemed to be a low, warm trust she wasn't sure she dared chance breaking—she ventured, "Joss?"

Joss glanced at her in question when she didn't go on.

"I meant to say—" She gathered her courage. "Last night? I... you were so—thank you. You were—are—so...kind. I know it's childish to be afraid of the dark—"

"No, Aidan." It was a remote protest, as if most of her mind had followed her gaze back across the damp, dark fields. "If it's childish, it's that children have sense enough to fear what deserves fearin'. It ain't the dark they fear so much as what they can't see comin' at 'em out of it."

"I never was, before—" Self-consciously, she touched her belly. "But I—I remember it. What he—I remember, and it—it I get—it drives the sleep from me. And today—Captain Slade—" She rubbed a hand across her forehead. "I don't know what, saving that I hope I can sleep tonight."

What Joss examined was not the fields or the distant hills, but the still-disturbing memory of drowsing from sleep to find Aidan in her arms; she had never shared a bed with anyone, or considered how deeply intimate that might be. She had awakened as Aidan had, confused and cautious, to realize that the soft warmth in her hand was her cousin's breast, and she had moved that hand as quickly as she could without disturbing Aidan . . . but Aidan had murmured a sleeping protest, her hand searching for Joss's, returning it to that warmth, and Joss, with her hand full of that silken roundness, felt smooth legs close around her thigh to draw it near to that most private warmth; she felt Aidan's breath deepen, and heard her sleeping murmur: *you feel so good—*

There had been no more sleep. She felt the pulse of her palm, and the fullness it cupped; she knew her awareness of Aidan snugged into the curve of her. She searched how her breasts and belly felt, pressed close to that silk-clad back; she breathed the scent of her hair, and brushed that hair aside to let her lips find the smoothness of her cousin's neck, and knew the purr of unconscious pleasure her kiss drew from the woman in her arms. "I hope you can too," she whispered, and took a last hot taste of her cigarette and dropped the end to the ground and stepped on it, and looked up to find blue eyes heavy-lidded in their consideration of her.

"I felt so safe with you holding me." Aidan's voice was soft as the song of night wind in grown corn, the sound of the night's cool invitation. "I felt so...treasured." She looked away, and so did Joss. "As if nothing could ever hurt me again, because you wouldn't let it. And he would have, but you stopped him, and..." She faltered; her face felt hot with some unnamed embarrassment.

"I wanted to kill him when he touched you." She didn't dare look at Aidan; she picked at a scab on her knuckle. "I knew he'd take it too far, or not show you decent respect, or—an'—it was like I was jealous," she said softly. "I've never been jealous before. Ethan told me what a God-awful thing that was, for me to know what to name it now. He said it'd make a person's guts feel like... like swallowin' hot coals, an' that's how it felt to me, when he touched at you."

Something twitched at her belly; Aidan stood, not knowing why she needed distance, only knowing she did. She went to the end of the porch, hugging the post there. The chickens argued in the yard; the horses, Charley and Fritz, stood somnolent in the pasture, sharing tails, ignoring the placid cow. The gray cat walked the top rail of the fence under the willow tree. She closed her eyes against the markers inside that fence, forcing back a burn of tears. The porch floor squeaked and she knew Joss was behind her. "I begged my father to end this pregnancy," she whispered. "I begged him, Joss. His answer was to try to beat the fear of God into me." A harsh laugh jittered from her. "Doc says he will, if I decide in the next two weeks, and I don't know what to do. I don't know what to do! That's a baby, a child inside me that I don't want—Joss, can you keep me safe from this? Can you keep this from hurting?"

Hands closed around her shoulders. "I know what to say as much as you know what to do." Aidan felt the warmth of breath against her neck. "I only know to say that you're welcome here, Aidan. Whatever you decide, you're welcome here."

Her throat fluttered with tears. She swallowed, trying to hold them back. "Do you have an opinion?"

"Yes. But it'd be wrong to tell you, an' always wonder if I swayed you. You're my blood kin. If you go with Doc, I'll love you. If you go without him I'll love you both."

It was too hard to cry alone; she turned to the shelter of Joss's warmth. When it seemed she might have her control she tried to pull away, for she was embarrassed by so many tears in such a short time, but Joss kept her in her arms. "Let me hold you—" It wasn't a demand, just an invitation, and she couldn't refuse it. "I don't know this hurt, but I know how hurt feels to have it alone. Please, Aidan. Let me hold you."

She saw the little graveyard, its markers blurred by tears, and wondered how many times Joss might have wished to be held when no one's arms were there for her. "You asked if I'd ever been loved," she whispered into the worn-soft cotton of Joss's shirt. "I don't know, Joss. They'd say they did" —a pained laugh escaped her— "usually just before he'd beat me for my own good. That's what they said. It was for my own good. But it didn't feel like love. It felt like—like I was a mistake they made and had to put up with. I don't want this baby to know I didn't want it the

61

way I know they never wanted me. I never mattered to them—to anyone—" She swallowed. "Until now. Joss, tell me how you feel. I'm so confused. I don't know what to do."

The hands that framed her face were as hard-palmed, as rough-skinned as the hands of a working man, but they were as gentle as a mother's. Her voice was unsteady. "Decide as you will, but stay with me. Aidan, you don't just matter to me. You're all that matters. You, an' the baby—" Too late, she tried to catch it back.

"Oh, Joss!" Aidan jammed her forehead into Joss's throat. "You want me to keep it? You don't know! What he did to me—"

"No," Joss whispered. "I don't know what he did to you, Aidan, any more than I know their minds when they call it your fault. I know it wasn't. Aidan, please...is that Doc's crop out there just 'cause he planted it? It's my land, my sweat to come, my heart beatin' an' the good Lord's will if the corn grows tall an' the beans set on—sowin' ain't reapin', Aidan, an' nothin' more to the Scripture savin' how you care to read it."

She didn't know what she felt, besides cold; she didn't know what she heard besides the hard pulse of her cousin's heart. She didn't know where the words came from, or why, when they came: "A floor," she whispered. "Please, Joss. I want a floor in the kitchen."

Joss's arms closed hard around her. "I can give you that."

CHAPTER FIVE

The rooster had crowed half an hour past on the morning of a Sunday that already promised to be hot. "Joss," Aidan said almost timidly, when her cousin emerged dressed in her usual Levi's and one of Ethan's shirts—it had probably once been red, but had faded to a dusty rose, and it made Joss look sharp and clean and feral in the morning light—"won't we be going to church?"

Joss finished pinning up the black mane of her hair. "Didn't go to church when I didn't have a quarter to do o' what I got to get done today, an' already off to a late start. Rooster's crowin' on one wing this mornin' or I'm lazy, one." She took a speckleware cup from a nail on the wall over the sink and went to the stove. "Meanin' no disrespect for church-goin', Aidan, but I got yardful o' livestock out there that'll be a lot happier to see me gettin' in the hay than spendin' the mornin' gettin' to town an' back an' listenin' to that gasbag of a Baptist in the middle o' the mess." She licked a finger to tap on the side of the coffee pot, like checking an iron for hotness, before she poured the cup full; she looked into the big kettle of water that always simmered on the back middle burner of the stove, and lifted the lid of the hot water tank, and checked the fire, finding everything in good morning order. "But I'd hitch you up the wagon if you wanted to go."

Aidan knew how to drive a shay behind her mother's gentle Morgan, but she had never been comfortable with the reins; she couldn't imagine piloting a buckboard behind the immense pair of draft horses any more than she could imagine walking unaccompanied into the Washburn Station Baptist Church for the first time. "I couldn't possibly. But surely you're not going to work on the Sabbath? Joss, it's—"

"Cousin, I'll ask the good Lord's mercy on how I go about survivin' the situation He put me into Himself. He rested on the seventh day 'cause He had the job done. Next Sunday, if that hay's all teddered, mayhap we can be restful an' church-goin', but you need to know it ain't a habit o' mine. If it's one o' yours an' you want to go on with it, I'll teach you to drive the wagon. Won't take no time. Charley knows what to do an' Fritz goes along." She tasted her coffee and went to the milk pail under the sink; she skimmed off some cream to stir into her cup. "I don't mean to offend you, but I got my differences with how the Baptist reads the Scripture. I see Marcus an' the Jackson boys restin' of a Sunday, but Earlene puts a fancy board in front of 'em at four o'clock, an' God ain't doin' the cookin' or washin' the dishes either, an' both o' them chores always felt like work to me. All I ever seen settin' around on Sunday was the menfolk, an'—Damn! Milk's soured." She dumped her coffee into the sink and got the pail out from under it. "Chickens'll get it, I reckon; I ain't got time to fool with cheese this week."

She put the pail on the edge of the porch, where the milk would clabber in the day's hard sun, and stepped back into the house for her hat. "Guess you got your Sunday sermon after all. Sorry for runnin' my jaw. I'm goin' to milk the cow. If it's against your thinkin' to work today, it won't put me out o' chirk, Aidan. Suit your own believin'."

Aidan leaned against the sideboard by the sink, remembering the fine Sunday dinners that had welcomed her family home from church, remembering her father blessing the food that the Lord had provided— "The Lord in the personage of Matilda MacGuire," she murmured, and put a stick of wood in the stove to bring the oven up for biscuits. If that devoutly Catholic woman who was the Blackstone's cook could work on a Sunday, so could Aidan Blackstone.

There was a metronome in the field by the road, that nine-acre plot surrounded by barbed wire to keep the livestock out of the hay; Aidan sat on the porch, her needle working in rhythm to the swing of the pendulum that was the scythe wielded by her cousin Joss. Step-sweep, step-sweep, step-sweep; hay fell in neat rows as Joss worked her way down the length of the meadow. She had been at it for hours, pausing only to drink from a bucket at the dooryard end of the field, and the swath she had cut was discouragingly narrow.

When she was almost back to the near end, Aidan put down her mending and drew fresh water from the well. She and Joss arrived at the fence at about the same time. "Aren't you an angel." Joss leaned her scythe against the wire. "I was thinkin' on that stale water an' not likin' the idea much." She poured the first dipper over her head and drank the second one. "I quit sweatin' a few minutes ago. That's a shade too dry for my likin'."

"It's too hot for such work today." Aidan refilled the ladle. "And you're still not completely well from your sickness, Joss. You mustn't overdo."

"I'm well enough. An' this don't hold a candle to hayin' in August." She held out her battered felt hat like a bowl; Aidan looked at her in question. "Fill it right up. Workin' hay in August, you know what the good Lord's got in store for you for workin' on Sundays," she grinned, putting on the filled hat; water cascaded over her back and shoulders.

Aidan wished she could smile back in complete appreciation of the teasing. She had justified cooking as a necessary evil, and mending as keeping her hands from idleness, but she wished Joss, had she felt compelled to do something today, might have chosen to make a new egg basket (or at least repair the one that was falling apart), or whittle an axe handle, or find some other chore that would allow her to sit in the shade and pretend she was enjoying what she was doing. "This is a pleasure next to August," Joss added, as if she'd been listening in on Aidan's thoughts. "Don't even feel like work."

"Don't add purveying untruths to your sins," Aidan said dryly, as Joss took a long whetstone from her pocket and touched up the edge of her blade, "or the Lord might not even see fit to provide you a stone to sharpen the instrument of your eternal torture."

"That'd be small of Him." Joss wiped her dripping face on her sleeve. "I've been talkin' to the Lord out here, Aidan, an' I got a feelin' He understands me pretty well. He made them beasts in the pasture, too, an' knows they're countin' on me for their bed an' board come winter." She stuck the stone back into her hip pocket. "I know the Book says to remember the Sabbath an' keep it holy. I can pray an' cut hay at the same time, but the hay ain't goin' to cut itself, an' I ain't testin' the Lord by askin' Him for no private miracles. Says not to, right in Matthew. I thank you for the water."

"Don't work beyond its lasting. Eternal damnation is long enough for you to know how sunstroke feels."

Joss touched the brim of her hat in acknowledgment of the warning and took the snath in her hands. She turned and stepped and swept, and the blade hissed an eighteen-inch swath through golden grass. A clump of hay fell to her left, the start of another six-hundred-foot windrow. Aidan, seeing how long it had taken her cousin to clear a ten-foot path through the square field, suspected that the rest of Joss's week was going to blur into a drone of repetition as dreary as the sound inside a train that was taking its passengers to places they had no desire to see.

It takes men to run a place. Effie Richland's voice came back to her as she watched Joss pace slowly down the field: step-sweep, step-sweep, step-sweep. She turned with a small, soft sigh, wishing she could disbelieve the acidic storekeeper.

"Will you look," Joss murmured, looking at the golden roasted chicken, and at the woman across the table from her; slowly, her glance touched the empty chairs at the table. "A whole damn chicken an' not but two mouths to peck at it."

"What may I serve you?" Quietly, Aidan asked.

Joss slipped her napkin from under her fork; carefully, she spread it on her lap. "I'm used to a wing." Her voice was soft and rough. "But if Ethan's sick of a Sunday, or gone, I'll sometimes have a drumstick." A brief ghost of a smile haunted her face. "He's got to be a right smart o' sick or busy to miss Ma's Sunday chicken. Yankee chicken, Pa calls it. Says she never could fry chicken like a decent Southern woman, nor try to, even, but he sure can eat his fill o' that Yankee chicken."

Aidan didn't think she'd ever seen a human being who had as much right to be tired as had Joss Bodett that evening. She had worked from seven until five, taking only enough pause to eat lunch and smoke a cigarette before she was back to the scythe; her only concession to the simmering heat of the afternoon had been to linger a few moments in the shade of the massive oak trees at each end of the field when she got to them. Aidan had called to her at four, trying to bring her in; she got a wave of response, but half an hour later when she looked Joss was at the far end of the field, the lowering sun flashing off the straw-scoured blade of the scythe. Aidan attacked the triangle at the end of the porch with the irritation of any woman whose afternoon in the kitchen has been greeted with yet-empty chairs at the table, even though dinner was almost an hour from being ready, and Joss was on the porch ten minutes later, her hair damp and her rolled-up sleeves wet at the distal ends from her quick wash at the trough. "Dinner already?"

"Dinner after you've had a bath. I've been near enough to

67

hay to know you must itch, though I'm sure I couldn't know how horribly."

"Bath?" Joss blinked at her. "I just had one last night."

That was a piece of Kansas custom Aidan meant to change on the parcel of post road real estate over which she had influence, however minute: that business of a bath on Saturday night whether it was needed or not, but no more often whether it was needed or not. Joss's sweat was fresh and honestly-earned, but tomorrow it would be old; by Saturday Aidan knew she would have been giving her cousin wide berth for several days. "Your tub's all made. No sense in wasting such an amount of hot water." She plucked a clean shirt and jeans from the sideboard; Joss took them more out of reflex than wanting to. "You can have your privacy, or I'll wash your back for you."

Joss eyed the clothes in her hands. "Well," she murmured. "I guess you got told, sister." And now, clean and freshly-dressed, she considered the drumstick and thigh of chicken Aidan had put on her plate with the same expression she had aimed at the clean clothes: disbelief at the oddity of such a thing.

Aidan added a spoonful of fresh peas to her cousin's plate. "Eat. If you work like you did today without food enough to sustain such effort, I'll be back where I started this uncommon adventure: nowhere else to go and you collapsing before my very eyes." She cut into the pan of cornbread she had made. "I don't know about this johnnycake. I followed your mother's recipe, but it doesn't look like any johnnycake I ever saw."

Joss broke off a corner and tasted it. "I'd wager you used grits, not corn meal. It don't taste bad; it's just a little—" She stopped in the name of diplomacy; it was hard as a brickbat. "Corn meal's in the lard tin with the C on the lid. Grits is marked with a G." Diplomatic again, she added, "Them two look a lot alike, don't they, Cs an' Gs."

She ate a piece of the unusual bread with what Aidan had served her, and another piece with a wing of the chicken, and a fat slice of pecan pie (that morning Aidan had opened a lard can she hadn't dared unlid before, fearing what she might find, and discovered it full of shelled pecans). "Flora Washburn's got a whole orchard," Joss told her when she cut the pie. "Must be a hundred trees. Ethan was goin' by one day an' on a whim he stopped an' asked what she'd get for a flour sack of 'em. 'Boy,' she says, 'you can take home whatever you can carry,' thinkin' he only had that one sack he'd showed her. Well, he'd been on his way to the miller—that's Mister Nissen; he gives a penny apiece for sacks back. He must've had a quarter's worth of 'em. T'ain't hard work or he'd've never picked 'em all full. He said Flora like to died laughin' watchin' him try to hang all them sacks o' nuts all over Charley. We was all the winter crackin' his damn pecans. The shells're good to light the stove in the mornin', though. Flare right up on the leastest coals."

"I hope the pie's better than the cornbread," Aidan said; Joss was touching the rolled edge of the crust with a tine of her fork, trying to get it to flake. "I used to help Mrs. MacGuire fill the shells, but she'd never let me touch the crust."

Joss forked a healthy bite into her mouth. "Damn near good as Ma's," she allowed, and cleaned up the first piece and had another small sliver. "Let me know next time an' I'll help you with the crust. You got this one almost right. A tad short, but pie crust's awful hard to learn."

Clean, her belly full, her back warm from the dying woodstove, Joss was nodding before Aidan finished stacking the dishes. "Stay put. I'll do them," Aidan said gently, and when the dishes were washed she woke Joss only enough to make her easy to lead from the table to her room.

"I c'n do it," Joss mumbled, fumbling for buttons when Aidan would have helped her out of her jeans. "Ain' all that tired."

She let her try; she ended up doing it anyway, and she turned back the covers and guided Joss into the bed. "Sleep well," she said at the door; she knew Joss hadn't the night before or she never would have been in bed past the rooster's alarm. Joss made a noise that might have been a response or the beginning of a snore, and Aidan closed the door and went to finish the last small details of cleaning up her kitchen.

The Bull and Whistle was a quiet place on a Sunday night; most of the wives of Washburn Station forbade their men to take a drink or play a card on the Sabbath, but there was a desultory game of two-handed cribbage in progress when Doc Pickett wandered in. He sat with the players and nodded to Jack Bull when the barkeep held up a beer mug. "Two, four, an' eight's a doz," Ottis Clark counted. "That's a buck, Marcus b'hoy."

"Oh, for Chr—crackin' ice." Marcus Jackson held his curse in deference to the day and tossed his cards face-up to the felt. "Look at that son of a snake, too."

Doc shook his head in sympathy at the hand that had come too late to count: pairs of fours and fives, four points turned into twenty-four by the six of hearts on the cut. "It's a pretty hand anyway," he offered.

Ott cackled. "Pretty hand's like a pretty woman. No good if you can't peg'er. You 'member that, don'tcha, Doc? Post the pony, Mister Mudsill."

"You callin' me Mudsill's like gettin' called ugly by a toad." Marcus tossed a dollar across the table; Ott traded it to Jack Bull for a shot of rye and some change. "Seen Joss out there today slayin' hay," Marcus said. "When you gonna talk some sense into 'er, Doc? Don't make no sense to save 'er from the grippe just so's she can kill 'erself tryin' to do three men's work."

"God-damn girl's just as stupid as she's stubborn," Ott muttered, "speakin' o' women you can't peg."

Doc tasted his beer. "No talking sense or anything else into Joss if she doesn't want to hear from you. You boys know that. I'll give you stubborn," he aimed at Ott, "but she's a far cry from stupid. She could give old Flora a run for her money, if she had to start with what Flora had when the old man bought the farm. All she's lacking is hands."

"An' all she gets for a hand is a Yankee oven with a bun already cookin'." Ott scraped up the cards to shuffle, aiming a sly grin at Marcus. "Cousin on 'er mother's side, ain't it? Guess some things run—"

"A word on Jocelyn out'n that ugly hole you call your mouth

70

an' I'll sew it shut for you." Marcus spoke the interruption genially, but Jocelyn Bodett's clear head and quick hands were the only reason either his wife or James, his second son, had survived the birthing of the brawny mite who'd decided to come breech, and Marcus wouldn't hear ill spoken of her. "Doc prob'ly lend me a needle an' thread. Who cut an' give you the deal?"

Grudgingly, Ott put the deck between them.

"See you've got your first crop tedded." Doc didn't direct it; both men's meadows were cut and windrowed. "Your beans look good, Marcus, and a lot of them."

Marcus won the cut. "Felt like a bean year." He shuffled awkwardly, being mostly left-handed since an unfortunately-timed meeting of a hammer, anvil, and the two middle fingers of his right hand some years back had virtually ended his job as farrier for Jackson Bros. Livery. "Get that hay in, sure like to see a couple days o' rain next week."

Doc took a swallow of his beer and squeegeed foam from his mustache with a finger. "That'd be just in time to leave Joss looking at a week's work with the scythe gone for naught. Expect it'll take her all week to mow it. Most of a week to get it in. Long job for a little hay."

"My kitty, Ott! Merciful baby in the bulrushes, do I got to watch you every second? Throw them damn cards over here." He looked into his empty shot glass; Doc signaled Jack to bring the bottle. Ott emptied his glass in a quick swallow. "I'll send the boys over tomorrow," Marcus said when the glasses were full and Jack was gone with Doc's Seated Liberty. "Got nothin' to home that can't wait a day. She ain't got but eight, nine acres there. Get that done—well, maybe two days. One with a little more help."

They waited for Ott to ante up his sons, but he studied his cards, chewing on his mustache. Marcus applied the hard side of his boot to Ott's shin under the table. "Kick me again, son of a bitch, an' I'll settle your hash," Ott said evenly. "I heared the question an' you got my answer."

Slowly, Marcus folded his cards. He took the shot of rye Doc had bought him. Even mostly left-handed, he was still quick

71

with his right, and Ott's drink was in his belly before the other man's hand could close on the air where Marcus's wrist had been. Marcus put the glass down, his smile asking an ungentle question, and Ott stared at the big-shouldered part-time farrier for a considering moment before he drew in his quills and let it go.

Marcus stood to draw a handsome gold watch from his pocket. "'Bout time, was I to acknowledge the corn," he mused. "Tomorrow, Doc?"

"Early." Doc stood, too, and they left the Bull and Whistle, leaving Ottis Clark chewing his mustache over an empty glass and the cards of a game that had been called.

Aidan heard the ruckus before she was well awake; she staggered from bed to peer bleary-eyed out the window. The barnyard was a jumble of horses dragging reins, the near end of the hayfield a beehive of men with scythes and rakes. "What in heaven's name—?"

She heard Joss's voice like a profane echo from the other end of the house: *What in the joe-fired hell?*

Joss could protest, but she couldn't dissuade the strong-backed men of Washburn Station who had assembled. Marcus Jackson was there with his five sons (Gideon, his eldest, had courted Joss for two years, and Marcus had fervently hoped the match would be made, for that would have given Gideon one of the best full sections in the Station. But as Doc had said, there was no talking anything into Joss that she didn't want to hear, and Gid hadn't had the words she was listening for).

Hank Richland was there, handing out scythe stones liberated from his father's store. Ezekiel Clark was there with four younger brothers and an eye that was rapidly swelling closed. "Who laid the hand on you?" Joss asked.

"Called Pa out," he said tersely. "Doc'll be along directly, soon's he sets an arm."

Joss touched the swelling with a woman's gentleness, and clapped his shoulder with a peer's admiration. "You whupped your weight in wildcats there, Mister Clark!"

There were young men Aidan didn't recognize; she would meet them during the day as she offered rare lemonade (Doc, when he came, brought a sack of lemons) to boys who took off their hats and wiped sweat from their eyes with shy grins as they accepted much-welcomed drinks: "Will Grant, ma'am." Will Grant fled, too shy in the presence of a handsome woman to linger for conversation. "Thank y'ma'am. Daniel Washburn. Yes'm, Flora's my grandma." He offered a hand to be shaken; Aidan pegged him a born politician. "Much obliged, ma'am. Nathaniel Day; we live past Jacksons t'ward the Post. Ma's after gettin' down to see y'all, but spring's awful busy." Aidan assured him that she understood about spring and chores that wouldn't wait. "Pa's pa was from up Maine," Nathaniel added. "A silversmith, he was. No'm; I can't recall the town."

The hay fell under their relentless step-sweep, step-sweep, Joss and the elders handling the scythes, the younger boys raking the grass into windrows. Aidan despaired of feeding them all; Doc produced a quarter-side of beef and made a fire in the pit by the barn, and spitted the haunch. She squeezed lemons, and Doc drew water from the well and boiled up a sugar syrup on the stove to add strength to the drink.

The workers jostled for position when Aidan took a bucket of lemonade to the fence, but no one jostled enough to spill any of the precious potion. They were mannerly, introducing themselves if no more formal introduction had yet been effected, thanking her for her concerns for their well-being in the heat, brushing off her thanks for their assistance: "Ain't but neighbors," Gideon Jackson said. "Hay's a hard row an' we got ours in. One day more don't matter to the pokeweed in the beans." He lingered until the lad behind him protested; he gave Aidan a slow, dark-eyed smile, seeing the rise of her blush before he went back to his scythe.

The haunch of beef was bones when they were done with it. Some of the workers had been accompanied by dogs, and those lean mutts snarled and gnarled over the remains as their masters returned to the field. Aidan and Doc washed dishes Aidan hadn't known she had. "How did this happen?" she asked. "They'll have it done before dark. I know you had something to do with this."

He wiped the last of the flatware and rattled it into its tray; he hung his towel on the wire over the stove and sank the dipper into a bucket of lemonade and poured for them both, and took Aidan and the glasses out to the porch. "Joss isn't understood by many in this town," he said when they were seated in the creaky cane rockers, "or even liked by some, but she's respected by most. No one wants to see her go down." *Except Thom and Effie Richland and Ottis Clark*, he added silently.

"What happened to Ezekiel Clark?"

Doc raised a mild eyebrow. "Boys call out their fathers. It happens every day."

"Did he win or lose?"

"Oh, he won."

"And how shall Mr. Clark respond to that?"

"I assume Mr. Clark shall respond with the healthy, albeit somewhat grudging, respect any grown man would afford a sixteen-year-old boy who sustained no more harm than a circumorbital hematoma in the process of breaking his father's arm and dislocating his shoulder before leaving him eating the dirt of his own paddock."

Aidan traced the condensation from her glass with a fingertip. "Can Ezekiel go home?"

"That's up to Zeke."

"And if he opts not to?"

"Then Ottis owes him a sound horse and saddle, a double eagle, and a handshake."

"But no open door?"

"It's usually extended. Ott Clark's a hard man."

"Should we—"

"He's a good lad and well liked. If he leaves his father's house but wants to stay in the Station, he won't go lacking a roof over his head. I'd not recommend it be this one."

Aidan understood, but she grumbled: "And we the ones who could most use the back of a boy strong enough to put Ottis Clark on the ground. What shall I feed this hard-working crew for supper, Doctor?"

He stood. "In my buggy, dear lady, I have a shoat who had the unfortunate luck to be vested of an evil disposition. James Jackson walloped him between the eyes with the flat of an axe Friday afternoon, and not a moment too soon; it seems his intent was to make a meal of one of his smaller brethren—Jim's brethren, not the shoat's. Earlene's done the dirty work; Sir Shoat is at the parboiled point. We need but spit him close to the coals and give him a spin now and again."

"I just had one last night," Joss protested.

"It's drawn. I'll be hanged if I'll waste such a great lot of hot water. Get in."

"An' I'll be hanged if I know why you waste such a great lot o' hot water anyway," Joss grumbled, peeling out of sweat-damp clothes behind the screen by the tub. "A rinse in the trough was plenty for me an' less work for you." She was just as worked as she had been the evening before, but not nearly as weary for knowing it was done; all that was left was to get the hay into the barn. Gideon Jackson and Hank Richland, both as true as the sun in the morning, had promised their presences on Saturday, earlier if it smelled of rain; Ezekiel Clark, grown from a boy to a man that day in the eyes of most his peers and all of his elders— and grimly unimpressed by his newly-won stature—had matched their offer. "I done fit for it," he said. "Might's well see it through. I'll be here, Joss."

Aidan offered Joss a fresh bar of soap and a washcloth once she was settled into the water. "You'll sleep better with the work off you."

"An' you? It was no work feedin' that army twice, I suppose?"

"I've bathed." She'd bathed out of a basin in the sink, Doc on the corner of the porch guarding both doors against untimely visitors. She knew she would sleep tonight; she wasn't sure about Joss, who had been out to the meadow four times since dinner, marvelling at its clean-mown stubble and straight windrows

75

of tedding hay. "Your towel's here over the screen, and your nightshirt beside it. Can I get you anything else?"

"No. I'm...fine. I'm fine."

Aidan was halfway to the table and her daybook before Joss spoke. "Aidan—"

She turned.

"Thank you." Joss's voice seemed almost reluctant. "You say you had nowhere else to go, but I know you didn't have to stay, an' I'm glad you did. Not just for the help. That's grand, but I—I just—"

"I'm glad to be here," Aidan said quietly. "I truly am, Joss."

"I don't know that you'd counted on quite such an education."

"Anyone who counts on their education is bound to be surprised."

"I hope I never surprise you too much."

Tiredly, Aidan smiled. "I don't know that you can, Joss. I'm fast getting beyond the point of surprise."

May, 1876

I sleep, but my heart waketh: it is the voice of my beloved that knocketh, saying, Open to me, my sister, my love, my dove, my undefiled: for my head is filled with dew, and my locks with the drops of the night.

Song of Solomon 5:2

CHAPTER SIX

Dear Mother & Father (Aidan spoke aloud as she wrote):

> *I trust this letter finds you both well & that you will accept my apologies for not having sooner informed you of my safe arrival in Kansas. All was not as expected when arrangements for my visit here were made. I am deeply grieved to tell you that Cousin Jocelyn passed away 21st March due to an outbreak of influenza that also carried away her beloved husband Harmon & their sons Seth & Ethan, within six days of one another. Their daughter Jocelyn, who is called Joss, met me with the news & graciously asked me to stay despite her deep sorrow at her loss. That very day she also was stricken with the influenza, but owing to most modern attendance by Doctor R.J. Pickett of this village she has recovered her robust health & now goes vigorously about her chores.*

"I asked you graciously? It's a sin to lie to your parents." Joss got away with tipping her chair back at the table; anyone else who did so on that oiled dirt floor received Aidan's coldest look. "I seem to recall behavin' as boorishly that day as a human body possibly could."

"You were ill and grief-stricken. I had precious little excuse for my own rudeness. Hush, now, and let me do this."

I have fallen quite in love with Kansas. It is a place of exquisite beauty & I should not mind to spend my life here, saving how awfully I should miss my loving parents.

"Speaking of lies," she added dryly, not looking up to see Joss's bitter smile.

Though Joss tells me that the land changes rapidly west of here, the Missouri River Valley so reminds me of my own dear New England. The air is sweet & pure & the earth as black as any I have ever seen yet an hour's ride away the soil is as red as rust! A most amazing place!

What it does not seem to offer is tea. We should be most grateful if you might send us several tins as Cousin Joss, Dr. Pickett & myself should be bereft without our thrice-weekly ritual of high tea. If one cared to dabble in merchantry, I suspicion his profits on tea alone would most handsomely buy his tobacco & brandy!

"Tell 'em to send it by the case," Joss suggested, pushing her luck by rolling a cigarette; Aidan, disenchanted with her affection for tobacco, had finally asked her not to smoke in the house. "Bein' a tea dealer in this town o' sorry merchants would be a right nice supplement to our income."

"Someone might think to take up the ice trade, too," Aidan grumbled. "I daresay we'll be lucky to see a tin of tea without a ride to Leavenworth, knowing my father. If you light that stinking thing in here, Joss Bodett, I'll pitch a proper fit."

We are attentively protected by a Cavalry troop quartered at Fort Leavenworth & commanded by one Captain Argus Slade, most recently of Philadelphia, who honored us with a personal visit. He

*humored my request to learn how to fire a pistol & spent quite too much
time ensuring my success. He is terribly handsome with his flowing
moustache & dashing uniform, & seats his fine steed superbly. Should
he call again, perhaps he might humor a request for the benefit of his
equestrian expertise to improve my notoriously poor seat.*

"You need a bigger shovel," Joss drawled, "to spread manure
so thick. The attentive Captain, may he rest in peace as soon as
possible, more resembles a toad on a stool than a knight on a
steed—an' you'd have as good a seat as any cowboy if you'd only
wear trousers when you ride. Not that you should ride at all, in
your condition."

Aidan blushed. She was used to Joss's swearing, and could
even do some of it herself now, but her cousin's casual use of such
words as trousers (and her insistence that chickens had breasts
and thighs, not white and dark meat) could still raise a flush to
her cheeks. "I'm not even evident, and I certainly shan't wear
sit-down-upons. It suits me for them to think I've an interest in
staying here, as I'm most certain it suits them." Aidan dipped her
pen. "But I couldn't write this in the morning without vomiting
most dreadfully, I fear."

"If you long continue your admiration of the pestiferous
Captain Slade, I fear I shall be required to join you at the dreadful
end of the porch." Her mimicry of Aidan's accent was ruthlessly
accurate; Aidan gave her tall cousin a gentle shove. Nimbly, Joss
saved her own balance and righted the tipped-over chair. "Can I
smoke this in here? Just this once?"

"No. Next you'll have your feet on the table."

"I'd never! But I enjoy your company so much, Aidan, an' you
won't be done for hours at the rate you're tellin' fibs. Please?"

It was hard for Aidan to resist the appeal in the dark eyes,
playful as they were; she managed. "Out, Joss. I fear I must insist."

*We've cut our first crop of hay—in April! The rhythm of life is
so different here, at once faster and slower. I imagine the lilacs have
blossomed all across New England by now. We importuned Dr. Pickett*

for the largest of his volunteers before he applied the bush-hook to them, as we had none in our yard here & he has both white & purple. We put four small bushes about the house, & while I may never see them bloom, it should serve to make more fond my memories to know lilacs blossom here for my silly insistence. I fear my dear Cousin Joss must find me frivolous at times, but she so graciously accommodates my Eastern desires.

"Your dear Cousin Joss takes eternal delight in your Eastern frivolity."

Aidan had to smile back at the laughing affection in her cousin's eyes, a smile that lingered despite her displeasure with this letter. "Go have your smoke, dear cousin, and let me finish this horrid exercise. It seems easier to ride to Leavenworth for tea than suffer this."

"You'll not ride so far even in Levi's. You do intend to see our lilacs bloom, don't you?"

"I intend to fill this house with them, and never mind silly superstition. And I shall ride to Leavenworth if I so decide."

Joss grinned. "Let me know when you plan to go. I want to see you try to saddle Charley." She dodged the swat Aidan aimed at her as she passed and struck a match on the doorframe, pausing there to light up.

Aidan smiled as fragrant smoke drifted back into the house. It was the repartee she enjoyed more than the tobacco she disliked, though the smell of it in the mornings could make her stomach roil uneasily; that was why she refused Joss the privilege of smoking in the house. But it was comfortable of an evening to sit on the porch while Joss had her smoke; she was graceful with it, and it seemed as if that smell on the evening breeze might let all to sense it know there was someone here who would brook no trouble...and it was oddly stirring to discover that rich scent in her hair, and on her breath, in those times when chance or quick affection brought them close to one another.

Her gaze lingered at the door as she remembered how long she had watched that morning as Joss started an arduous day of splitting wood. It hadn't been long before she had broken a hard sweat, and there had been something compelling about the widening line of wetness soaking the back of an old shirt with its sleeves and tails torn away, something magnetic in the power that coiled and sprang with each swing of the axe, and the flash of pale skin at her waist as that tool reached the apex of the swing. When finally she sat to rest in a breath of breeze Aidan had turned from the door, sensing that to be caught in her attention by those dark eyes would be like being found at something intensely personal.

Now, seeing the winking fire of that cigarette and the handsome profile of the smoker, some warm, alien thing stirred in her belly. "Away from the door, please," she called gently, blaming her sensitive digestion, but it was a moment after Joss had stepped from the porch before she could bend to her letter again.

Given the circumstances, all is well, my dear parents. There is much hard work to be done, which Cousin Joss & I share as equitably as we are able. When something simply demands a man's strength we importune our friend the Doctor, & if he cannot manage it he sends round someone who may—most often our neighbor Gideon Jackson, who is handsome as any black Irishman and delights in proving his youthful manliness to me! With few exceptions I find the folk here likeable & generous, & sympathetic to our situation; most gladly lend a hand if able—with the exception of procuring tea! Never would I have dreamed that such a simple matter could be made so tiresomely complex. We eagerly await your generous gift in that regard. Hoping this letter finds you both in good health & spirits, I remain—
Your loving daughter, Aidan

"Just send the damned tea," she grumbled, blotting the page before she folded the letter into an envelope. Doc would take it whenever he came round next; it was written, and that was the labor of it.

Joss watched from the door as Aidan addressed the letter, able to imagine that fine hand laid across the paper; her own writing was legible at best. There was so much that was so different about Aidan, she mused; good penmanship was but the tip of it. She was refinement, even with her new habit of swearing delicately, and she knew things Joss had never thought to imagine: last night the northern lights had shimmered in the sky; Joss had called her out to see, and she had said—what? "It looks how the strings of the orchestra sound when they're tuning for the symphony." Joss had heard two fiddles played lively at a barn dance, but she couldn't imagine forty of them all in harmony—or pianos in parlors, or fireplaces in drawing rooms, or gents retiring with cigars after dinner (though her banishment to the porch for her smoke seemed close). She had no concept of a debutantes' ball, or shaking white-gloved hands with senators, or dining with the President, all things Aidan had known in her nineteen years; Joss at twenty-four couldn't imagine prettily-patterned paper on the walls, or running water in the house, and until Aidan had railed at her about the kitchen floor it had never occurred to her that her house might have boards underfoot (their board porch was, on the post road, considered an Eastern frivolity).

She knew those things existed. It simply had never struck her that they would exist in her immediacy. Her mother had rarely spoken of home; for all the East had influenced Joss's life until Aidan came into it, Jocelyn might as well have been born and raised in Washburn Station. Joss had never been across the river into Missouri, or west of Topeka; Aidan had seen Paris and London, sailing on a ship as big as a city. "Aidan," she said softly, and blue eyes came to hers in question; she studied that enigmatic being who was of her own distant blood. "Why would you stay here? What is there to hold you?"

It seemed long before Aidan set down her pen and smoothed her hands across her face. Wearily, she found the pins in her hair, setting loose a lush tumble of gold. The lamp, still writing-high, made her silk gown diaphanous when at last she stood, making her approaching suppleness a shadow inside it before she slipped into Joss's arms. Bewildered—for Aidan never asked for her comfort, and sometimes refused it when it was offered—Joss

83

could only hold her, feeling the firm warmth of her before Aidan shook her head, her fingernails painfully hard at Joss's ribs, and at last came the catch of breath that meant tears.

"Aidan, what? Please tell me."

"Why did— Oh, damn—" Joss waited, allowing her to regain the threads of her control, or at least gather enough of them to allow the words. "Why did I have to come so far to find someone who could forgive me a sin I didn't commit? No, I've never been loved; not until you. You gave me the chance of blood—and damn their hearts that they couldn't give the same chance to someone they should have loved without condition!" She broke away with a harsh laugh, seeking the warmth of the stove instead. "Without condition, indeed. Even without this delicate condition, they couldn't even pretend to love me."

Joss leaned wearily against the doorframe, staring at the floor, her hands in her pockets. "Damn our blood," she murmured at last. "It's a family tradition, Aidan. Your child an' I will have some things in common. Most notably our bastardy."

Aidan looked up in amazement; Joss smiled tightly. "I've almost told you ten times earlier. It never seemed like just the time." She brushed at hair that had escaped its pins, pushing it back from her face; she left her hand there to shade her eyes. "You had Ma to come to—at least in thought. They put her on a train with a one-way ticket—no money—not even a letter of introduction. Lord knows what they thought she'd do, save be a whore in some poker parlor. She got off the train in Kansas City an' fainted. Harmon Bodett rescued her then an' never let her go, but it surely might not have gone so easy for her. Or for me."

"Oh, Joss." Aidan sank to a chair at the table. "Have you always known?"

"Since I was old enough to understand." She went to sit across the table from Aidan, her forgers finding the pen, toying with it. "All the Station knows. They've long since found new gossip to spread, but they know. Ma thought it best I hear it first from her, instead o' the likes o' Effie Richland—I got it there second." She laid the nib of the pen to Aidan's blotter, watching the slow spread of ink remaining in the quill. "Pa was a hard man, but he was a good man," she said quietly. "He never separated me from Ethan an' Seth. To me he was my father. Whatever man convinced Ma he loved her so he could leave her a grass widow when she told him she was with child..." She laid the pen on the table. "He was no father to me. Just a damn poor farmer, sowin' seed with no regard for where it grew."

"But she—Joss, did she love him? That man?"

"Yes, but she was raped sure as you were. Takin' a spirit must be as much a sin as takin' a life. All we had o' her was a shadow, betrayed everywhere she looked back." She unpinned her hair. It slithered down in lamplit shimmers, blue-black and gold as she shook it out; obliquely, Aidan wondered at the difference between the tersely efficient farmer that was Joss with her hair pinned up and her battered old hat shading her eyes, and the feral, feline femininity of her with that ebony mane wilding around her shoulders: they seemed extravagantly different people.

Joss flicked the wealth of hair back over her shoulders. "The first you heard me say o' Pa was harsh words," she said quietly, and Aidan came back from her wondering to listen, "an' true. He was far too fond of his whiskey, an' ofttimes he shirked work, but he spent every night o' my memory in this house or had fair reason for his absence. He'd lay the rod to me an' the boys for our education, but never for meanness, an' I never knowed him to raise hand nor voice to Ma. What was left o' her cared for him, but he loved her. He loved her with every bone an' drop o' blood in his body, an' I thank God that he died before her to never know the pain o' losin' her—an' that she died with the hopes o' three livin' children."

She got up to open the china closet; in the soup tureen was a bottle of whiskey. She poured a jelly jar half full. "May I do this here, or would you rather me out for it?"

"Stay." Aidan had heard the unsteady jitter of glass on glass as Joss made her drink. "Smoke if you want to."

Joss gave her a glance of weary gratitude for the generosity. "Women should never predecease their husbands." She tasted her whiskey, letting its bite serve as excuse enough for the roughness of her voice. "Nor children their mothers. It's not the order o' things people stand well."

"And what of the child losing everyone?" Gently, Aidan asked. Doc had said he'd never seen Joss cry for her family; she stayed with them while they died, and for long enough after to be sure; she prepared them for burial, and buried them, refusing his help (*God damn you, tend to the living! I'll tend the dead*), and made their markers, those carefully-carved boards inside the fence between the corn and beans. But she didn't cry.

Joss touched the coolness of the glass to her cheek, looking at or past or through Aidan for a drawn moment before she drank. "What of it?" Her voice was soft and raspy. "God calls the tune. You dance." And she took a wide turn of thought, returning to the road they had started down. "How could I not accept you? To refuse you would be to refuse my mother—to refuse myself. I had no choice but to care about you, Aidan. To find how much I care for you—" She emptied the glass; the whiskey whispered its warm song to her. "I'd love you if you were no kin to me."

Slowly, Aidan shook her head. "Joss, I've never had anyone I could trust. I've never had anyone I knew I could turn to without wondering if they'd really be there. I've never known how it feels not to be lonely, and now...How can you think to ask why I'd stay? What you give me—!"

Joss scuffed the toe of her boot at the worn-hard dirt surface of the floor. "Yuh. Everything a city girl might ever need or want, right here in Washburn Station, Kansas."

"It was good enough for your mother."

"No it wasn't. It's just what she got."

"Lord, you don't listen—" She scraped back from the table, scarring the dirt with the legs of her chair. "You, Joss Bodett. I have you." She went to Joss and took her face in her hands. "Don't you understand? Be we cousins or sisters or whatever we may call it, what we give each other is love back in our hearts. No floor can ever mean more, Joss."

Be we cousins or sisters— That was the kiss Aidan touched

86

to her mouth, but Joss had to grope for the reins of emotions charging away with her: she had never known a debutantes' ball, or a symphony, or a president's handshake; she had never known the pure ache of desire for a lover's kiss—

Until now. It took of all her will not to bury her hands in Aidan's hair, not to bend her head to that trusting warmth and ask with her kiss if cousins or sisters was all the love there might be between them. "Yes—" It was an unsteady breath into that fragrant hair; precariously, she held her, absorbing the frightened shiver that had started deep inside herself. "Yes, Aidan. I do love you."

CHAPTER SEVEN

At first Aidan didn't know what it was that night that drew her from sleep; she curled into the quilt she had grown to love for its history (the dresses Jocelyn had worn while she was pregnant with Ruth, too painful to wear and too dear to discard; Ethan's first-day-of-school shirt; Seth's first-ever shirt; Harmon's back-from-the-War shirt; Joss's I-hate-dresses dress) and listened drowsily; finally she heard the scrape of chair legs against the hard dirt floor. Softly, she sighed: Joss, up again.

The first few times it happened she had gotten up, going to ask what was wrong. "Nothin'," Joss said, looking haunted in the flickering golden glow of the lamp. "Go back to bed. No sense in the both of us bein' up."

Nights after that she lay wakeful as Joss stirred around the house: out to the well for fresh water, or to the porch for a smoke; sometimes she heard the clink of the neck of the whiskey bottle against the jelly jar Joss favored for her drink, or the hiss of a book being drawn from the case Joss had put by Aidan's door, and then the soft rustle of pages. Sometimes came the sounds of a stove being stoked by a hand cautious of the sleep of another, if the night was cool. Or—most often—just the slow, metronomic tick of her glass meeting the table as she put it down, glass against oilcloth-covered wood as she sipped an hour away.

It happened, on the average, every other night.

This night she heard a drink made, and smelled the hint of a cigarette on the porch, and when she heard the scrape of a chair at the table she pushed back the quilt and slipped into her wrapper. She went barefoot to the door she always left ajar and saw Joss at the table, the jelly jar in front of her, her forehead rested on one hand, the fingers of the other ticking a slow, slow measure against the oilcloth: little finger, ring finger, long finger, forefinger.

Little finger. Ring finger. Long finger. Forefinger.

Harmon. Jocelyn. Ethan. Seth.

Joss sipped. The glass touched softly against the table. Little finger. Ring finger. Long finger. Forefinger.

"Joss," she said quietly.

"Go back to bed." She didn't look up.

"Joss, can't you tell me?"

"Go back to bed, Aidan."

She turned, and stopped, and turned back; she went barefoot to the table and stroked her hands down the mane of black hair glinting gold in the lamplight, and bent to press her lips to the top of her cousin's head. "I love you, Joss," she whispered.

She was on the edge of sleep, drifting in and out, when she sensed a presence near her; she opened her eyes to the night and felt a warmth of breath near her face: hints of whiskey and tobacco, and then fingers gentle in her hair, lips soft against her face, a naked whisper: "Thank you."

She reached to find Joss's shoulder, the curve of her throat, the tangle of ebony hair so seldom loosed. "Stay here, Joss. Stay with me."

"I can't."

"You can't do this, either. You work too hard. You need to sleep."

Palms found her face, a brief, needing caress; softly, lips brushed hers. "If only I could tell you what you mean to me." And Joss was gone, leaving behind her the echoes of tobacco, and whiskey, and critical loneliness.

CHAPTER EIGHT

"Joss! Oh, Joss, look! In the corn—"

Her hair pinned up but yet barefoot in the morning, Joss abandoned coffee and Cervantes to see where Aidan pointed. Unworried by their morning noises, a plump doe deer grazed in the new-sprung corn, cropping at tender shoots near the woodlot. "Damn! You dare eat my sweat?" It was her father's deer-in-the-corn indignation, but her own labor over that black earth she defended; she plucked the Winchester from its pegs over the door and whistled sharply between her teeth. More curious than cautious, the doe raised her head, ears swiveling forward in inquisition.

"What are you—oh, no! Joss, no!"

But Joss was a quick shot, and a good one. Pure grace in living motion, the doe collapsed in the ungainly surprise of sudden death, her throat exploded by the bullet, and Joss turned with the small smile of a hunter's pride in a long shot and a clean kill.

"Damn you!" Aidan's fury was so electric, so unexpected, Joss didn't have time to dodge the slap that lashed across her face. "She was so beautiful! I only wanted you to see her and you *killed* her!"

Bewildered, Joss reached for her stinging cheek. "Aidan, it's meat! What—"

"Meat!" Aidan spat it back at her. "Is that all Mrs. Browning would be to you, then? Meat and never mind the poetry? Damn you, Joss Bodett!"

"Aidan, you don't understa—" But she was protesting to a back; the door that slammed between them was definitive. "Aidan, you—oh, God damn it!" Just in time, she reined in the impulse to heave what she had in her hands across the room. The instinct that made her a good shot had made her ready for another if it was needed: she had reflexively levered the spent shell from the rifle, another round jacking into the chamber, the weapon cocking itself. She let the hammer down and banged the rifle to its pegs over the door. "No poetry in a chicken, I guess," she snarled at Aidan's door, "or a pig whose ham you enjoy of a Sunday mornin' an' never mind how fond o' the damn pig I was!" She jammed her feet into her boots. "Ain't no butcher shop in Washburn Station, Miss Eastern city girl!" That was resoundingly more than a snarl as she slammed out the door. There was no time to argue, or try to explain; there was no time to waste in hot weather if a kill was to be more than a murder.

She sent her knife into the deer's white belly, splitting the skin in remaindered anger at her cousin's lack of vision, but when its paunch and hot blood smell spilled out something potently visceral stabbed her as sharply as she had driven her knife into the deer. Her breakfast lurched in her. She fought its rising and lost, and gave it to the dark earth of her cornfield. "God damn it," she whispered on her hands and knees, when she could; she coughed, and tried to spit the bilious taste from her mouth (and had a weirdly slanting moment of sympathy for her cousin, who had suffered this indignity almost daily for a month). "Damn your blood, Aidan! Did you have to hit me?"

She wiped the cold sweat of sickness from her face, and drew a hard breath and turned to the deer to touch a flank still warm, still almost vibrant under her palm. "Yes, you were beautiful," she said softly, "an' yes, you were a poem. But a poem ain't food in her belly or mine, an' it's the good Lord give me the taste for meat an' not my fault to get slapped for it. I thank you for your poetry an' for the meals you'll put on our table."

Grimly efficient, she finished dressing the deer, knowing the coyotes would clean up the leavings before the sun rose again. Aidan's door was still closed when she took the heart and liver into the house; tight-lipped, she covered the bowl and stored it in the cool space under the sink before she went to draw a bucket from the well. She scrubbed sticky blood from her hands and arms, and buried her face in a double-handful of icy water; her cheek still burned with the memory of Aidan's hand. "Damned frivolous city girl," she muttered, and went to drag the deer to the woodshed. By the time it was hung on the game pole she was awash with sweat, bloody again, and simmering with resentment.

The skinning had long been her job, for her fine touch with a blade; she approached it now for no more satisfaction than knowing what a stretched hide was worth to Thom Richland, and that was something: salt to replace what she'd use today, or flour, or cotton or linen for dresses and shirts, or boxes of bullets, or part of the promised kitchen floor...

Or part of a train ticket East.

The thought lurched her stomach. She tried to shove it away, but it twittered at the edge of her consciousness, taunting as the malicious singsong of children in a schoolyard; it made her feel the way she'd felt as a child when that vicious ditty had been aimed at her: *Joss is a baaas-turd, nyah, nah, nah-nyaah nah*— "Nyah nyah yourself," she muttered. "Go to hell an' leave me be."

Methodically, she worked.

She was aware of Aidan long before she spoke, but she'd be damned if she'd break the silence; even less than she had expected the slap had she expected to be so hurt by it. The only person in her life who had ever struck her had been her father, and on those rare occasions his reasons had been well-defined. Immediate, raw anger had never been one of them.

At last, softly: "Joss, I'm sorry."

"It don't matter." A simple apology might have sufficed an hour ago, but now, with the hurt in her as thick as the smell of sweat and blood in the day's rising heat, nothing would be simple. She smiled bitterly, knowing the work that faced her today—and for what? Would Aidan concede to eat this meat? Would she even be here to eat it?

"Joss—" The hesitant brush of fingertips at her back stilled her hand. "I was wrong to criticize you, and—" Joss closed her eyes, hearing the catch of Aidan's voice, feeling the unsteadiness of the hand on her shoulder. "I'm so sorry I struck you. Please forgive me for that. Please."

Joss swallowed hard. *It's a bigger effort she's making than you could do yourself. Would you wait until she cries?* She forced herself to yield, to turn, and found the ache in Aidan's eyes; behind that came a blinding image of the belly of the deer as she had split it with her knife. That knife spilled from suddenly nerveless fingers. She reached, catching her cousin roughly into her arms. "Oh, no. No. Aidan, come here—"

Aidan buried her face into Joss's shoulder, tears contained for the effort of the apology breaking now in its acceptance. "Joss, I'm so sorry, I hate it that I struck you, I'm just another damned Blackstone—"

"Aidan, no. Don't cry. It's all right—" It wasn't all right, but she knew that if this reunion hadn't come now it mightn't have come at all, that they might have traded spoken jabs and slashes until the hurts swarmed like mosquitoes, buzzing and biting until further exposure was unthinkable and flight was the only answer. "I'm sorry too, Aidan. I do things an' expect you to understand, an' knowin' this is all still new to you." She pressed her lips to the curve of Aidan's shoulder, tasting sweat and dust and last night's soap, and those mingled essences shivered something into her, a feeling like taking whiskey raw from the neck of a bottle, or coming from hours of January outdoors into a kitchen Sunday-dinner hot, or jumping from the haymow and seeing, halfway down, the rake glittering tines-up in the stack below. "I love you—"

It was barely a whisper, but she felt Aidan's fingers tighten against her back; more than she heard it, she felt the breath of words returned: "Joss, I love you, too—" and Aidan raised her head as Joss bent hers.

She had thought only to press her lips against her cousin's hair, to allow herself that brief indulgence, but what her kiss met wasn't golden hair but Aidan's lips, parted with the beginnings of some word or words, a thought caught back with a soft breath of surprise at the meeting.

Aidan didn't withdraw, or retreat; her fingers brushed Joss's throat, turning into a palm laid against her face. It was magnetic; it was opposite and alien and unthinkable; it was undeniable. Joss felt her arms, her hands, full of Aidan, the fit of their bodies together, the tentative inquiry of the lips under hers...

She stood again in the shadowed door of the livery on the seventh of April, watching Aidan take her first look at the mean street of Washburn Station. She felt the pale, uneasy weight of Aidan in her hands as she took her from the wagon in this yard, and remembered wanting to hold her then, to make her know it would be all right. She struggled from the phantasms of fever to an awareness of this head asleep on her belly; she saw flickers and flashes of question and courage in the blue eyes, heard the laughs, held the tears, caught the smiling sidelong glances.

She didn't know her kiss had deepened. She didn't feel Aidan's slow question. She only knew the raw flame that flared in her as the corners of their mouths sought, avoided, knew, denied...she found Aidan's lips again, fully this time, and there was a searing flicker that was their tongues meeting.

"Joss—" It was a shivering breath as Aidan broke from her. "Oh, Joss, no. No."

No...no—? No!? What— "Aidan, I'm sorry, I don't know what—" *came over you? You damnwell know what did! and catching her by surprise doesn't mean she meant to kiss you back (but she did, she*

95

did—) *and now you've frightened her witless and unless you've got the luck of Ethan Bodett at poker she'll be on the next train East.* "Aidan, I—" She drew a ragged breath, tasting her own hard earthiness and Aidan's soft, clean scent...and some deeper essence that was of them both, raw and private to the point of secrecy and she backed away: from Aidan, from that hot, subliminal awareness. "Aidan—" It was a plea, struggling between them like a rabbit caught in a spring-freshet river, freezing to death even as it tried to dodge the tumbling chaff of the current.

Aidan didn't look at her. "I'll make the stove if you want tea—?"

"No. Thanks." It almost strangled her to have to say so normal a thing; nothing was normal, not the hard flush she could feel on her own face, not the way Aidan's hands were knotted in her apron—and surely not knowing that those lips had parted under hers, that the sharply-drawn breath had been as much quickening desire as it had been shock—and knowing that desire had been clamped down on, lidded, locked behind a door as impenetrable as a bank vault. "But make up the fire. I'll need hot water all day." She heard her voice: rough, like an order. "Please," she amended, and wondered when, short of burying her family, she had done as hard a thing as watching Aidan walk away from her, watching as she drew a pail from the well and took it to the house—

"Dear God, what have I done," she moaned, and turned to the wood for a lost battle with the panic breaking in her. It drove her to her knees, her hands over her face, raw fear welling out of her: "Aidan, don't—oh, merciful Jesus, please don't let her leave me—"

The fire had burned down to a thick bed of coals; the sticks of oak Aidan coaxed into the firebox caught quickly. Heat bloomed in the kitchen, but she didn't feel it. She dumped water into the big kettle on the back middle burner, where it would heat to almost, but never quite, boiling. If the stove was to run she might as well make bread; she got the mixing bowl, and set milk and lard to heat, and opened the barrel of flour; she measured salt and molasses and flour into the bowl, and sank into a chair at the table to wait on the milk and lard...and buried her face in her hands. "Oh, Joss! Oh, my Lord—"

Had she been mistaken in what she had felt? Had their lips really parted, had their tongues really touched, had that leaping flame of—what had it been?—really happened in her belly, and if it had, what had it been or meant or...?

You know what it was. You know what it meant. You've known- "Oh, Joss," she whispered. "Oh, dear Jesus, help me." *—since the night she held you. You've known.*

Her instinct smelled the lard hot on the stove and she retrieved it, and set about her bread, and as she mixed in flour and stirred in the starter and added more flour she could only remember the metamorphosis of that kiss, the warm question of Joss's tongue, the willing parting of her lips.

She shivered, and paced the kitchen, and went back to the bread and was helpless with it. "Help me," she begged the side of the woodshed she could see from the door. "Joss, please help me with this—"

"Whatever else has happened," Joss whispered at last, "you've killed, an' you'll not commit the sin o' wastin' the flesh of a beast you caused to die." She felt her pocket for tobacco, but her little sack of makings wasn't there; she sat on the chip-scattered ground, trying to work up the courage to go to the house to get it, and couldn't. She drew a breath and got up to address the deer with the knife.

Sometimes the skin came off a deer as easily as she'd take off her own shirt. Sometimes—and this was one—the membrane between meat and hide seemed as sticky as half-set glue, and every inch had to be coaxed away. Halfway through, the point of her knife slipped with unanticipated ease through a layer of fiber she had expected to resist, and the blade sliced through the hide. "God damn it all to hell!" She stabbed the knife into the end of a piece of stovewood and paced, fuming, around the woodshed; an intact hide was worth a gold eagle, and a punctured one worth not a picayune. She filled her arms with an excuse of wood and stalked to the house, finding the kitchen empty, bread rising under a cloth on the table. She listened hard for Aidan and heard no hint of her, and wrestled the wood into the box and slapped her makings from the sideboard.

Back at the woodshed, she rolled a cigarette; the making and the smoking helped calm her, and by the time she had ground the end of it under the heel of her boot she was able to check the hide for damage. It was a small nick; maybe Thom wouldn't notice (maybe Margaret Milk Cow would jump over the moon; maybe double eagles would be picked from cherry trees). She tested the knife against her thumb, stroked it on the steel, checked it, cut herself; she sucked the blood from the cut and started again.

"Oh, damn your clumsy hand!" Another slice in the hide, her sight blurred by the memory of the shadow of Aidan's slimness inside backlit silk. She took no more caution with the skin; it was ruined (and of course came off without further damage). She tossed it to the wood and leaned against a stack of split oak and elm, her stomach jumpy; still headed but denuded of its hide, the deer looked like an obscenity hanging there, its eyes glassy with death, its tongue lolling. "You worry about her eatin' any of it," she swallowed. "Your own taste for venison ain't holdin' up so good."

She shivered a sigh and took the kindling axe from its pegs inside the woodshed. "All right, deer. You'll be work an' not short, but I'll be hanged if you'll die for naught." She started the quartering, Aidan flickering around her thoughts as persistently as the fat flies drawn by the scent of the blood, and more distracting. There was no satisfaction in the job; it only needed doing. She knew she'd think beyond the kill when next she pulled a trigger.

She wished she could shake off the vision of Aidan in the house, gathering her belongings, packing her trunk, preparing her exit from the life of someone who had finally done one arbitrary thing too many. She wished she could dispel the image of the house empty of her gentle warmth: it was a meaner emptiness than had been there before she had come, an absence hollower and more—

"Will you eat?"

Her hands and her thoughts had been miles apart. The quiet question jolted them together, jarringly unsynchronized; she jumped, and the knife blade she had been working between two vertebrae snapped from its haft. She stared at the bone handle in her palm. "Damn," she said, tight-jawed, and worked the blade out of the deer's spine. "You been a hard luck son of a snake from the start, deer. Pa give me this knife." She touched the broken ends of the blade together, and blew a sigh, and closed what was left of the blade and slipped the Barlow into her pocket.

"Come eat." Aidan's voice was low, controlled. "There's fresh bread."

Joss looked up, finding eyes to match her cousin's voice: cautious, bridled, something hidden that she wanted to keep that way, and she wondered: would a woman on the verge of flight spend the morning making bread?

"Come have a wash and a cold drink, and you'll feel more like working."

She didn't want to go inside, to see the bare spaces she was sickly afraid would be there: the china closet where Doc's teapot had been, the shelf by the side door where Aidan had kept daybook and ink bottle and quill, the bookcase she had put by Aidan's door, where *Don Quixote* and *A Christmas Carol* and the poems of the Brownings had resided. But Aidan turned; reluctantly, Joss followed. Halfway to the house she stopped, her belly squirming like worms in a tomato can, her heart screaming for one answer. "Aidan—"

Sun glinted on golden hair when Aidan turned. Their eyes held long in the hard noon light. "Are you—" She swallowed, and forced the question out. "Have I driven you away now?"

There was no knowing what flickered in her eyes, but her voice, when finally she spoke, was calm. "Don't be foolish, Joss. Come eat."

"That's no answer."

"The question scarce deserves one. You've done nothing to offend me, save ruining a shirt that looked so good on you. Will you have your wash on the porch, please? I've a sink full of dishes. I've left you a clean shirt."

Joss washed, and left the bloody shirt to soak in the basin and went in, her fingers fumbling with buttons, her eyes seeking the china closet, the shelf, the bookcase, and she breathed a taut sigh, seeing teapot and daybook, Cervantes and Dickens, the Brownings open at the end of the table. Buttoning her cuffs, she paused at the book of poetry.

If thou must love me, let it be for naught
Except for love's sake only. Do not say,
"I love her for her smile—her look—her way
Of speaking gently—for a trick of thought
That falls in well with mine, and certes brought
A sense of pleasant ease on such a day"
For these things in themselves, Beloved, may
Be changed, or change for thee—and love, so wrought,
May be unwrought so. Neither love me for
Thine own dear pity's wiping my cheeks dry—
A creature might forget to weep, who bore
Thy comfort long, and lose thy love thereby!
But love me for love's sake, that evermore
Thou may'st love on, through love's eternity.
When our two souls stand up erect and strong,
Face to face, silent, drawing nigh and nigher
Until the lengthening wings break into fire . . .

Too aware of Aidan watching her, she turned from the book; she put the pieces of her knife in the china cabinet next to the Baptist hymnal.

They barely spoke through the meal. "It's good bread," Joss said.

"I didn't sun the flour, and I've cut into it much too soon. I'm surprised it's fit to eat." There was a faint smear of blood on

Joss's chin. Yesterday Aidan would have wet her napkin with her tongue and reached to wipe it away. Today—

"It's good as Ma's. You've turned into a good cook."

"Thanks to her recipes." She watched as Joss carved the heel from the other end of the loaf she had opened for dinner. It was still warm; a thick spread of butter melted to accept sugar sprinkled liberally on top of that. Joss ate it standing up, looking out the window over the sink. *I love thee with the passion put to use In my old griefs, and with my childhood's faith...*

"Damn cat's got a rabbit," she said, and wiped her hands on a towel and got the kettle from the stove to fill the dishpan. "Watch he don't try to bring it in to show you."

"Don't bother with those. I'll do them." Aidan stood, smoothing her apron. "Can I—is there anything I can—I've never—" She sat again. "I suppose I'd just be in your way."

Joss turned. "What?"

She didn't dare look up. "I—is there anything I can do to help you? With the deer? I know I've never done it before, but—"

Slowly, Joss came back to the table; she sat to roll a smoke with careful precision. "I've never done it alone before." She licked the seal of her cigarette. "About all we can do is can it an' jerk it. Prob'ly it's too hot to try cornin' any, but I don't know what else to do with it. Hard to keep meat with no ice." She stood, going to the window again; Aidan knew she was looking at the split-rail fence between the corn and beans. "Wasn't thinkin' clear when I shot it," she murmured. "A deer'd hardly last two weeks before. Lucky to have enough to make jerky, an' lucky to get any o' that away from Ethan." A humorless laugh bit from her. "Get all I want now."

She went to the porch. Aidan heard the creak of cane and the scratch of a match, and smelled smoke; reluctantly, not sure her company was wanted, she went to the door. Joss rocked slowly, her cigarette between her forgers, her elbow on the arm of the chair and her chin on her thumb as she stared at the little graveyard. She sipped at her cigarette, barely moving; smoke leaked from her nostrils. "Come sit," she said quietly.

Aidan wrapped a corner of her apron around a finger and wet the cloth with her tongue. Gently, she wiped the smudge of blood from Joss's chin.

Cane creaked. A faint breeze toyed with the leaves of the elms. Up on the wooded hill, a woodpecker hammered an incessant rhythm on a dead tree.

Joss shot her cigarette end into the yard with a thumb-powered forefinger and sighed to her feet. She scanned the simmering sky; there were no clouds save high, useless wisps. "God-awful weather. Need some rain." And she stretched, her shoulders popping. "Well. It ain't doin' itself."

"Joss—"

One foot on the first step down, Joss turned.

"I brought this for Seth," Aidan said softly, offering the scrimshaw-handled folding knife from her apron pocket. "It's from Germany. A sailor on Nantucket—that's an island in Massachusetts—did the carving on the ivory. I know it can't replace the one your father gave you, but..."

Slowly, Joss picked the knife from Aidan's palm. She turned it over in her fingers, and opened it, and tested the blade against a few hairs on her wrist; it shaved them off cleanly. "It's a good blade," she murmured, and closed it again to examine the finely-detailed hunting scene on the handle. "Almost too pretty to use, it seems." She cleared her throat. "Seth likes pretty things. He's always pickin' up little rocks an' shiny things, an'—an'—thank you." Abruptly, she turned; she was halfway to the woodshed before she could open her fingers enough to slip the knife into her pocket.

Hot.

The scent of fresh death called flies that buzzed thick, dull songs in the blood-smelling afternoon as they landed on the— *God-damn flies*—meat, crawling over the blood-sticky surfaces— *first they visit the shithouse then they walk on your dinner—* "Damn! Git! God damn it, go on—"

"Whoa, Joss! Jeepers, gal, settle down, you got that deer

about dead by now, I'd say! Come on—oof! Damnit, Joss—hey now! Settle your feisty self down before I—whoa! Joss, put the knife down, Josie, this is Hank, come on, you know I'm your friend—"

"Th'only one calls me Josie is Doc an' ever'body else come to visit lately's wanted somethin' I ain't about to give up. I don't expect you're any damn different. Speak your piece an' get th' hell out."

All that was between him and three inches of German carbon steel was a felt Stetson hat. It was better than nothing; he held it there. "I'm s 'pose to be askin' you to marry me, but I know you don't want me so I won't offend you by the askin'," Ephrenia Richland's oldest son said softly. "I won't bother your cousin neither, though I was told to an' the good Lord knows I'd marry her if it'd put me close to you. I know what he'll go, Joss. I ain't sayin' sell. I'm only sayin' I know what you can get out of him, an' a sight more'n he's offerin' you."

She read twenty years of shared history—and their mutual distaste for his parents—in Hank's eyes before she lowered the knife.

He backed away, glad to be intact; he'd known Joss Bodett long enough to know she had days when she wasn't much less crazy than her brother Ethan had been. "Got a long day comin', workin' up a deer." He found two rolled cigarettes in his tobacco pouch and offered her one.

"I's realizin' the lack o' hands when you came by." She accepted the cigarette and the light that followed it.

"I'd stay if I could, Joss. I'm headed for Leavenworth."

"You could bring me a bottle o' whiskey an' know I wasn't askin' for more help than I got."

"She workin' out?"

Joss bristled. "She's my kin, not my God-damned lady-in-waitin'. You got news for me?"

Hank was a handsome six-footer, broad-shouldered, slim-hipped, the easy-smiling heartthrob of most of the girls in western Leavenworth County; it had been his bad luck to fall hard in love at twelve with Joss Bodett, who had broken his nose once and his heart more times than he could remember. Right now he wanted to kiss her; he was sure that if he tried she'd run her knife between his ribs with no more thought than she'd need to slick the meat off that deer's bones.

He named a figure and grinned at her double-take. "An' Flora said she'd top him just for spite. I heard Mr. Carpenter at the bank tell Flora he'd lend you money against knowin' she'd be good for it."

"Jehosephat," she breathed. The idea that Mr. Carpenter, with his pinstriped vest and gold watch chain perpetually straining at his enormous belly, would lend her money against her farm was boggling. "Pa'd come back to haunt me if ever I borrowed a dime, but what a thing to know!" She pushed her hair away from her face with her wrist. "Lord have mercy, Hank!"

"Ain't it, though? Say, I could fix your hair so it'd hold better," he offered, and she looked at her bloody hands and nodded. He unpinned the ebony length, and apologized for his own comb; more slowly than he was able, treasuring the chance to touch her, he made a French braid. "I don't suppose you would," he murmured, halfway done.

"Would what?"

"Marry me. You know I love you, Joss. I always have."

"I thought you wasn't goin' to offend me with the question."

Finished with the braid, he reached into his shirt pocket for the pins. "You'd make me spend my whole life alone for not wantin' anyone but you?"

"You done it yourself by keepin' on with it when I said no the first time."

He coiled the braid around itself, pinning carefully. "I'd make you a good husband, Joss. I wouldn't let you do work like this."

"You wouldn't let me?" Coolly, she laughed. "That's the trouble I see with marryin', Hank. A man gets a wife, but a woman gets a master." She tasted her cigarette and spat a shred of tobacco from her tongue. "No, Hank. Not you. Not anyone. Not me. Not ever."

CHAPTER NINE

"Don't move, Joss."

She had been thinking about Aidan, wondering about Hank, worrying about Aidan, thinking about Ethan, Effie, Ottis Clark, Gideon Jackson...mostly, her mind had been sidling around the edges of her thoughts about Aidan. The soft command froze her in momentary confusion. Fingertips touched her shoulder, staying her. "Don't move—" She heard water meeting water and was suddenly warmer; she came to her senses, almost groaning in the pleasure of the bath.

"Don't move." Aidan's aim with the teakettle was unerring: everywhere a part of Joss wasn't, hot water went. "Just soak. Soak out the day."

She had spent all the daylight with the deer: skinning, quartering, boning, starting the corning, slicing strips to soak for jerky, grinding the toughest parts for canned meat (as if it all wouldn't be tough, disallowed the luxury of hanging time) and cursing Tucker Day, the deceased ice man, for falling off the church roof and breaking his damned neck. The work had kept most of her mind from Aidan, even when she was close beside her at the stove, or just across the table, or on the other side of the big kettle as they took meat and brine to the barn for the corning crock, and she had a new, weary respect for her mother and brothers, who had always done this labor before, Joss doing enough to know how to do it now but escaping the heaviness of it, as Aidan had escaped it today. She finished bone-tired and aching, bloody and irritable, sweaty and reeking and hungry, and Aidan met her on the porch with hot water and hard soap and her third shirt of the day, the scent of frying liver with chives wafting from the house.

Half-clean, she savored liver and bread and greens from the kitchen garden, and when she finished her smoke her bath was ready. She luxuriated there now, breathing a sigh of appreciation for the pampering...and for the absence of the precarious shyness that had quivered between them for most of the day. "You're good to me," she murmured. "Better than I deserve."

"Don't ever think you don't deserve it." That voice, like the susurrous murmur of night breeze in ripe corn ... hands, wet and intimate, traced her shoulders, and some visceral thing inside her slipped, a tilting warmth that suspended her breath and made all of her thoughts one name as fingers found her neck, soothing the knots work had left there, tying new ones under her heart. She knew she had never been touched the way Aidan was touching her now. She knew she had never been so intensely aware of another human being. Delicately, fingers tracked the lengths of her collarbones, brushed the hollows above them, wandered below them to stroke the soreness from hard-used muscles; softly, they drew up her breastbone to measure the vulnerable, exposed line of her throat. The warmth in her belly blossomed to a low, urgent heat. Stop, she knew she should say, but too much of her was pleading *don't stop, please don't stop*—

"What would you say—" It was a breath of words in her ear;

106

if she turned her head Aidan's lips would be there. *But if you did and it wasn't the question...once might be named a mistake, but twice and she'll name it goodbye and you know you can't live without her.* "—to a cup of tea? I'll even make you a cigarette." A low, soft laugh. "I'll try to, anyway."

Tea?? Lord above—! She searched for her voice, hoping it would work, hoping it would say what it ought to instead of what it wanted to. "Make that a drink o' whiskey an' a cigarette an' I'd be a happy woman." *Aidan, it's you I want. Can't you see?*

"Whiskey and cigarettes!" That throaty laugh again. "Whatever shall I do with you, Joss Bodett?" Hands cupped her face; upside-down from behind, a kiss brushed the corner of her mouth. "You know those aren't proper things for a lady, heaven forbid in the house! But if they'll make you happy...you shall be a happy woman if I can make you that, my darling cousin."

Joss lay there in the tub, her jaw still clenched against the desire that had almost overpowered her when Aidan's lips had touched her own, her skin alive with the memory of Aidan's hands, her heart hammering painfully. *Find the reins, Joss, or tie a noose in your rope. She's just being Aidan—your dear cousin Aidan— and means nothing more. This is how it has to be.*

"I didn't know you were so religious, little cousin," she said when Aidan came with whiskey in her favorite jelly jar and a smokable cigarette, and she was surprised at how easy and playful her voice sounded. "You an' Ethan wouldn't have got on well at all. He taught me all the sins that pass my lips."

Aidan's eyes met hers. "It seems a bit late for protest of what's touched your lips," she said softly, "liquor or otherwise." She struck a match on the base of the tub and offered the flame between them. "I'll leave you to your sacrilegious habits, dear cousin. Call me if you need hot water."

Half the cigarette burned down between Joss's fingers before the hiss of ashes falling into the tub made her remember she had it; she snapped out of a reverie of repetition *(lips that touch liquor must never—)* and dared a look at the table, where Aidan sat writing. Joss revived her cigarette, and regarded the glass in her

107

hand; finally, she tasted that, too. "What do you write?"

"A fat deer in the corn this morning is in jars and brine and our bellies tonight owing to the hard labour of Cousin Joss. *Et cetera.*"

A faint smile twitched to Joss's lips, there and gone; she nibbled at the rim of her glass, wondering about the *et cetera*. She had never opened Aidan's daybook or diary—had never considered doing so—but she wondered, sometimes, what might be there.

Aidan's daybook read as she had spoken. It was her diary she wrote in now.

Joss shot a deer to-day. Misguided, I was horrified, & said vile things to her. Worse yet, the ugliness of the Blackstone blood arose in me: I slapped her. Horrified again, & utterly unable to face her! Tho' I knew her feelings were most grievously wounded, it took far too long for me to reconcile my immediate knowledge that I owed her abject apology, & the good sense of the kill. I feared she would deposit me on the next stage bound for L'worth & the most express train east, but at last I found the courage to go to her. Had she sent me away I would have been broken-hearted! Never did I anticipate such dependence upon another soul for all my happiness, but I know that without her I would surely die for lack of sustenance to my heart, I love her so.

In accepting my apology she kissed me in a way I neither expected nor understood. I do not understand it now beyond the certain knowledge, borne by the tenderness of her touch, that naught but love & respect for me underlay it, but even as I feared she would send me away she seemed to fear I might go of my own accord, & has been shy & uneasy with me all day. I think were I to speak of it she would come quite undone, but I feel I must, or come undone myself! I am at sixes & sevens, not knowing what to make of my feelings. But the page is near done & so is the day. Sleep shall certainly clear my mind.

A deer is a great lot of work!

While Aidan wrote Joss soaked, and sipped, and she was calmer but no less confounded when she stepped from the tub and into the towel Aidan held for her. It was fresh from the line; something hollow touched her in its familiar smell and feel as she hugged it around her. She forced back the tears that stung her eyes, but the memory of her mother hanging laundry on a dry, windy Monday lingered in the smell of the flannel.

"Sure," she murmured, when Aidan came with a shirt to find her staring blankly at the floor and asked if she was all right. She turbanned her hair in the towel and slipped into the offered shirt. It was crisply ironed, but still worn-soft; she would have known blind that it was Ethan's. He had favored Saturday-afternoon barber shaves with liberal applications of bay rum, and that sharp, spicy scent lingered in the cloth.

"He's so tall—" She sniffed a pained laugh, feeling the tails of the shirt brushing her thighs. "By the time he's fifteen the sassy rogue's callin' me little sister, an' me three years older."

Aidan squeezed her shoulder in silent understanding of her missing those so freshly gone. "Come," she said quietly. "Sit. I'll do your hair for you."

Joss sat. Aidan draped her shoulders with a towel to keep her shirt dry and unwound her hair; patiently, her fingers an occasional, gentle massage against her scalp, she towel-dried the thick black length. "Your hair is so lovely," she murmured. "Like a crow in the sunlight, so black it's blue."

"An' as much a trial as a crow in the corn," Joss grumbled, irritable in the wake of too much work and too many emotions. She didn't know how many times that day she'd tried to scrub her hands clean enough on her jeans to put that unruly mane back into its pins; even Hank's braid hadn't lasted through the job. She had wished it gone each time then, and she wished it gone again now. "I wish I could be shed of it. I wish I could just have it cut right off short like Doc's."

She felt Aidan's lips touch the top of her head, and the breath of her whisper: "Silly. It's what makes you beautiful, Joss."

Joss blew a derisive snort. "First time I ever heard me an'

beautiful in the same breath."

"You are, you know."

"I know what I ain't better than I know what I am, an' I ain't ever been or ever goin' to be beautiful." She started a cigarette, needing something to do with her hands. She felt the comb, and the tug as its teeth met a snarl—and with that tug, she was out of patience. "Cut it off!" Tobacco spilled across the tabletop. "I'm past my tolerance for it! Women keep long hair for God or men. I'll take my chances with God, an' if I wanted a man I'd have him by now!"

"Joss, this is your whiskey talking—"

"Whiskey, the devil! A man doin' my work would scarce bother with such as this!"

"Joss, you can't cut your hair! My stars, what people would say—"

"Hang what they say! They say now I'm the hell-bound bastard daughter of a Yankee whore with the bathtub to prove it. When they gossip of me they leave some other soul be. Aidan, please cut it for me. It's a trial I've no time for."

"Oh, Joss—" Helplessly, she gathered the black thickness into both her hands, loving it for itself and for the nightly transition it effected; she understood the request, but was afraid of it. "Saint Paul said—"

"Oh, Saint Paul! Paul said the man was the glory o' God, an' the woman the glory o' the man. He didn't hold a woman to be no more than chattel, an' ain't no man owns me. He said this damnable tress was given me for a cover for when I pray unto God?" Her voice was thick with scorn. "I prayed unto God with all this hair an' all my heart, an' all I got for my prayers was four fresh graves. God don't give a damn about me or my hair." She shoved back from the table, four steps taking her to her belt and the sheath knife there. "I'll cut it myself, then. Damn the gossip an' damn God if He can't admit a short-haired woman to His Kingdom."

"Joss, that's blasphemy! Oh, Lord, forgive her—"

"He'll have to forgive me without this insufferable hair."

110

She knew the knife was sharp; the last thing she'd done before sheathing it was hone it, and now, this moment, that unruly mane had to leave her neck, her waistband when she tucked in her shirt, her face when she chopped pokeweed or split wood or shoveled stalls. She wound it into a damp, taut twist.

"Joss, no!" Aidan caught her arm. "Not that way, Joss, please! Sit. I'll do it—"

"If I sit you'll but try to dissuade me. I know my own mind, Aidan."

I prayed unto Him with all this hair and all my heart and all I got for my prayers was four fresh graves. "No," she said softly, and knew she would see the inside of the Washburn Station Baptist Church only for the rare weddings and funerals Joss felt a need to attend. "No, Joss. I'll just cut your hair."

Joss sat, watching warily as Aidan got her sewing basket for the shears and scissors there; Aidan put those tools on the table and finished combing out the dark mane. She tied it back with string and rested her hands on Joss's shoulders. "Are you sure?"

"Yes." *No, Hank. Not you, not anyone, not ever, and with this gone no man would think to want me. All I want is to be left be.* "Please. Just cut it."

There was a breathless realization that it was too late to change her mind when Aidan's almost-moan chased the crunching bite of the shears: "God forgive us both—" and a two-foot-long damp black ponytail came around her shoulder to be placed gently on the table.

"It's too late for regrets." Joss tried to appease Aidan, but she was almost queasy at the evidence before her. "Finish it. Like Doc's, up around the ears an' close to the neck." *I'm sorry, God. I'm not strong enough to bear all my crosses and that hair too.* She settled in the chair, too distracted by what Aidan was doing to be too aware of her touch. The blades of the scissors were cool at the back of her neck as Aidan sculpted the first brutal hack. "Hank Richland came by," she said at last.

"I thought that was his horse. What was Hank about?"

"He asked me to marry him."

The scissors hesitated, and finally clipped again. "And?"

"Would I be gettin' a haircut if I'd said yes? I told him to go shit in his hat an' pull it down over his ears. That's how many times I've told him no."

"Oh, Joss! You're *so* vulgar." It was a helpless laugh; the scissors paused their whispering around her left ear for a moment. "Does it occur to you that he might truly love you? He seems a gentle fellow."

"Oh, he's gentle enough, an' a good friend, but lovin' me's his misfortune. Can't you see me in that white getup, holdin' a bouquet o' tumbleweeds an' sayin' I do when I don't want to? That'd be worth hirin' the picture-taker for." She blew a brief, moist raspberry. "He says he'd make me a good husband by not lettin' me do hard work. Such goodness as that I can live well enough without, an' watchin' my farm go to hell for havin' a storekeep not know how to run it nor let me, either."

"You do work too hard, Joss."

"I live on the face o' God's green earth. A farm's hard. Wish I could've took on Zeke Clark for a hand—Flora got him for bed an' board an' a half-eagle a month, Doc says—but I'd've made a hard enemy out've Ottis if I had. He's still all up in a froth over that hayin' business, like it was my fault Zeke called him out. Gid was the one tellin' him just cause his Pa's a ass ain't no reason for him to be one too, an' him almost growed." She chuckled. "It was that 'almost' that got Zeke all het up, Gid said. Ain't sixteen a age for a boy to be! All horn an' howl an' not a lick o' sense in a wagonload of 'em."

"I don't care for Ottis. There's something...coarse about him."

"Look at them eyes," Joss agreed. "Man's meaner'n a snake." She resumed the making of the cigarette she had started earlier. "Marcus is about the only one that don't watch words around him, I guess, but Marcus's big enough to hunt bear with a switch, an' he don't miss them fingers none in a fight. Ma always says it was the good Lord's doin' that put the Bodetts 'tween the Jacksons an' the Clarks or there wouldn't be nothin' left but the bones."

"Turn your chair; I need to get at your front. Thank you." Aidan stepped between Joss's knees so she could reach. "Tell me about Flora Washburn. Everyone talks about her, but I've never met her."

"Flora's a queer ol' bird. She'll give a boy a hand up one day, like Zeke, an' hold another one under her boot the next. She let Ethan have go at all them pecans, but not a week later she like to wore the hide off'n Nat Day for fillin' his poke with what'd dropped over the fence. He picked a hundred bushels o' nuts to pay for that pokeful, an' his daddy barely in the ground."

"Ethan asked her. Nathaniel didn't."

"I suppose. Seemed harsh to me. He didn't jump into the orchard." She fingered her unlit cigarette, keeping her eyes closed, but she could still smell the clean, soft scent of Aidan too close to her. "She's about eighty, they say. Older'n Methuselah, anyway. Don't look it. Still rides, an' drives her own buggy. Surprised she ain't showed up yet. Maybe she's waitin' on me to present you. Suppose we could dig out the finery an' pay a call one afternoon. I ain't wearin' no dress, though. She wears breeches. Only reason I ever got away with it."

"You'd have done as you pleased with or without Flora Washburn. Tip your head up." She touched a finger under Joss's chin and gave her a critical look one side to the other; dubiously, she shook her head. "I'm as done as I can do. Mayhap the barber will take pity and finish the job."

Joss let her fingers have first look; it felt like what she had asked for. It felt exotic and free and comfortable; it felt frightening. She wondered if she'd dare to take off her hat in town for the next—oh, six or eight years. She stood, brushing hair from her shirtfront, and lit her cigarette.

"Aren't you going to look in the glass?"

"I will. I need to shake out this shirt, though. I feel all itchies." She went to the porch and stepped out of the light; Aidan heard the snap of the shirt, and in a moment Joss came back, still doing buttons. "How's it look?"

"Don't ask me. See for yourself."

113

"Suppose I've got to," Joss murmured. "Feels so good I hate to, though." Reluctantly, she went to the mirror.

"Mercy—" It was a soft breath of shock. "Moses on the mountain, look at Ethan," she whispered. "A rat's-tail of a mustache an' I'd be Ethan Bodett."

Weakly, Aidan smiled, recalling her arrival in Washburn Station and her first sight of the slim and handsome cowboy who had approached her; she had assumed that person to be Ethan, had known he was Ethan. Two of the deepest shocks of her nineteen years had been her father's dry, "You're with child," and that cowboy's equally dry, "I'm Joss Bodett." Looking at Joss now, she saw that darkly handsome cowboy again, and it stirred something vaguely uneasy in her.

"You did a fine job of it, Aidan," Joss said softly. "Thank you." And she smiled: it was an Ethan-smile, glinting and wicked. "We'll tell Saint Paul I got the lice. Maybe he wasn't lookin' tonight an' we'll get by with it."

"Hush," Aidan protested, not at all comfortable with the possibility of Saint Paul's opinion. She hung the hank of hair on the wire over the stove and got the broom and dustpan. "Do you really look like Ethan now?"

Joss found a damp four-inch lock of hair on the floor and stuck it under her nose. "Ethan. I wish you'd've known him." Her mustache disintegrated as she spoke; she sat, brushing hairs from her lip. "An' I say that—" She drew on her cigarette and found it dead; she scratched a match under the table, raising an eyebrow in request for permission. Aidan nodded, and Joss lit up and exhaled smoke in a soft sigh. "You'd love Seth. He's like Ma—quiet an' sweet—even if there's somethin' in the both of 'em to make you wonder if they ain't just resigned. But Ethan—"

She frowned at her jelly jar, finally swallowing the rye left in it. "I don't expect you'd've cared for him in the long run." She picked a hair from her tongue and flicked it away. "You'd've fell in love with him at the first; he's such a charmer. But he don't understand—" She groped for a word. "Fences? Restraints. Or— limits, I guess. An' you'd have saw that. He was fun, but he just wasn't reliable. Had he not died of the grippe, it would've been by the hand of a jealous man, or one beat at cards—fair, though. Ethan didn't need to cheat; he was God-blessed lucky at them pasteboards. But he lived what parts o' life he enjoyed an' never mind the rest. Today he'd've likely shot the deer an' been gone, as if good aim was work enough an' I couldn't've did it."

Aidan, remembering her own response to good aim, turned to the stove with her dustpan, not wanting Joss to see the blush. "Land sakes, girl, don't burn that great lot of hair," Joss protested when she reached for the lid lifter to raise a burner plate. "It'll stink to high heaven." She rescued the dustpan and took it to the porch, winging its contents to the night— "No, cat. Stay out where the mice are." —and came back brushing off her hands. "But still, I wish you could've known him."

"As do I. All of them." Aidan sat at the table; she trimmed the lamp to its softest light. "Poor cat should have a name," she murmured. Finally she looked up. "Joss, this morning...I hate it that I slapped you. I didn't understand—"

Joss looked away; there was plenty about today that she didn't understand, or dare to approach. "It's all right, Aidan. Let it be. Let's think up a name for the cat."

"Orion, after the constellation; he hunts in the stars, like the cat. And it's not all right. I saw something beautiful, and for a moment I despised you for killing it, but I had no leave to do what I did. We call it Blackstone blood and we damn it, but I don't want this child to learn those ways. I need to remember how it hurt us both that it happened."

Joss tipped her jelly jar to its side. "Did you empty the bottle?"

"Not quite."

Joss went to the china cabinet and the soup tureen there. She got the bottle from it and came back to the table. The cork squeaked as she drew it from the neck; a quick shiver chased up Aidan's spine. "You'll remember," Joss said quietly, emptying the amber liquid into her glass. "It's the only time I've ever saw it true that it hurt you worse than it hurt me."

"I don't believe that. I can still see how you looked. I didn't hurt your face, Joss, I hurt your heart. And I hate that."

"I've got an' given worse. Let it go, Aidan."

Aidan sighed. "Would that I could. Perhaps had the others been here to share the work—but I was of so little use to you! This morning I saw a murder. Tonight I see so much hard, hard work for little more end than keeping a frivolous city girl alive—"

Joss sent her an aggrieved look, remembering muttering those same accusing words that morning. "Aidan, you're not—"

"—and I want you to know how dearly I appreciate it. At home there was meat on the table and we ate it, or we went to market and bought it." She looked up from under a fringe of dark lashes. "Butcher shops by the dozen in those big Eastern cities," she teased gently; Joss managed a pained smile. "I deserved that. But here, saving chickens, whatever I've eaten was killed and tended to before I came—until now. I know what it cost now. I know good aim was the easy part and hardly work enough done, and had Ethan been here and left you with the work after the killing, I'd not have fed him tonight. Maybe from him, I'd have still seen it as a murder."

Joss gave her a weary smile. "Ethan would shoot for the pleasure o' shootin' well, but I never saw him kill just for the pleasure o' killin.' I think was we required to eat all we killed we'd live in peace, but you can't tell some men that. They enjoy the killin' too much."

"Argus Slade," Aidan murmured. And she stared at her cup; it wasn't just Slade. It was Jared Hayward, and his father, and her own; it was the newly-crowned man who was Ezekiel Clark, who had taken grim pleasure in the beating he'd given his father—and it was his father, and the soldiers who had accosted her when she had stepped from the train her first day on the western side of the Missouri River. They could fight a war to free the slaves, she thought, because they knew they still had women. She knew a man—Ethan or most any other—would make his kill and expect his women to clean up after him.

But Joss? Joss was as good as a man at man's work, but she

116

thought like a woman: she assumed nothing, as likely to lend a hand at the dishpan or stove as she was to mend fences or split wood; Aidan felt like a partner, not a slave, to this enigmatic being who in the space of a morning could kill without compunction and then kiss her as gently as—more gently than—

Any man.

That strange and frightening kiss had been how a man might have kissed her...if men thought like women, and knew to stop when a no was said.

She looked up to be startled by a short-haired stranger, but she knew the warm, dark eyes. "Joss—" But the words wouldn't come; she looked away. When at last she spoke, her voice was very soft. "Joss, I...what happened to us this morning?"

The short end of her cigarette suddenly demanded attention; Joss took a last hot taste of it and got up to put it in the stove. "What d'you mean?" She felt exposed in the thigh-length shortness of Ethan's shirt. There came a sudden, pungent memory of that rogue brother of hers, laughing wickedly after his first trip to a Kansas City whorehouse, telling her about it: *they licked each other, Joss! Would you ever do that, kiss another woman between her legs? They liked it, too, both of 'em. I could tell they did.*

"You know damn well what I mean," Aidan said, and Joss almost jumped.

"I—" She made meticulous adjustment to the stove lids, her blood roaring in her ears. *They licked each other. Would you—* "I don't know, Aidan. I..." She swallowed. "I don't know."

Aidan's gaze was so gentle that at last Joss had to meet it, her own look pleading that this be left alone, and for a silent moment their eyes held; it was Aidan, finally, who looked away and said quietly, "I suppose I'm ready for bed, then. You must be tired."

Joss breathed a tiny sigh of relief. "Yuh. Long day."

Aidan cupped her hand behind the chimney of the lamp; in a puff of breath the night closed around them. Joss stood cautiously in place, waiting for her eyes to adjust. "Isn't it dark tonight." Aidan's voice was closer than when the lamp went out. "New moon?"

"I'd say." Her nerves screamed at her, memory adding to the chorus: *stay with me, Joss, I'm so afraid of the dark—*

"Will you walk me in?"

"I—yuh." Aidan's fingers found hers, a touch like sunrise and moonshine, like heat lightning shimmering across August afternoons, or stars shooting to their deaths through midnight skies; Joss was acutely aware of her nakedness under the worn-thin old shirt. "G'night," she whispered at the bedroom door, and tried to turn, but Aidan kept her hand. "Aidan—"

"Stay with me," Aidan said softly, and Joss's belly took a painful leap toward her heart. "Please, Joss."

"Aidan, I can't—" She rescued her hand and tried to put it in a pocket she wasn't wearing, and then didn't know what to do with it, or its companion; she stuck them into her armpits. She wished she hadn't had the whiskey. She wished for more of it. She wished for a cigarette. She wished she had on trousers. She wished she was out in the barn, out in the beans, out in the night—anywhere; just out of this precarious place.

"Joss, don't leave me alone with this. Please. I know you don't want to talk about it, but—"

"It's not the talkin' I'm afraid of." She raked her hand through what was left of her hair, a breath escaping her that felt as if it had been held in tight rein all day. "I'm sorry if I frightened you," she said softly. "I didn't intend that, Aidan. None o' this. This mornin'—I don't know what it was. I didn't mean to do it. It just...happened. It won't again."

"Joss, I've never felt—" She drew a breath. "I can't pretend it didn't happen. Not when—" She bit that off, as if it were an admission too close to the truth to reveal. "Joss, I—"

Joss waited, but there was no more. "I wish I could lie to you, Aidan." She ran a hand over her face, and through her hair; she shook her head. "How I kissed you—" The words tasted odd and liquid; she had to stop, to absorb their intimate, unfamiliar flavor. "It's how I feel," she said quietly. "About you. But I never meant for you to know."

"Joss, why? Why would you keep that from me?"

"I'm afraid of it! It's only part of how I love you, an' if it'd cost you leavin' me—"

"Leaving you!" It was a strangled laugh of disbelief. "If you told me to I'd go, but if they came for me, I wouldn't." She abandoned the support of the doorframe, took a step into the bedroom, turned back. "All the time I was growing up they told me I'd find a nice man and fall in love and live happily ever after. And then Mother would tell me about a wife's duty. She'd say all a woman can do is suffer it. Well, I suffered it once! You didn't frighten me, Joss. Jared Hayward frightened me. He hurt me and he humiliated me, and I'll never let a man touch me again."

"Aidan, he was but one man an' a bad one. You can't say that. It's like—"

"Don't tell me I can't! A wife's duty is naught but the worst of a life of slavery, and I'll be damned first!" She fumbled pins from her hair and threw them at a basket on the stand by the bed; shielded by the dark and the thick fall of her hair, she searched for her composure. "I don't know what I've thought today, but leaving you never occurred to me. And I can't bear to be without you tonight. Could I let you go I would, but—" She shivered; she had never been so honest. "I so need for you to hold me," she whispered. "I need to feel safe, the way I felt when—oh, Joss. Please—"

Silently, Joss went across the bedroom; she took Aidan's face in her hands, slipping her fingers deep into her hair. "I can't just hold you." Her breath was rich with tobacco and the warm, subtle hint of liquor. "The first time I did I knew I'd never be able to again. You don't understand how I think about you, an' I don't know how to say it, but—"

"Joss, you're all I've thought of! I don't know what to call this, and I'm afraid and confused and I know you are too but Joss, I want you with me. I need you with me. When you—how it felt when you—I didn't want you to stop. As soon as I said no I wanted you back, but I was afraid—"

"Aidan, you don't know what you're sayin'. You don't know what you're askin' for. Stop this now, while we can."

119

She touched her fingers to Joss's lips. "I'll never forget how it felt when you kissed me, Joss," she said softly. "I'll always want to feel it again."

"I can't—oh, God! Aidan, I can't just kiss you. You don't know what I want, to know if you want it too." *Would you ever do that? Kiss another woman between her legs?* "Oh, no." Something halfway between a laugh and a groan jittered from her. "Lord, no. I can't say that to you."

Aidan tasted the length of Joss's back with her palms, finding the washboard of her ribs, the sharpness of her shoulder blades, rediscovering the startling absence of hair at her neck before her hands found Joss's face, turning from palms to fingertips against her skin. Delicately, she traced Joss's lips with a finger, feeling a barely-controlled shiver of response there. "Whatever you want, I want it too." It was hardly a breath; there was hardly a breath between them. "Kiss me, Joss. The way you really want to."

"Aidan, you don't know—"

"I don't know the words, Joss. I don't know how to say it any more than you do, but I know how I feel! I can't be without you tonight. I can't. I've never wanted anything as much as I want to be close to you. Joss, please—"

"Oh, Aidan—" It was almost a moan. "I wasn't born with strength enough to say no to you. God forgive me—"

It was a kiss like the morning, but daring to, this time; it was the soft question of lips tasting hers, and the press of fingers at her cheek as that gentle mouth sought her more closely; it was the query of Joss's tongue asking if she might part her lips. It had never occurred to her that a lover might want that from her; now there was nothing she wanted more than the smoky warmth of that tongue against her own. She buried her fingers in Joss's hair. Hands drew her closer; the warmth of that hard, lean body against her made some hot and liquid thing surge in her. "Joss—oh, how you touch me—"

"Everywhere," Joss said softly. "Aidan, I want to touch you everywhere—" She buried a deep, wanting kiss into Aidan's throat, her hand coming to cup one heavy breast in gentle possession;

Aidan almost shuddered with the feel of it. "—with my mouth," she whispered, and Aidan's breath deserted her in helpless shock. "Will you let me?"

There was no answer she could have said that would have been more honest than what her body spoke as Joss's thigh pressed between her own. "Is that how—oh, Joss—" She shivered, in terror and in aching want; Joss's tongue sought hers again, and she imagined that probing tongue finding her *(everywhere? Oh, God, can this be right? Can it be wrong?)* as hard-palmed hands stroked to her waist, holding her close as that hungry mouth tasted her lips and trailed across her cheek; Joss's tongue slipped delicately into her ear, pulling a moan from her. "Joss, this is—oh, you make me feel so—"

"Put your arms around my neck," she whispered; Aidan did, and Joss raised her into her arms to hold her tight against her chest, finding her mouth, her hunger, her urgency. "To hold you this way—" The feel of teeth against her throat made Aidan arch against her, tearing harsh breaths from them both. "You don't know how I've wanted this, Aidan. You don't know how much I've wanted to touch you—" It was a husky admission. "Since the last time I shared this bed with you, I've wanted this—you, this way."

That look, that morning—yes, it had been different, some secret behind it—and yes, that had been the moment she had fallen in love with Joss Bodett. "Whatever this is, it's what I want," she whispered as Joss gave her to the bed. "It's all I want. Joss, I need you so—oh, Joss!" Questing lips at her breast pulled the gasp from her; with no thought for the time it might take to sew the tiny buttons back onto her gown, she tore open the throat of the silk. No lips had ever touched her breasts, nor any hand their nakedness, and more than she needed to breathe she needed to know the feel of Joss's mouth there—and with that touch there came a feeling so intense, so fervid and foreign, it pulled a cry from her as she held that close-shorn head there, her fingers buried in the thick dark hair as Joss drew her hardened nipple into her mouth. "Joss—oh, my Lord. Joss—"

121

Delicately, Joss's tongue sought her, both her hands coming to embrace her breast, and when teeth closed there with exquisite gentleness Aidan remembered the morning and that hot liquid surge when Joss had kissed her only because "Oh—" it exploded "—my—" in her "—Joss! oh love oh my love don't stop—" now as if it had been some real thing inside her heart and mind and belly, a straining bubble filled with warm honey or sweet cream, bursting to spill itself into her as a peach hot from a summer tree would spill its juice into a mouth as hungry as the one against her now. "Oh, Joss," she wept, and then had to assure her that she was all right. "You didn't hurt me," she whispered around concerned kisses, clinging to her, still trembling. "It felt so good—" *are you sure?* "I'm sure." *Aidan, are you sure I didn't hurt you?* "God didn't strike you dead, did He? Joss—" She stretched against that hard body, thinking of peaches; one always made her want another. Still uncertain, Joss leaned over her. "I want to feel you against me," she said softly. "And I never want to sleep without you again. Will you always sleep with me, Joss?"

"I'll do anything you want me to," Joss whispered, as Aidan undid the buttons of her shirt and slipped her hands inside it, tracing fingertips across her breasts, brushing the hardness of her nipples. "I'll do anything at all."

"That's what I want you to do." Aidan drew her head down to her, offering her mouth, her want, her need. "Anything you want. Anything at all, Joss."

There were dozens of tiny buttons down the front of her gown; patiently, Joss freed them, hands and lips murmuring across skin bared by their defeat, lingering where her touch made Aidan's breath come short, brushing a kiss at the compelling scent of hair, wandering down one smooth thigh; when at last she could spill open the silk she eased beside her to feel the length of skin on skin. For a moment they could only hold each other, absorbing the wonder of their naked warmths together. "How I've wanted this," Joss whispered. "Lord, how I've wanted this. To feel you this way—"

Aidan had never known that hands could be so gentle, that a

mouth against her own could make her ache with want, and when Joss's hands and mouth found her breast again she wept with the depth of her love—and the bitter wish that her virginity could have been given to this tender, patient woman. For she could feel the effort of control in the body so close to hers, in the lips that brushed her skin as if it was their desire to taste every inch of her, in the palms that explored her curves and hollows with a wonder she understood, for she felt it, too, touching a body so different and yet so much the same it was almost like another vision of herself, and when at last fingers trailed up the tender inside of her thigh (and oh, they were such long and slender fingers, precise, delicate, gentle with everything they touched) she shivered in her need, and when Joss's mouth found hers with a whispered question: *Is it all right?* she rose to meet that hand in her answer, and when fingers touched her smooth, wet warmth she was helpless; she heard Joss draw a breath, almost moaning her name at that first discovery, and something newly familiar, something ripe and unrestrained, pulsed and ached and grew in her as lips found her breast "Joss—" and then her belly "Joss, please—" and that tongue traced the hollow inside her hip "Joss! Yes oh my love Joss yes—"

And knowing there was no one but Joss to hear, she allowed to come ungoverned the scream that spilled from her as that gentle, probing tongue proved what Joss had meant when she had said that she would kiss her everywhere.

CHAPTER TEN

When Doc Pickett rode past the Bodett place at nine the next morning there was no smoke coming from the chimney; he spurred his mare into the dooryard and tossed a rein over the porch rail on his way to the door. "Josie!"

The curse from Aidan's room made him suspect; he had suspected all along, but he grinned in certainty when Joss burst out with one of Ethan's old shirts on inside-out. He'd have laughed, but for the shock of her close-shorn head. "Christ in a carriage," he goggled. "What happened to your hair, Joss? Lice?"

"What're you doin' bustin' in here? I could've shot you, you damn fool!"

"Not 'til you move your Colt into Aidan's room," he grinned; the sidearm hung on its peg by the door. "No fire at nine is why—and Joss, your hair is beautiful!" He was recovering from the haircut, but not from the delight of knowing where she'd slept last night (or, rather, stayed; from the look of the delicate bruises around her lips, precious little sleeping had got done). "Where's Cousin Aidan, Miss Josie?"

"Abed," she managed. She had spent some barely-awake moments in the night scouring her mind for the admonitions of Leviticus, and hadn't come up with enough to confirm any sin in what they had done—but still, it felt as odd as the space between waking and sleep, as alien as the sky before a tornado, as precarious as being on foot and too far from home in a blizzard...

It felt as right as snow on Christmas, as healing as rain in April. Doc couldn't get rid of the grin; it seemed stuck to his face. "I might have been our good friend Argus Slade."

"You might've been fish under my corn, too, an' none the wiser—nor the sadder, in my humble estimation. Are you idly rounding, or about more serious matters?"

"Delivering the mail. Aidan has a package. Four tins, from the heft of it. One will keep my mouth shut," he leered, and saw the relief in her eyes before the fire of her humor flared in them.

"So will my Colt, Hippocrates. I'm not bound by your oath to do no harm. Be useful since you're here; start the fire." She took the bucket to the well and came back wet-haired, spraying like a dog on the porch. "Doc—"

He looked up from adjusting the stove dampers.

"I wonder if—um—is there any—in our—will we cause any trouble—any danger—damn! The baby," she managed. "Will we harm the baby?"

He closed the oven damper and nudged at the one on the side. "Not as long as you're gentle, Josie. After the seventh month don't insert anything into her" —she gaped at him; he smiled at her innocence— "saving your fingers, and be damn sure they're clean with or without the baby." She sat hard in a chair at the table, red to the roots of her hair. "You asked," Doc said gently. "Let me mortify you all at a time and get it over with. Try not to have an apoplexy."

She learned more from his quiet lecture on what they could and couldn't do for the baby's sake than might have occurred to her on her own in five years; at last she sat back to run her hands through her damp hair. "Lord," she breathed. "An' here I thought just lovin' her was all there would be to it."

"This may not be a widely-held opinion, but it's my opinion that there's nothing in loving that's wrong as long as you both agree to it. But some needs wait until the baby's born. What seems inconceivable now might sound like fun when you're more comfortable with one another—mayhap next summer, when the corn and cucumbers are ripe," he grinned. "I hear an ear of corn's the—"

"Oh, make the coffee!" She fled, his laugh following her, and went across the bed on her knees to deliver damp kisses from Aidan's neck to her hip, admiring her nudity, trying to restrain fractious thoughts of cucumbers and ears of corn. "It's Doc. Wait til you hear the things he told me! An' you got a package. He thinks four tins. Are you awake?"

"Mmmmm. Package?" Her voice was muffled by the pillow and her pure satiation; she had never thought to know how good it was simply to be alive and have Joss tracing soft kisses across her back. "I love you so much," she whispered. "I can't face Doc and not have him know it."

Joss rested a hand at the curve of her waist. "We needn't hide from Doc," she said quietly. "He loves us both."

When Aidan came shyly out Doc's eyes convinced her; if they hadn't, his softly-mustached kiss would have. He held a chair for her. "I might've known, seeing your corn so tall so soon. Shaman planting isn't always shaman growing."

Joss, adding wood to the firebox, dropped the burner plate and lid-lifter with a crash; she turned from the stove to look at him. "Shaman?" *There's men, too.* She heard Ethan's voice: Ethan, the sexual encyclopedia. *Men who do it with men. Injuns call 'em shaman, like a priest. Read Leviticus. Says right in it. Says don't to do it, but injuns ain't Christian. Don't matter to them what ol' Moses said.* "You?"

"Need I ask where you learned the word? Mercy, Joss, is there anything that boy didn't tell you?" He leaned back in his chair

126

with a small sigh. "One thing, it seems, and that to his everlasting credit. Joss, Aidan...this must stay between us. No one will suspect the two of you—no one suspects passion of a woman—but mere suspicion has been the death of more than one man of my stripe. As the two of you are, so am I."

Wide-eyed, Aidan looked at him. "But you told me the War—"

"I needed your trust and I needed it quickly. Was I to offer such truth to someone I didn't know? I've no fondness for tar, feathers, or a ride on the next rail out of town."

Joss retrieved the lid-lifter, dropping it again when it burned her hand. "Damn!" She wrapped the tool in a towel and seated the plate over the burner. "Ethan knew this?" She didn't look at Doc; her voice was low and cautious. "How did he know?"

"Not what you're thinking." His smile was pained. "Ethan caught me. *Flagrante delicto*, as it were."

Joss turned, an eyebrow raised in question.

"In the act."

"I know what it means. How the thunder did he catch you?"

"It was afternoon that Tucker Day fell off the church roof. Ethan knew Tuck was bad hurt. He didn't waste time knocking."

"How'd you keep him shut up?"

Doc leaned back to accept the cup of coffee she put in front of him. "I didn't," he said quietly. "I said, 'Ethan, you've got my life in your hands.' He turned his back and said, 'Tuck's hurt real bad. You'd better come.' He was on my elbow all afternoon, more good help than in the way. When Tucker died he sat with me for a long time. Finally he said, 'If that's how it is to have someone's life in your hands, I ain't cut out for it.' Three days later he was knocking on my door with his pockets full of poker money, asking where he could buy a bathtub for his mother. We went to Kansas City and never a word of it passed between us, and I knew no word ever would." He tasted his coffee and grimaced. "Did I make this? Lord have mercy, that's coffin varnish!"

"You know where the milk is."

"A little loving and you've turned flat lazy," he grumped, and

127

came back from the barn with a pail brimming with milk, Aidan's mail under his other arm.

The package held eight half-pound tins of tea and a letter. Aidan opened the page and read, her lips thinning until at last she threw it to the table. "Damn you! You may take your demands of me to perdition!" She shoved away from the table and stormed to the bedroom, leaving Joss and Doc looking wonderingly at each other, and at the letter. Reluctantly, Joss picked it up.

Daughter: Enclosed find a bank draft for two hundred dollars. Leave half with your cousin & make immediate arrangement for your return to Portland. It is unthinkable that you remain in Kansas without male protection or suitable chaperone. Arrangements for your travel to Bangor, where you shall stay with your mother's cousin Rosa Snipes, are making. Our heartfelt sympathy & deepest regards to Cousin Jocelyn the Younger. We hope she & the doctor shall enjoy the tea.

"Well, thanks for the invite, Cousin Adrian," she drawled. "I appreciate all hell out o' your heartfelt concern for li'l ol' unprotected—an' apparently unsuitable—me." She tossed the letter across to Doc, studying the bank draft while he read; she'd never seen one before. It was hard to believe a piece of paper made in Maine was good for Kansas dollars. She wondered if it would really work.

"What an insufferably pompous son of a bitch." Doc's disgust interrupted her ponderings. "Get me paper and ink, Joss. A rude country doctor is about to admonish a city physician about the delicacy of his daughter's condition."

He was done his letter by the time Joss coaxed Aidan from the bedroom, and read it to them: "...and although I appreciate your apprehension of what may appear to be an unworkable situation, I respectfully submit that you lack understanding of the peculiar capabilities of Western women. Your daughter is as well-protected with Miss Bodett as she would be with any man. She is as true and bold a shot as she is a judge of character. But that is not my deepest concern, sir. As her physician, I forbid my patient to travel such an onerous distance in her delicate condition. I trust that I may thank you in advance for your regard of my professional judgment. Respectfully, Robert James Pickett, MD, Columbia College of Medicine, 1860." He folded the letter into his coat pocket. "I'll post this tomorrow—and expect Dr. Blackstone within the month."

"It was a token protest," Aidan said wearily. "He doesn't care enough to come after me."

Tight-lipped, Joss tapped the crisp edge of the bank draft against the tabletop. "What o' this? It was meant for her travelin' expenses."

Doc hadn't liked Adrian Blackstone's ostentatious stationery, or his cramped, prim handwriting, or that he hadn't had the grace to address his daughter by name or sign off on his letter; most of all, he hadn't liked the dull certainty of Aidan's words: *He doesn't care enough.* "Damn his intentions. It's in Aidan's name. Cash it posthaste."

Shakily, Aidan smiled. Saving her refusal to marry Jared Hayward, defying her father was nothing she had ever done—or even thought to do—but much of what she had thought yesterday had cartwheeled off into the depths of last night, never to return. "Thank you, Doc. To me, it looks like a board floor."

"I said I'd build you a floor!" Joss pretended insult and won a smile.

"Floors! Does this mean I can tip back in my chair?"

Aidan looked at him in mock horror. "And scar my wood? Never, Doctor!"

Joss made a leisurely breakfast that would serve Doc for lunch. They spent the bank draft a hundred ways, knowing the money would go into the tobacco tin under Joss's bed. Doc caught them up on Leavenworth gossip, where he had been the day before: the Cavalry was mobilizing, and would leave for the Dakotas within a fortnight. Captain Slade was making the rounds of civilian homes under his protection; Joss heard his unspoken warning.

They saw him off with a venison steak and the heart of

the deer. He wasn't to the track on his mare before their eyes locked and their hearts followed and they were back in bed, a tangle of arms and legs and desires and but one concession to the possibility of Argus Slade: on their way, Joss took her Colt into Aidan's—their—room.

June, 1876

Let all bitterness, and wrath, and anger, and clamour, and evil speaking, be put away from you, with all malice: and be ye kind to one another, tender-hearted, forgiving one another ...

Ephesians 4:31-32

CHAPTER ELEVEN

The fortnight passed with no sign or news of Captain Slade. The days rose hot and clear, the nights cooled mercifully, and their lives assumed a rhythm: Joss rose quietly at first light, leaving Aidan to sleep, and started the fire before going to the barn for her early chores there, milking and feeding and cleaning, having low conversations with her animals, turning out the horses and the cow. She checked the corning crock in its pit in the barn, and climbed to the haymow to see to the jerky turning wizened and hard in that dim, dry heat, and she would cut off a piece of the spicy leather to tuck into her mouth; the rest of the strip went into her shirt pocket.

Finished in the barn, she headed for the fields, working there until Aidan rang the breakfast bell. Recalling the silence save requests for salt or butter that had been mealtimes with their families, they used the time to talk, to laugh, to plan; they ate leisurely, drank their coffee, retired to the porch for Joss's cigarette. (Doc kept her supplied with tobacco, since Thom and Effie Richland, with their situational brand of morality, refused to sell it to her. Effie had barely spoken to her since her first sight of that scandalous haircut, but the colored barber had a laugh as big as his substantial belly and trimmed her ragged ends for free; Joss watched him closely and reported his methods back to Aidan.)

After breakfast she worked the crops until the sun was unbearably hot, then retired to the shaded side of the woodshed, patient in her assault against wood her father and brothers had blocked. Firewood was a back-of-the-mind worry to her. Half of their claim was forested, but Charley, that good and gentle horse, liked nothing less than snaking a tree out of the woods; only Seth on his back had kept him from jug-headed skittishness at the task, and she didn't know how she might keep him calm without Seth. Fritz was no good alone; he was just as liable to lie down in the traces if Charley wasn't hitched beside him to prevent it.

Sometimes she would lean on her axe, staring at empty fields, thinking about all that had to be done and how little time there was to do it, and she'd have a moment of irritation with Seth and Ethan for not being at their chores... and then she would remember, and attack the blocks of oak and elm, sending stove-sized chunks flying around the woodyard.

When the sun was highest and hottest Aidan would ring her in for cold biscuits and milk and meat. She had lived her life with a hot mid-day meal, but she'd lived it not worrying about winter's wood; a cold lunch saved three sticks of wood every hour for six hours...and spared Aidan the rank heat of the kitchen in the thickest part of the day.

When the meal was done and her cigarette smoked, there was always something to be mended: a harness, an axe handle lost to a block of twisted elm, a bit of oakum to be chinked into a light-showing space between logs in the cabin half of the house, a board to replace on the porch floor. (Aidan, watching her make a board one sultry afternoon with axe and adze and froe and

133

drawshave and sweat, resolved to say no more of floors.) When the rank heat abated she returned to the crops, weeding through the lowering afternoon, watching from a corner of her attention as Aidan tended the garden or took in the morning wash or the evening wood. By the time she got to the end of forty acres, tall weeds jeered at her from the start of them. Her hands grew shiny with calluses, as tautly curved as the hoe-handle; her monthly bleeding was but a distant memory.

Men came to talk. She listened out of courtesy and sent them away, but when they were gone she did sums in the sun, figuring the contents of the tobacco tin under her old bed and the profit on beans and corn after the winter's store was removed. She wondered why she had planted beans and corn, when wheat and oats demanded such less labor; she wondered if she could afford to plow under forty acres and reseed with the grasses, and if she did, if she still had time to get in two crops. She wondered if Mr. Carpenter would really lend her money if she needed it, or, if he wouldn't, if Flora Washburn might...or if Harmon would return to haunt her if she asked either of them.

She wondered why her family had been taken, and why she had been spared. She wondered if there was any gold left in California, and if a woman would be allowed to stake a claim if there was. She wondered and figured; she chopped weeds and wood, and the days blurred together in mindless similarity.

Out in the beans one mid-morning, she heard a wagon in their track and squinted to see who was coming to call. "Boy howdy. I'm in for it now," she groaned, and trudged in from the field fully expecting a tongue-lashing from the irascible Flora Washburn.

"You look like you been workin harder'n three darkies." Four-foot-nine, eighty-two years old, Flora quivered with too much irritable energy to sit with the tea Aidan had made for her; her steel-gray hair corkscrewed out in all directions. "Work's good for a body, but you're takin' it a sight futher'n the good Lord intended—like He gives a rat! We ain't but a gnat on a bull's ass to Him. Not a lick o' fat on you! I s'pose you work it off faster'n this'ere Yankee can fork it into you. Smell o' this house they's a good cook livin' in it. Kitchen garden looks good. Effie says she's lah-de-dah, but Effie wouldn't know bootblack from her own bunghole. I'd oughten chaw your chops for not bringin' 'er by to make a decent hello to a neighbor, but I don't 'xpect you've had time for a fair squat since the family went acrost. Place looks better'n I figured it would. Now! Out back o' the wagon—an' that puke over to Leavenworth calls hisself a lumberman! I ask for lath enough to plaster up a dinin' room an' he sends enough, all right, if your dinin' room's in the God-damn White House— what's left over's out back o' the wagon. What the merry hell am I s'pose to do with it? I'm too damn old to bust it up for kindlin' an' damnwell tired o' lookin at it, an' you don't batten up the board end o' this house an' this little Yankee girl o' yourn'll be all winter sweepin' snow out'n the bedrooms. Your daddy never had a lick o' no sense to him, boardin' an' not battenin'—God rest'm an' all that Baptist blather, I know you miss him but you got to admit. Under the seat's a box o' them bitty little nails. Take that, too. Go on! Go get it; I ain't got all day to fiddledy-fart 'round here with the two o' you. Twitch your tail, little girl; it's easier work than you been doin'. Git!"

"Yes'm." Joss managed to get outside before the laugh welled out of her; she leaned against the side of the house, her hand clamped over her mouth to keep it as quiet as she could, tears leaking from her with the effort to keep it contained. "Oh, Aidan! God help you, stuck in there with her!" She hiccupped a ratcheting breath. "That's Flora Washburn, little cousin. Aren't you glad you asked?"

"My stars," Aidan whispered, dazed, when Flora had tornadoed out of their yard, her horses running as if for their lives in front of her whip. "I had no idea she was so—oh, my stars!"

"Ain't she, though! But you got to think on Flora. She accused you o' good cookin', complimented your garden an' your housekeepin', gave me a nod, an' saved us more shiverin' than you can imagine. Ma's been peckin' at Pa forever about battenin' the bedrooms. Oakum don't stick 'tween the boards, an' Lord knows we tried it. She give up on him an' made quilts. Hell, we put what's the corn this year in cotton a few years back, an' she used up most of it just quiltin'. Hung 'em on the walls. I ain't never growin' cotton again! One crop o' that an' I know why the rebs fit to keep the slaves. She's got a good heart, Flora has; she's just a trial to have in the kitchen—an' God help the faint o' heart. She's cruder'n a Saturday night at the Bull an' Whistle."

Marcus Jackson came one day, emerging from the trail cut by the energies of the Bodett children and their Jackson counterparts through the years and the woodlot the two farms shared. Joss was sitting on the chopping block, waiting for her muscles to ease their overworked quivering so she could roll a cigarette; she heard movement on the trail and assumed it would be Gideon. He had been Ethan's best buddy, and came sometimes to visit or lend a hand, bringing gossip and big eyes for Aidan and, if he had been to Leavenworth, Joss's standing order of whiskey and tea.

She rolled her cigarette, waiting for him. She supposed she ought to take time to go visit with Earlene, but as much as she hated to admit Argus Slade had been right about anything, leisure was indeed a precious commodity for her. "Never mind," she grumbled to herself. She loved Earlene, who had made her midwifery debut at the age of fifteen with the delivery of Jocelyn Bodett the Younger and had attended every birth, successful or not, to follow in the Bodett household. Until Doc Pickett's arrival ten years ago, Earlene and Jocelyn the Elder had swapped midwifery the way they swapped recipes and scraps of cloth, until their children were born, their kitchen books identical, their quilts bearing as many pieces from the one household as the other.

But it was her father's best mate, not her brother's, who emerged from the trail. He shook his head at her haircut and her cigarette, but he knew Joss well, and respected her as he had respected her mother.

He sat on the block of wood she would split next and quietly, they talked: of guns, for Marcus's had frozen, and she tinkered with it while they spoke; of horses, for Fritz seemed listless (damn horse ain't but flat lazy, the farrier said); of beans and corn and wheat and oats, and firewood, and finally of money, and Marcus went away shaking his head again.

"You ever been to California?" she asked Aidan late that afternoon. In from the corn, almost immobilized with weariness, she was too spent even to wash off the heat of the day. Aidan, a curl of hair escaping its pins to hang damply against her cheek, looked at her from the stove; Joss shied her eyes from the unspoken question. "You went to Paris an' London an' Rome, all them old places. You ever had a yen to see a new place?"

"Who came today?" She had seen no horse or visitor, but Joss only mentioned California when someone had tried to talk her into selling the farm.

Joss took a dipper of warm water from the tank at the end of the stove and splashed it into the washbasin, and tackled her hands and face and hair. When she was done the water was grey, her hair dripping, her face a few dusty shades lighter. Aidan offered a towel. She buried her face into the flannel and spoke so softly that Aidan had to study the muffled whisper to realize what she had heard: "Marcus Jackson."

Aidan closed her eyes, a brief, hurt breath escaping her. "Oh, Joss. What did he say?"

Joss towelled her hair with exacting thoroughness; she took her comb from its crack in a log over the sink and did what the fat barber had recommended. "Seems Mr. Carpenter's ready to front money to anyone I'd sell this place to." She stuck the comb into its crack and went to the table to sit, looking as weary as she had before the wash. "Marcus'd leave my family buried decent. If I was to sell it to him, Gid might marry that Newtonville girl he fancies when he ain't busy fancyin' you, an' they could set their babies down in a decent house 'stead o' that back claim shack. We could go to California—"

Aidan blew a derisive snort. "And do what? Pan gold?" Impatience edged her voice. "What might we do in California, save marry out of desperation or be whores for the same reason?"

"I can pass for a man. No one'd know we wasn't man an' wife."

137

"I'll never agree to such a lie, Joss! And I'm not going anywhere until this baby's born. If you'd let me help you—"

"The hell! If you weren't with child—"

"Next year I won't be with child. Joss, I'm not—"

"Next year you'll have a child, an' twice the work under this roof you have now an' too much already! Do you think I don't know how you sweat in here? Do you think I reach for a shirt not knowin' your labor in boilin' an' hangin' an' ironin'—an' why you iron 'em!"

"I iron them for loving how you look in a pressed shirt, however long it may last. I'm not overworked or I'd not do it. What did Marcus say?"

"He said it'd grieve Pa for this land to lay fallow but how there's nothin' but that to do with it, an' how I'll kill myself tryin' an' he's right—"

"Then let him farm it!" She knew that if she felt betrayed by Marcus's offer, Joss must be writhing under the ache of it, but the words had flared unbidden from her; she went on with it. "Gid Jackson's a strapping boy! He could have that claim shack looking like a home in short work if he'd but put his back into it, and if they're so joe-fired heartsick at the thought of land laying fallow, let them pay for the privilege of planting and harvesting it. It's called rent," she snapped. "Even in this godforsaken backwater, they must be familiar with the idea."

Joss's eyes showed a brief, baffled hurt before that familiar dilation of temper blazed in them and Aidan knew: *too much, too far, too harsh...* "Joss, I'm—" Joss's chair tumbled halfway across the kitchen when she uncoiled from it. "—sorry!"...*and too late.* "Joss, I didn't mean—

"I don't want your pity for my trouble no more'n you ever wanted mine for yours," Joss snarled. "If you're stayin' in this godforsaken backwater for pityin' me, you can go the hell back to Maine!"

The momentum of anger carried her across the yard, her long legs eating the uphill distance to the woodlot she shared with Marcus, but by the time she got to the coldwater spring where she always took her wounds, she knew she had dealt as much hurt as she had been delivered. She collapsed to the soft moss beside the spring to knot her fingers in her hair, trying to make enough physical pain to overwhelm the other. "Aidan, I'm sorry—" She crowded back the tears the way a sheepdog refuses its herd the wrong gate; she gave her hurt the eye of that capable dog, baring her teeth with the warning: I won't cry, so don't even try.

"Marcus, why? Why you? You was Pa's best bud; you'd have to know how I feel about it! Jesus, why—" *(hast thou forsaken me)*

At last she drew her makings from her shirt pocket, but it was long before her jittering fingers could roll a cigarette; when it was made and lit she leaned wearily against a huge old oak, a sigh shivering from her. "Go apologize before she takes you at your word," she whispered, but the hurt still squeezed hard in her chest, and she was afraid of it; she knew how hurt spilled from her. It came out sounding like anger, with all of anger's destructive force, and harm enough was done already and too much. "Damn your hot Blackstone blood—an' hers too. Damn us both for it!"

She drew up one knee to rest her wrist on it; her cigarette smouldered away, smoked only enough to keep it going as she searched for stability. When the butt was too hot at her fingers she took a last taste and buried it in the damp moss. "Godforsaken backwater." Wearily, she shook her head. "Would that I could argue the point." It hurt as any hometown slur hurts one whose roots are deep, but she knew who had delivered the killing stroke: Aidan, with her sweet shepherd's stew simmering on the stove, was innocent—and too right about everything else, from babies to California. "Damn you, Marcus!"

You can't understand how it felt. Ethan's voice whispered to her from the not-so-distant past: too many hands of cards, too much to drink, too much else to think about when at last he took the girl upstairs to discover that what should have worked, wouldn't. *So I busted the Dutchman's nose. Just bail me out, Joss, an' don't try tellin' me what you know, 'cause you don't know this.*

"Shit." She jittered a laugh. "I think I got an idea of it now, Ethan."

She knew it, and knew she was wrong. They were two, where five had fought to hold the same pace they kept now. The second crop of hay was in the barn thanks to the Jackson and Clark youth, but she knew their efforts on her behalf had given her a hard adversary in Ottis. The beans were choking in weeds, a dry spell would take them to ruin with no hands to water—and the hands spared for the occasional haying bee would not be spared in a drought. There was no long wood in the yard behind the shed, the corn was lodging one plant in ten to cutworms, the promised floor was yet unmade and money was part of why not. The cash in the tin was dwindling; without crops to sell, they would survive the winter at no level above pure existence.

She had given Aidan only cursory instruction with the rifle. It was imperative she be able to shoot, and shoot well, but she didn't enjoy the innate ability with the carbine she had at the Colt, and cartridges were dear. The last rain had proven a leak in the roof that she hadn't been up to find; the handle on the axe was the last one she had, and she hadn't found or made the time to seek out an ash tree to cut and carve. Flora's generous pile of lath still sat beside the house; she told herself the breeze sifting through the walls was appreciated in the hot summer nights, and that she'd do it before the chill of fall set in, but she knew it wasn't done because too much else drew her away from it. "Fuck," she muttered. Ethan had taught her the word; it was satisfying in its raw coarseness even if Harmon had liked to flail the skin off her back the once she had said it in his hearing.

She brooded at the calm surface of the constant spring. When Ethan was alive it had sometimes harbored quart bottles of beer to be shared with his sister in that cool, private place. He had been able to talk to Joss about things, and talk her into things; they had pals in Gid and Hank, but she had been his best friend, and he hers.

She turned the cap of one of those old beers over in her fingers. In the matter of work Ethan had been nigh useless, in thinking of it or doing it, but in the impotence of not being able to, he'd be good to be around, and she missed him with a low, throbbing ache, like the one she saw Aidan's hand reach for low in her back time and again in a hard-work day. "I need me a Dutchman, Ethan," she whispered, a bitter little laugh choking out with the words; she found a twig to break into pieces. "Hell, I prob'ly couldn't even bust a drummer's nose was he here stickin' it out at me. I'm tired, little brother. I am some damn tired."

She tossed the crumbs of twig into the spring and leaned back against the tree. "Can't hardly keep my face out o' my dinner of an evenin', an' asleep 'fore my head hits the pillow. She ain't gettin' no comfortin', an' you was the one said disappointin' the lady was what set you off, so don't tell me what I don't know. Woman or man or ever what the hell I am, I ain't enough."

You might think about takin' a day o' rest now an' then. Like the Sabbath.

"I ain't got time to rest."

You ain't got time not to. She'll be thinkin' that damn dirt means more to you than she does. You ain't the only one gettin' weary, little sister. You tell her about how Ma was resigned—hell, that was with Pa givin' her Sundays. Her rest was havin' him fetch the wood an' water an 'dry the dishes for her, an' bein' there to talk to her an' keep us kids out from under her skirts. What looked like lazy to us was help to her, an' what felt like work to her seemed like rest to him.

"Yeah, an' next she'll be wantin' to go to town an' hear the Baptist."

So give her the damn Baptist! He was so near she could hear his hard-edged laugh. *That Blackstone Methodist'll weary o' him quick enough an' be glad to spend a Sunday mornin' readin' the Psalms to home, long as you're there readin 'em with her. Go make up, girl. Them pressed shirts ain't goin' to last long lessen you do.*

"Oh, Aidan—" Aidan, who pressed her shirts for no more reason than liking how she looked in morning creases soon faded to sweaty limpness, who did all the hard work Jocelyn had done plus a fair share of Seth's: countless trips across the yard, hundreds of pails of water drawn from the well, thousands of sticks of wood

141

wrestled into the stove, sad irons hotted, linens laundered, meals cooked, dishes washed, weeds pulled in the kitchen garden, when her life had once been hardwood floors and pianos in parlors and symphonies and—

How long before she tires? You promised her floors all through and haven't even given her one in the kitchen—but here you sit at your sulking-tree, smoking money while she makes your supper on a bare dirt floor.

"I'm sorry," she said in the dim golden glow of the kitchen lamp, thick-voiced, her sheepdog struggling to contain too big a herd of tears. "It's not your fault an' I'm sorry I put it on you, an' I—I didn't mean—when I said—"

"I know you didn't, and I'm sorry too." Aidan delivered her dinner with calm control; Joss would have rathered the bowl hit the table with a bang. They might have fought, then, and had some release. She ate, but the stew was like noon dust in her mouth.

After supper they pretended to read, but when one looked up the other looked away, and the words on the pages swam like huddled fish in a drought-dying stream. She got up from the table, finally, and went into the room Seth and Ethan had shared, closing the door behind her.

She opened the drawer of Ethan's armoire and touched things in there, and at last she picked up the little mahogany casket that held things he had treasured, guarding them in his life and since his death. She sat on his bed with the tiny chest cradled in her hands, searching for the heart to open it.

He had died in the morning. They all had, four in six sunrises, as if the rooster's crow was the voice of the angel come to lead them home. She smoothed a finger across the glossy red wood of the treasure-box, wondering why they would struggle through the long, dim hours of the night, crowding back death (as she had crowded back sleep, as if her watchfulness would see them through) only to close their eyes and hearts and breaths to the new dawn. Was the brightness of day too much to dare after the peace of the dark? Or was the night too dark to go into alone?

With a soft sigh, she worked the catch on the lid of his treasure-box. She had admired the casket the night he came home from the Bull and Whistle with it filled with his other poker spoils, mildly hoping he might give it to her, for he was often generous with his winnings, but he had said jokingly, "I'll leave it to you when I die. Can you wait that long, little sister?"

"I'd've waited, Ethan," she murmured. "I'd've waited a right smart o' longer, little brother." Slowly, she raised the lid.

She sat for a long time on his bed, studying what she found there. When she heard Aidan close her book she put a few things into her pocket, and the rest gently back into the casket, and she stood.

They slept together that night, but Aidan didn't reach for her; hollowly, Joss didn't dare try to hold her. They may as well have been in separate beds, separate rooms, separate worlds.

CHAPTER TWELVE

Aidan woke groggy and grumpy, missing Joss's warmth; for all Joss thought she slipped away mornings without disturbing her lover, it was a rare day that Aidan didn't feel her leave the bed, but this had been one. Had she ever known a hangover she'd have remembered it now; she was headachy, thick-mouthed, queasy for the first time in weeks. But that wasn't what nagged at her; she felt an absence, and sat up to listen for its source.

There was a fire in the stove. Occasionally when Joss built it and left for the barn it died of a downdraft, and Aidan knew the feel of her house with or without a fire.

Margaret was milked and the pigs were fed, else they would have been clamoring by this much light.

There was heat and silence: a built fire and contented animals, but no sound of a hoe in the beans, no scrape of shovel or fork in the barn, no crack of axe against oak. She caught her wrapper from the end of the bed and went to the kitchen pulling it over her nakedness. "Joss?"

Margaret drifted across the pasture, seeking something succulent; early sun shone hard on empty fields. Orion dozed on the porch rail, the headless corpse of a field mouse presented on the top step. Wind rustled through the woodlot and stirred dust in the yard; a squirrel chattered busily in the oak just behind the outhouse. Bewildered, Aidan turned back to the kitchen. The kettle had boiled nearly dry. She filled it, neglecting to make her tea first, and stoked the stove and went to the door again. "Joss!"

Finally she realized the wagon was gone from its spot by the barn; she was so accustomed to seeing it there that she had seen its memory when she looked. Charley and Fritz were also absent. She stared at the spaces those missing things left until the kettle rumbled on the stove; a small part of her mind commanded her to set it back to a cooler place. She did so, a much larger part of her mind asking a hollow question: *Joss?*

She had never been alone there. She didn't think it; she just knew it. She had never noticed how little scope there was in their valley, a wise choice for a house site to protect from the weather, but no place to see a distance; her eyes probed the hills and saw outlaws, Indians, those James boys from Saint Joseph—but Doc said they never robbed widows; she invented a late husband and wished her pregnancy was more than a soft rise at her belly.

She looked for the Colt on its peg. It was gone, along with the wagon and horses. Feeling intrusive—it never bothered her to hang his shirts after Joss had worn them and she had laundered them, but this seemed different, somehow—she found Ethan's gunbelt in his armoire; she loaded the revolver and paced back to the kitchen with it, shivering. She realized her nudity under her thin silk robe and fled to the bedroom to dress. She made tea, drank a cup, and lost it miserably off the end of the porch. Alone, she recovered, shivering, sweating.

She tried to recall a time in her life when no other soul had been within her reach. Touching distance, certainly. But no one within earshot?

If she screamed—if she had reason to scream—who might hear? Marcus and Earlene across the woodlot? Too many trees. The Clarks down the road? A harsh laugh spiked from her: down the road? The Clark door from where she stood took twenty minutes in the wagon, not that it mattered a whit whether they could hear her or not; she knew that neither Ottis nor his thin and razory wife cared for her any more than she cared for them. Ottis had proven himself an ass, and Mrs. Clark wouldn't speak when they met in town—and she and Joss never passed the Clark homestead without hearing Pamela's voice raised in shrill harshness, and the wail of at least one unhappy child.

She allowed herself to scream at night when what Joss did with her hands and her mouth made her lose herself to that exquisite, wordless pleasure. And Joss had never said not to, never said someone might hear—

No one would hear.

"Joss...?"

"Why'd I want it smooth both sides? Ain't but one side fixin' to be up."

Something about the lean farmer bothered Jacob Hart; he couldn't put a finger on it, but whatever it was, it didn't hide the fact of hard dark eyes clearly saying *don't try to screw me.* "I'm makin' a floor," said the farmer. "Don't want my baby gettin' slinters in her knees, but I don't reckon she'll be crawlin' on the bottom o' the damn thing. Take the money from a man can afford it, hoss, an' sell this plow chaser what I'm askin' for."

Thinly, Jacob smiled. "Stationer, are you?" He could tell a Stationer; they wore their rank poverty like a badge of fierce pride. "Got a name?"

"Bodett." The Stationer's thin, clean-shaven smile had a curve like the business edge of a Bowie knife, and Jacob's smile expanded: no more warmth, but much more ingratiation. The only Bodett he knew of was Ethan, and if rumor had it true, a wilder, meaner son of a bitch independent of a bandanna across the face had yet to be born. He'd imagined Ethan Bodett to be

146

a bigger fellow, but rumor tended to inflate a man, and size be damned: from the look in those black eyes, marrying hadn't much settled him down.

He hastened to smooth any feathers he might have ruffled. "Wellsuh! If you're making a floor, you want hardwood flooring, not a regular three-surface plane. Shame to go to all that work and not do 'er up right. She'll cost just a little more—"

"I ain't got 'just a little more.'"

"Let's calculate 'er out both ways. With real flooring you won't have cracks to let the wind in, or any nails showing on the surface."

A dark eyebrow raised in mild disbelief.

"That's for true. Look here." He offered scraps for inspection.

Hands emerged from pockets to accept the wood, and the lumberman double-took at the size of the diamond embedded in a massive gold ring on the farmer's right hand. He didn't know much about jewelry, but he knew no piece of glass had ever sparked that way in the sunlight . . . and neither did he think he'd ever seen such supple hands on a man. They were scabbed and scarred as any farmer's hands would be, but they seemed almost delicate in their graceful length. *Dealer's hands*, he thought. *Right off the bottom of the deck and the ice and gold to prove it.*

"Well, I'll be hanged," Bodett mused, fitting the tongue into the groove. "Nail it in here, then stick this into it an' just keep on, yuh? Hell, a body could oughta build th' whole damn house this way an' never mind battenin'."

"It's been done." Hart was grudgingly impressed by the quick study. "How big's your room? Let's have a look at numbers."

But when the numbers were figured and he put the tip of his pencil to the bottom line, those graceful hands lifted in a regretful shrug. "Too much?"

"Too much." The diamond gave a blue-flame wink. "Guess I got to settle for cracks an' showin' nails."

Jacob Hart cleared his throat. "Let's don't be hasty, Bodett. Might yet be a way."

"Dad-damned pokeweed, I know why she cusses it!"

There had seemed to be nothing in the house to demand her attention once the panic of solitude had seeped from her; Aidan chose the hoe and beanfield to occupy her time, hoping to also occupy her mind, but chopping weeds was drearily mindless once the novelty wore off. That had happened but minutes into the exercise. Then she found herself picking through yesterday, searching for reasons for Joss's absence today.

She knew Joss had been bitterly wounded by Marcus's vote of no confidence, however fundamentally justified. And 'godforsaken backwater' had been uncalled for in the extreme. "Meanness," she muttered, hacking a particularly overgrown weed to pieces. "You are your hateful father's daughter, Aidan Rose."

She suspected the crack, meant or not, had been a last straw on a camel's-back of impending failure; real or imagined, it had been failure—or fear of it—to send Joss into flight last night. But today...?

Today she was simply gone, and beneath her concern Aidan simmered with resentment that Joss had left without word or note or reason. If she was going to be like Papa, bingeing on her bad moods and ending up in the booze, disappearing and staying gone for days—well, the lie that would serve the James boys if she needed it was the one that had been meant to serve in Portland anyway, and she could blamed well go back there—they had to take her in, didn't they? Joss had said so herself, in the fever delirium Doc said his shaman brethren believed was the voice of the Great Spirit speaking through a Human Being.

And Doc! Where was he? He always came for Friday breakfast; of all the Fridays he could have chosen to be absent! "Blame him, too," she muttered, and straightened up with a groan, a hand reaching for the small of her back. How did Joss stand this days on end?

She looked at her palms; soreness an hour ago had turned to puffy blisters. She suffered the handle of the hoe to carry it to the barn. The bail of the bucket, when she got water from the well, was more than uncomfortable; she stopped midway across the yard to use the end of her skirt to pad the rope, not caring who might see her legs.

She wished they had a big yellow dog, with jaws like an alligator and a deep voice to warn her of comers, and comers of consequences. "Damned pokeweed," she growled; it was all she could think to damn save Joss, and Joss kept herself in danger enough of eternal damnation without being helped along that unholy path.

She sat on the porch step, her skirt hiked up over her knees to let out the heat, and examined her hands. They had sprung a crop of blisters more quickly than pokeweed grew back behind the hoe; some had broken. Tight-lipped, she tipped the bucket to splash water over her palm, knowing Joss would pitch a fit that she'd been in the beans. She hadn't accomplished much in two hours, but it was more than had been done when she started, and short of blisters, a sweat-soaked dress, and a back that felt as if she'd been beaten with a legal stick, the work hadn't hurt her. That was what she'd tried to tell Joss last night—

"Oh, shoo." She hauled the water into the house. There was warm water in the tank of the stove for a sink bath; she knew she'd feel better clean.

"Collie! Buck! Rassle up three hundrit foot oak floor an' underpinnin's for Mister Ethan Bodett," Jacob Hart bawled, the bright diamond glittering on his pinky, and Joss hid a smile behind her hand as millhands abandoned tea and biscuits in favor of appeasing the celebrated temper of Mister Ethan Bodett. She hadn't given Hart any name but Bodett; he had taken it upon himself to surmise, and the scrambling of the millhands proved that the news of Ethan's death hadn't yet reached the county seat. She wished Ethan would be home when she got there, for her to jibe about his good name in Leavenworth; it was fine to know that he was alive somewhere, if only in the fawning, wormy soul of Jacob Hart.

149

Whistling as she went about her other chores, she got good prices. Only the gunsmith noticed that the smudge over her lip was dirt instead of stubble; he inquired after Doc Pickett and set about what she had asked him for, and admired her aim when she tested his work.

Ethan's memory settled into her as the horses, heavily-laden, worked their patient way down the post road. Of all of them, it was Ethan's loss that tore at her heart most often. He had been crazy, so wild around the eyes on Saturday nights that he scared her, but he had been of her heart, a soul of her soul...and notorious at twenty-one. He'd taught her how to smoke and cuss and drink, and shared the secrets of Kansas City with her when he came strutting back so full of himself that he took Harmon's tanning without a thought of calling out his father; it didn't dent his pride a whit. What did he care about a whupping? He'd rode to Kay Cee, plundered the whorehouses, spent more money on a night than Joss had spent for boards that would last her lifetime and that of the baby whose knees she had defended in the buying. It was because of Ethan that she had known what to do (or at least, what to think of doing) when Aidan had come to her at last...

And if Ethan nagged at her, the thought of Aidan made her squirm on the hard seat of the buckboard. Sure it was Friday, sure Doc always came for breakfast Fridays, sure she had counted on that in her leaving, but if he hadn't...

Gossip said the Cav was a week away, but Slade was only one speculative man who might happen into their yard of a Friday morning with her gone and Aidan not knowing where she was or when she would be back; had she been out of her mind? Aidan could shoot bottles off fenceposts all day long, but would she be able to blow a hole in a man if she had to? Would she have thought to find Ethan's Colt, or be in reach of it if she had?

"Yo, Charley! Get along, you Fritz!" Reluctantly, for they were far too heavily loaded, the horses stepped up.

Thinking of Aidan alone made her remember how innocent she was—not helpless; heaven help the fool who dared suggest that Aidan Blackstone was helpless—but innocent, a refreshing innocence borne of the trust that rose naturally from a trustworthy soul. But behind her stubbornness, Joss knew Effie Richland and Argus Slade were right in warning of the perils lurking for women alone on the remote post road, and she knew Aidan's ingenuous trust might serve her ill more quickly than it might serve her well.

She remembered how Slade had looked at her, as if it would suit him if his next meal from soup to nuts was Aidan Blackstone. His God-damned smile, the eyes it never reached, those flinty eyes that followed her every move—

But she knew that was how men would react to Aidan. How liquored up might the malignant Ottis Clark be, should he take a mind to come have his say? Or any rank of drummers or tinkers, silhouette-cutters or other peripatetics, hunting work or whiskey they wouldn't find—or a woman they would? "Hie, Charley! Keep up, you lazy Fritz!"

Charley looked back at her and rattled his traces, and hied.

By eleven Aidan was freshly-dressed, her palms coated with the foul-smelling balm Joss used on Margaret's udder, catching up her diary at the kitchen table. Ethan's Colt was near, unholstered. There was laundry to be done (but no hot water, with Joss's daytime fire restrictions); the floors were dusty, in need of oiling *(not with these hands, I'm not)*; the stove was cool enough to clean and needed it *(I'll get to it)*. The butter was nearly gone, but blisters meant biscuits with cream for a few days. The woodbox was empty, and her mending basket was full; Joss was hard on clothes. She wrote: 'On this, the last day of my 19th year, we take a day of uncivil rest. Joss is gone off in foul temper somewhere. I mean to do little today save prepare an evening meal, should she be here to eat it.' She reached to dip her pen.

"Excusing, ma'am—"

"God in Heaven!" The ink bottle skittered across the table. She had heard no horse in the yard, no boot on the porch, yet here was a colored man at the door, hat in hand, an ill-kempt beard straggling over his shirtfront. "Who—" Her heart galloped

151

in her chest; she reached a hand to cover it. "Who—"

"Levi, ma'am, you not to fright, maybe work to trade for bite? Beans you hand to poke they need—oh, not needing, ma'am!" he begged in alarm as her hand stole toward the Colt. "Honest ask work for meat, biscuit spare one you if not or on the way, you say, no harm I'm ask?"

Perhaps he was thirty, possibly fifty; he was painfully ragged, and once she had untangled the words she realized that his garbled speech was but a gracious request to swap labor for food. He was patient at the door, as if he knew he'd startled her and was giving her time to recover. One of his feet lifted to worry an ankle and she saw that he was barefoot; no wonder she hadn't heard a step on the porch. *Why, he's harmless—and hungry*, she thought, as his glance stole sidelong to a basket of yesterday's biscuits on the sideboard. "When did you last eat?"

He scratched at an odd streak of pure-white hair over his left ear. Helplessly, he shrugged, and she suspected he had no sense of time. She stood, pausing to right the bottle of ink. The black smear would be a horrid mess to clean up, but she left it in favor of making him a plate of cold meat and biscuits. She set it on the table, but he wouldn't come into the house; he wolfed it down on the porch with unwashed hands that he wiped on his denimed thighs when he was done, refusing seconds. "Work you now? For?"

"You're right in saying the beans could use a hand to the poke. There's a hoe just inside the barn door—"

His smile was wide and bright as the nearing noon, his dark eyes soft as a deer's. "No ma'am, no hoe. Broke poke grow mo' poke."

He loped toward the field. She stood with his plate in her hand, watching him, a tall barefoot man with no meat on his bones stooped across a row, his fingers picking pokeweed faster than even Joss could chop it. She looked at her raw hands and wished Levi had come along three hours earlier.

And wearily, she smiled; three hours earlier, she probably would have shot the poor fellow where he stood. She turned to take his plate back into the house.

Joss didn't need to speak to the horses; a pull on the reins and they held, shaking their manes against the flies in the blistering early-afternoon sun. She squinted across shimmers of heat to see her bean field. "I'll wear you out, Aidan, if you're choppin' poke," she warned, still too far away to know any more than the fact of a human figure in the field. "G'up, Charley." Wearily, the valiant Charley stepped out; lacking options, Fritz went too.

Joss watched the figure in the beans, her squint turning to a scowl as her sight defined a dark scarecrow of a man crabbing steadily down the row. "Pullin' weeds? Sweet baby Jesus—an' who in Sam Hill is it? Dad dang it, Aidan—"

"Come wagon!" Levi didn't straighten up; he had heard the wagon coming before it crested the hill, heard it stop and start again, and knew it would turn in; when it did he announced it, recalling the fright he had given the good lady who had fed him once and might again. "Come wagon one man two horse come!"

Aidan raced to the door—and then, indignantly, she composed herself. She would *not* fly out to greet someone whose absence in the first place was inexcusable. She waited, the ire that had been stewing in her all day warring with her relief that Joss was home and safe. On another, idly curious level, she wondered what was making such an unholy racket in the wagon.

Joss swung lightly down, bringing a box from under the seat, and jerked her head at Levi in the beans. "Who's the darkie?"

"And a very good afternoon to you, Miss Bodett." She bit the words off coldly; relief might have won out over anger had Joss greeted her civilly, or had a gentle word for good help of any color. "So nice of you to call. I trust you've kept well since last we met?"

A dust devil skittered across the yard, rising a column high into the air before it collided with the barn to collapse as if in surprise; peripherally, she saw it. More directly she saw the bewilderment that flickered in Joss's eyes, and she knew as suddenly as the tiny cyclone had risen that her cousin's greeting hadn't been meant uncivilly. It had been logically curious, colored by her upbringing, rendered brusque by the filter of her own irritation—an irritation she had managed, now, to pass along.

"I got you a kitchen floor in the back o' the wagon. Happy birthday." Joss brushed past her into the house to put the box on the table. *Oglethorpe Orchards*, its endpaper read. *A-One Georgia Peaches*. Aidan noticed that as she had noticed the dust devil, a sidelong distraction to the thinness of Joss's lips. "Got crazy an' thought you might like water in the sink, too. Like to killed the horses gettin' the pipe here. Take it back if you don't want it."

"Joss, I'm sorry. I've spent the day worried about you. It's made me edgy, so I barked. It was uncalled for, and I apologize."

Joss shrugged a little. "It don't matter." But Aidan knew by the set of her jaw that she was still wounded. "Let me see to the horses. They've worked damn hard."

Aidan let her go; she knew odds would be odds until Joss had time to even them in her thoughts. She watched from the window over the sink *(water in the sink?)* as Joss coaxed Fritz and Charley to back the wagon into her desired position by the house; they did look weary, dark with sweat that was ringed with dried salt-whiteness. Joss unhitched them and led them to the barn, and it seemed forever before Charley emerged into the pasture to ruin his new good looks with a thorough roll in the dirt, and longer before Fritz burst from the side door of the barn to do the same. Joss trudged across the yard slapping her gloves against her thigh, looking as tired as the horses before their care. Aidan met her on the porch with water drawn fresh from the well and a kiss against her throat. "You taste like faraway places and the heat of the day, my love. How was the road?"

"Be glad you didn't go. My back feels like a bedspring in a whorehouse."

Helplessly, she laughed. "Joss Bodett, you're *so* vulgar."

"I know," Joss grinned. "I'm sorry."

"You're not in the least bit sorry. Have you eaten?"

"Not lately. Who's that feller in the beans?"

"Levi, and now you know as much as I do—except he's simple,

I think, and hasn't stopped since he started three hours ago on a charge of biscuits and cold venison. What's in the box? And what's this about water in the sink?"

"Got to thinkin' on the way to town. Water always run downhill last I noticed, an' we're downhill from the spring. Seems like all we needed was pipe enough to get from there to here. Hope I guessed right on distance. Worth a try, anyway." She hung her hat on its peg by the door. "The box is treasures from the East Coast to the East Indies. If you'd make me what you made your friend Levi, I'd show you." She let a hand trail down Aidan's arm, squeezing her hand; Aidan tried to catch back the flinch but couldn't, and Joss caught her wrist again, turning her hand to look. "Aidan! What in tarnation have you done?"

"Nothing you don't do every day—"

"I told you to stay out of the God-damned beans!" she roared, and their fragile truce disintegrated. "Aidan, you're with child! You can't—"

"With child, but not helpless or useless," Aidan blazed back, "and you don't own me! I'll not be commanded like a wife or a slave for I'm neither to you and don't you dare think I am, Joss Bodett—and don't you ever curse me again!"

"I cursed the beans! Aidan, I'm tired an' hungry an'—"

"And you left without so much as a note to say where you'd gone or when or *if* you'd come back, and when you do you treat me like some—some—oh, make your own damned dinner!"

Joss grabbed for her arm and missed. "Aidan!" She came up short as the bedroom door slammed in her face. "Damn it! Aidan, what do you want from me?"

"Leave me alone!"

She bit her lip hard enough to taste blood. "I'm sorry! Is that what you're waitin' to hear?"

Silence.

"This don't settle jack shit!" she yelled at the door, and turned to take four steps with an ache building inside her like the charge in the air that advanced a tornado before something in her splintered (*so I busted the Dutchman's nose. Don't try tellin' me*

155

what you know, 'cause you don't know this) and she wheeled to drive her fist full at the wall.

Pain roared from her knuckles to her shoulder. It ripped her breath away, and took her legs out from under her; she buckled to her knees, tears burning at her eyes, stars twittering at the edges of her vision. "Aidan—oh, God," she moaned, touching one searing, bleeding knuckle, wishing she hadn't, and she felt a hand at her shoulder and didn't have time to apologize before she was hauled up by the shirtfront and planted hard against the same wall she had hit. "Wha—?"

"No hurt! Good lady hurt do I you, you no hurt! Hurt you no here be good in lady house, you mister man!"

"What—? This is my—who the hell—oh no! Let go oh no please Jesus let go—" He was a ragged scarecrow, but his hand around her injured knuckles was inexorable; the pain seemed bottomless. There was nothing in her stomach to rise but bile; it bittered in her throat as her knees deserted her again.

As dimly if they were behind closed doors in another room, she heard Aidan begging him away. She cradled her scorching hand to her belly, trying to fight the faint, her stomach lurching; the dirt floor was cool at her palm as it rose in her fracturing vision.

"It's just a bad sprain," Doc decided after Joss passed his tests; he'd missed breakfast but come for high tea, finding Levi in a sobbing panic on the porch as Aidan tried to get Joss to her feet without jarring the damaged hand. "Aidan, fetch me some brown paper and a bowl of vinegar, and we'll draw it out."

Aidan headed for the barn, and Doc closed his fingers hard around the wrist of Joss's uninjured hand. "What in the name of all Christ's disciples is wrong with you? If you'd hit her that hard you could have have killed her!"

"Doc, no! I couldn't hurt her—"

"And this is supposed to prove it? From what she said, you started this day off stupid and it hasn't gone but downhill from there. Lord above, Joss! You can't leave her here alone with the

Cav gone, or hardly with them here, for the love of—"

"Doc, it's Friday! You always come Fridays, that's why I—"

"I come if I can! Today I couldn't. You listen!" he spat, hard against her beginning protest. "She wasn't telling tales on you. She just said what happened. You might act the man around this farm, but if you need a daddy to teach you how to be a better man than your brother was, I'll be that now. You'd damn well best learn to admit it when you're wrong, and not go off half-cocked like this—and if *ever* you raise your hand to her, you'll never touch her again, from your hand to the sight of her in your eyes. I promise you that. You're as good a man as any, but you can be just as fucking stupid as one sometimes, so I'll talk to you like one. You hear me, Joss."

"I'm a better man than many, an' well more able to listen." Her voice and her eyes were flat and cool and even; it was the dead composure of fear, not anger. "I hear you, Doc."

It took time for Aidan to convince Levi that Joss belonged in and to the house, but when at last she did, Joss knew that anyone setting foot on Bodett land for as long as he was there would have to explain themselves to that stolid, uncompromising being. He was abject in his apology for hurting her, and adamant in his refusal of her femininity: "I think he needs to see you as a peer," Aidan offered hesitantly, "as much as a white man and a colored one may be peers. If he hurt a woman—a white woman at that he's disgraced himself more than he could bear. If you're a man, he did the right thing by protecting me."

Joss didn't feel like a peer to much besides the coyotes howling at the moon. "If you say," she murmured, the fingers of her left hand comforting the darkening bruise that was her right. She had finally been able to eat for the first time that day since cold biscuits slabbed with butter for breakfast. Pain had roiled her stomach for the afternoon, and the whiskey she had taken to try to dull the hand had but further distressed her digestion, and done nothing for the throbbing ache.

Hitting the wall had been stupid; she wondered how much

157

additional damage the protective Levi had done in his defense of his good lady.

"Aidan—" She picked a shred of tobacco from her tongue, and licked her smoke where it was coming undone, smoothing it in one-handed concentration before she looked up. "Please be honest," she said softly. "Have you ever feared I'd strike you?"

"Joss, no." It came with such calm assurance there was nothing to do but believe her. "You've a vile temper, but you'd hurt yourself before you'd hurt me. I can take as proof what Doc denies." Her touch was light and cool on Joss's hotly swollen hand. "Him and his old wives' vinegar! Ice would pull the fever from that. Levi!"

He was sitting by the well, as dejected as Joss, sifting a handful of pebbles from one palm to the other. "Levi, can I have a bucket from the bottom of the well? Please?"

He scrambled to his feet; the water was delivered in less time than it would have taken Aidan to draw it. "Bucket," he announced. "Hot hand bucket mister Joss-man make small fever hand." He grinned helplessly, shuffling his feet in his new boots; Harmon's had fit him, as had Seth's jeans and shirt, and his pleasure in his new gear was as evident as his guilt for Joss's pain. That she'd hit the wall meant nothing to him; to him, he had caused it all. His largest uncertainty was why the lash hadn't yet been introduced to his back. He didn't remember much from the time before the rifle ball had laid the crease across his skull that left the streak of pure white hair, but he remembered the bite of ropes around his wrists, and the crueler snarl of leather against his flesh; he remembered being too proud to scream, or even to cry, and didn't know if that pride was still in him. His nerves ached in waiting for this white man's verdict.

Joss slipped her hand into water icy from the depths of the well; fire stitched to her elbow and subsided to a level well below what it had been. "Lord above. Thank you, Levi," she breathed.

His smile went shy and confused; he had seen many miles and much work since the end of the War, but few white men had thanked him for anything. "Sit with us." Joss indicated the porch step with her good hand; he looked cautiously at Aidan. She nodded, not so much permission as confirmation, and gingerly, he perched on the edge of the step.

Joss offered her bag of tobacco and he looked at it in wonder. "Go ahead," she said quietly. "My Pa fit for the Blue, Levi. I got the wrong words sometimes, but you ain't but a man like any other an' I know that. Sorry if you'd ruther a chaw; I ain't got that."

"Grace," he whispered, and touched as little of the tobacco as he could in the rolling of his smoke, and accepted the flame of the match she offered him as he might have accepted Communion, had it ever been offered him. "Thankin' you, Mister Joss."

"You like a smoke, I'll double up my order with Doc. Ain't got much else to pay you save three hots an' a squat an' a bed in the barn. That's good fresh hay there, just cut."

He drew on his cigarette, treasuring the taste; tobacco had often appeased his belly and his soul when there had been nothing else to fill them. "Need up go loft," he murmured of the hay, and added absently, for sometimes his caution left him: "Young get sons maybe soon."

It was the good lady who chuckled; the sound of her laugh was low and soothing to him. "Maybe a son soon, Levi; yes. But long before he can pitch hay into the loft."

"So Levi," Joss said, flipping the end of her cigarette across the porch rail into the yard. "Tell me why you pull the pokeweed instead o' usin' a hoe."

He scrubbed fingertips at the scar over his ear. "Broke poke grow mo' poke." He said it patiently, as if he were talking to a curious child. "Even no, hoe so slow. Hurt hands."

"Broke poke ...? What d'you mean?"

He studied the field in the moonlight; he had returned to it after the fracas of the early afternoon, pulling more pokeweed in three hours than Joss could chop in a day, guilt driving him to try to please her. "Break by hoe? Night water part mo' grow poke. Pull by root, sun die forever."

Joss frowned. "You sayin' each part o' the plant runs a new plant?"

"Cha! One three break three, break three make—?" His hands, deft in the fading light, did the multiplication. "Nine. Damn no good Station farmer."

Wearily, Joss smiled; she could take no offense at his offer of a county-wide opinion of Stationers. "Damned if I ain't. Go ahead on an' pull it, Levi. You done a fine job of it today. Got more done than I could've in three days," she said, and he wriggled like a puppy in his pleasure at her praise.

"There's a treasure untold," she said quietly, when he had finished his smoke and excused himself with awkward, oddly-spoken grace. "That crease on his head tangled his tongue, but it didn't relieve him o' any aces, an' he's a strong back we could sorely use."

Aidan was still amazed that Joss had agreed so readily to his staying. "I wished for a big yellow dog," she murmured. "It seems better to feed a being who can pull weeds." And she looked at Joss, sensing her still feeling small. "Having fed you at last, love of my life, what's in the box?"

"Box—? Oh! I forgot all about it." She got up to bring the peach crate to the porch. "You didn't peek?"

"Not even a little bit—but oh, how I wanted to!"

"Well, you know about the floor an' the water. Be a week 'fore I'm able, Doc says, but the makin's is all there." Levi had tied a tarpaulin over the wagon; under the lumber were two dozen ten-foot lengths of cast iron pipe. Hart had cautioned "Ethan" that his horses couldn't haul it even if his wagon would bear the load, but the horses were Belgian and the Jackson brothers built one hell of a wagon.

"Tea, out of habit—" She set two tins aside and dug for a paper-wrapped package. "They tell me this fellow's all the fashion back East." Aidan split the wrap to find *The Adventures of Tom Sawyer*, and she exclaimed in delight; she had loved *Innocents Abroad* back in Maine.

"An' this!" Joss's fascination was obvious as she pulled an odd contraption from the box. "It's like nothin' I ever saw! Hold it here—" She handed it over. "Turn the crank—see the little cages

160

go round? Can you imagine what it's for?" It had occurred to her that this ingenious device might be everyday back East, but Aidan was bewildered, turning the handle, watching the mechanics of it. "It's an egg beater! D'you see? Put eggs in a bowl an' put the cages in an' spin the crank—Aidan, he made egg whites thick as whipped cream! Merry-goo, he named it. Hell, he made whipped cream that stood straight up, in just a minute! It's the damnedest thing I ever saw, an' it only cost two bits."

"We'll have whipped cream every day. I can't wait to try it." She didn't mind beating eggs with a fork, but whipping cream that way was a trial, and she'd never seen whipped cream stand straight up. "But Joss, the money—two bits, yes, but books are so expensive! I could go without—"

"Not on your birthday, you couldn't." She reached into the box again. "I could've got this at Richland's, but I hate givin' them money." She offered three wrapped packets; Aidan opened them to find broadcloth, ten yards each by the heft of the fold. "It seemed you'll need some new dresses," Joss said shyly. "I'll help with the makin'. Sewin's a good thing to do on a Sunday."

"But there's way too much here," she protested. "And such good cloth for dresses I'll never be able to wear again—"

"We can cut 'em down after the baby's born to where you'd never know it'd been made big. I used to do it for Ma. I got enough of each for a dress for you, a shirt for me—I like the feel o' good cloth, too—an' some extra. Curtains an' quilts an' such. Earlene'd prob'ly like some, if we got left over." It was a gentle warning; Aidan let her fiscal protest go unsaid.

There were boxes of bullets for the Colt and the Winchester: "cheaper there than here. Thom might've chose storekeepin' over stage robbin', but he's still a bandit." There was a handsome English etui with a large compliment of needles; Aidan shook her head in mute resignation and wondered if there was anything left in the tobacco tin under the bed, but was glad of the needles; she only had four left that were of a useful size.

"Praise God Ethan was lucky at the poker table," Joss said, as if she had heard Aidan's thought. "Pa'd cuss him for takin' rings an' watches instead o' cash money, but the money would've been long spent. I found the fancies last night. When the floor's laid we'll be walkin' on a diamond ring. The water pipes are a gold watch. This odds an' ends o' stuff used to be a ruby ring—" Awkwardly, she dug her left hand into her right pants pocket. "Hold out your hand," she requested, and Aidan received eight double eagles into her palm. "That's change from the rings, an' jewelry left."

It was the first time she'd been to Leavenworth alone, and surely the only time she had been there with spare money in her pocket. There were hair ribbons for Aidan, and a new hat for Joss; Aidan tied a fluttering length of lilac ribbon around the crown, winning a smile from her lover. There were horehound drops in a paper bag, and a bottle of French brandy: "A drink fit for a lady, should you care for one of a Saturday night." There was a new diary for Aidan, a tin of lamp oil, a three-quart saucepan...and Aidan realized that with a pocketful of money, Joss's indulgences had been miniscule, and largely practical.

"And," Joss said with a note of finality, her hand hesitating in the box. "Mayhap you'll think I'm loony for this." She offered something gleamingly blue-black in the darkness; Aidan accepted leather and wood and cold steel, heavy and solid in her hands, and sucked in a breath of surprise.

"It's Pa's," Joss said. "I had a fellow put new grips on it. Said carve 'em down till they feel a shade small for me an' they'll be just right for you. He done a pretty job. That's cherrywood."

She had feared it, fired it, depended on its comforting presence by the door—and now it fit her like the handshake of an old friend. "Joss, I can't—oh, Joss! I can't take this from you. This was your father's—"

"I loved Ethan, too. I'll carry his. Aidan, you ain't worth sour owl spit with the Winchester. You need a Colt an' you know this one. I know it's a odd sort of a thing to give a woman—"

"Oh, Joss," she murmured, touching the cold security of the gun in her hands. "I've turned into an odd woman, compared to who I was when this year started. Will this kill a deer?"

"It'll kill what you're close enough to hit true, from here t' the barn. Mean to kill when you pull the trigger." She offered a box of Leavenworth bullets and her tobacco pouch. "Might you make me a cigarette?"

She watched Aidan's concentration, and scratched a match on her boot when Aidan licked the paper; she lit and drew, and smoke leaked slowly from her nostrils. "Before Slade we had a good Captain," she said at last. "He'd come an' sit here on the porch an' talk to me an' Ethan—Seth was wee, an' not yet sick; he didn't have time for the stories of an old man." She chuckled. "All o' thirty, he was when he came here, but to Seth, all o' six, he looked old, I suppose. To me he looked like Jesus in a short beard. Ethan asked once to see his sabre an' Cap'n said, 'What would you have me kill? If I draw it, it must shed blood before it's sheathed again.' He said it was a tradition o' soldiers that a sword never be drawn but for purpose, an' the only purpose of a weapon is to kill." Softly, she laughed. "Ethan was about nine. 'Well, you could kill Joss,' he says, just all lit up for wantin' to see that sabre an' what it could do. Cap'n had quite the talk with Master Ethan that day."

"From what you say, it sounds as if Ethan did some listening."

"I'd say he did." She glanced at Levi, cross-legged by the well, his hands limp in his lap, and knew he was hearing all they said. It wasn't that he listened; he simply absorbed. She looked back at Aidan. "Know what you're aimin' at, when you aim. An' when you shoot, know you want somethin' to die by your hand." She reached to move the barrel of the pistol; it was pointed at her knee. "An' no matter what you think you know, it's always loaded. Unless it's broke down into parts on the kitchen table, it's loaded an' able to kill. It may be your companion, Aidan, but it ain't your friend. A friend won't maim you or kill you for one mistake of attention."

Aidan opened the revolver's loading-gate; she half-cocked the hammer and spun the cylinder, holding it so the last light showed through its empty chambers. She slipped rounds into five of six chambers, leaving the hammer resting on the empty one. It was how Joss had carried it, when Harmon Bodett's pistol had been hers. "Thank you." She took it into the house and came to sit again. "How does your hand feel?"

"Numb. Better. How are yours?"

"I soaked them in salt water and put balm on them. They stink, but they feel fine." They were stiff, but not tender to every touch as they had been earlier. "Joss—" She touched a puffy blister with an exploratory finger. "I see a problem with Levi," she said softly. "I—we've never had to be concerned with—ears. When we—" She looked up shyly. "In the night. But the way he came in when he thought—"

"Oh." It was a self-conscious sigh. "I expect you're right." She stood, taking the bucket in her left hand; Aidan watched as she gave it to Levi. He emptied it in a spraying gift to the kitchen garden and made a good hitch with the well rope around the bail. "Levi, I got somethin' to say like we was one fellow to another—"

Aidan heard no more than that as Joss walked him to the barn, talking quietly, her good hand cupping the place where the masculinity he expected of her might have risen; he appreciated that male gesture, and the frank, gentle confidence she shared with him. He heard her respect for the good lady, and her ungrudging regard for him, and he gave her a bashful grin and a shove on the arm, and pulled the barn doors shut. Joss went back to the house shaking her head, not quite comfortable with what she had said... but knowing she'd be a damned sight more uncomfortable if the protective Levi burst into their room to save Aidan from her first cries of impending fulfillment. "Lord," she sighed. "I'm not used to bein' thought a man, but it's been my life today. I'm not so sure I'd like livin' it forever."

Aidan breathed a soft sigh, sensing California farther away than it had been last night. "What did you tell him?"

"That's between us fellers," Joss teased, sinking to her chair.

"Oh, you—" She leaned to brush her lips against Joss's, and found a brush wasn't enough when Joss's mouth quickened on hers. "Oh, my," she breathed at last, the heat stirring deep in her belly, her breasts pressing full and tight against her chemise. "What did you say to him? Tell me, Joss."

"Let's just say he'll forever believe me to be a man now."

"All to the best." She parted her lips under the sweet aggression of Joss's tongue, to its gentle exploration of the secrets of her mouth. "Take me to bed," she whispered, when she could; the kiss had deepened until she had to break away, to gasp for breath—and then gasp again in want as Joss's teeth bruised softly against her throat. "Now, Joss—"

She soothed Joss's injured hand with kisses before she wrapped it in strips of old sheeting, snug enough to compress but not so tight as to bind. In the bedroom, she let her lips graze across Joss's throat, tasting dust and sweat. Joss clean from the bath made her gentle, but the smell of a day's work on that hard body ripened something deeply subliminal in her; it made her remember that first electrifying kiss in the woodshed when Joss had been soaked with sweat and the base, animal smell of blood. Sometimes when she first heard the sound of axe against oak she would go to the door, watching as the sweat started and grew on the back of Joss's shirt until the cloth stuck to her in the heat, and she would imagine the ripe slickness of that wet body next to her own, her own heat rising until she had to turn away, shivering with the knowing that if she watched any longer she would call her to the house . . . and be naked (or nearly so) in the time it took her lover to come across the yard.

"What," Joss asked softly, feeling that smile on her lips as Aidan eased her suspenders from her shoulders and her sleeve over the wounded part of her, dropping the shirt to the floor, that tiny, secret smile still touching her. She stroked a finger under Aidan's chin, bringing her face up so she could kiss that smile. "What makes you this way?"

"You," she whispered. "Remembering the first time you kissed me—" That smile was more than reminiscent now; it was almost speculative, almost adventurous.

"An' what else?" But Aidan only smiled as Joss found the pins in her hair and loosed them one by one, golden length tumbling over her hand, and she drew Aidan close for a lingering kiss, her wrist at the back of her neck holding her there. Aidan's mouth was quick and hungry on hers, her nails raking against her ribs as Joss's left fingers tried to learn about buttons. Her kiss distracted from their clumsiness; by the end of tiny buttons on Aidan's dress they were deft. Her hand sought skin and found her chemise instead. "How do you stand all these clothes!"

But when Aidan shed the dress she was lovely in the flimsy silk, the soft glow of the lamp coloring her honey and cream; Joss reached to stop her hands on the laces. Slowly, she pulled the bows herself, loosening the cloth that stayed the fullness of her breasts. Aidan's hands caught hard at her ribs as she bent her head to the exposed rise of that heavy warmth.

Aidan trembled under the touch of lips there, caught her breath when that tongue traced the line of the silk, cried Joss's name softly when teeth closed lightly on tender skin in a promise of what they might do when they found what was still hidden; she found the buttons of Joss's jeans and tore them loose, and Joss kicked out of the jeans as Aidan's nails scratched hard against her back. "Let me—" Aidan's voice was husky with desire. "Let me, Joss."

Careful of the hurt, Aidan drew her down to the bed, taking her gently to her back. "Let me, Joss," she whispered against her lips, her silk-clad breasts a caress against Joss's bare skin. "If you could know how I need you—"

There could be no refusing the softness of thighs that embraced her hips, or the lips that found her mouth, her throat, the small hardness of her breast; there was no denying the lush hair that swept across her belly, or the hands that took their measure of the slender muscularity of her shoulders, the leanness of her ribs, the slimness of her hips; Aidan's lips followed her hands, finding the tenderness of a breast, the ticklishness of the bottom rib, the soft hollow inside her hip before her tongue flickered damply back up to Joss's throat to trace her lips, allowing Joss a momentary capture before Aidan kissed her with a dizzying thoroughness that left Joss searching for breath, rising to meet the silk-hidden feel of Aidan's breasts against her own nakedness.

Aidan felt the appeal of the hand at her breast and loosed the lacings of her chemise, a slow, deliberate exposure in the soft light of the lamp, loving the need in Joss's eyes. She lowered herself, offering that fullness to the hunger of Joss's lips, and she had a sudden image of herself swollen with milk, this woman's mouth tasting her in a thirst that was tonight and the first time and something deeply more, and when Joss's lips closed on her nipple she could only arch into her touch, holding that close-cropped head against her, gasping her name as waves of sensuality shimmered through her like heat over the fields at midday: "Oh Joss, this is so good it feels so—oh Joss please—"

"Come to me," Joss whispered, her hand gentle against her hip, a promise of knowing their desires. "Let me taste you—"

Aidan could only submit, if submission was what this driving want was; she gave herself to the fingers that eased the silk aside, to subtlety of the mouth against her, the lips that found hers, the tongue that sought and probed and drew from her the gasping moan that would swell to a scream of gratification as she braced into the intimacy of its knowledge of her, a scream she tried to stifle and couldn't as Joss's kiss took her to a place where there was no sound or silence, no light or darkness, no memory or future; there was only being, a sinuous tapestry that surrounded and consumed her, a rich cloth woven on the threads of two women's lives.

And she came back from that place wanting only to take Joss there; it was a trembling moment before she could move, but when she could she found Joss's lips, shivering at the musky essence of herself there. A part of her was heavy with satiation, but in another part a thirst still burned, and she took her lips to Joss's ear, tracing it with her tongue. "Let me. Allow me, Joss."

Her palms sought every curve and hollow, every softness and hardness of her lover as her mouth took a long and wandering way down the spare landscape of her body. She found the soft curls at the tops of her thighs and breathed deep, inhaling her essence; she drew her cheek across that damp froth of hair. "Oh, my love—" It felt like a prayer as her palms slipped down in slow measure to find Joss's hips. "Oh, Joss. Let me taste you—"

Joss gasped at her first exquisite touch. Captured by the delicacy of that kiss as it flirted with the limits of her control, she began to understand why Aidan wept and cried and screamed when— "Aidan! don't stop please don't stop—oh, Aidan! please, right there—"

The fire could find her just by touching Aidan. When that small hand had found her in their love before, she had thought nothing could ever kindle a higher flame; if Aidan's fingers against her then had been the hot blaze of tinder, what her mouth did now was the liquid explosion of a flaming pine knot in the place where the fire in her lived, and she let it take her, gave herself to its consuming intensity until that knot burst into a final, searing flame, blazing until it was but a glowing memory of itself. Spent, struggling for breath, she felt Aidan's lips on her face and caught them with her own, tasting them both in the mingled essence of that kiss until she could only bury her face in thick golden hair and breathe a shuddering sigh of helpless gratitude. "I'll try to deserve you. God, I'll try to deserve you—"

Gently, Aidan shushed her; she kissed her lips, murmuring her love as they found the comfort of their fit together. She thought to turn off the lamp, but couldn't bear to leave their closeness, and sometime in the night a breeze strolled through the room to gutter the flame down and then out, and they slept entwined in the darkness, secure in their love and their lives.

July, 1876

Then I will give you rain in due season, and the land shall yield her increase, and the trees of the field shall yield their fruit.

And your threshing shall reach unto the vintage, and the vintage shall reach unto the sowing time: and ye shall eat your bread to the full, and dwell in your land safely.

Leviticus 26:4-5

CHAPTER THIRTEEN

"Come one soldier man come horse!" came Levi's announcement from the corn; Joss straightened up from the shoulder-wrecking job of bucksawing stove-length blocks from one of the three massive oaks Levi and Doc had felled a week ago. She was ambidextrous enough that left-handed operation of the saw was possible, but it was awkward and slow. She had been arguing with her pride, trying to convince herself to ask Levi for help with this most difficult part of the wood, when he let out his yell.

Squinting up the hill, she saw only dust. She shook her head. Levi saw the world in black and white, but he saw more of it with his hawk's eyes than she could. She left the saw in the kerf and wiped a forearm across her face, depositing as much sawdust as she removed sweat, and went to warn Aidan of the impending arrival of Argus Slade.

Aidan was churning butter with one hand, holding *Tom Sawyer* in the other; Joss took the handle of the churn. Aidan abandoned it without protest. "Your attention to Mr. Twain is required to delay. Levi says soldier man one horse, an' I can only assume the scurrilous Captain Slade."

Aidan made a face. "And just in time to be fed. Why couldn't he have ridden with Custer instead of Terry?" Doc had brought them the news of the rout at Little Big Horn, and Aidan had opened her bottle of brandy. They had a thoughtful drink, more commemoration than celebration, but she knew both Doc and Joss took grim satisfaction in the disaster even though they knew the retribution of the Cavalry would be both swift and vicious. "I don't have time to amuse him at his convenience," she grumbled. Suddenly extremely pregnant, she was miserable in the spell of hot weather they were suffering, and her disposition proved it at times.

But the soldier who arrived in their yard was a stranger. "Captain Malin Leonard, replacing Captain Slade," he said from his horse; his voice was thick with the accents of Kentucky birth and Virginia Military education, his gray eyes almost bashful, his hands calm on his saddle horn. He was barely taller or broader than Joss when he was invited to the porch, where he shook her hand with the firmness he would afford a man—offering his left, seeing her right still bandaged—and gave her the courteous half-bow a gentleman would offer a lady; he did the same for Aidan. "Miss Bodett and Mrs. Blackstone, I trust. Is my horse welcome at your trough?"

"As you are at our table. Will you join us for a simple dinner, Captain?"

"Perhaps a cup of tea—" He produced a tin from a saddlebag. "My arrival at mealtime is unhappy coincidence. I deplore the habit of officers inflicting themselves upon the civilians of their territory. It smacks of quartering. I've come but to introduce myself, and lay rest to rumors of the decimation of the entire Cavalry in the unpleasantness at Montana."

He showed his horse the trough and returned to the porch.

"This heat must be heavy on you, ma'am," he said in his liquid accent to Aidan's now-obvious pregnancy. "If your stove's not built, I'll thank you for the offer and accept some other time. Cold water will do as well on such a day as this."

He wouldn't hear of them starting a fire for no more than a kettle of hot water, nor of either of them drawing a bucket from the well; he did it himself, and brought it to the house for his use now and theirs later.

Argus Slade, he said, had resigned his commission and was gone to parts unknown (his tone suggested that departure was to no one's especial dismay). The situation with the Lakota Sioux was not good, but the trouble seemed to be keeping north of the Kansas border, at least this far east. He spoke his news with the churn between his knees, his hand easily metronomic on its dasher until it was ready; he savored a glass of buttermilk before he helped them with the washing and gathering and packing, and rinsed the churn over Aidan's protest but to her satisfaction. "A soldier can be of more use than killing," he smiled. "Take pity on a man without a wife in whose chores he may assist—especially those he so enjoys." His grin was easily self-effacing. "Butter is so like playing in mud. The man doesn't mind cleaning up when the boy is through his fun."

"They're sayin' had Custer survived he'd've been court-martialed," Joss said, when they were back out in what breeze there was to be had on the porch. It was a daring statement, but it was what Doc had said rumor had, and she was curious about both Custer and captain. "Relieved o' his command, if not his commission."

The captain packed a pipe. "It's difficult to discern the decisions of the dead, but easy to criticize them. Will my pipe offend you, Mrs. Blackstone?"

"Not at all, Captain Leonard." It was common knowledge around the Station that she was a grass widow, and common knowledge fast became common gossip; she appreciated his use of a title that afforded her propriety no matter what he may have heard.

172

He lit his pipe with studious attention; fragrant smoke lingered in the air before the sulky breeze took it. Joss had watched him, listened to him. Now she asked quietly, "Cap'n Leonard, what's your opinion o' the Indian trouble?"

His dark gray eyes were pensive; it was a long moment before he spoke. "Rarely does it behoove an officer of the Cavalry to speak his heart." His smile was weary. "But some crocks don't stink until they're stirred, Miss Bodett, and there will always be those who live to smell that stink."

Faintly, Joss smiled. She drew her sack of tobacco from her pocket and rolled a neat cigarette. "Will it offend you if I smoke, Cap'n?"

He struck a match, cupping it in his hand for her. She accepted the light and leaned back in her chair. "We start up the stove around five," she said, studying the hills that framed the farm. "Eat a bit late to escape the heat. It'd honor an' please us if you'd find our home some evenin' in time for supper."

Shyness touched his eyes again. "It's an honor and a pleasure to be asked," he murmured, and stood. "Your crops look better than some I've seen. You have some protection from the wind—a two-edged sword to be sure, on a day such as this. My Navajo scout prognosticates no rain for at least a fortnight."

"Then your Quartermaster's hard pressed for winter." Harmon Bodett, like most farmers in the Station, had sold his crops to the Cavalry Quartermaster, albeit through the exorbitant brokerage of Thom Richland. Joss wondered if this captain might provide a source of kinder transaction, should she have a crop to sell.

"Buffalo or beans is of no mind to the belly of the Army. It's farmers such as you who have my concern." He raised a corner of the tarp covering the wagon by the house, idle since Joss had hurt her hand, and sent them an apologetic smile. "Please forgive my curiosity. I thought I smelled oak."

"An Eastern frivolity," Aidan smiled. "A floor, as if we needed one."

"One want satisfied can hold many others at bay." He returned her smile, and she was comfortable in it. "A floor is a fine thing to set a foot on when the day is spent in dirt."

The time he spent with them seemed short; he left with directions to Doc Pickett's place and fat biscuits slabbed with new butter and cold corned venison, fed whether he took it in their company or not. "What a wondrous surprise is our new captain," Aidan said. "And to know Slade is gone—"

"It renews my shaman faith in the Great Spirit," Joss grinned. "I should get back to my wood, since the good captain left me day enough to do somethin' with." She stood. "Hey, Levi!" she yelled across the yard; in the corn, the gangly fellow looked up. "Come take one end o' this saw for me, will you?"

CHAPTER FOURTEEN

It had been relentlessly hot for a week on the day they were visited by Captain Leonard, and that sullen weather held; heat shimmered from the land all the time the sun was in the sky, and there were no evening rains to lay the dust or relieve the crops. Joss got up one morning to discover big footprints leading from the barn to the road, and Levi nowhere to be found. He wasn't back for supper and they stayed up late, but at last they went to bed, and when he was still gone in the morning they could only assume he had drifted out of their lives as easily as he had drifted in.

Joss, on the porch with coffee and cigarette, regarded her fields. A light breeze rustled the leaves of crops that were silver-gray with thirst; it was a nervous, brittle sound, like gossip at a banker's funeral. She flexed her still-lame hand. "No fool, our Levi. He hightailed it before I got out the buckets."

"Let me help," Aidan said softly. "Joss, please."

Joss leaned against the porch rail; she took the last taste of her coffee and the last drag from her cigarette. "Ma lost Baby Abraham to buckets an' we still lost the crop. I'll be God-damned if I'm carvin' another board this year." She settled her lilac-ribboned hat onto her head. "It would've been a fool's errand with Levi here. He knew it. An' he knew I'd've tried with him here, 'cause I'm a damn no good Station farmer doin' it how we always done it an' not smart enough to think up any other way? Watch me fool you, Levi." She stepped off the porch and looked back at Aidan. "I meant to have water to the house by now. I'm sorry we don't, an' now it's got to go to the fields. First soakin' rain, I'll bring it in."

By the end of the week Marcus Jackson and Ott Clark had seen the green of her fields and had come to gape at her irrigation, thinking what the price of beans was going to be. The sky was an eerily glossy silver, no rain forthcoming. "God-damn Bodetts. Nigger-riggers to a man of 'em," Ottis grumbled, forgetting for the moment that Joss wasn't a Bodett man; she just seemed like one in her relentless capability.

The weeds thrived with the beans. Joss pulled them, finding a new set of muscles to ache at the end of each day. The crows got after the corn; Aidan made a dark and lanky scarecrow that so resembled Levi it spooked them both every time it caught the corners of their eyes. It spooked the crows, too, so they left it, and spoke often of that gentle, absent friend.

The scarecrow didn't bother the raccoons. As soon as ears set on the stalks they began their nocturnal raids. Joss, on the porch for a smoke one early evening, saw one lumbering from the woods toward the corn; perfunctorily, she shot it in the head. "Surely you won't just leave it there?" Aidan asked, when she made no move to retrieve it.

"The coyotes'll clean it up."

Aidan regarded her for a long, silent moment before looking away with a tiny sigh.

"Well, y'don't eat the damn things." Joss rammed a cleaning

176

patch down the bore of the Winchester, cross in the censure of Aidan's silence.

"I see. You just kill them."

Tight-lipped, Joss got up. She cleaned the coon and skinned it, and stretched the hide, and dredged her memory for the time Earlene had told about being so short they had to eat coon; it wasn't bad, she'd said, if you soaked it in salt water for a day and roasted it like a turkey. "Mind you git off all the fat," she had warned, "else you'll bite into somethin' turrible bitter now an' agin."

Not bad was an understatement. It took Joss but one taste to sidestep her instinctive objection to eating varmint. After weeks of beans, canned venison, the occasional rabbit, and chicken every other Sunday, it was as welcome as it was tasty.

She had to think long when Aidan asked why such a perfectly meal-sized creature would be ignored in the diet of a family that largely existed on meat that was canned, jerked or corned. "I suppose because they're meat-eaters," she finally said. "Ma wouldn't feed the hogs meat scraps. She said it made 'em mean—that's true enough—but she'd never let Pa shoot a bear, either, 'cause it was a—a—I'm wrong here—cannibal?"

"Carnivore," Aidan suggested.

"That's it. She an' Pa got into it one time—he'd shot the bear, y'see, an' she wouldn't even let the heart an' liver into the house—an' she said how the Bible says about eatin' the flesh of a beast that ate flesh, an' he come back just that smart with the part about cloven hoofs an' cuds an' how she never seemed to mind eatin' off a hog or a rabbit—one's got the split hoof but don't chew cud, an' one chews the cud but don't have a hoof at all, an' Moses didn't leave room to mistake what he thought about that. Well, she just went stubborn on him. Said if he wanted bear he could cook it outside an' eat it outside an' sleep in the barn." She shook her head, amused memory flirting with the corners of her mouth. "Ma with her back up, now, that's to see. Ott got the bear, Thom got the pelt, an' Pa never shot another bear that I knew about."

She nudged at a sliver of meat on her plate with her fork before she put it in her mouth; it was tender and succulent and she had no trouble swallowing. "All that Leviticus stuff, what you can an' can't—the last month or so, I been readin' that over. More I study on it, more it seems to me God was tellin' His people that some o' that stuff—sayin' this or that, an' doin' this or that—wasn't so much sinful as it was against how they was supposed to keep their religion. He says, 'After the doin's o' the land o' Egypt, wherein ye dwell, shall ye not do, an' after the doin's o' the land o' Canaan, whither I bring you, shall ye not do, an' neither shall ye walk in their ordinances.' Ain't He sayin' that the Israelites got their own ways an' He wants 'em to keep separate from the ways o' the land they're movin' into? He laid down the ethics with the Commandments. This other stuff, why, mostly it's just common sense, relations with near kinfolk an' the like; that throws sickly babies, same's it does with cows. He ends up by sayin' 'whosoever shall commit any o' these abominations shall be cut off from their people.' He don't say nothin' about bein' cut off from their Lord."

Aidan laid down her fork and touched her lips with her napkin. "By that interpretation, then," she said quietly, "are you supposing He wasn't averse to men laying with men as with women?"

Joss gave her a slight smile; she had detected a bit of distance between Aidan and Doc since the doctor had made his admission. "He said don't do it, but I ain't so sure He was allowin' as to how it was a mortal sin. He said about not eatin' anythin' that ain't got fins an' scales that moves in the rivers an' the seas, 'cause they was an abomination unto us, an' that's the same words He uses about men layin' with men, but Ma talks about eatin' lobsters an' clams an' oysters, an' ain't none o' them got both fins an' scales as far as I can tell from the pictures I seen. You ever eat them things?"

"Yes..."

"Eatin' them things was an abomination unto you, accordin' to Leviticus, same's Doc layin' with a man. You feel as if you're goin' to Hell for eatin' a lobster?"

"But it says and 'surely they shall be put to death' for laying with a man as with a woman. It seems a larger abomination, given the penalty."

"Ought I take you out an' shoot you, then? Leviticus offers up the death penalty for cursin' your father, too." She took a biscuit from the pan and broke it in half, slathering butter onto it. "An' Jesus said, 'It is not that which goeth into the mouth defileth a man, but that which cometh out of the mouth, this defileth a man. Those things which proceed out of the mouth come forth from the heart, and they defile the man.' Jesus wanted people to be kind to one another. An' it seems God in the Ol' Testament was sayin' He wanted His chosen people to behave in a more comportly manner than the Canaanites an' the Egyptians—like sayin', 'look here, Joss Bodett, Ott Clark beats his horse, an' maybe he ain't goin' to Hell for it, but that don't mean I want you followin' his customs just 'cause you live next door to him.' But if I did beat my horse, would He turn His back on me?"

"I can't imagine you beating your horse."

Joss bit into her biscuit. She knew Aidan wasn't being obtuse; Aidan was simply dreadfully uncomfortable with the turn the conversation had taken. "All o' that bein' what it is," she said, flicking soft biscuit crumbs from her lip and her shirtfront, "this ol' raccoon don't taste half bad. Wonder what Thom'll allow me for the hide."

Captain Leonard appeared a few days later; Aidan was making bread so the fire was up, and he had his cup of tea. She asked him if he had ever eaten raccoon.

"You ask a Kentucky boy if he ever ate coon?" He laughed. "Why, my best friend when I was a lad was my old bluetick hound. We kept meat on the table and money in my pocket."

"And you weren't concerned about eating the flesh of a beast that ate flesh?"

He glanced at her across the rim of his cup. "Poor folk haven't much room to worry about the next world, Mrs. Blackstone," he said gently, "busy as they are trying to survive this one. A raccoon

179

would feed my family, and I'd get five dollars for a coonskin hat."

Joss came in from the barn in time to hear that. "I saw one o' them once! Boy howdy, that was nice. You really know how to make one?"

In an hour, so did she. The Captain taught her how to make a bag of the raw pelt; filled with oak gall and water and hung from the game pole, it would tan in a week. He hewed a chunk of oak into a rough block that she could smooth down later with her drawshave. He told her how to block the pelt, and stitch it, and knew by her hands that she understood.

"I've a fair contingent of Blue Ridge boys in my troop," he said, picking at a sliver in his knuckle; Joss got it between her fingernails and flicked it away. "Thank you. They might provide a bit of a market if someone made a good coonskin cap."

"What's one worth anymore?"

"Twenty years ago, with every other lad in Kentucky making them, I asked and got a half-eagle. It would seem that their paucity here would make one worth at least double that." He folded his knife against his thigh and stood to slip it into his pocket. "Hard to say. Test your market and charge what it will bear. You must tell me what you've done with your crops, Miss Bodett. This is the only piece of the post road that looks as if it remembers what life and breath mean, and I know you're not getting help with a bucket brigade. Everyone else is too busy trying to save their own."

She told him about the irrigation. He followed the pipe to the spring and was still grinning when he emerged from the woods. "That woman of yours," he said, turning bread from the tins for Aidan; Joss had noticed Fritz limping, and was out coaxing a stone from his foot. "She'll have water in your kitchen sink a day after the first rain. Lord, but the two of you are a grand union." That won him Aidan's thoughtful study for the next hour; he left saying he thought he'd go see if he could find Doc.

Doc came the next day for high tea; Aidan asked if the Captain had found him, and Doc blushed and grinned and finally admitted. "Nothing serious, you know soldiers, but..."

"Is that a difficulty for you?" Joss asked her that night, holding her; Aidan had seemed shy with Doc all afternoon, and Joss knew Doc had noticed. "Doc an' the Captain? Seems they might care about one another same as we do, given enough time an' the same grace as Doc's given us."

Aidan sighed. "Nothing I believed in before I came to Kansas seems to fit here," she said softly. "Everything's been turned upside-down. I love Doc, and I like Captain Leonard very much. Perhaps I need leave it at that, and leave God's judgment to God."

They ate raccoon until they were sick of it. Pelt-bags hung tanning from the game pole, from the woodshed roof, from tree branches, until Aidan wondered how Joss kept track of them—and how there was a coon left in the county, but each night, lured by the corn, one or two fat bandits fell to the Winchester.

It rained ten days after the irrigation had been set in, a hard, two-day rain that kept Joss out of the beans while they dried; she moved the water to the house. The system for the crops had been balky, and wouldn't work at all in its first incarnation to the house; she spent most of a morning walking from the spring to the house and back, her hands shoved into her hip pockets and her hat raked back on her hair, staring at the pipe as if it might give her answers. She cut a forked branch from the cherry tree and dowsed down from the spring; the witching said its underground stream came within feet of the never-failing well. She squatted there to draw in the dirt with a stick. She went to the house to draw in the margins of a newspaper with a pencil, and Aidan could make no sense of her pictures. "Won't a pump work?"

"Would, but I ain't got one, an' Pa'd never put one in even with all of us to run the pickaxe. We ain't got but a foot'n a half o' topsoil; under that's as much o' clay that's hard as Effie Richland's heart. Then three foot o' somethin' harder than that. Frostline's some ol deeper'n what I care to dig a pipeline."

Six feet, Aidan thought uneasily. *She knows too well what the first six feet look like, four graves later.* "Gravity won't just feed it down?"

"That's what it's doin' now, but it don't work into here, an' even if it did it'd freeze up come cold soon's you turn off the water an' stop the flow. Then you got no water an' busted pipes. I don't know that I want to have it runnin' day in an' day out in the sink."

"I don't," Aidan said definitively; she had lived with dripping faucets, and didn't want a constantly-running one.

Joss went to sift through her box of couplings, coming up with a T; she stared at it. "Gentlemen, hush," she murmured, looking narrow-eyed at the well. "Will this...?"

She didn't know what she was doing; there was only a gut feeling that it would work. She laid pipe past the house to the well and elbowed a four-foot section upright, leaning it against the well; she sawed a foot off the end of a full length, and fixed the T sideways to the top of the upright and added the short piece to the top of that, water gushing onto her feet. "Outflow's lower 'n the source an' higher'n the sink," she confirmed, not sure why that was important, only knowing that it was. She drew a deep breath. "Please, Jesus," she prayed, and hollered, "Aidan! Open the pipe in the sink!"

She knew before the whoop of success that it worked, for the flow at her vented pipe gurgled and stopped. "Hail Caesar! It won't freeze 'cause it runs all the time–an' back into the well so even if it does freeze we'll have water. We can tap it for irrigation do we need it again, an'—Hi! Is that ol' pickle barrel still in the barn?"

By the time she was done not only did they have water in the kitchen, but there was a cooling tub by the well; no more would butter or milk or meat need to be carried to and from the spring. She chiseled a hole in the side of the well for an overflow pipe from the tub, with a coupling that would allow her to channel the overflow to the kitchen garden. Finished, she could only stand there and stare at it. "I'll be damned," she whispered. "I'll be God-damned if this don't work."

And for a long time that night she laid awake, her fingers stroking a rhythmic caress against the blonde head sleeping on her breast as she listened to water burble from the pipe into the cooling tub. No symphony would ever play sweeter music to her ears than the sound of running water in her front yard.

CHAPTER FIFTEEN

The floor went so quickly Joss was sorry she hadn't done it sooner, forgetting that her sprained hand would have disallowed that much work with hammer and saw even a week ago. "How will you move the stove?" Aidan asked, watching Joss lay her framework under the cast-iron behemoth. "Or will you?"

Joss glanced up at her. "Give me a long enough lever an' where to stand an' I could move the earth." She wiped sweat from her forehead before it could run into her eyes. "Somebody said that first. Some Greek schoolteacher."

"Archimedes." Aidan remembered Captain Slade's remark about a ration of civilized education behooving the youth of Washburn Station and wondered where Joss had encountered the quote. There was nothing to suggest such education in the books that had been in the house when she arrived, and now that Joss had read *Don Quixote*, *A Christmas Carol*, *Tom Sawyer* and the poems of the Brownings, she spent her reading time browsing the Bible in no apparent order: where it fell open in her hands, she read.

But the Greek schoolteacher hadn't mentioned balancing that three-quarter-ton monster once she had it off the ground; Joss was sweating more from nerves than exertion by the time she got her block set so that the stove seemed to balance when she gave it an exploratory raise on the old iron whiffletree she'd found in the barn.

"Stand away as far as you can, Aidan. For God's sake, don't put any part o' you under any part o' the stove. If I yell, jump away an' no questions. Just move." She sketched a hand across her forehead, catching sweat; her shirt was soaked. "Doc or Gid could come along just now an' I'd not refuse their damned help."

"Stop worrying. Lean on the bar."

They both knew that the missing part of the equation was a long enough lever. Joss had to put all her weight on the whiffletree to get the stove far enough off the floor for Aidan to slip the next board into place, and Aidan was glad to be out from under and Joss glad she was by the time the stove was standing with its four legs on oak boards—and of course they were barely done when they heard a horse in the dooryard and Doc sauntered in to exclaim, first in delight at a floor at last, then in admonition that they hadn't waited for him to help with that most dangerous part of the process.

"Pooh, Doc," Aidan chided gently. "If we always waited for you, we'd get naught done and quickly. Do please excuse me; I must check the chickens."

Doc examined the job so far. "Looks damn good," he said. "Flora Washburn would be jealous if she saw it, Josie. This is a fine job."

"Flora Washburn'd tear my head off for not havin' the battenin' done yet. Pa'd call me a pure fool, spendin' money on such a thing."

"Mayhap, but your mother would sing your praises, as will

Aidan, each time she sweeps or drops a biscuit. It's a woman's house now, not a Station claim shack." He took off his coat; there were unwieldy objects yet in the way of floor-building. "Let's move the china cabinet while she's in the outhouse or she'll make us empty the damned thing first."

It took a long day to set the frame, and a longer one to lay the boards; that night they trod its alien length and breadth, marvelling at its cleanliness, at how the lamp cast so much light against the paleness of the oak, at its sweet scent. "I'll hate the first stain or scratch," Aidan mourned. "Please, Joss, can we try to keep it clean until I can get a coat of wax on it?" It wasn't pegged, but it was oak and it was hers, a gift of love in answer to a request born of pain, and she loved it, and its giver.

"Hart said shellac it, steel-wool it, do that again, then wax it. Do a little work now to save you a lot later. I only believed him cause he threw in the shellac. He ought to've, for what he charged me for the damn lumber." She stretched; she had thought to get the first coat on tonight, but she was tired and sore. "Tomorrow," she promised.

The next day she worked at the floor until her hand protested; it wasn't all healed, and she had been using it hard. She rested, smoked, had a whiskey, went back to it. By the end of the job she was quite tipsy, but the oak glowed in the lamplight, and she sat cross-legged between the table and the bathtub, massaging her aching hand, satisfied with the job and how Aidan moved in the kitchen across its glossy surface, barefoot and loving it; a smile settled onto her when Aidan went to the sink and drew water to put in a pan with potatoes from the kitchen garden. The succulent smell of roasting chicken masked the odors of shellac and wax. "My dear cousin Aidan," she said softly, and Aidan looked up at the odd gentleness of her voice. "A floor in the kitchen an' water in the sink. You'll have me thoroughly civilized yet."

"When you start wearing skirts, I'm going back to Maine."

"I'll wear skirts when you accept a proposal o' marriage from the hopefully late an' utterly unlamented Argus Slade."

Aidan rolled her eyes. "A classic impasse, if we're waiting on those eventualities." She watched Joss get up; even with one whiskey too many she was graceful as a cat. At first Aidan had been afraid of the liquor, too many memories of her father too strong for her comfort, but in the past Joss's occasional daytime drink had only made her a little more talkative, her humor against Argus Slade or Effie Richland a little more biting. Aidan knew today's excess had been to dull the ache in her still-bruised hand; now it (she assumed the whiskey, anyway) had given a deep smile to her, a look that tugged at her as Joss came across the floor. "Do you know how much I love you?" Aidan asked quietly, and some strange answer flickered in the dark eyes, in hands and then arms gentle as Joss brought her close for an embrace that made her forget there was a world beyond their doors. She had never been held the way Joss held her; she had never known she was so treasured; she had never been so enveloped with the warmth and being of another soul. "I do, Joss," she whispered. "More than I know how to tell you."

"Without you—" The tenderness of her hands, and the lips she pressed to Aidan's hair, was almost frightening in its intensity. "Without you I'd've long since been up a tall tree with a short rope," she whispered. "You gave me back wantin' to live. I'd have wallowed here—" A laugh jittered from her, a laugh as frightening as the tenderness. "Smokin' in the house, feet upon the table, drinkin'—bein' Ethan. A week, a month, I don't know"—she buried her face in the curve of Aidan's shoulder— "tiltin' at my windmills until they tilted me too far. You gave me—" Her voice broke. "You—oh, Aidan. Lord, I'm sorry—"

"Joss—" She sank with her in her slow collapse to the floor. She had never seen Joss cry: not when Levi had mauled her hand, not in her hurt and anger at her thoughts of failure with the farm, not when she had been delirious with fever, and to have the tears come now, on the heels of the accomplishments of the water and the floor, was bewildering. "Joss, what? Tell me—"

But Joss could only cry; Aidan could only hold her, rock with her, assure her of her love.

"Ma—" It was a rasping sob. "Oh, Ma! God damn all those men! Why did she have to—" She drove her face into Aidan's belly. "He could've gave her this! Rings an' a watch won at poker an' a trip to town, that's all it took an' she spent her love on a fucking dirt floor—oh, Ma! I miss you so much—"

Aidan had never felt so helpless as she did with Joss's face buried against her belly, knowing nothing to do but hold her as she wept for the loss; she had never been so bitter as she was in knowing that if tomorrow's mail brought the news of her own mother's death, she would have no such tears to cry. Tears, yes, but not this anguish; not the loss of such a rare and unconditional love. "Joss—" She hated knowing nothing to say that could help. "Oh, Joss. I'm so sorry—"

At last she quieted, a few hiccoughing sobs leaking past the end of the storm, but it was a while before Aidan understood what she was doing: one hand at the small of her back, one cradling the growing roundness of her belly, her head pressed there, she was listening to the baby, or feeling its restlessness. "Can you feel her?" Joss nodded a little. Aidan slipped her fingers through the dark waves of her hair. "Are you all right?" Joss nodded again, a huge, unsteady sigh escaping her. "Can I do anything?"

A shake of the head was all the answer she could give; she curled into Aidan's warmth, needing only her closeness while the hollowness subsided.

"Damn—" It was a raspy remnant of a voice; she sat up to hold her head in her hands, and sniffed and found her handkerchief to wipe her face and blow her nose. She stared at the floor, and reached to smooth a hand over its golden surface, shivering at what it had stirred in her. "It was so easy to do," she whispered. "It ain't like she ever asked for it, but Lord, you'd think a man'd see his babies crawlin' in dirt under his own roof an' feel some shame. It didn't cost as much as he drank in a year." She ran both hands through her hair, and sighed and got to her feet, offering Aidan a hand, pulling her up to hold her for a grateful moment. "Thank you," she murmured. "Might I'd've done that well ago, an' not let it eat at me so long."

"You did it when you could, Joss."

"I guess." She leaned in the door, staring at the dark, listening to the water in the yard. "We've 'proved this claim more in a month than he did in twenty years." Her voice sounded hollow, remote. "He did what he had to—he did good to start, buildin' on with boards, an' a porch—but after that? Fix what's broke an' promises, an' never a new thing. Marcus, Ott—the whole damned lot o' this place, they're all the same. God-damned Station farmers an' all they'll ever be. Earlene fixin' to put a baby down on that same dirt six others crept on? Dirt don't hurt the baby none, but it'd hurt my heart. Your baby comes an' we'll have floors through if I have to kill every coon in Kansas an' sell more hats than Stetson. The only dirt this child's knees'll touch'll be in the damn yard."

"Don't be hard on him, Joss." Aidan slipped her arms around her cousin's narrow waist, resting her cheek against her back, holding her. "He did what he knew to do, and he loved you. He loved your mother."

"He loved us as much as he knew how to, I guess. He just didn't put much imagination into it." She rested her arms over Aidan's. "This is about the best farm in the Station. Best soil, best lay of the land, best woodlot. The spring. A well that's never gone dry. He chose it well, an' then he treated it like—" Tight-throated (for she had loved the man she had called her father), she shook her head. "Like Stationers treat things," she whispered. "Like a wrong man treats a right woman. An' I'm damned if I will, it or you. It can be a good farm, Aidan. It won't make us rich, but it can be a good farm."

189

CHAPTER SIXTEEN

"Stars, girl, wouldn't your momma be proud," Earlene Jackson breathed, coming into the kitchen to see the oak floor glowing under its second coat of wax. Joss had seen her on the road and hailed her for tea, knowing the only time Mrs. Jackson enjoyed a cup of that was in other people's homes. Marcus had plenty of whiskey money, but Earlene couldn't afford tea, and put her babies down on dirt.

Earlene knelt to brush her fingers across the glossy surface of the wood. "I never seen anything so tight, Joss! It must have been—" Her eyes widened when Aidan freshened the kettle from the pipe in the sink. "Saints be praised, you put in water! Marcus said you had it to the crops, but Joss! Water in the house?"

Joss hadn't meant to show off, only to afford Earlene a cup of tea; her mother always had, if they had tea. "We've got the spring," she said apologetically; surface springs were rare, and rarer still the sort that didn't run a brook on the downhill side. "Made it a right smart o' easy just to pipe it on down—short o' almost killin' the horses gettin' the pipe here. I witched the water down, an' the spring runs smack into the well. We feed the flow back into that. Can't see how it'll ever go dry."

It occurred to her that all three bedroom doors were open; she saw them from a visitor's perspective and knew no woman who kept a house could miss the fact that only one of them was seeing daily use. "When's your wee company comin', Earlene?"

"Save me another baby carried through the summer," she grumbled; she had indeed noticed the bedrooms, and wondered why they slept in the same bed when body heat in July wouldn't be welcomed. "October sometime. How you bearin' up under the heat, Miz Blackstone?" She slurred the title enough for politeness; Jocelyn had been her dearest friend, but she had been a Blackstone and Joss a bastard (likely explaining her being the only brains in the Bodett family), and at some point one had to wonder if the behavior just ran in the women of that family—except Joss. She was a case, was Joss, not a mite of interest in the boys and never mind Hank Richland and Earlene's own Gideon chasing her all through the schooling years; she'd known that what they were chasing had more to do with prime acreage than her feminine charms.

"I spend every minute I can with my feet in cold water," Aidan confessed, and Earlene haw-hawed in heartfelt empathy. "Do you get the headaches, Mrs. Jackson?"

"Headaches! Girl, you take a day the sun shimmies on the dirt an' I ain't worth a fart in a tornado, but with seven sittin' supper an' glad to feed 'em—" After what had happened in this house in March, she'd never curse the board she laid three times a day. "Good Lord give me a girl amid all them boys. She's a help to her momma, an' I'll be hanged if I'll let some b'hoy knock her up at fourteen th'way Marcus done me. Two years short o' forty an' still at this taradiddle? It's agin God's law, I told him, an' the last of it. You needin' help gettin' in the beans, Joss? Lord knows we ain't got enough to worry about."

191

"I ain't turnin' down help, but I'm good for two, two an' a quarter acre a day, an' we ain't got but twenty. Wood, now, I'd take help with. Levi could make Charley snake out a tree, but hell if I can. I'm some sorry about your crops, Earlene. Save that spring, an' we'd be cryin' here."

"You cried plenty this year. I know there's some grudge you that water, but Jacksons ain't among 'em—an' who gives a soft crap for a Clark? Been hard enough for you 'thout losin' the crops too." She stirred her tea. "We saved about five acres. Plowed the rest under, both claims. Planted again after it rained. All a farmer can do. Good Lord give us season enough for two crops."

The Jacksons had two forty-acre claims, as did the Bodetts. Harmon had built his house on the edge of one and put his barn on the edge of the other, thereby improving them both; the lay of the Jackson land had precluded that shrewd technique, so Marcus had 'proved his second one up just enough to keep it, building a cabin that had seen lackadaisical maintenance since then. "Leaves us startin' from behind just like any spring, but only one crop comin'." Any farmer's wife would have recognized her short, soft sigh. "What with Ethan gone, Gid's the best poker player 'tween here an' the Fort, I guess. Mayhap it'll make a difference."

Joss shook her head. "Not if you count on it. Time we trusted on Ethan an' he'd come home with his pockets inside out. But he got us the floor an' the water with his rings an' watches. God rest 'im, he passed in the middle of a hot streak at the Bull an' Whistle."

Joss rocked back in her chair, took a look from Aidan, set back down on all fours. She wanted a cigarette. "Devil's pasteboards or no, them cards is the only reason there's a crop out there. Gid takes a hard urge to roam, that's when to stake him, if he's like Ethan." Her smile tightened. "He'd get all wild 'round the eyes, Ethan would. Get to pacin' like a springtime bull. Bust outa here like a cat outin' a cage. Come home three days later smellin' like the bottom o' the barrel an' his pockets right full o' double eagles an' diamond rings an' somebody else's daddy's watch."

Aidan and Earlene could only watch, knowing it was coming

by her eyes, her voice, how her hands fisted on the table. "Not worth a continental with a hoe, nor plow a straight furrow to save his mortal soul, but give him a bottle o' rye an' a game o' draw an' a promise from a pretty girl an' he—" Her voice broke; she scraped back in her chair. "Marcus or the boys headshoot a coon, I got a dollar for a raw pelt," she rasped, and the screen door banged behind her as she fled.

"Bless that child," Earlene said softly. "There's lots here was hard—there's hard 'hind every door o' every house—but there was care enough to make up for it, an' for her that cock-wild Ethan hung the moon. Is she holdin' up?"

Aidan didn't know Earlene had Effie Richland's nose for gossip but none of her mouth; she had seen those curious eyes probe the bedrooms. "She drives herself," she said tightly, aching to go after Joss. "Floors, the water—it's all part of the driving. At least if she stays in with me she's able to sleep. Alone, she was up all night walking ruts into the floor. I just feared she'd wear down."

"Be a right smart o' comfort in a body on the other side o' the bed," Earlene nodded, wondering why she hadn't suspected that; tough on the outside didn't pass a good heart able to hurt. "Marcus can be common as dogshit, but he's a good man, same's Harmon was an' all their faults. Just puttin' my hand out, times, to know he's there..." She shook her head with a little sigh. "Lord only knows what the dark's got in it for that girl." Her eyes met Aidan's, frank and direct. "Or for you, child. Ain't none o' this was your idear, was it, from the gettin' to the givin'."

Tiredly, Aidan smiled. "Why I'm here was no choice of mine, but staying is. How could I leave her alone? She's my blood kin, Mrs. Jackson."

"Earlene."

"Thank you. I'm Aidan."

"Well, thank your momma; I always thought that was too pretty a name for a boy. You go find your cousin, Aidan. I'm flirtin' late on supper already. I thank you for the tea—an' if I can't stand admirin' your floor from where I set, I may come do it here, if you don't mind a call of an afternoon."

"I'd treasure it, Earlene. I'm starting to get nerves about the baby."

"Laws, child, if you're like Jocelyn—an' you're built just like her—that baby'll pop right out 'fore Doc can hear an' get here, 'less your man was tall as Lincoln an' fat as Grant. What me an' her done was swap horses the last month before. Come time, you have Joss turn that horse out with a sharp slap an' he'll come right on home an' I'll know you're ready. I'm fair closer than Doc! I brung Joss into this world, girl; I can bring this one. Say grace you ain't got a houseful o' men! God love Marcus an' rest Harmon, but we'd fain send both of 'em down t'the Bull an' Whistle for four days an' give us some rest durin' an' after the doin'." All of this was said on her way to her wagon; she stopped there and gave Aidan a brusque hug. "Ain't nothin' to birthin' a baby, child. It's the next twenty years is a hard row. Be you lucky, when you die they grieve you hard. Means you was a good mother. Now you go find young Joss. Practice some motherin' on her. She's missin' that bad, if you could only scratch the flint."

I can scratch it if I can find it, she thought, scattering indignant hens as she ran barefoot across the yard and up the old trail to the spring, seeing leaves and humus fresh-turned by recent heels; old hurts went the old ways, and the path wearing down along the pipeline was too new for instinctive flight.

She found her cross-legged by the spring, unmoving at her approach; Aidan touched a gentle hand to the back of her neck. "Would you rather be alone?"

"Why is he so hard?" She had been clamping back the tears; now they came. "I thought he was too mean to die that way! I thought he could spit in the devil's eye an' live to laugh about it—God above, all the things we ever did together an' diggin' Ma's grave was the last—"

A floor in the kitchen, water in the house—things your mother should have had, things you've given me—things you could give me thanks to Ethan, who hung your moon. If you could have made him come to good in his life you would have, but death was the only chance at goodness he had and you took it. Grieve him, now, and let him go. She held her, feeling the heat of her tears and the cool dampness they left at the shoulder of her dress.

"This ain't goin' to happen again," Joss whispered finally, shakily. "I ain't such a—"

Aidan heard the self-deprecation coming and cut it off. "You can't have such pain and not cry. It's not the tears you cry that drown you, Joss, it's the ones you don't cry. It's not a weakness."

"It feels like one."

"The first night you held me while I cried, did you think I was weak to cry, or to ask you to stay?"

"No! Aidan, you were so hurt—"

"And now it doesn't hurt the way it did. It was no weakness of mine, any more than you're weak to hurt in the loss of people you loved. If you know love and death as part of life, you have to know the pain they cause, too."

Joss studied her cousin, not comprehending her; a cigarette end in a coffee cup could send her into a snarling irritation, and yesterday she had been reduced to tears by a piece of wood that refused to fit into the stove until the house was full of smoke. She wrote to her parents out of duty, and was rewarded with tins of tea and letters as cold as a tax collector's smile; she burned the letters, drank the tea, and mentioned Maine and the people there as if they had been a dream she'd had once, long ago, and yet— "How did you come to know so much o' love? You were raised up with so little of it."

"What I know, I've learned by knowing what I've missed that you've given me." Aidan reached to tuck a straying curl back into the thickness of Joss's hair. What Earlene had said came back to her; her smile was small and sad. "If we're lucky, when we die this baby will grieve her family the way you're grieving yours. It'll mean we were good mothers. I'd rather the grief of losing a loved one than to die knowing I was never loved."

"Better to have loved an' lost—"

"Yes. Come, and I'll trim your hair. You're getting shaggy."

Aidan tried to coax Joss into the tub once the haircut was

done, thinking if she was clean and freshly-dressed she might take the rest of the afternoon at leisure; there was nothing Aidan had to do that wouldn't wait, save making supper, and as for Joss and the weeds—well, the weeds would be there tomorrow. But Joss, shaking the hair out of her shirt, decided there was too much daylight left (and too much wasted already this day) to indulge in a bath yet. "I'll just tighten up that section of fence by the road," she said, and Aidan sighed and got her sewing basket. Joss couldn't seem to touch barbed wire without damage to her clothes or her person; she could wear shirts that had been Seth's, Ethan's and Harmon's, but all three men had been broader-beamed than she was, and she was wearing her last intact pair of Levi's.

On the porch, she ripped the side seams out of a pair of Seth's jeans that were nearly new and measured them against a pair of Joss's that were nearly rags, keeping an ear tuned for the treacherously musical scream of a breaking strand of barbed wire; the last time Joss had mended fence, Aidan had been required to mend her. The scar across her back was still fresh and red, and Aidan dusted with the remains of the shirt.

Joss straggled back to the house two hours later, her shirt sweat-stuck to her and blood leaking from her in several places, none of them serious; she collapsed to the other rocker on the porch. "Lord, but that's miserable work!" It was, and harder still for knowing too well how fast one of those thorny strands could sing back to give her its vicious embrace. "I ought to've listened to you an' quit this day a while back."

Aidan got up to get her a glass of water, standing behind her to massage her shoulders while she drank it. "I wish you'd wait for Doc to help you." She didn't add the rest of her thought: that having the doctor on hand would be provident should a strand break again. She knew her cousin had gotten away lightly the last time, saved by a combination of feline quickness and a shirt thick enough to have afforded meager protection.

"If I wait for someone to help me with everythin' hard I'll never get anythin' done. You said that first, an' I take too much help anyway."

196

She bent to touch her lips to Joss's hair. "You're so stubborn."

"I'm a Blackstone by birth an' a Bodett by raisin'. Stubborn's my nature." She tipped her head back, smiling upside-down at Aidan. "You don't think you're tamin' me at all? Here I am sittin' on the porch callin' the day done an' it ain't but four o'clock—an' I know you'll have me in the tub when I just had a bath day before yesterday."

"You need the bath. Have I tamed you enough to get you to church on Sunday?"

She meant it as a joke; she'd long since given up on church, and was amazed when Joss shrugged. "If you'd like. I ain't wearin' no dress, though. Good Lord'll have to save me in the same clothes I wear for my sinnin'."

"You'd really take me to church?"

Joss raised her palms. "You want church, we'll go to church. I ain't closed to it, Aidan; I just been busy."

"My stars. What a surprise." Aidan sat in the rocker beside her, fanning herself with her apron in gentle exaggeration. "What might you do if we weren't to go?"

"Well..." Joss found her tobacco pouch in a shirt pocket and rolled a cigarette. "There's a brown ash down in the branch section I'd had a mind to get before someone beats me to it. It's enough for a dozen axe handles an' makin's for a new egg basket too." She scratched a match on the sole of her boot and lit her smoke. "An' Gid said he caught a nice stringer o' trout down there the other day. I sure am fond o' the taste o' fresh trout." Not looking at her cousin, she broke the match and tossed the pieces into the yard. "That's a right nice spot for a picnic. Figured we'd take the spider, catch some fish, cook 'em right there, an' maybe some corn to roast in the coals...yuh, I thought we might just have us a lazy day, but if you'd ruther go to hear the Baptist—"

"Joss Bodett, you don't have an ounce of shame. Making me choose between church and a picnic! Not a smack nor a scrid of shame do you have."

Joss slid her a sidelong grin. "I should be ashamed, offerin' you a picnic?"

"You should be if you're only offering it to get out of going to church."

"Cousin, you hurt my heart even thinkin' it. If you want to hear that hellfire an' brimstone Baptist spout his brand o' preachin', we can go to church an' come home an' have the picnic too."

They didn't go to hear the Baptist. On Sunday morning Aidan made a pecan pie; while it was baking off she packed a basket with bread and black raspberry jelly and fresh corn, a jar of milk and a smaller one of butter, a cloth and napkins and plates and flatware, and finally the pie on top, and Joss lifted her to Charley's broad bare back and strolled the mile to the brook with the halter rope loose in one hand and the basket easy in the other, her shoulder brushing softly against Aidan's knee. Orion followed them for a while, winding around Joss's feet and staying clear of Charley's massive hooves until a squirrel caught his attention and he tore off into the woods to hunt. "He'll find his way home," Joss said when Aidan worried about him. "He always does."

The brook was a clear, quick rill, no more than ten feet wide at its broadest, overhung by the branches of tall, brooding trees that dappled the sunlight on its glittering surface; there was a bent-boled cedar sweeping halfway across the water, and a clearing on the bank center-pieced by a circle of blackened stones around the ashes of a hundred old fires. Joss held a hand over the fire ring; the design of the ashes told her more than she thought Aidan needed to know, but they were cold, and she trusted that the Pawnee who had paused there for a meal was well away.

She received her cousin from the horse into her arms, gentling her to her feet. "This is a nice spot. It always feels cool here, even on the hottest day. Flora owns it, but she's never minded us usin' it." She spread a blanket, setting their basket and her poke of tools on it, and put the corn into the stream to soak in its husks.

Aidan studied the fire ring. "I read—of course, it probably wasn't true; so much of what I read in those silly dime novels has long since been disproved—that the Indians make fires that leave patterns in the ashes when they burn out. Do you suppose an Indian made this one?"

Joss glanced at her; she looked more curious than cautious. "Suppose it's possible," she allowed. "But I can make a fire like that, an' so can Gid, an' he was just here. Ethan taught us. He was pals with a few Pawnee bucks. Made good sense, makin' friends. Ott's always losin' stock, but we ain't had a lick o' trouble." She paused to cut a long branch from a willow tree. "The day after Ethan passed on, I got up an' found a funny little pile o' rocks on the porch," she said, stripping bark from the branch in deliberate curls. "Doc said it was a Indian mournin' thing, that they was payin' their respects an' tellin' me I'd get no bother from 'em. That's that little bunch o' stones on his grave—you remember, I asked you not to disturb 'em while you was pullin' the weeds from around the boards one day. I put it there soon's I got him buried, as close to how I found it as I could." She whipped the branch in the air, testing it. "I like it bein' there."

Aidan considered the tangle of forest across the brook. "How did your mother think of them? The Indians?" she asked, turning; Joss was tying a line to the end of her willow branch. "Was she afraid of them?"

Joss slipped her knot below the first knuckle of the fishing rod she was building and tested it. "I don't think Ma was afraid o' anythin' except rattlesnakes—which I ain't ever seen but two of in my whole life—an' this brook in spring freshet. Zeke wasn't the oldest Clark boy. Their firstborn drownded about a mile downstream. Fishin', an' the current caught him down. Drug out his body halfway to Newtonville. What's a brook now's a regular river come spring." She tied a hook to the end of her line. "Ma said they doomed Ott Junior, namin' him after a dead son. Give a name once, she said, an' let it go with the child if needs be." She spat on the knot and drew it tight. "You been thinkin' on names for yours?"

Aidan found a stick and drew an X in the ashes of the fire ring. "Not really. Not yet," she said softly. "Do you have any ideas?"

Joss's hand snaked out into the tall grass beside her; she turned her back to spare Aidan the sight of her making bait out of the grasshopper she had caught. "Guess it depends on if it's a boy or a girl. I like Esau for a boy. A cunnin' hunter an' a man o' the field, an' he'd have no brother to plague him like Jacob done."

"And if a girl?"

"I don't know. I got named after my mother, an' you've got a right pretty name. I never gave enough thought to havin' babies to worry about namin' 'em."

"You didn't want them?"

Joss toed off her boots, her socks staying with them, and stepped into the stream. "Babies are nice enough. I helped Ma with Seth an' Ruth enough to know I like 'em. It's all the foo-fraw that goes with bein' a mother I never cared about. Husbands an' all their orders an' demands. Do this, be here, make that, go there." She tossed the hooked grasshopper into the current. "Don't know where I fit, but not there. Seems to me a husband or a son ain't so much different. All want to be coddled. Ma was always chasin' an' waitin' after Pa an' Ethan, an' Seth more like a daughter to her, an' me—Lord knows what I was. Some o' both, I sup—whoa, fish!"

The green willow branch bent double; a brawny trout fought line and air and current as Joss played him, tired him, coaxed him to her hand, finally catching him to ease the hook from his mouth and hold him in an oddly spiritual moment before she broke his neck and tossed him to the shore. "There's your dinner! Now I but need catch mine."

She fished around the stream bed with her hand, coming up with a crawdad to use for bait.

She didn't go back to her train of thought, and Aidan didn't quite dare pursue the question of how Joss saw herself. Joss whistled while she fished, a song Aidan had never heard and thought was mournfully beautiful until her cousin gave voice to it:

When this cruel war is over,
Mother I'll be comin' home to you.

Well, I've eaten all the chicken, Mother
But I saved the bones for you.

"Oh, you!" Aidan tossed a pebble at her. "How can such a lovely tune have such horrid words?"

Joss dodged the unmeant missile. "I didn't write it, I just remembered it. I s'pose you'd ruther I sing a Baptist song, seein's how you got cheated out o' your churchification by my picnic." She deepened her voice—she really had a fine voice, true and clear—and intoned,

So I'll cling to the old ragged bay
till in the traces at last he lays down;
I will cling to my nag of a bay
And exchange him some day for a roan.

"Joss, you're terrible! How can you be so sacri—"

"Hi! There's a fish!"

Watching her play the trout on a crude willow rod and a line of white carpet thread, Aidan thought of her father's fine and mostly idle fly-fishing rig from England and wished for it for Joss, who seemed to care for the stream and the sport and the fish, once it was in her hands; she held the heavy-bellied trout almost mouth to mouth to her, saying some soft something that Aidan was sure was a benediction before she broke its neck in a clean, spare motion. "God can't be too displeased with me." Joss splashed across the stream with the fish in her hand. "He allowed me my dinner." She knelt by the water, opening the scrimshaw-handled knife Aidan had given her, and cleaned the two trout. "This is a good knife," she said. "Seth had a good hand with a blade. He'd have whittled you some pretty thing, or a whistle. I ain't much good for that, but I like a good tool. Did you know a fish tastes better if you leave it set wrapped up in grass for an hour or two before you cook it? Ma always said so, anyway. I'm goin' to go get that ash tree. I asked Flora could I have it, an' I think God'd be too surprised if I didn't do some little piece o'

201

work on the Sabbath."

She was wet to the thighs from the brook when she went after the tree; she was soaked through her shirt with sweat by the time she had dragged eight feet of the butt end of it back to the clearing. "Hope to hell Charley'll haul that home without too much fuss," she panted. "That's two or three good baskets if I can find time to make 'em. There was some Shaker group along where Ma lived when she was a girl—"

"Yes! At Sabbathday Lake; I've been there many times."

"She said they made the nicest baskets, an' glad to share their ways. She'd set Seth to beatin' on a ash log with the back of a axe 'til the year rings broke apart, an' she'd split 'em down again so they felt just like silk an' then weave 'em up. She made this one." She aimed a thumb at their glossy-patinaed picnic basket. "I hate to let her ol' egg basket go, but it's served its time, I guess. Past my fixin', anyway, but I can make a new one."

"We needn't throw it away; I can use it for cloth scraps. My grandmother—your mother's aunt—lives near the Shakers. She's friends with them, and she'd take me to visit. They do make a lovely basket, and grow the most wondrous herbs. They're a fine, God-fearing people."

"Ma said so—but a funny folk, not believin' in relations between men an' women. Can't see how they'll last."

"They take in orphans. Had I bowed to Father and gone to Cousin Rosa in Bangor, this child would have likely gone to them. A worse life could be had by a babe unwanted elsewhere."

"An' a better life could be had than bowin' to your father for the rest of it. Your babe ain't goin' to lack wantin'." She stood. "The other half o' this log back there yet is my axe handles. Let me drag it up an' we can go on with our picnic."

Joss showed Aidan how to lay a fire that would leave the star-like pattern of ashes that had been in the fire ring when they arrived. "But you can't touch it once it's lit. They make the young braves do it that way to teach 'em patience an' stillness, Ethan said. I like to tease a fire—you know, poke at it with a stick an'

202

such. An' o' course it don't work when you're cookin' corn in the coals."

She spread the checkered cloth on their blanket, and set out the plates and flatware and napkins. "Let me wait on you," she said when Aidan protested. "You do it every day for me."

"I don't think of it as waiting on you, Joss. It's just my part to do."

"An' you don't get tired o' the same part every day in an' out? I sure as hell do." She used two forks to turn the trout sizzling in the skillet, and gave an ear of corn a quick squeeze, and sat; for a moment she tapped at the toe of her boot with the stick she had been using to stir the fire. "Will you be wantin' to go to church next Sunday?" she asked at last.

Aidan looked up from the tiny grass basket she had been making just to have something to do with her hands. "I think not. The more I hear about this Baptist, the less he appeals to me. Our minister didn't go so far as to advocate free will—Father wouldn't have stood for that—but neither was he of the fire and brimstone school. I only said it hoping you might take a day of rest, Joss. I don't want to drag you there if you don't want to go."

"Well, I don't. I ain't the most sociable o' critters anyway, to go minglin' about the church yard with folk who don't give a damn for me savin' what gossip I can provide 'em, an' I hear that preacher go on an' wonder if he's even readin' the same Book as me. Accordin' to him we might's well all just curl up an' die 'cause there ain't no hope for our sinful souls anyhow. How's he figure that? The Gospel accordin' to John the Baptist says, 'for God sent not his Son into the world to condemn the world, but that the world through Him might be saved,' an' that if you believe in Jesus you're not condemned. Well, I do, so I ain't, an' that preacher ain't preachin' the same brand o' Baptistry that John was as far as I can see, so I don't care to listen to him. I ain't ever intentionally hurt anyone in my life, 'less you count a couple o' noses I busted when I was in school, but I've mostly turned my other cheek when people was cruel to me an' let 'em be cruel again, an'" —her laugh was small and hurt— "an' I inherited my earth. I've questioned God, an' I've cursed Him an' took His name in vain, an' maybe I ain't kept the Sabbath like I'm s'pose to, but I ain't ever forgot it. An' I done pretty good on the other Commandments. I figure me an' God can settle up when my time comes. He'll know my heart for what was in it when I sinned."

Aidan wove a strand of grass into her basket. Joss prodded at the fire. "Joss," she finally said, softly, "do you think we're sinning? When we—oh, Joss. I've thought and thought about it, and I've prayed, but I just don't know. I worry about it sometimes. Not just for us, but for the baby."

"Do you love me?"

Aidan looked up. "Yes."

"I ain't ever seen anything in the Bible that says love is wrong. Saint Paul said, 'I know an' am persuaded by the Lord Jesus that there is nothin' unclean of itself.'"

"But Leviticus—and I love Doc, Joss; I love him as dearly as a brother, but it's so explicit! And I wonder how His word can condemn such love between men and not condemn it between women. It almost seems implied."

"Aidan, I said before that I believe there's a difference between what Moses calls unclean an' what God sees as sinnin'. There's a difference between what makes the neighbors frown an' what makes God frown. I see that takin' your own life is a mortal sin, an' I was considerin' that before you came. There wasn't nothin' left for me. If lovin' you saved me from that, how can it be a sin?" Joss took the skillet from its perch on the rocks lining the fire. "I'm goin' to live my life an' let God decide if I done it right or wrong. I ain't countin' on the Baptist or any o' his flock to decipher the word o' God for me. If He sets me to cuttin' August hay for all time, I'll swing that scythe an' remember how it felt to have you here lovin' me." She set the skillet into the grass beside the blanket and eased a fish onto Aidan's plate. "Ain't nothin' in my life ever felt as good as havin' you close to me. I'll bet on that an' take my losses if I'm wrong."

CHAPTER SEVENTEEN

It was sweetly cool when Aidan awoke, Joss gone from the bed and a fresh breeze coming in the windows; she stretched in satisfaction. Their loving had been long and slow and sweet: once on their blanket by the stream, again after they got home—again and again, she thought, her smile soft and smug in the memory.

She stroked both hands over the child-roundness of her belly, her smile deepening at the memory of Joss's kisses there, delicately gentle as she loved the baby, too; gentle was all Joss ever was with her, even when their desires were so urgent it almost hurt to wait. A delicious shiver rippled through her at the memory of that long-fingered hand against her, caressing as Joss whispered against her lips: *Doc says some women like to have a cucumber there? Can you imagine, hot out o'the garden...* The words had jolted a moan of helpless anticipation from her, accompanied as they were by a probing finger—and then another whisper, another possibility: *or maybe an ear o' corn? Imagine how that would feel, so slow and easy...*

Her fingers told how slowly and easily she might do that; they told so well Aidan had almost felt it, a feeling that had taken her in a gasping rush so intense the memory of it now made her breath come quick and shallow in her, made her wish desperately for Joss, but there was only her own touch and the image of them both naked in the bed, sweating in the heat of the night and their desires, the lamp casting a shimmering glow over them as Joss's mouth found her breast, her hand leading a ripe and golden ear of corn to the willing parting of her thighs before slipping it easily into her readiness—

"Oh, Joss! Oh, my darling, yes—"

Deep, rich, crawlingly familiar, the drawl from the door froze her. "Well, I'll be damned if there ain't a woman who got it once and needs it bad again."

"Mother of God! What—" *If he's*

here—

Where

oGod please Jesus where's

Joss?

Know what you're aiming at, when you aim.

"Captain Slade"—Aidan's hands were full of cherrywood and blued steel— "you're not welcome here."

The memory of exploding whiskey bottles flickered in his pale eyes before the faint, sarcastic smile traced back to his lips. "You may have the aim to hit me, my Yankee whore." Lazily, he pushed away from the doorway. "But you don't have the ballocks."

And when you shoot, know you want something to die by your hand.

"Yes," she said softly. "Yes, Captain Slade, I do."

He didn't believe her.

He should have.

It was the peculiar brotherhood of soldiers that had led

Malin Leonard to spread a thin veil of propriety over the sudden civilianship of Argus Slade, the new captain allowed: soldiers tend not to reveal the flaws of their fellows even if the fellows are but marginally respected before their warts are discovered. In Montana, Slade had committed— "Let me say unspeakable acts, and leave it," he said to his small audience: Aidan, pale and shaken on Doc's porch glider, Joss close beside her, Doc in the doorway with one ear on the conversation and one alert to the patient in his small, neat home. "He was relieved of his commission. War is brutal, but never does it justify the individual acts of brutality at which Slade was found. No one will doubt you, Mrs. Blackstone. They'll only wonder why you spared his life."

Slade had pulled open his trousers, and Aidan had pulled the trigger. She didn't know if it had been outrage or anger or fear that had tightened her finger; she didn't know if it had been courage or the memory of Jared Hayward that had bathed her nerves in something as coldly liquid as water from the bottom of the well. She did know she hadn't meant for him to be alive twelve hours later. Wanly, she smiled. "Joss says we should have to eat everything we kill. I guess I didn't want to eat him."

"Innate human decency has affected more aims than yours." Wish though he might that her aim had been truer, her bullet had gone wide of the killing zone, exploding the shoulder joint; luck put Doc at his side almost as soon as the shot was fired. That morning Joss had found Levi in the barn, his eyes bruised shut, sipping the painful breaths of broken ribs, unable to make her understand what had happened to him. She went for Doc. They had just turned off the post road onto the Bodett dooryard track when came the potent whump of a sidearm discharged within the confines of a building.

Joss beat both men to the house, skidding across the waxed oak floor with her Colt drawn to find Slade gray-faced and bleeding into the dirt floor of the bedroom, his trousers undone, Aidan naked on the bed with her pistol trained on him, apparently content to watch him bleed to death. She had meant to kill him, she said; when she knew she hadn't, she cared neither to finish the job nor to get close enough to him to help him.

Now Slade was in Doc's disgusted but capable hands, delivered to his house with no particular gentleness on Joss's part. They'd met Gideon Jackson on the road and sent him for Captain Leonard, who came with a trio of guards; the guards were a distance off, their cigarettes winking like fireflies in the dark.

The captain knelt in front of Aidan; someone passing might have thought he was proposing to her. "Are you all right?" That she had pulled her aim was one thing. Had she not been able to pull the trigger...

He hadn't told even Doc of Slade's unspeakable acts, or that he had been the one to find him at them; Doc only knew that whatever had happened in Montana, the memory had more than once made his lover wake in the night with screams barely caught back and cold sweats that lasted long past the awakening. Aidan looked at him in the dark, seeing enough of that in his eyes to know how well she had chosen in shooting. "He would have killed me?"

"Yes," he said, much more simply than the dying would have been, and Joss felt the hard shiver that drove through her.

Aidan took his hand. His male touch, and Doc's, were gentle enough for her to bear today. "I had a choice today. Last time I didn't—and might not have taken it had it been there."

"I think this hard country makes hard choices easier—or perhaps it forces one to make them quickly. The element of pure survival is so much nearer—"

He almost pulled his hand away when she opened his fingers and led his palm to the rounding warmth of her belly, but then he understood; his breath stilled in helpless awe as he felt the movement under his hand. "Mother of God—to feel it! To know its life—how beautiful. How very incredible, Mrs. Blackstone."

"It hasn't always been beautiful to me. May I ask, Captain, if you might be comfortable addressing me by my Christian name? I'm not, nor have I ever been, married, as I'm sure you know. All the man had to do with me was a moment's subjugation of my will. Knowing that the next nine months or twenty years—the whole life of this child—was to be my burden...it was so terribly frightening until I met Joss, until I knew she loved me. This morning there was no choice. There was nothing to choose between."

"What happens to him now, Cap'n?" Joss asked quietly.

He stood. "Doc will save him," he said, "so that I may hang him. Aidan defended herself, and her child. The Army will deliver the justice."

"Why didn't we just let him die, then?"

The captain looked across Doc's moonlit yard. It was dead clear; the sky was ablaze with stars. He could see his soldiers leaning on the paddock fence, talking quietly to each other and their horses. "That would serve justice," he supposed slowly, "but through the side door in the dark of night. To let him die when he would live with proper care casts the doctor in the role of executioner." He drew his pipe from his pocket and packed it. "I could put him in the wagon and take him to post—"

"That road would kill him as effectively as my neglect," Doc said dryly.

"—which would make me his executioner by my choice, assuming the outcome of the trial to which he is entitled." *And I'll be damned glad when he's dead and buried and I can stop finding myself having to choose not to kill this rogue.* "I'll do it as civilly as such an uncivil thing may be done, but I'll take the responsibility for his blood. That's what my hands are for."

Doc turned abruptly, going into the house to check on his patient.

"Might one o' your soldiers see us home?" Joss asked, seeing the captain's look linger where Doc had been. "I ain't all that comfortable goin' past Clark's place this time o' night."

The captain watched them out of the yard. He had memories of many places, many people, many acts of cruelty and kindness, but he wondered, if he lived to be eighty, if he would ever forget Joss Bodett taking both his hands in both of hers, raising them to her lips to kiss his palms, one and then the other, with a benedictory gentleness that made his eyes sting with tears. "Such a beautiful night," she said softly. *"Ad astra per aspera.* Thank you, my friend."

To the stars through hard ways. "No, Joss," he murmured, listening to the creak of the wagon in the night, feeling his hands warm with the absolution only the understanding of women can give. "I thank you."

Given what else he had to do, Doc had given Levi only a cursory patching-up that morning, smoothing out his nose and binding his ribs; there was little else to be done for him. Aidan did as much with cold water and tenderness when they got home, soothing his bruises and his heart.

"What happened to you?" She understood little of his garbled answer, but she knew what he meant when he asked cautiously, "Blue man go die?" for Slade had still been wearing his uniform, albeit raggedly worse for wear. He curled a lip when she shook her head. "No good Station farmer Mister Joss call joke. No good soldier him, no call joke."

He had tried to stop Slade from going into the house, and took a coiled rope across his already-broken nose for the attempt. Gagging in pain on his knees, he understood why Mister Joss had fainted when he had squeezed that already-hurt hand: hurt on hurt multiplied like broke poke, and as much as he wanted to defend his good lady, his legs wouldn't work and he couldn't see, and then Joss charged into the yard and it was over—save guilt that he hadn't been able to protect her, guilt he had spent the day with as it squirmed in his guts.

Joss touched a booted toe to the black stain on the bedroom floor. The day had been hot; the room smelled thickly unfamiliar. She remembered the look in Captain Leonard's eyes when he had answered Aidan's question and knew he had spared them something blacker than bloodstains in his guarded talk of Argus Slade. *Had she been asleep when he came, had she not had the Colt there by the bed, had she not dared—if all of that, if he'd had his way, if*

210

I'd just come home and found her or what he left of her—

But she wasn't. She did. And she dared. Joss gave the room a weary smile. "Remind me to tell your daddy not to worry about you, little cousin. Any fool that tries you might best expect to be catawamptiously chawed up."

But before they slept again in this room or in this house, Argus Slade would leave it. She got a spade and two buckets and dug six pails of blood-darkened dirt from the floor, taking them up the track to pour the dirt in the ruts of the post road. She dumped half a box of matches into the hole, and fired one with her thumbnail and dropped it in; the acrid smell of sulphur rose as the matchheads flared. With her hands in her pockets and her thoughts blank, she watched the tiny bonfire burn itself out.

There was oil of camphor in the medicine chest; she sprinkled half the bottle into the hole, sneezing at its pungency, and then filled in the hole with dirt from the bean field, and had salted and oiled it and was tamping it with patient application of her own hundred and twenty pounds when Aidan came in from the barn. She looked up. "Is Levi all right?"

"He's badly bruised, but mostly he's embarrassed and angry. Talk to him tomorrow, Joss."

"I will. Did you get any answers out of him?"

"Not out of his mouth. But whoever did this to him was left-handed, I think. It's all worse on his right side."

"I'll want to have a look at Ott Clark's hands tomorrow, then. He ain't never had a good word for a colored man, an' he'd look on Levi as our colored man. You know how dear Ott holds me." She sat on Aidan's Saratoga trunk at the foot of the bed. "What about you? It ain't like this's been the finest o' days for you, either."

Aidan leaned in the doorway, considering the memory of the morning. Slade had surprised her, but his intentions hadn't; she had known before Malin Leonard confirmed it that he would have killed her. She knew that before she pulled the trigger, though she was quite sure she'd shot him as much for not knowing what he might have already done to Joss. "I think I'm fine," she said.

"Maybe I'll go into shock in the middle of the night, but Joss, I think I'm fine." She sat beside Joss on the trunk, stretching out her legs; they ached, and her back ached, and her head ached— but she felt good; she felt calm and strong and composed.

"I've always had someone to take care of me," she said quietly. "They've done it with varying degrees of competence or desire, but they've always been there. It's good to finally know that when push comes to shove I can take care of myself. That I needn't—to borrow one of your choicest vulgarities—take the fucking. Again."

Joss studied her for a long moment; she wondered if she had ever really seen her, or if this was a new Aidan to be seen. She reached for Aidan's hand. "I knew I loved you. I knew you mean more to me than anything ever has, or ever will." She closed that small hand in hers, feeling the strength in its returned squeeze. "But when I heard the shot, my first thought was like it was all one word: Aidananourbaby. I've studied that all day, tryin' to remember if I thought you an' *the* baby, or you an' *our* baby. An' it isn't that I think as if we're—I mean, we're both women an' there's no husband or wife to it, but—"

"But she's our baby," Aidan said gently. "A bad farmer in Portland planted this seed, but it's you who'll tend the crop. And no, there's no husband or wife about it, but if she turns out to be a boy, he'll not miss a father for having you to teach him how to do the things men do" —she sent Joss a sidelong, elfin grin— "the way a woman wants them done."

August, 1876

Yea, though I walk through the valley of the shadow of death,
I will fear no evil: for thou art with me.

Psalms 23:4

CHAPTER EIGHTEEN

"What do you pay Richland over in the Station for beans and corn?" Malin Leonard asked the quartermaster over a hand of cribbage one night, and suffered patiently through that officer's disparaging commentary about Station farmers before figures were finally named. He took the numbers to Joss as an offer; she accepted, and asked that the Jackson beans—what of them there were—be allowed in the sale. "Clark's too?" the captain asked.

Joss spat into the dust of her yard. "Fuck Ottis Clark. They'd ought to crop that hammerhead's ears, like they do a bad horse."

Malin blinked at the hard-edged vulgarity. "I didn't know the blood was so bad, Joss."

She jerked her chin toward the fields. Levi was picking beans, a cotton sack slung over his shoulder and trailing half-full behind him. "Ott's the one took after him the night 'fore Aidan ventilated Slade."

The captain frowned. "You know that for sure?"

"Jack Bull—you know Jack? 'Tween Pa an' Ethan they kept him open, I suspect—anyway, Jack tells me Ott got all horns an' rattles into the corn, there, a few days after all the pucker. Ott said if I'd been born the man I look like I should've been, he'd've give me what he give Levi. Said he didn't figure he'd get by with that so he give it to my nigger instead—those ain't my words. Jack says Ott said it was a good thing he didn't come after me 'cause my whore of a cousin prob'ly would've shot him like she shot Slade, an' I already cost him a busted arm." She spat again, as if there were words left she needed to get rid of. "His boys done give me a lot o' help, an' I expect they took their licks for it. I'll help 'em back anyhow I can, but I ain't turnin' a word nor a hand for Ottis Clark. You want to buy his beans at the price you're givin' me an' give the difference to Zeke 'tween that an' what Thom pays, I know Zeke'll take care o' his brothers an' mother. Find him up to Flora Washburn's. Give it to Ott an' it won't be but corn down his gullet like any damn scraggledy rooster, hoggin' the feed an' crowin' all hours."

Malin rubbed the backs of his fingers against the day's growth on his chin; he liked the pay and privilege of his captaincy, but not the politics. "How long before you're picked off?"

"We'll be done it by midweek next."

"I'll send a wagon." He watched as Levi picked a plant clean, pulled it, shook it, dropped it, and moved along. "Putting in a second crop? You've got time for a pod dry."

"Price o' wheat's up, I hear; I'll put in ten acres an' rent the rest to Marcus. He needs it, an' he's got the hands to mess with beans an' corn. I don't."

"You know right where you stand," he said quietly. "I admire you, Joss."

She took her bag of tobacco from her shirt pocket. "Don't."

"Gentlemen, hush!" said the driver of the quartermaster's wagon when he saw Levi wearing one of Joss's coonskin hats; he had worn it non-stop for four (fortunately cool) days since she'd

215

given it to him. "I hain't seen one o' them since I left Tennessee! How'd a nigger come by that?"

"I made it an' I give it to him." Joss had been picking and shucking and sacking beans for a week; her back ached like a bad tooth, and she cared for neither the heavy-set soldier's looks nor language. "That pass your muster, gen'ral?"

He studied her from the seat of the wagon and decided that this narrow-eyed, short-haired, Colt-wearing female wasn't anyone he cared to cross. "Your hat, lady. Your nigger. I'us just wonderin' if you might have another one."

"Hat, or colored man?" She came down with cool emphasis on the last two words, and he damned the fact that in Kansas a man never knew how a body might think on that delicate set of issues that boiled down to Blue and Gray. "Hat, ma'am. Hear it gets a right smart o' cold here come winter."

"You heared correctly, an' a double eagle's what you need to save the top o' your head an' the tips o' your ears."

He looked at the jaunty ringtail sweeping Levi's back as the gangly fellow bucked sacks of beans into the wagon. "I ain't got but fifteen."

"I'll take fifteen if you get your wide Rebel ass off that seat an' help my hired man with the loadin'."

The Tennessean worked side by side with Levi for an hour. Joss took his money and gave him his hat and he went away, and she looked at the coins in her hand and took Levi by the wrist, turning his hand palm-up, and planted the ten-dollar gold piece into his palm. "Called you hired. Means I got to pay you."

"Food me sleep I work you pay no this got need do," he stammered, trying to shove the eagle back to her. "Barn sleep food pick bean pay fine!"

"Just take it," she said crossly. "Sew it into your shirttail for hard times or somethin'. An' take off that damn hat if it gets hot, will you? One true August day in that thing an' all you'll be good for is soap."

The next day three bashful, grinning soldiers showed up in the yard. For an eagle apiece and three felled and blocked oak trees, they went off with coonskin caps and full bellies, and Joss reluctantly adjusted her opinion to allow the possibility that not all Cavalry soldiers were swine.

She and Aidan were both nursing the blisters left from shucking dried corn on the mid-month morning that Joss went out to find handsomely woven cornhusk mats at each door and footprints in the dust leading to the road and to town. "Damn," she murmured, and went back to the house to break the news to Aidan that Levi was gone again, and they knew they would miss his ingenuous smile and his garbled speech...and his strong back.

On the evening of the day the Cavalry hung Argus Slade, Captain Leonard showed up with a wagonload of oak flooring and a bottle of scotch whiskey. Joss relinquished the agreed-upon diamond ring from Ethan's treasure-box, and she and Doc and the captain commenced to the serious pursuits of tonsil-lacquering and three-handed cribbage, swapping silver dollars and increasingly rude insults across the table until Aidan lost patience with them and went to bed.

She found the bottle empty and its emptiers in various stages of poverty and wretchedness when she yawned awake the next morning and drifted out to the kitchen to make the fire. She had no sympathy for them save making the coffee strong enough for bootblack; they each had two or three cups and staggered around the kitchen until she threw them out. They staggered around the yard and finally launched a competitive attack on the woodpile, Joss losing to Doc but beating the captain in timed assaults on blocks of green oak; Joss won back all the money she'd lost to Malin at cribbage before Aidan rang them in for a hearty drunks' breakfast.

"Men," she muttered, banging their plates to the table, and they gaped at her, amazed that she could damn Joss so effectively in one word that was, at best, misapplied. They ate raccoon and eggs and fried corn and fat biscuits with gravy, and drank another two pots of coffee, and hauled the furniture from the bedroom the women shared and had the floor nailed down by dark.

The men stayed the night. Without hangovers, they had the other two rooms floored by suppertime. "We do good work, men," one of them would intone every so often, and they'd have to let the laughter pass before they could continue. Aidan let them have their joke. She was getting floors through the house, and if they wanted to make that small jape at her expense, it was worth it.

But when the men were gone and the woman damned in the same breath as them was left, that woman stood leaning against the porch rail post, her lilac-ribboned hat low over her eyes, arms folded across her ribs, her booted ankles crossed, watching the dust they left as they rode off, dust that hung long in the close August air before it settled sulkily back to the earth, and still she stared after them. When Aidan emerged from a kitchen still hot from the preparation of supper Joss didn't turn; she asked her question in a low, neutral voice, as if she asked it of the yard, of the wagon track that led to the post road, of the memory of the dust. "Is that how you see me, then?"

"Is what how I see you?" Aidan sank into one of the rockers on the porch, fanning herself with the Leavenworth newspaper Malin had brought and she hadn't yet had time to read; it was scarcely cooler outside than in.

"As a man." She flipped her cigarette end out into the dirt of the yard. "Short hair. Trousers. Doin' a man's work. Smokin'. Takin' too much pleasure in drink." She turned to regard her cousin with hat-shaded, unreadable eyes. "Is that what you see when you look at me? Lackin' the part of a man that hurt you, but a man all the same?"

"The part of the man that hurt me was his certainty that I existed only as a vessel for his desire, and there's none of that in you," Aidan said quietly. Short hair and jeans be damned, there was nothing masculine about the supple body leaned against the post—except, perhaps, the cock of her hat. "I've never seen you as a man, Joss."

"You called me sir when first you met me."

"Which misconception lasted only until it was corrected, and never was renewed. I expected to be met by a man. I'd never seen a woman in trousers, never mind wearing a gun; what else might an Eastern girl have thought? Joss—" Almost hesitantly, she went to her, touching her face; she smelled of dust and sawdust and sweat, of shellac and floor wax and tobacco, as Doc and the captain had smelled when she had hugged them goodbye, but the underlying essence of this person was redolently female. "Joss, I'd never say such a thing save as the joke I meant it to be. You laughed with them—"

"Was I to weep in front of 'em?" She retreated from Aidan's touch, abandoning the shade of the porch in favor of the sun-drenched yard, and kicked at a stone with the toe of her boot. "I may not be a usual woman, but I'm no damned man. I do a man's work because it needs doin'. Am I to wear skirts to muck stalls an' split wood? Does takin' up a shovel an' a axe over the cookstove an' washtub make a man o' me? I'd be doin' cookin' an' laundry if you weren't here to relieve me o' the burden. I'm woman enough to want a bath when I'm as worked as I am now, an' clean clothes, an' more meal than biscuits an' beans every night o' my life. My rogue brother taught me to smoke an' swear an' drink liquor, an' I enjoy those things, but does that make me man enough to go to the Bull an' Whistle an' have a drink or a hand o' cards? A man save all the privilege?"

"Joss—"

"I'm not man enough to buy a quart o' whiskey or a tin o' tobacco in this town! In Leavenworth, where they don't give enough of a damn for a Stationer to know fourteen of us died this miserable spring, I ride on Ethan's reputation 'cause I look so much like him, an' 'cause it gets me better lumber than they'd sell me as a woman, an' 'cause I can walk into the Green Front Saloon an' buy my bottle—I let 'em call me Mister 'cause it serves me to let 'em think I'm Ethan, an' 'cause it keeps him alive in some small part, but damn it! It don't please me that they look at me no closer than to think me a man."

The day had been blisteringly hot, and Joss had worked hard:

her hat was sweated through, her shirt still plastered to her after an hour's rest. Years of labor had left her whip-slim and rangy; what small breasts she may have had with an easier life had long since given over to muscle. Her dark-tanned face was smudged with the grime of flooring nails, giving her a faux beard-shadow; had Aidan known Ethan she would have seen him standing there, but she hadn't. All she saw was Joss, wounded and angry and bewildered. "I've never seen you as a man, Joss," she said quietly. "I've never thought of you as one. I named you with them out of pride in you—no, you're not a usual woman. Side by side to a man you're as good as any and better than most at their own games, even to holding your decency with a bellyful of whiskey. And you're as good as any woman at the things expected of us. What does it matter whether you wear pants or skirts? What matters is who you are. You're strong and fierce, and you've made me strong and fierce. Were I to go back East I'd be like an animal in a cage. You've taught me independence and—and cussedness, and—"

"An' I treat you like my father treated my mother! Stuck in that fucking kitchen, doin' my cookin' an' cleanin'— How do I treat you but as a housemaid, Aidan? You came here so you could take your dignity back home an' I—"

"What dignity would I have there, Joss? I'd rather be called a grass widow here than a strumpet there. Dignity here is weighed by a different measure, and a truer one. Accomplishment matters here, not appearance. Who in this town has time for a woman who faints at the mention of legs instead of limbs? They may not approve of my condition or your haircut, Joss, but saving Ott Clark and the Richlands—and who cares a whit for them?— there's not a soul in the Station who doesn't respect what we've done with this farm."

Tight-lipped, Joss stared at the ground. The last offer she'd gotten on the farm had been from Marcus Jackson, almost two months ago; had they stopped because she'd said no to everyone interested, or because she'd proved herself?

"Last week Flora herself buttonholed me in Richland's to

sing your praises—oh, and didn't she make sure Effie heard every word!—and a note for me, for blowing a large hole in a small target. She thinks you're the best farmer this town's ever seen, and if the men would take a leaf from you maybe they'd be able to hold up their heads in Leavenworth County. Does she care if you wear your brother's shirts and gun? Not a whit does she care. Does she see you as a man? She sees you as a person, Joss. Tenacious is what she called you. A tough, tenacious human being, able to do what needs doing—and doing a damned good job of it."

Joss jammed her hands into her pockets and kicked at the dirt. Praise from Flora Washburn was notoriously hard to come by, as anyone who had ever worked for her could attest, but unexpected approval from Flora couldn't dispel the quivering feeling of near-desperation she had been carrying for two days, a distortion of her inner vision that made her feel hollow and thickly magnified, a panicking loss of her grasp on her perception of herself that had happened when it seemed Aidan saw her as just another man, so scathing had been the denunciation Joss had heard. That single muttered word had delivered a kick that sent cartwheeling the can of worms that was self-doubt in Joss's mind, and those loosed worms of question had squirmed too far into too many corners of her thoughts to be gathered back now by Flora's praise and Aidan's calm assurances. "I don't treat you well," she said hoarsely. That was no worm; it was a snake, thick and lethal and coiled around too many thoughts: He treats it the way a Stationer treats things, she had said of her father and his farm. Like a wrong man treats a right woman.

Like you're treating Aidan. Just like a wrong man treats a right woman. Just like a man—

"Joss, what are you talking about? I've never been so loved, or so respected. When I feel mistreated I'll tell you. Joss—" Aidan went to her, taking those slim, hard shoulders in her hands. "You misunderstood me," she said softly. "I never meant you to think I see you as anything but a woman. I love you, Joss. I—"

"But who is it you love? What am I, that you can love me?

Some—some—hermaphrodite, neither man nor woman an' a poor excuse for either—"

"Joss, stop this! You're the most capable, the most kind and caring person I've ever known. I could never be as happy as I am with you. One of us must run the house and the other the farm; we do what we're best at. You've been forced to assume the role—"

"No one forced me! I love this dirt! I love my water pipes! I love the barn an' the woodpile an' hittin' my thumb with a hammer—" She pulled away from Aidan. "An' none o' that feels womanly to me! For God's sake, I lay with a woman at night—"

"So do I! Does that make me a man, or mean I wish I was one?"

"Or does it but mean you wish I was one?"

"If you were a man I'd not be laying with you." Her voice was cold in the bruise of her cousin's accusation; she felt that and looked away, waiting for the sharpness to subside. "Joss, no man could awaken in me the things you do," she said softly, when she could. "It's because you're a woman that I love you. You can do the things a man does, but you feel things—you understand things—as a woman, and that's the difference. You can cry, where a man wouldn't allow himself to admit the pain."

"But I don't feel like a woman." It was a rasping hiss between her teeth. "My hair was all I had to make me feel womanly an' I was glad enough to see it gone, but ever since—" She fisted her hands deep into her pockets; the pain that ricocheted in her mind couldn't mask the dread that one of those hands might flare out suddenly—

I get afraid of what I might do, Joss.

Ethan. She remembered the wildness that had come over him, and knew his need to flee when that turbulent thing happened in him: *I want to break all the dishes, and kick out the windows, and burn down the house and barn —I need to hurt something, and I have to take it away from here.*

She swallowed around a breath too pent to escape, glad for the brim of the hat to hide her eyes, knowing what was there;

she had seen it too many times in her brother. She brushed past Aidan, reaching for Ethan's Colt, buckling it on and tying the thong around her thigh, barely aware of what her hands were doing.

"Where are you going?"

Joss knew the tone, and the struggle behind it; she'd heard it from her mother times enough, asking after Ethan with a woman's fear of what a man might do. It grated at her, as she knew it had grated at him; it grated at her that she would know so surely how that man had felt. "I don't know." It was Ethan's answer, low, cold, rude—but not as rude as its alternative: *that ain't none o' your fuckin' business.*

"Joss, don't do this." It was an echo of Jocelyn's eternal supplication of her perilously-balanced middle child: *Ethan, don't do this.* The sense of déjà-vu was blindingly disorienting; did this conversation run in the family?

Ethan's reply was all she could give: a simmering look under the brim of a sweat-stained hat, dark eyes so flat and deadly that the woman who had borne him had stepped back from the danger there. It was Aidan's first glimpse of that virulent look, and it drained her courage and her color from her. "Joss—"

The whisper of her name—and that she didn't take the backwards step Jocelyn always had taken from Ethan—penetrated the ferity; Joss groped for her voice. "This isn't you." The words felt like fishbones in her throat. "Whatever it is, it's in an' of me, an' I need to be alone with it. I'm afraid—"

I'm afraid I'll hurt you. The knowledge turned her on her heel. A sharp whistle around her thumb and finger brought Charley from a far corner of the pasture. She used his mane and the fence to boost herself onto his broad bare back and put her heels to his side hard enough to startle him into flight.

CHAPTER NINETEEN

Night settled nervously around the house. Aidan sat on the counter with her feet in a sink full of water that had been cold when she had drawn it from the tap, her forearms on her knees, her head weary on her own shoulder, her Colt close enough if it was needed.

She had watched the sunset, recalling Joss saying that when there was such a rage of orange in the sky there had been a dust storm to the west of them, a fury of wind out in prairies she had only heard of, where trees faded to long grasses shimmering gold in the ripe summer. That tempestuous sunset was long since gone to the thick, muttering darkness of a night pregnant with storm, and still she stared out the window, listening in the dark for Charley's odd gait (a pacer, Joss called him) bringing her cousin home; she listened, too, for a hoofbeat less familiar, perhaps more dangerous.

She heard the grumble of distant thunder; she heard owls in the woodlot and coyotes beyond the rises, and tree frogs shrilling their evening complaints; she heard the clock ticking on the shelf. She didn't need to watch it; long minutes ago it had struck ten, and would soon announce the half. The living sounds outside made her wonder who had told her, or where she had read, that stalking Indians communicated with perfectly-mimicked noises of the night. She wondered briefly, and put the thought away.

All through the house, until the light had faded too far, oak floors gleamed. In the flurry of furniture-moving—Seth's and Ethan's beds had gone into Joss's old room, and Joss's bed to an empty stall in the barn in case Levi returned—a dusty cradle had emerged from the barn to go into the room the Bodett boys had shared, the room she and Joss had shyly started calling the nursery. Malin had polished it to a loving shine with a waxy rag Doc had abandoned. Only Seth had enjoyed the rocking bed, Joss had said; she and Ruth and Ethan had berthed in the bottom drawer of the armoire in the room she and Aidan now shared. None of the rest of the babies had lived long enough to get out from between their parents on the bed.

Joss, are you all right? Where are you?

She had agonized with guilt over Joss's flight; guilt had tipped over into the brittle rage of desertion, but it was an anger too brittle to last too long. Now, there was only a dull ache of fear.

The first time she had been alone at the farm she had been terrified; now, even in the dark, she wasn't afraid; not for herself. She had blown a large hole in a small target once, and coldly, she knew she could do it again. But those eyes: those dark, haunted eyes...

I'm afraid— An admission caught back, hanging between them like a horse thief caught in the act.

Of what, Joss? I felt it; I felt your fear as sharply as a blow.

Somewhere in the dark she was alone: tenacious, capable, cock-wild as her beloved Ethan, but still a slight and vulnerable being against the creatures of the night. In that dark were savages with two legs or four, and the appetites of animals who roamed the night were more predaceous than those of the beings of the day; night creatures craved fresh meat, or dark excitement.

She traced a finger over the cool steel of the Colt on the windowsill. If she stepped out the door and let go a round into that blackness, would Joss hear and come?

If she heard, she would come. With deep certainty, Aidan knew that...but only if she heard.

Just a mile away was the brook where Joss sometimes took her, always to the same lush-grassed spot; not too far from there was Marcus Jackson's cobwebby claim shack, where they had spread a saddle blanket and held each other in the shadows of a dwindling Sunday afternoon, daring to kiss and then to touch— her hiding places, Joss called them. Had she chosen one of those places tonight, where she might still hear a shot from the house? Or had that simmering thing behind her eyes taken her farther?

Whatever it is, it's in and of me, and I need to be alone with it.

She left the pistol where it was.

The baby kicked, protesting her position. She straightened up. She'd been on her feet most of the day, and her back ached mercilessly. Sitting on the hard counter wasn't helping, she supposed. She got down carefully; Doc and Malin, in their zeal, had waxed the kitchen floor to slick perfection.

She sighed into her rocker on the porch. Nestling her Colt into the folds of her skirt, she settled in to wait.

It was an old trail, familiar to them both; Joss gave Charley his go. He drifted through the darkness, his horse's memory recalling the crispness of autumns past when he had carried Harmon or Ethan or Joss as they hunted the thin trail that led to Newtonville.

Too tired to stay awake, too wounded to sleep, Joss seethed a restless doze on his back. A rain-scented breeze rippled its fingers through her hair and she started awake, reaching for the hat that had been taken from her a few miles back by a low-sweeping tree; she had ducked, but not enough. That cedar had stolen her Stetson before; she knew where it was.

She remembered the day Slade had taught Aidan to shoot: how he had treated his horse in his departure, and her own suggestion that the pony take him under the sweeper at a dead run; she smiled hollowly. "Should've. Saved a lot o' people a lot o' trouble."

She settled back into long journey looseness, groping for the reins before she remembered there were none. She wove her fingers into Charley's thick mane, loving the generous smell of him, and let him pick his way.

You're strong and fierce, and you've made me strong and fierce—

"You're crazy, an' you make me crazy." It slurred out as if she were drunk; Charley shook his big head at her voice, his halter slapping gently against his cheeks. "Yuh, Charley. S'awright."

There was a saloon in Newtonville, and a double eagle in the watch pocket of her jeans. She wanted to go there. She wanted to be mistaken for Ethan, to drink straight whiskey and play draw poker and monte; she wanted to be drunk enough to let a hard-edged saloon woman take her upstairs and be surprised at what she found under the sweat-stained shirt and trousers....

"Merciful Jesus," she muttered. "You're too stupid sober to be allowed to drink."

She wanted to ride blind and trust Charley to take her home. She wanted to be home, curled with Aidan in their bed, breathing the scent of her, feeling the heavy warmth of her breast in one hand and the swelling roundness of the baby against the other. She wanted to rest her head there, to listen to the vibrant pulse of that blossoming life, to feel its nudging protest of her weight; she wanted to know her hands gentle with Aidan in the night.

She remembered the coppery taste of the need to lash out, to spray the hurt away from her; she remembered why, and felt the bitterness again, and didn't turn the horse.

She remembered how it felt to be fifteen, to have Hank Richland and Gideon Jackson pursuing her with dogged gentleness, Gid with wildflowers picked in the ditches, Hank with candy stolen from his father's store. She remembered their shy smiles and tugs at her braids in school, and the righteous retribution of their fists when the inevitable taunt *(bastard)* came her way. She remembered—

Charley shied at something and the Colt was in her hand, all her senses probing the darkness while her intellect tried to catch up. There came no sound or shadow; they both listened until Charley looked back at her as if in apology for the false alarm. "S'okay," she muttered. "I respond to threat like the tough an' tenacious human bein' I am. Any normal woman would do the same." The horse danced a nervous sidestep, not accustomed to the harsh tones of sarcasm. Joss holstered the revolver, gave him a soothing pat on the neck, and in ten horse-steps was back in her dozing reverie.

—knowing if Hank hadn't defended her, she could have defended herself, as good as any boy in a schoolyard brawl. But Gid...flowers. Buds

Budding breasts, so aware—and the afternoon Hank had tried to kiss her? He'd courted her for two years. She had known he would, hoped he would...and she had belted him, a solid right hook that had bloodied his nose, blacked his eye, broken his heart.

"Moment o' truth," she mumbled, and firmed her grip on Charley's mane. Gideon had retreated, too, and no other boy had stepped in to woo her. One more called her a bastard; she broke his nose and jaw for his lack of discretion. The brawl had driven a wedge between herself and other girls her age; fighting at eleven was one thing, but at fifteen? She didn't miss their company. All they talked about was boys and clothes and getting out of Washburn Station, and she cared for none of those things; if she looked into her future, she saw her life unfolding on that post road acreage, and she was content with the vision. She assumed some defect of her personality made her unattractive to boys, and uncomfortable to girls, and tried to accept her mother's gentle wisdom that no one different is well-received by those who would wish themselves peers, that lack of acceptance didn't mean she wasn't a good and generous spirit, that the one she might love, and who might love her, would come along someday—

228

"An' on your deathbed you call me your son? Ma, you might've died without sayin' that." She fished in her shirt pocket for her bag of makings and rolled a cigarette, and fired a match with her thumbnail, the small process easing her mind from the sharpness of the pain those words had caused her—bad enough it had been said at all, but for Doc to hear it! If that was how Ma thought of her, what would have been her reaction to her feelings for her cousin Aidan?

Aidan. She closed her eyes, smelling smoke and impending rain, remembering whispered words: *and now I can't let you go*—and how the knowledge of love had squeezed into her, swelled around her, permeated her with the knowing that all she'd never wanted from Hank or Gid, she wanted from Aidan, an understanding that had consumed her with the want to return that offering.

It's all I've been able to think of, Joss— how it felt when you kissed me, how it felt when you stopped—because I didn't want you to stop.

The memory could still ignite a slow fire in her, a heat rippling through her being the way ripe, heavy-headed grain rippled across the prairie. She felt that visceral surge, and the rhythm of the horse's strong back between her legs, and the night breeze that cooled the tracks tears had left on her face, and sickly, she remembered riding the quivering verge of raising her hand—

All those thoughts—they're like a unbroke horse, Joss, a Wyomin' mustang an' I've lost the reins, an' it's crazy to be free an' there's no way to break the run. All I can do is let it run itself out.

The tormented Ethan by the spring, bruises from his last desperate race with his wildness not yet faded before he felt a new one coming on. *If I could just find the reins*—

He had never admitted what those thoughts were about. Something made him that way; some hurt inside him started the churning; he started out hollow-eyed and aching with the pain before the anger rose around it, sending him boiling out to find the places where men spent their rages: saloons and whorehouses, card games and fistfights.

"What about me, Ethan?" Tautly, she asked the darkness.

"Where does somethin' like me go when I can't break the run?"

It's because you're a woman that I love you.

"Aidan, I know it's you I should turn to but Lord! if ever I hurt you—" Ethan had slapped his mother once, a lashing response to her plea that he not leave. Jocelyn hadn't told her husband, but Ethan, writhing with guilt, had told his father. Harmon hadn't bothered with a strap in the woodshed; he took his son's shirtfront in one fist and balled up the other and hit him as hard as he was able. Ethan's knees buckled and his eyes rolled back, but he didn't go under; Harmon drew his fist again, not hearing his wife's protest, or Seth's cracking plea of 'Papa no,' not seeing Joss ready to put herself between them if it went too far—but he heard Ethan's hoarse whisper. *Kill me, Pa. Please.*

It was the only time Joss had ever seen her father cry.

She'd never ridden the mustang then, to understand the awful deadness in her brother's eyes when he whispered those chilling words, but she knew now. "If I ever—"

He hadn't wanted, or meant, to hurt her. She had just been in the way of the rage. She had forgiven him; the mother's love forgave her son before his hand was back at his side, but Ethan's last words before he died were *I'm so sorry I struck you, Mama . . .* even though, rasping and shivering with sickness, he had helped Joss dig her grave.

"If ever I—" It was a sick, hollow protest; it hurt too much to think it, let alone say the words. She forced them out. "If ever I struck her—"

I've never been so loved, or so respected—

"No! Not if! If you allow the if, it'll turn into a when—" The shudder came deep in her belly, an orgasm of pain racing through her like Ethan's lunatic mustang, tearing the strength from her; she slipped in barely-controlled collapse from the horse to her knees and elbows on the trail, almost choking on the sobs. "No! No ifs! Aidan, I promise you—"

You feel things—you understand things—as a woman, and that makes the difference. You can cry, where a man wouldn't allow himself to admit the pain.

Ethan hadn't cried the day his father had hit him, that day Harmon Bodett had wept for his alien son. He had allow that anguished man to hold him; he allowed his mother's tear forgiving, and his sister's ministrations to his broken nose—

Ethan, can't you cry? Jesus, can't you let it go? There's places you can go where no one would see—

It doesn't matter if anyone sees, Joss. I'd see. I'd know I was weak.

You need a daddy to teach you how to be a better man than your brother was.

She choked a laugh into the hard-packed dirt of the trail. No one but Ethan could have taught her about being a man; they were too much alike for anyone else to have taught her that. "It's not a man I need learn to be! I know that well enough an' too much!"

While she cried, it started to rain.

Aidan jerked awake, barely choking back a near-scream of Joss's name; unreleased, it echoed wildly in her mind, and her heart tripped and stuttered in her and her blood roared in her ears. It was long before she could sit back, and much longer before she could rest her senses from their probe of the night. *Joss, come home. Damn you, just come home! This is—*

The easterly skies were gray with impending dawn when the rooster made his announcement; she struggled awake to see Fritz in the pasture looking around as if he wondered where Charley was. Charley was still absent. Aidan shivered in the dewy morning chill and felt an irate kick from the baby. She rose stiffly from the rocker, scanning the close hills. "Oh, Joss," she whispered wearily, and heard her voice leaden with the beginnings of grief.

She started the fire and sat at the kitchen table to wait for the kettle; she awoke an hour later with the kitchen steam-muggy and the kettle boiled dry. She set it on the tank to cool before she refilled it, and knew by sensing that she was still alone. She went to check the pasture anyway.

No Charley. Fritz came to visit worriedly with her; she stroked his velvet nose. "What good are you to me, handsome e?" she whispered. "You lazy son of a snake. Oh, Fritz—"

Joss had lifted her to him bareback for a gentle ride to the ranch one day, but there had been less baby then; now, she idn't think she could mount him, let alone stay on him bareback for the ride to town, and she knew she didn't have the height to swing the saddle to his back, nor did she know how to adapt a double wagon harness to one horse.

Fritz shook his head and nudged her shoulder with his nose, and lowered his head to poke it through the fence, stretching for the greener grass on her side. "Wait?" she asked helplessly. "Fritz, I can't! What can I do?"

She checked the clock when she went back into the house; it was just past six. She made a cup of tea and drank it cautiously, making sure one sip would stay down before she took another.

She walked to the top of the first hill on the trail Joss had taken with Charley, carrying her Colt, her apron pocket heavy with bullets; she sent three rounds into the air, protecting her ears with her shooting shoulder and her other hand, and waited, straining to hear answering shots. None came and she repeated, and listened, reloading in slow silence, remembering to pick up the brass; Malin gave them a penny a dozen for spent casings.

Even covering her ears, after twelve shots her head rang and she knew she couldn't have heard a distant response. She trudged back to the house and sat in the porch rocker. The clock struck seven.

She heard leisurely hooves and bolted from her chair, letting a yell go up the track; Malin and Doc trotted into the yard, Doc dismounting when he saw her face. "Aidan, what is it?"

"Joss left angry last evening. I can't ride—" Doc's look sharpened, a probing visual examination for physical evidence of the quarrel. "Don't even think it, Doc! Just find her. She left across the rise toward the branch, bareback on Charley."

"Did it rain here in the night?"

"Past midnight, half an hour of hard rain."

"Damn. Malin, a mile past the branch the trail forks. Check Jackson's claim shack; I'll take the south fork. Two shots if you find her; pause and one more if you need me. We'll both end up in Newtonville eventually. You've got your Colt, Aidan? I need to borrow your Winchester."

"Joss was shooting coons; it's light," she warned; he slid the magazine full from a box on the sideboard and they were gone, leaving her to wait—and wonder why he would want the rifle when he carried twelve rounds at his hips, favoring the gunslinger look of crossed pistols.

"Just the one got away?" Doc asked Malin at the top of the hill; the captain's call, while he needed little excuse to visit the Station, hadn't been entirely social.

"That's what the sheriff in Newtonville said. They were after horses when there were seven of them, but a lone buck—" He looked back at the house. "She'll be all right alone?"

"No Pawnee will bother this farm or anyone on it, but it's the farm that's marked, not Joss. Away from it, she's naught but another paleface. Check the claim shack. I've got to skirt the swamp; we'll come out about even. I wish to God we had your scout."

"If wishes were horses. Be careful, R.J."

"Beggars might ride. And you, my friend."

She sat on the porch in the rocker, her Colt in the folds of her skirts, not sure what she guarded against, only sure she should guard. She rested her head against the high caned back of the chair she favored, her eyes scanning the tops of the hills beyond the fields, her mind wandering; she remembered a conversation with Levi before he left. He had called Joss 'Mister' one more time than she could bear. "You do know Joss is a woman," she'd said gently, across the row of tomatoes in the kitchen garden. "You know that, Levi?"

"All cats are gray in the dark," he said, and she stared at him; shyly, he ducked his head, and found a fat hornworm to drown in the kerosene. They picked bugs and pulled weeds in long silence until he added, "Mayhap him him. Or her, or—but kind you papa still make small inside! To. He do. He—she. Do. Kind—God damn my head! Goddamn Station farmer. Hornworms!"

Remembering it now, tears stung her eyes. Yes, she would make the baby a kind papa—but only if she came home. Only if they found her. Why had Doc wanted the rifle, heavy with all fifteen rounds?

She watched the hills, dozing, but her ears never slept. When the clock struck six she made a small fire to heat water for tea and a wash; listlessly, she ate cold meat and a day-old biscuit. She retired to the porch to watch the sunset, and the close horizon.

The last light was fading from the sky when the sound of horses snapped her awake; she strained to see through the gathering darkness.

Three horses, one empty *Joss no oh Lord Jesus God please* no—but then she saw Charley was ridden double, Doc and a bloody bundle in his arms, and that was worse than one horse empty.

"Hot water," Doc grated, an order as he brought in his burden without giving Aidan time to see anything but the limpness in his arms and the awful dark stain across his shirt. "Aidan, move! I need hot water and I need it now. Alcohol—whiskey's fine— Malin, get my saddlebags. Aidan, I need hot water and whiskey! In Jesus's name amen, woman, will you move?"

Aidan spent two hours swallowing tears, swallowing knowing she would vomit, swallowing knowing she would faint; somehow, she didn't vomit or faint. She did cry, but with quiet, grim control, and not so much that she couldn't be a nurse for Doc as he worked patiently to suture a huge flap of Joss's scalp back into place.

Malin had found her under the sweeper, her face as white as the bone that showed through her wound, her Colt empty in her limp hand, four dead coyotes scattered around her. Two of them had died from her bullets. The third was crush-ribbed, Charley's hooves bloody.

The fourth had an arrow buried in its throat.

He had thought her dead, partially scalped by the lone Pawnee warrior who had brought him to the county's corner. But as he was gathering up her body to bring it home fresh blood

234

had run, and he fired his pistol twice in the dim hope that Doc would hear. Reluctant to leave her, he signalled over and over; twelve rounds later, he heard answering shots. He scouted in his wait, finding the nervous dance of Charley's shod hooves...and the natural track of an unshod pony, the almost-barefoot sign of a moccasined foot. On a sharply axe-sheared branch stub of the sweeping cedar was a bloody clot of dark hair.

She had been asleep, he surmised, letting the horse find their way home; Charley, eager to be there, cleared the tree and expected his rider to duck. She hadn't, and hit that slicing stub hard. Why her stiff new hat hadn't saved her from the brutal injury, he couldn't imagine; it was there on the ground beside her. (Later, Aidan would turn that pale hat over and over in her hands; there wasn't a drop of blood on it.) There was no way to know how long she had been there, save that the blood on her was dry when he found her.

The Native sign—? Over that, he could only shake his head.

Finally Doc came, and cleaned the wound with water and whiskey and bound her head as best he could with a shirt from Malin's bedroll before they brought her in, not daring to hurry for fear of starting the bleeding again; her shirt and the dark stain on the trail were evidence enough that she had lost too much blood already.

Stitching the wicked wound closed now, he was as gentle as he knew how to be, but the whiskey burned and the needle stung as the chloroform wore off; Joss flinched and moaned, pain penetrating her unconsciousness. Aidan held her head and Malin her ankles.

Doc was almost finished when she opened her eyes and whispered roughly, "You might have shed a tear, you stubborn son of a bitch. What else did you think could cleanse your soul?"

"Hold her," Doc said quietly, and they did; Doc sank the needle and her eyes rolled back in a pain-faint that almost took Aidan with it. "Aidan, I need you," he said tersely. "You can faint when we're done. Move your head; you're in my light. Clip her hair there. Easy—"

At last he was finished. He gave the whole job a last wipe with a whiskey-soaked cloth. No blood seeped from the wound, and he decided not to bandage it for now; he adjusted the pillows to keep her from moving her head and sat back with his bottle of antiseptic to take a hard pull from the neck of it for himself. "Heal, Josie," he said wearily. "I've done what I can for you, my friend." He thumped the cork back into the bottle. "All she needs now is a bath."

"You both need sleep," Aidan said, and they took their hint and left the women alone. Malin managed to get his boots off before collapsing in exhaustion to Seth's bed, but Doc had held Joss in his arms for eight miles before spending the better part of two hours placing dozens of tiny stitches; he barely made it to Ethan's bunk before he was snoring, his booted foot still on the floor, his wooden leg enjoying the mattress. Aidan got her water quietly, so as not to disturb her men.

But it was a moment before she could begin; she sat on the edge of the bed, biting her lip to hold back the tears, wondering how long Joss had been awake with what must have been mind-reeling pain: long enough that the coyotes scented the blood. Long enough to defend against them. Long enough to know how deeply endangered she was: no one knowing where she was, on a trail little used save in the cold fall for hunting, terribly hurt and unable to get back onto Charley, who would have brought her home—

She recalled coming awake on the porch while the night was still hard dark, after the rain but long before the dawn, choking back a cry of unknown panic; had it been then? Malin said he had found her just past noon—ten, perhaps eleven hours she had been there; how much longer could she have lasted? Or had it been too long, had she lost too much blood, would she—

"You will," she whispered fiercely. "You will, Joss Bodett!" She kissed cool lips and felt no twitch of response, and put her face into the blood-smudged curve of Joss's throat and wept.

At last she was able to sit up, to wring out the cloth in the basin of warm water; gently, she wiped blood and dirt from Joss's face, finally getting down to sleek, even tan; more gently, she worked at the blood that had dried in her hair, and when she had gotten what she could without moving that damaged head the water was a brackish, rusty brown. She changed it, silently barefoot on the gleaming oaken floors Joss had given her.

Her scissors were still on the nightstand. She cut through the collar of the shirt and split it to the tail, easing the ruined garment out from under her patient, freeing her arms from its sleeves. She smiled tightly to see the cleanliness of Joss's forearms above her bloody hands; she had washed the dishes after dinner yesterday, Doc rinsing, Malin wiping, Aidan putting away so she'd know where to find things when the job was done.

She dropped the pieces of the shirt to the floor and started at her neck, working from dark-tanned skin to the startling paleness of breasts and belly untouched by the sun. Joss's natural complexion was the creamy flawlessness of the Irish, from her mother—and very possibly from her natural father too, given the breathtaking good looks and smooth salesmanship of so many Portland Irishmen. Adrian Blackstone had forbidden his daughter to see what he called Galway boys, mistrusting the very smoothness that had earned his cousin Jocelyn her trouble. "God bless your trouble, Jocelyn," she murmured. "Your heartbreak is the only love I'll ever know."

Well away from the damaged part of that love, she scrubbed the strong, slender arms, removing blood and hard-work dirt.

She changed water and came back to tug off Joss's boots and ease her dusty jeans away. It occurred to her that this bath was nearly more intimate than their loving; she smiled hollowly and left a gentle kiss against the curving crest of a hipbone. Joss stirred briefly, and her breathing went soft and slow again.

She didn't even consider trying to get her into a nightshirt. She pulled the covers over her and checked the wound for bleeding. Patiently, she emptied the basin and wiped it out, and hung the cloth on the wire over the stove.

She relieved Doc of his boot and lifted his good leg to the bed, not interrupting the rhythm of his snores. She glanced at

Malin in the other bed and found him watching her. "Soldier." Her smile was weary. "Ever vigilant."

"She'll be all right, Aidan," he said softly. "She's strong."

"I know she is."

"I'll sit with her if you want some rest."

"No. Thank you, though—and Malin, God bless you for finding her."

"I love her, too, Aidan. There's something in her that heals me."

CHAPTER TWENTY

There was a daguerreotype on the wall across from the bed, its silvery tones washed with gold in the early morning light. It was a picture of Jesus. Joss studied it, bemused. The Bodetts had never been long on churchgoing, making it into town for Easter and Christmas but not much more often. "Church is s'posed to be a hospital for sinners, not a storehouse for self-appointed saints," Harmon had grumbled of the churchgoing populace of Washburn Station, who eyed the Bodetts with haughty disapproval when they did show up. "Treatin' us post roaders like we's too sinful even to be in church?"

He had known it was because of his two Jocelyns: one turning away their sanctimony with gentle grace, the other withdrawing in frustrated hurt when children who were her chums at school refused to play with her under the eyes of their parents. So the Bodetts dressed up like church and took their weekly dose of

Bible at home, sharing a hymnal that said Washburn Station Baptist Church on the inside cover in someone's elderly hand. Ethan swore the hymnal was the only thing he'd ever stolen in his life, and he didn't think God would object a whit, since He could surely see how His churchgoers treated His post-roaders.

And the daguerreotype of Jesus hung on the bedroom wall. Joss puzzled over it; something about it was different, and she ought to know; it had been there most of her life, that she would notice a difference now.

It was a daguerreotype, not a painted picture! How could there be a photograph of Jesus? And there'd never been anyone in the picture with Him before. Jesus was laughing—she'd never seen any picture of a laughing Jesus—and He had His arm around someone's shoulders like they were pals. He wasn't wearing His usual robes, either; He had on a plaid shirt and a sheepskin vest, His wavy brown hair and beard flowing like always, and that happy grin on His face as He laughed at the also-grinning face of—

Ethan? Jesus and Ethan Allen Bodett, sporting it up in a daguerreotype on the bedroom wall?

That don't make no sense at all, Joss. Ethan chumming with Jesus Christ and the photograph to prove it? You look again, you'll see that painted picture of Jesus that Pa brought when he came home from the War, and looking like He ought to with His robes on and no silly grin.

But when she looked again it was Jesus and Ethan, looking as if they were ready to raid a whorehouse or raise hell at a poker parlor, God's sun beaming on them as they grinned for the camera, and Joss watched that daguerreotype for as long as the sun shone full on it, fighting sleep until the shadow cast by the edge of the window slipped across Ethan's face, for she had never seen him look so happy. When she opened her eyes again the picture was in full shadow and it was just Jesus, white-robed and reverent-looking, a painting of the Lord Jesus Christ and no foolishness, but she couldn't shake the memory of Jesus and Ethan together...or the smug feeling that neither Jesus nor His Father had minded a whit that Ethan had liberated a hymnal from the Washburn Station Baptist Church so the Bodetts might have their worship at home.

She faded into the other-worldly landscape of dreams, and out of it, and into it again.

She was sitting on the porch smoking a cigarette, gazing over her fields, when Flora Washburn rode into the yard. "Looks like I'll be dust ere you decide to batten this damn house," she snapped. "I'm on my way to the boneyard. You comin'?"

"Got all the bones I need," Joss grinned. "I'll get right on that, Flora. Stop back by an' have some tea with us. My cousin likes to hear you cuss."

"She'll be cussin' you, you don't get them laths nailed up. Come with me or get your ass up an' runnin', but don't sit there playin' polly-wolly-doodle all the day."

It was dark save the golden glow of a lamp. At the foot of the bed was an angel, looking up at the picture on the wall—just that old painting of Jesus, she assured herself quickly, before the angel commanded her rapt attention.

She'd always figured angels would have a fairly momentous set of wings, but none showed on this gleaming being. There was the expected white robe, and a tumbling flow of golden hair, and the requisite halo—but no wings. Could angels be like birds? she wondered. Eagles had broad, powerful wings, but if you saw one sitting in a tree it was always a surprise when it took off, unfurling a magnificent span that had seemed but a part of its torso until it decided to fly. "Angel?" she asked cautiously, not sure how one might address an angel—or if one should address an angel at all.

When the angel turned Joss saw that she was crying, and it so disconcerted her that she closed her eyes, pretending to sleep. She wasn't sure she could fool an angel, but she was willing to try; it had never occurred to her that an angel might weep—even though Jesus had, in the Gospel according to John, just before he rose Lazarus back from the grave. "I love you, Joss," the angel whispered, and the words infused her with such a depth of

.nowing she could only whisper back: I love you, too.

And she learned that the touch of an angel's lips was real, and exquisitely gentle; she learned that angels did cry, and that their tears were as warm as human tears when an angel rested her face against a human woman's naked belly for her sorrow. She discovered that an angel's hair against her skin was softer than anything she had ever imagined, making her senses think of springtime and the brief, precious fragrance of lilacs. Hoping it was all right to dare to touch such a being, she let her fingers find that wondrous hair, but she was too weak to offer the comfort she had intended; shyly, she let her fingertips rest against that golden head, and wished there was more a mortal human might do to console a weeping angel.

It was bare and brown and brittle, slate-skied; nude tree branches chattered like teeth in the bone-biting cold. She was glad of the thin gray line of smoke rising straight up from the chimney as she looked toward the house, glad of that fire even as she knew that such a straight rise of smoke meant the cold was killing...and she was glad of the cold.

Levi emptied a box into the bed of the wagon and put it under the spout of the overflow pipe by the well. It was about half the size of the peach crate she had brought home filled with treasures from Leavenworth one day. Its sides were slightly flared, its seams sealed with pitch; it didn't leak much as it filled with water so cold it seemed almost thick. There were a few dozen of the boxes lined up by the well; some of them, filled but moments ago, were already skimmed with a layer of ice: ice as thin as a Spode teacup, ice thin enough for a horse to cut a lip on. The ice was the color of breath in the air, the color of the sky and the smoke that dared into it.

She muscled the last of the solidly-frozen boxes to the back of the wagon and upended it, thumping a gloved fist against the bottom. The block of ice broke free and Levi wrestled it into position, tossing a handful of straw over it. The wagon was almost full, its load gleaming diamonds and gold in the deep-winter afternoon. She put the empty box beside the one that was filling and waited, studying the new log cabin in the elms behind the house, and pushed the box into place with her foot when it was time. When it was full she closed the valve and heard the overflow splash into the depth of the well.

Washburn Station Ice Company, said the side board of the wagon. *J. Bodett, Prop.*

"Joss..."

She looked up from a particularly gnarly burl of oak that had been resisting her best efforts to split it, studying the sound of the hot summer afternoon, wondering if she had heard her name or not.

"Joss, I need you in here..."

She picked at her sweat-saturated shirt, trying to unstick it from her skin, and leaned the axe against the chunk of wood and trudged to the house—and what she found was the angel, clad only in an expressively loosened chemise, coming to her with a look that removed any doubt of her intentions for the next hour. "But I can't—you're—"

"Would you deny me?"

"I—oh, Lord. But I'm all sweaty," she protested weakly, as deft fingers defeated the buttons of her shirt.

"That's how I want you. Wet"—small hands slipped under the shirt, seeking her back—"and slick"—palms indulged themselves in that hard wash of sweat, slipping from her waist to her shoulders, bringing her closer— "and here"—the touch of whispering lips at her throat was enough to convince her; that tongue tasting the slick saltiness of her neck, and the press of barely-clad breasts against her, left no time to spare—"and now. Right now, Joss. Right here."

The kitchen table was clear save a basket of husked corn. When the angel wrapped her arms around Joss's neck and her legs around her waist, the table was as far as they would get. By the time she led Joss's hand to the corn, neither of them questioned what she wanted, and no one was near enough to hear

hen she panted her desire and gasped her need and screamed
er fulfillment into the heat of the day.

Lord above, did I do that to an angel? No, I couldn't have, but—oh,
you're going to Hell, Joss Bodett...if you ain't already there. Something
feels awful desperate wrong here.

She peeked through her eyelashes for the picture of Jesus;
it was there, and just Jesus, sunlight splashing across His pious,
handsome face. She breathed a sigh of relief—surely no picture
of Jesus would hang in Hell—and almost yelped at a deep and
gentle male voice. "Well, Joss. Have you joined us at last?"

Uh-oh. First He's sporting around with Ethan, and now He's
talking to you. This ain't looking so good for your earthly self, Josie.
She dared to open one eye.

If that was Jesus standing by the side of the bed, He was quite
a lot shorter and slighter than she would have expected, and He
didn't have His long hair, or much of a beard, but she remembered
her mother saying that she didn't think the Good Lord would
have put a lily-white baby down amongst all those dark people of
Israel, no matter what the pictures of Him showed; maybe Jesus
looked like what He had to so as to fit in with the appearance
of His flock. She hadn't expected that He'd wear a uniform *(you*
didn't expect Him in a plaid shirt and a sheepskin vest, either). She
didn't know how to address Him any more than she'd known
how to address the angel *(oh, that angel—what you done! Lord, I*
hope You're in a good mood—); it seemed a bit presumptuous to
say, 'Howdy, Jesus, fancy meetin' you here,' especially given the
likelihood of His disapproval of her recent behavior with the angel.

"This don't none of it feel right nor real." Her voice felt like
molasses in her mouth.

"I shouldn't think it would," he said soberly. "It's been a
hellish week all around, my dear."

His choice of words didn't make her feel any better; He
looked as if He were trying to decide what to do with her. "I
didn't hurt her," she whispered. "Should I have denied her? She
asked me—"

He sat on the edge of the bed. "Tell me, Joss," he said softly

"That angel. She—I—" She felt the tears start, tears of utter helplessness and confusion. "I was just tryin' to bust down that burl, an' she—I didn't mean but to try an' please her! I had to answer, didn't I? It ain't my mortal place to try an' outguess an angel! She asked me to, Jesus; wasn't you watchin'? It was rough but I swear it wasn't against her will, I ain't no Sodomite—"

"All right, Joss. It's all right—" His hand at her shoulder was gentle, but his voice had the sharpness of command. "Robert!"

Something thickly warm and bitter met her tongue. "Merciful Jesus," she heard, as deep and warm and bitter as the drug. "Don't do this to her."

She struggled to focus on the ethereal beings at either side of the bed, or on the picture at the end of it. "No! No, she asked me—please! She asked—she—"

"We called him wild"—Doc's voice was hoarse from sleeplessness; Aidan looked gaunt and hollow to Captain Leonard as he nursed the last of her bottle of Leavenworth brandy— "but what he was was periodically insane." Quietly, he spoke of Ethan: of the uncontrollable, almost cyclic craziness that had come over him, spewing him out into the dark places where he could let his madness go; he spoke of the innate goodness of him, goodness not strong enough to overpower the surges of rage; in speaking of Ethan, he spoke of Joss. "There's too much of that in her, and ever been thus. What she says when she wakes, Aidan—I don't know if it comes from the blow she took, or if we're hearing the part of the Blackstone blood you damn so often that lives in her. Ethan laughed at it—called it his mustang—but he knew his madness, as did she. I only wonder how much she knows of it in herself."

Aidan looked at him. "Will she live?"

He averted his eyes. "I don't know," he said softly. "If she will, or if she should."

Malin looked up.

"If this blow to the head were to exacerbate that streak of

nacy in her—Good Lord, Aidan, she was talking about raping angels. I'd fear for your safety."

Aidan jammed back the hot flare of her own Blackstone blood; she stood. "You've ever been so damned ready to believe she'd harm me! You treat her injury," she said coldly. "I'll treat her madness."

"'In the beginning God created the heaven and the earth. And the earth was without form, and void, and darkness was upon the face of the deep.'"

She started from the beginning. There was nowhere else to start.

"'And there came two angels to Sodom at even, and Lot sat in the gate of Sodom: and Lot, seeing them, rose up to meet them; and he bowed himself with his face toward the ground; and he said, Behold, now, my lords—'"

"They get that all wrong, don't they?"

"What?" Aidan looked up from her reading; it wasn't the first time Joss had seemed to be asleep and surprised her with a comment, although this one didn't make much more apparent sense than any of the others.

"They'd've took after them angels, an' no regard for who they were or what might come o' their rashness. Ain't that it?"

She was talking about raping angels. Aidan closed the Bible on her finger. "What, Joss?" Softly, she asked. "What are you saying?"

"Either they was sayin' 'Bring 'em out an' let us molest 'em as if they was women,' or they was sayin' 'Bring them foreigners out an' let's see what they got to say for 'emselves.' Either way, they wasn't showin' no hospitality. They mistrusted 'em just 'cause they was different, like Thom an' Effie damnin' a free-stater. Sell the tea an' never mind forcin' yourself on people! Ain't that what it was about? An' I knowed I never hurt you." Her fingers fisted around a handful of quilt. "I don't know why you're here," she whispered, "unless I'm fixin' to cross, but—please, could you

246

read me about Ruth an' Naomi? 'Entreat me not to leave thee, for whither thou goest, I will go—' Lord, those're such pretty words."

"Don't be so hard against him, Aidan." Malin Leonard sat at the kitchen table, brooding over the shaving mug and brush Aidan had given him, listening as she railed against Doc. "He doesn't deserve your wrath."

"And why not?" She banged a pan filled with pared potatoes onto the stove and slammed a lid onto it; Zeke Clark had arrived in the early afternoon to have a terse conversation with Doc out on the porch, about what she didn't know; she only knew Doc was gone, and she could speak freely—and had to, before she exploded. "So she's a Blackstone!" She lifted the lid to toss a palm's-measure of salt in with the potatoes. "I'm one, too. If my birthing goes awry, will he advocate letting me die as if I were no more than Argus Slade—whom he treated as gently as if he were worth saving for no more than to hang! Would that he'd give Joss the same courtesy."

"That's unfair. He's done everything he knows to do for her, Aidan."

"To the exclusion of boring a hole in her skull, thank you very much." She had nipped that suggestion in the bud—vehemently— the day before. "Given his talk of madness, I'm not so sure he's convinced she has swelling on the brain as much as he might give credence to that charlatan Dr. Rush's belief that drilling a hole in the skull releases the demons." The oven door screeched as she opened it to check on the chicken she had roasting there; she spooned its own fat onto it and drove the shelf in again. The door squawked shut; Malin gritted his teeth and made a mental note to find the oilcan. "You said there was something in her that healed you. Mayhap even madness can heal, by showing us what could be in ourselves, that we might be grateful it isn't." She turned. "We don't know her thoughts, Malin, or her dreams, to know if what she says makes sense to her but not to us—and how is she to make sense anyway, the way he keeps her dosed with opiates? I only know she's never hurt me, and I don't believe she ever would, and for him to question the rightness of her survival—what sort of god does he think he is, to even entertain such a notion? He sounds like my father!"

Wearily, Malin smiled. "I'll assume that's a most despicable insult. Aidan, I was as stunned as you were to hear the words fall from his mouth. It sounded so little like the Robert I know, for I know he loves Joss—and you with her—as if you both were his own flesh and blood. But he's desperately tired, and feels hamstrung at his inability to do more for her, and I wonder if perhaps that has clouded his thinking. But for Joss's sake, I'd dose him with laudanum and force him to sleep."

"You might as well. Joss is in God's hands." She speared the liver of the chicken from a pan on the stove and mashed it with a fork, mixing in a spoonful of baked beans, the yolk of a hard-boiled egg, and enough cream to make a smooth, soft paste of it; she added a dollop of spinach to the plate, chopping it until it, too, was a creamy paste. Over it all, she sprinkled a generous dusting of pecans that she had reduced nearly to powder. "Mind that oven gauge if you would, and prop the door on a piece of kindling if it gets too hot," she said, knowing that the captain didn't deserve her curtness visited upon him for the sins of his lover, but she was unable to keep it from her voice; she took the plate and a cup of corn tea to the bedroom

"I'm sorry, Malin," she said gently, back from Joss's care with an empty plate and the sheets she had replaced on the bed; she dropped the bedding into the washtub that had lived for the last week in a lightly-trafficked corner of the kitchen and put a pail to fill under the spigot in the sink. "I railed at you for something that's not of your doing. Please forgive my rudeness."

"There's naught to forgive. We're all tired, Aidan." He traced a finger around the top of the shaving mug that was still on the table in front of him; he supposed he should use it, but he rather liked the look of the week's growth of beard that had softened on his face.

He opened the tin of shaving soap and sniffed of it, and closed it again. "She ate well."

"Yes, with much coaxing."

"Did she speak?"

She started to lift the pail from the sink; he scrambled to his feet to do it for her. "How can she remember Levi and yet look at me as if I were a stranger to her? A welcome stranger—she looks at me with—I don't know; it seems almost like adoration—but it seems she sees me as a stranger nonetheless."

He poured icy water onto the sheets and set the pail under the tap again. "A head wound is a curious thing, Aidan. I've seen wounded men who knew me, but not their own wives or mothers, and men such as Levi, who comprehend everything said to them but can't express their thoughts save with the greatest difficulty on their part and dedication on the part of the listener." He leaned against the sink, feeling grubby in clothes that hadn't seen but his back for eight days; maybe a shave would feel good after all. "When I was a young man, a fellow beat me senseless and left me for dead for having learned—through no doing of mine, might I add--that I preferred the company of men. He dealt me some fierce blows to the head. I spent several days not sure of who I was, let alone the people around me, but within the week I was myself again." He grated some soap into the washtub and emptied the second pail over the sheets (he was accustomed by now to the smell, but still not certain how Aidan could so casually deal with the reality behind it), and put the washbasin in the sink, getting a dipper of hot water from the stove so Aidan could wash her hands, looking out the window at a noise in the yard. "Here's Robert home."

"Testify for me that she seems more alert without the laudanum. She seems in no pain, and I see no reason to drug her if she's not."

"Have you forgiven him?"

"No. What Judas is he, taking his pieces of silver for the year's care of a family and then taking its sole survivor so lightly?"

"I don't take her lightly." Doc leaned on his forearms against the doorjamb, looking wearier than the two of them together. "Nor you, Aidan. And I'm no Judas."

The afternoon's anger boiled up in her again. "What would you call yourself, then? God? How could you even question if she should live?"

"I saw what hell he went through, and the hell he put others through! I stitched his wounds, and the wounds he gave others, I politicked the damage he did his family in the eyes of this town—"

"She's not Ethan!"

He turned from the door; they heard the awful crunching thud of his fist meeting a post on the porch. "Jesus God in Heaven! Why did You call me? Why?"

She applied brown paper and vinegar because he believed in it, and ice water from the well because she believed in it; Malin held him while grief shook his broad shoulders. Flora Washburn had died in his arms three hours ago: Flora who had, with her long-dead husband, founded Washburn Station; Flora who had financed the medical education of a Newtonville boy on no more promise than that he would practice in her town; Flora who had worn trousers first that Joss Bodett might get away with it next; Flora who had earned the fear and the respect—and the curious affection—of a village she had ruled for sixty years with a velvet fist in an iron glove. That noon she had left Zeke to the making of his own dinner, saying she felt puny and wanted only a cup of tea that he might make for her, and for him to sit with her while she drank it; by the time Ezekiel understood that she needed Doc's attention far more than his, it was too late.

Malin coaxed a sleepworthy dose of laudanum, thinly disguised in a cup of corn tea, down the doctor's throat. It hit him like Marcus Jackson's two-fingered fist; it took them longer to get his limp bulk to Seth's old bed than it had taken for the drug to knock him out.

God damn you, talk to me! I'll leave you, Joss, I swear I will, I won't go through this every time!

250

It was a desperate honesty screamed at her retreating back; she didn't know why she was running, but she could feel a writhing, volatile maze of hurt and anger and fear in her heart and in her guts, that dangerous combination that always made her run; she felt it as physically as she felt the ground under her boots, the dust in her throat, the sun on her back. The threat stopped her like a curb-bitted horse. Anger lunged up over the hurt and fear, but when she turned to lash something back, what she saw made her choke on the venom: the one who had screamed at her was the angel, and she was suddenly terrified in the coldest pit of her belly: she was terrified that if an angel said God damn you, God would listen.

She had never seen this kind of light before. She'd seen the preternatural brightness that preceded a tornado, and the glowering gloom before a blizzard; she'd seen the peculiarity of the July sky the year they got snow on the Fourth, and had the good sense to be afraid of all of them. But she'd never seen the flickering, mobile oddity of such a light as this; it drifted and swirled like a visible wind, there and gone, and there again, and she was more than afraid.

Is this what the light looks like in the place where the damned go?

She looked for the picture of Jesus, needing the reassurance of it. His painted gaze paid no attention to the light. "Lord above," she murmured, and wasn't entirely certain that those pensive brown eyes didn't touch hers in question before they returned to their study of a corner of the ceiling. "I seen some mightily strange things lately."

She had seen and dreamed, felt and sensed, until she didn't know when she opened her eyes if she opened them to daydream or nightmare. Jesus had known Ethan; she had known an angel; she didn't know, or dare to guess, what was right or wrong anymore.

She let her eyes roam the room. There was Jesus with His eyes that saw everything and nothing; there was the old and scratched armoire that lived in her earliest memories; there was the lamp that wasn't lit, and the window that showed the blue-green day. There was someone sitting by the side of the bed, nodding an uneasy doze. "Hey," she said; his eyelashes flickered. "Hey. What guardian are you?"

"Hmm?" He started awake. "Joss?"

"Which gates are you guardin'?"

He ran a hand across his face, humanly weary; he scratched at his beard, but understood her. "The gates between your sleep and waking. I'm Malin Leonard. Do you remember me?"

She studied his face. It was familiar and kind, and brought a flicker of memory: the smoky, warm breath of moors and heaths. "I think you was Jesus a while back."

He smiled. "An interesting thought, to one who believes in reincarnation as I do. You seem much better, Joss. How do you feel? Are you in any pain?"

She tested that, and finally allowed, "Not so's you'd notice." Her head ached, but it was tolerable. "Am I supposed to be?"

"Not if you aren't." He stood, stretching; she heard his shoulders pop. "Try to stay awake. I'll see if your lunch is ready."

She turned to watch him go, and a bolt of pain slammed into her head. "Oowww," she protested, reaching to explore, and groaned in the misery of her own touch. She struggled to sit up and wished she hadn't, but didn't dare try to lie down again for fear of making it worse. She rested her face in her hands and waited for the thudding ache to subside, fighting with her stomach; it felt as if it was lurching into her throat, and if just sitting up had caused such an intensity of pain, she didn't even want to think about vomiting. "That might be Jesus, Lord," she whispered shakily, "but this sure ain't my idea o' Heaven."

"Oh, my stars! Joss, what are you—"

Gentle arms offered support; when she didn't have to fight for balance, the pain ebbed. She clung to the angel—she knew it was the angel by the scent of lilacs (and had a confusing memory of sweat and corn and more kinds of heat than she could comprehend)—until her stomach stopped its roiling and the sick prickle of cold sweat relented. "Don't give me over to

252

this without lettin' me even know my sin," she whispered. "Please tell me what I did that you'd damn me."

"I haven't damned you." Lips brushed her face; she didn't know when she had ever felt such reassurance. "I'd never damn you, Joss."

She shivered, even though the room was hot and the body against her was warm. "I swear this is the mixedest-up I've ever been. I've got angels savin' me an' damnin' me by turns, an' Jesus in a sheepskin vest runnin' off with Ethan an' comin' back alone wearin' a uniform, an' me flittin' from hot to cold an' back again— an' if I try thinkin' on it I can't even half the time remember what I'm tryin' to think on. What scrambled my brains up so?"

"You hit your head. You've a bad concussion and a horrible wound, and Joss, you mustn't even think to try to get out of bed. You lost an awful amount of blood, and you're terribly weak. Give me your weight, now, and let me help you to lay down."

Once she was supported by the pillows the pain receded; three fuzzy angels merged to become one. "Ain't this how we started?" she asked; the words came seemingly independent of any conscious thought, and she wasn't sure what she'd meant once they were said.

But the angel smiled. "It surely is, my darling, and I'd be pleased not to need do it again."

"I wish I knew about anything," Joss whispered. "I keep thinkin' o' you as an angel, 'cause it seems that's what you are, but if that's so, you've surely been hoverin' over me for quite some time. An' it seems... it seems I keep runnin' to you, an' from you, an' stoppin' midway sometimes for not knowin' which way I'd ought to go." She closed her eyes, drawing a thin breath. "I liked that part about the ice, though," she murmured. "That was all clean an' sensible. Lord, my head hurts awful."

She heard the squeak of a cork being drawn from a bottle. "Open your mouth—" She grimaced at the taste of the laudanum, but she swallowed. "Rest, Joss." A gentle hand brushed her cheek. "I'll be here if you need me."

§

253

It felt like quivering near-panic; it felt like helplessness and desperation and prayer, the kind of prayer sent with promises attached: God, please if you do this for me I swear I'll never, or I'll always; it felt like washing her mother's body and putting silver dollars on her eyes and sewing up the shroud with tiny stitches blurred by a grief too barren to yield its tears. Names flickered at her in that fog of impotence, names with prayers attached: Doc, do something, please do something *(Aidan—)* Earlene, help her *(Aidan, stay with me—)* God, don't let her die, I swear I'll *(Aidan, stay with me! Please Aidan oh God no don't take her away from me—)*

"Aidan! Aidan please God oh God Doc do something please do something Aidan—"

"Joss! Joss, no, it's all right, I'm here—" She had been asleep, some part of her aware of Joss's restlessness in the bed beside her, but her utter weariness hadn't allowed her to respond to it until Joss almost screamed her name. "Joss, it's all right! I'm right here, darling. I'm here. Shhh—"

"I've got her." Doc's voice was low and calm in the darkness. "I've got her, Aidan." He held her, held her down, held her head; she fought him, but she was too weak to fight too much. "Light the lamp—Easy, Joss. Easy, girl. It's all right."

You talk to her like she's your damned horse. The thought flickered sourly through Aidan's consciousness, but she didn't say it; she found a match and lifted the chimney of the lamp. Light flared and she turned back the wick. "Joss, I'm here. Give me your hand—there," she soothed, her heart still thudding hard. "Tell me, darling. Tell me what's wrong."

It was Doc's hand at her chin, stabilizing her head; it was Doc's dark eyes she looked into. "She's goin' to have a hard time," she whispered. "Like Earlene with James that Ma said about. I seen it, Doc. Jesus, I was scared—let go o' me, you big son of a snake! I ain't goin' nowhere."

"You had a bad dream," Doc said, gradually easing his hold on her until he knew she was done struggling. "Aidan's fine,

Joss. The baby's fine. There's nothing to worry about." Joss had dreamed what she had dreamed, or seen what she'd seen; he'd had and heard dreams that had been more premonition than night-sweats. But Aidan's eyes were huge with apprehension; he spoke more for her benefit than for Joss's. "I've delivered hundreds of babies and only three breech births, and in all three cases, mother and child survived and thrived. She'll be fine, Joss."

"You take care o' her, Doc. If I ain't here—"

"You'll be here." He said it because he felt it; she was half-wild with the fear of what she'd dreamed, but she knew him, and knew Aidan; she was back in her mind, however much healing her body had yet to do. "I'll take care of her. I won't let anything happen to her."

She didn't say it, but he read it in her eyes: *You can't promise me that, and you know it.* "Give me some laudanum," she said. "My head hurts."

He let his fingertips trail from her cheek. "I'm sorry. You need to gut it out, Josie," he said quietly. "It's too soon since your last dose."

"No." Doc shoved the brown bottle into the inside pocket of his coat; Aidan was close enough—and angry enough—to slap him, and looked as if she was an inch away from it. "I know too well what the addiction's like, and I won't be a party to putting her through it. No, Aidan."

"Don't take your ire at me out on her! Give her the damned drug!"

Malin, leaning against the sink with one hand over his eyes, watched them through his fingers.

"It's you who's angry with me, not me with you. Aidan, two days ago you were begging me not to give it to her. Sit—sit down! Be quiet and listen to me." He sat at the table, letting her simmer until she knew he wasn't going to give in; she sat, glaring at him. "They took my leg at Manassas," he said gently. "I was a physician, so they left the bottle at my bedside, trusting me. And for two years I never passed a day without it. I arrived at Flora Washburn's one day—a hired hand had gotten his hand caught in a pulley and severed his thumb—and I bungled the job horribly because I was so drugged. A week later they took him to Leavenworth, but it was too late; he lost the hand to gangrene. Flora came back and beat me half-senseless with her crop, screaming that she'd wasted her money on a mindless puke with no more ballocks than a gelding. She chained me in a stall in her barn and left me there, shoving food at me once in a while, and for two weeks I envisioned more fantastic bugs and spiders than you can even dream. That's what laudanum can do. When the pain starts to drive her mad, I'll give it to her. Until it does—"

"You assume she's mad anyway," Aidan snapped. "How will you know the difference?"

"Ouch," Malin murmured, but neither Aidan nor Doc heard him.

"You're not listening to me. I'm trying to tell you—"

"You're playing God! You gave it to her when she didn't need it, and now you withhold it when she does—kindly explain your methods, Doctor, lest I believe her survival is something you still think you can control."

"You're a doctor's daughter, not a doctor," he snapped back, stung. "You're beyond your dinner-table learning now, Miss Blackstone, and I'll not explain myself to—"

"Stop this !" Malin roared. "Give me the God-damned bottle! Now, Robert, or I'll take it from you, I swear I will! Give it—give it—thank you!" He bounced off the doorframe on his way out, and fell down the porch steps and picked himself up and careered across the yard; Aidan and Doc heard the barn door crash open, and crash closed again.

"Now I control the drugs," the captain hissed, leaning on his hands on the table. "Aidan, go sit with her. You, Robert, take your ass to bed. I'm going to take a bath, and woe betide she or he who disturbs me for any reason saving the benefit of that patient! Get out of my sight, both of you. Get up in the morning and argue if you will over who's to do my laundry, but put this bullshit between you behind you!"

Aidan looked at Doc. He looked at her, and they both looked at the captain; he glowered back at them, and they went obediently to their rooms.

Joss was looking at her when she turned from hanging her dress in the armoire; to see the calm comprehension in her eyes was startling. "Joss?"

"The three o' you are better'n a God-damned circus," Joss grumbled. "Raise a tent an' print handbills. Sell tickets. Ain't I lucky to get all this amusement for free."

Aidan smiled. "You must be improving, if you're well enough to complain."

"You sure you want to spend your whole life patchin' me back together again? I done a good job this time, didn't I."

"You surely did. How do you feel?"

Joss touched an exploratory palm to the top of her head. "It ain't so bad," she allowed, "as long as I don't move around, or touch it much. Seems I took a God-awful lick. What happened?"

"Malin found you under a low tree on the north fork of the Newtonville trail. We assume you neglected to duck."

"The sweeper," Joss whispered. Memory flooded back: the screaming jolt of pain before she landed on her back in the trail, her head banging hard against packed earth; reaching to find the gut-wrenching feel of her scalp peeled back from her forehead; trying to put that precarious piece of herself back where it belonged. The ripe, sickening taste of blood, blood enough to blind her, a hot cascade of it over her face. Trying to stand, almost making it before her legs deserted her. The stupefying roar of pain as she struggled again to her hands and knees, panting there, waiting—and hearing (how long?) the close, hot snarl in the trees. Knowing she would die—but not by the dogs, not while she could help it; they could have her later, but she wouldn't let them eat her alive. A desperate hand scrubbed across her eyes, trying for enough vision to aim. She let instinct pull the trigger, hoping not to shoot the horse, her only hope, and heard the hollow click of the hammer falling on the sixth, empty cylinder. She remembered a sharp hiss and a thump before Charley took down the last of the dogs. Dimly, she recalled a dark face, a gentle hand, a voice as deep and soft as the warm night rain: *pale woman, bolder than night, shaman knowing sings deep in your blood.*

And then nothing. Nothing but the picture of Jesus and Ethan, and a jumble of disconnected dreams, and the lingering, unfocused questions they had raised. "Flora," she said softly. "I dreamed about her, Aidan, givin' me hell like always, but it was— odd. Real odd. Do we hear anything from her?"

Aidan sat on the edge of the bed, and Joss knew before she spoke. "Flora died two days ago," Aidan said gently. "I'm sorry, Joss. Doc was with her. He said she went peacefully."

Joss swallowed hard, blinking back unexpected tears. "Hard to imagine Flora goin' peaceful," she murmured. "God rest her. She had a rough mouth an' a rough life—an' a heart o' gold." She blew a soft sigh. "How's Zeke?"

"Taking it hard, Doc says. It seems Flora was more of a mother to him than his own mother ever was."

"Pamela Clark's a brood sow, not a mother. I knew they'd get along, him an' Flora. He's got grit, an' she demanded that. God knows she had enough of it herself for three men." She huffed another sigh. "I don't mean to be disrespectful, only practical, but that's a hard blow for us. Flora respectin' us was like money in the bank. It was nice knowin' it was there."

"We'll manage. My father won't let us starve."

"He can take his charity to hell with him. We'd' ve had to earn anything we ever got from Flora, an' that I'd've taken." She touched her head again, gently, and assessed the headache; it was a low, thumping irritant. "You tell ol' soldier blue out there to go to hell if he harps on you for goin' out an' gettin' my tobacco pouch. The way he was bangin' around an' ain't anymore, he'd ought to have all his manly parts under water by now. I'd sure enjoy a smoke, Cousin, if you'd not mind me havin' one."

Aidan smiled. "I suppose you want a drink of whiskey, too."

Joss grinned. "Well, since you mention it..."

Aidan rested against the wall at the head of the bed, her

ankles crossed, the saucer that served as Joss's ashtray balanced on one thigh. "It's good to have you back, Joss. I was so lonely without you."

Joss tasted her whiskey; Aidan had propped another pillow under her so that she could manage the glass on her own. "It does seem I've been gone somewhere. I had some awful strange dreams, Aidan. Leastwise, I suppose they was dreams. Don't know what else to call 'em—except one! Do I remember this right? Don't we got water now, to the house an' runnin' into the well, or did I dream that too?"

"No dream. You put it in a month ago. Why?"

"I thought! I saw it—I saw it clear as doin' it, an' the water part already done. Ice, Aidan! I can make ice all winter long. The water's there an' the cold comes like it or not. When Levi comes back we'll build a ice house, up in the elms behind the house, for shade in the summer."

"What a wonderful—oh, Joss! But you need sawdust to pack it in. Where will you—"

"Straw. I was goin' to plant the wheat anyway. Sell the wheat to Mister Nissen, save the straw for the ice. It'll work, Aidan. I know it will. I saw it plain as day—not Tucker Day, neither. I don't expect people've forgot what it feels like to have fresh meat handy, or ice in their lemonade. I'm goin' to make ice, Aidan, an' if he ain't got a better offer by then, I'll hire Zeke Clark to drive the wagon come summer."

"Ottis won't like Zeke having anything to do with us."

"Fuck Ottis. Zeke can do whatever the hell he pleases."

"Lord! How hard must you be hit to knock the vulgarity out of you?" Helplessly, Aidan laughed, holding onto the ashtray. "It's a wonderful idea, Joss—but how are you so sure Levi will come back?"

Joss shrugged. "I seen him. If he don't—well, I'll hire Zeke all the much sooner."

I seen him. Aidan traced a hand over the bulge at her belly. "Do you believe everything you saw in your dreams?" she asked quietly.

Joss tasted her drink. "I saw the ice, an' Flora" —she flushed;

259

Aidan didn't know why— "an' some other stuff that seemed awful real. I suppose there's some I don't remember, an' maybe for the best. I expect if I remember it, I got to give it some weight."

Aidan rubbed a flake of ash into her thigh. "Do you remember what you dreamed tonight?"

Out in the log part of the house, the clock struck; Joss listened. "Two o'clock. We're up awful late, ain't we?" She didn't look at Aidan; Aidan knew she was avoiding the question.

"Joss, please tell me. I'm terribly frightened."

Joss sighed. "James Jackson came breech. Ma delivered him, an' it was hard for Earlene an' caused her a God-awful lot o' pain, but there's James an' there's Earlene, just down the road. I said I saw it bein' hard," Joss said gently. "I never said I saw you dyin', honey; only me bein' afraid you might. I scare awful easy. I wish you'd just forget all o' that. I ain't in my right mind anyway, with my poor of brains all swole up an' agitated."

"You're shaman when it suits you," Aidan muttered. "You swear by your visions one moment and discount them the next."

"I swear by the ice vision 'cause it makes good sense with Levi or without him. Aidan, you can't trust that that's how it's goin' to be just 'cause I dreamed it. I heard that story too many times for it not to be a concern to me with you comin' onto your time." She found Aidan's hand with hers. "I dreamed about you next summer—or some summer. I saw you not with child, an' healthy. It's goin' to be all right, Aidan. You an' me both, an' the baby too." She took the last sip of her whiskey and ground out her cigarette. "I'm awful tired," she whispered. "Do you think you might just lay here with me for a while? Don't worry about our soldier boy. He'll wake up when his bath turns cold enough, an' mayhap he needs his time alone."

Aidan put the saucer on the nightstand; she bent to touch a kiss to Joss's lips. "I love you," she said softly.

Joss rested her hand against Aidan's hip. "It's good to have back some o' my grip on the truth o' things," she murmured, "but I still think you're an angel."

September, 1876

And Ruth said unto Naomi, Entreat me not to leave thee, or to return from following after thee: for whither thou goest, I will go; and where thou lodgest, I will lodge: thy people shall be my people, and thy God my God:

Where thou diest, will I die, and there will I be buried: the Lord do so to me, and more also, if aught but death part me and thee.

Ruth 1:16-17

CHAPTER TWENTY-ONE

Aidan had tried to keep her in bed for a few more days, but Joss threatened to get up and about on her own if she couldn't have any help with it, and Aidan relented; a month after her accident she was spending most of her days out on the porch, watching the progress of the beans and wheat Marcus and the Jackson boys had planted, carving axe handles, splitting down brown ash to make the long-overdue egg basket, obediently drinking the tea Aidan made from roasted cracked corn even though she didn't much care for it. When she was sitting, she felt well enough to work, but she never knew when she stood if she'd have her balance or not, so she contented herself with puttering at the things she'd spent the summer not having time enough to do.

She was filling in the belly of the egg basket one warm late afternoon, patiently weaving long strands of ash back and forth;

she liked making the framework and getting the ribs in place, but once that was done the rest of the job was tedious, and she was glad for the diversion when Doc rode into the yard. "Hey, Doc. Tell me you brought me some tobacco."

He tossed her a bag; she muffed the catch and picked it up from the porch floor. "Suppose I'll get my coordination back one o' these weeks," she grumbled. "Hope so, anyway."

"It'll come." He left the reins dragging so his mare could find the trough and sat in the other rocker, reaching to pick up the axe handle that had been her morning's work. "For someone who disclaims talent with a blade, you surely make a nice handle. How many have you made now? Enough to spare one?"

"Take that one. I've got eight done an' ash enough for more an' more of 'em."

"Thank you. I broke my last one the other day. Where's Aidan?"

"Havin' a nap. I had to swear on the Bible that I'd keep out o' trouble for her to lay down for a bit. She don't say so, but she's feelin' peaked." She fished another weaver from the pail at her feet and ran it between her fingers, squeegeeing water from its glossy surface. "Wish I'd never had that dream, or at least not had it so loud. She ain't been but nervous ever since."

"She'd be nervous about something else if it hadn't been that."

"Jesus! I wish you two'd quit snipin' at one another!" Joss flared. "Or else let me in on why you're doin' it! She ain't had a warm word for you since I've been awake, an' you sneakin' in the back door o' meanness with your speakin' o' her—"

"Joss, for heaven's sake! I merely meant that most first-time mothers are nervous in the last month. I wasn't—"

"An' the both o' you always got a explanation for your hard words. What the hell happened between you? She won't tell me."

Doc eyed her for a tense moment; finally he slumped back in his chair with a sigh. "I said something she rightly took exception to," he said quietly, his fingertips rubbing at his forehead. "I don't blame her for being angry with me. I won't blame her if she never forgives me. I'm ashamed of it, and hurt at losing her affection, and those things aren't excuse enough for my roughness with her, but they're all the excuse I have."

"Well, best you get over your roughness before next month. Earlene's due, too, an' might not be able to tend to her an' no matter what I dreamed. I always got sent off when Ma was birthin', an' don't know no more about it except what the cow an' sows do."

"It's all pretty much the same," Doc smiled tiredly, and for a moment he sat rocking, his hand rubbing a slow comfort at the junction between his leg and his prosthesis. "Perhaps the only way she'll forgive me," he said at last, "is if you can."

She rocked, and wove, and listened to his halting admission of the words he had spoken that had turned Aidan's heart against him. When he was done she opened the new bag of tobacco he had brought and rolled a cigarette; she lit it and smoked, looking out over her fields. The new crops were coming fresh and green as spring. "Mayhap it's easier for me to understand," she said at last, slowly, "knowin' Ethan as I did, an' my own wide streak o' nonsense, but I can't say it don't pain me, Doc, to know you questioned me bein' worth savin'."

"That's not what I meant by it. I don't know how to explain what I meant, but all I felt for you was love, Joss—and fear. I know your strength of character—and your gentleness, no matter how Aidan thinks I don't trust that in you—and I was terrified of you losing that. Of becoming the worst side of yourself. Neither you nor I can deny there's a darkness in you."

"Hell, Doc, there's darkness in all of us. Mine just stands out in close quarters." She held her basket at arm's-length, squinting at it. "That look even to you?"

"It's beautiful. You're as good at it as your mother was."

"Good teachin'." She put the basket beside her chair and drew on her cigarette. "I ain't mad at you," she said quietly. "Don't know if that'll help Aidan none, but I ain't mad at you."

"She's a good wife to you, Joss. She's reacting from that quarter."

"No. Yes, she's reactin' from somewhere like that, but sh—ain't a wife to me." She dunked her smoke in the pail of water and tossed the butt over the porch rail. "I don't know the word for what she is to me, but wife ain't it. That'd make me a husband, an' I ain't wearin' that name."

"I suppose not." He scratched the backs of his fingers against a day's growth of beard. "I hate to wake her if she's resting, but I have news that's for both of you, and sure to be welcome."

"Time she was gettin' up anyway. Just go in an' make up the fire; she'll think it's me an' come runnin' to make sure I ain't turnin' a damn lick o' anythin' but what I can do in this chair."

Doc rattled stove lids and Aidan came out yawning. "Oh. It's you," she grumbled.

"Joss asked me what was wrong between us." He opened the dampers so that the sticks of cedar he had put on the coals might catch. "I told her."

"Remarkably poor judgment, I'd say."

"At least she allowed me to explain what was in my heart, and accepted that. Be that as it may, please do what you need to and come out to the porch. I've news you both want to hear."

"Do you want tea?"

"If it's no trouble." He went back to the porch and leaned against a post, shaking his head slowly.

"I'll talk to her," Joss said gently. "Just remember how it takes time to turn an idea around in your head once it gets set there." Wryly, she smiled. "That's how all this trouble started, by me not bein' able to unthink somethin' soon enough to keep me from bein' all rash about it. Doubt's a bad weed, Doc. That seed gets planted, the damn thing'll grow anywhere."

"True enough."

"I wonder if it ain't like pokeweed. The more you try an' bust it up, the more it grows off'n its own parts. An' if you try pullin' it, it's got a taproot worse'n alfalfa."

Aidan handed teacups out the window over the sink; Doc held hers while she lowered her bulk to the rocker. She was carrying the baby high and forward, and a lot of it—or maybe, he mused, just looked like a lot of baby because she was so tiny. "How are you feeling?" he asked.

"Fat, awkward and ugly. Mostly ugly."

"Earlene says the same, and adds that hers seems to be trying to kick his way out—and with hobnailed boots."

"Both parties were wearing skates when she was conceived; it feels as if she got them, too. How is Earlene?"

"Just waiting. She's an old hand at this, six births later. Are you having any discomfort?"

"Less than yesterday, actually. I think she turned over and got her foot out of my lungs."

"And your bowels?"

"Fine. You said you had news?"

Doc tasted his tea and chose not to mention that he preferred it with sugar; he knew Aidan knew that. "Lemuel Carpenter read Flora's will today."

"An' now Daniel's a rich man and good-bye, Washburn Station," Joss said dryly.

"Yes he is—well over a hundred thousand dollars—and no doubt as good as gone. He was talking law school on his way out of Lem's office. But she left Nat Day the pecan orchard."

That surprised a laugh from Joss. "God love her! He earned them damn trees, Nat did, the way she abused his poor self over 'em last fall! Oh, that's just grand."

"It gets grander. She left Zeke Clark the farm proper—"

"No!"

"—with the provision that Ottis may never live there saving his complete infirmity."

"Hooray, Flora," Aidan murmured.

"Lord, that's wonderful for Zeke! I'll have to find another driver now, I guess! Oh, but ain't that goin' to stick an' fester in Ott's craw, his son a rich man an' him barred from takin' of it."

"There were a number of things in that will that showed a sharp cross between her sense of humor and her work ethic. If Nat or Zeke choose to sell within ten years, they must sell back to her estate at a fixed price, which is pitifully low. They'll have

266

to earn their winnings. But she knew a winning horse when she saw one. Nat, Zeke..." He smiled. "And you."

Both women stared at him. "Huh?" Joss finally ventured, cautiously.

"She left you the branch section, Joss. All hundred and sixty acres—"

"Good Lord!"

"—free and clear. Sell it next week if you want to, for whatever you can get for it from whomever you can get it, but until you do, you're one of the larger landowners in the Station, and that, my dear, is as good as money in the bank. Personally, I'd advise you to hold onto it. It needs clearing, but we can rally up a crew—"

"No," she whispered. "No. I ain't ever clearin' that land. If you're true an' it's really mine, it ain't ever goin' to get cleared while I live. Kansas got lots of fields, but she ain't got many forests. If I got me one, I aim to keep it."

"Then you have yourself a forest. I heard the will read." He scratched his back against the post. "Aidan," he said, grinning in spite of their difficulties. "While you weren't directly mentioned, she left your little skater the very tidy sum of ten thousand dollars in trust—"

Aidan gasped.

"—to assure the receipt of any higher education the child chooses. Lem said he'd come over this week to explain the provisions of the trust to you."

"And—oh, my," Aidan said faintly; her teacup jittered against its saucer. "And her family didn't contest this?"

Doc shook his head. "There's hardly a family in the Station untouched by her generosity. She spread her wealth around this town like Joss spreads butter on hot bread."

Aidan leaned her head against the back of the rocker, swallowing hard, her eyes closed. "Oh, Lord. Thank you, Flora," she whispered. "Thank you, you dear, rebellious old woman."

However little sense it made on the surface, by virtue of being the bearer of such wondrous news, Doc's stock went up with Aidan. She invited him for supper as if she might truly enjoy his company, and indulged in a few sips of the brandy he had brought to celebrate; by the time the dishes were done they had even managed to laugh together. He risked offering her a hug on the porch when he said good-night, and she hesitated only a moment before accepting it. "I'll stop by Jackson's on the way home and tell Gid to bring a horse over tomorrow," he said. "Even if Earlene can't serve as midwife, Joss can turn him out when it's time, and the boys will know to find me. Joss won't want to leave you—and she shouldn't be riding anyway, until her balance returns."

"Thank you, Doc." And he waited, for it seemed to him that there was more she might say, but finally she turned. "Good-night," she said quietly. "It was a pleasant evening."

Twenty-two

"Dead, but not dust, Flora," Joss murmured at the pile of lath stacked beside the house a week later, and found the box of itty-bitty nails Flora had donated with the strips of wood so that the board portion of the house might be battened before the bad weather. "I've got enough axe handles for two or three years, an' if I don't get this done you'll be hauntin' me."

It was easy work, as Flora had said it would be; the hardest part was that her eye-to-hand coordination was still variable, but the small nails didn't need strong driving, so she didn't have to swear too terribly when she missed a nail and hammered her thumb instead.

She worked a few hours before Aidan begged her to stop. "It sounds like a woodpecker on the outhouse door and me trapped inside. Please, if you need to be busy, mightn't you make me a garden basket? Something quiet while I take a rest. I feel a little colicky. Don't let me sleep past three. I've a chicken soaking for upper and must get it into the oven."

So she figured out a basket and carved a handle, and put it in the water tank of the stove to soak so she could bend it to shape, and got out her ash strips and pail, but when she got to the point of needing to insert the handle it was still too stiff to bend, and that brought her to a halt.

She paced, restless.

She went out to the pasture to talk to the horses: her own Charley and Fritz, and the jet-black Goblin, James Jackson's handsome gelding. She wasn't entirely pleased that it was James's horse that had come, but it was the horse the Jacksons had felt they could spare, and she appreciated the signal more than she mistrusted the possibility of the omen. She noticed a fraying strap on his halter and took it off to repair it, and then had hell to pay catching him so she could put it back on, and that occupied her for an hour.

At three, she debated waking Aidan and decided against it; she readied the chicken and put it into the oven, and scrubbed potatoes to bake.

She wandered back outside, saw the neat stack of oak flooring scraps, and remembered her ice molds; she assembled sawhorses and handsaw, block plane and folding rule, and measured the tray in the icebox. By the third try she had it figured out and was in production.

She heard Aidan stirring in the house and waited to be scolded for letting her sleep. She was less concerned about the scolding than she was about how erratic Aidan's sleep had become; she rarely got more than a few hours at a time before the little skater prodded her awake. Joss smiled a little. "That's just preparin' for after the birth," she murmured, marking off a board for cutting, "an' the babe wantin' feedin' all hours o' the night an' day."

"Joss—"

"Hi. Out on the porch."

"Joss, something's—oh, good Lord! What—? Joss! Joss, please, something's wrong—"

She dropped her saw, bounced off the sawhorse, staggered

through the kitchen door. "What—oh, Lord God, Aidan, your water's broke. Let me—" She stepped into the mess and her feet went out from under her; she landed hard on her back, banging her head against the floor. "Ow! Shit, ain't that just what I need!"

"Oh, Joss! Are you—let me—"

"Don't lift at me, woman; Christ A'mighty!" She struggled to her feet. "I'm all right. Oh, shit. What do I—oh, God damn, I ain't—God damned ears, quit ringin'!" She shook her head; it didn't help, but she managed to focus on Aidan. "Did you have the show? That little bit o' blood Doc said about?"

"Yes." She held her belly with her hands, trying to support it; Doc could give all the instruction he wanted, but he couldn't possibly have prepared her for what had happened in her body in the last fifteen minutes of the last two unusual hours. "I felt—crampy, like diarrhea, but with nothing—oh, what an awful mess I've made!"

"Don't worry about the mess. Just move careful away from it. What now? Lord, Doc give me a list, I put it somewhere—" She riffed through the Baptist Hymnal three times before she found it. "Here." Her heart was hammering in her chest. "Basins, binder, napkins, needles an' thread, safety pins, olive oil—damn! Effie never got that for me, the old bitch—old linen, all this stuff, I got all this stuff—hell, I've got to turn out Goblin an' have Gid go for Doc—"

"We've got time," Aidan soothed, calm by no means but calmer than Joss seemed to be. "He said from the time my water broke until the baby came might be as much as thirty-six hours. Maybe even more. It doesn't hurt yet, Joss. Let's get the bed ready."

"Right. Get the bed—damn! You're early by two weeks, Aidan, I ain't ready—"

"I don't think our readiness is of an issue here, my love. The baby is, and the bed must be. Let's go."

In the bedroom, trying to prepare things, her feet felt mired in molasses, but in the kitchen, zooming across the waxed oaken floor to get the things she or Doc or Earlene might need, she

271

twice hit the slick, wet patch of liquor amnii and ended up on her ass on the floor, trying not to hit her head, swearing when she did. She managed to stagger out to the paddock; Goblin laughed at her from the other end of it, and finally she cornered him and grabbed his newly-repaired halter in both hands and forced him to the gate. "Go home!" she screamed. "Go home, you worthless fucking hammerheaded black cayuse! Git! Go see James! Go! Go!"

Goblin danced and rolled his eyes and went, glad enough to be away from her.

"Noooo—! Not to town, you God-damned moron! Home, Goblin! Home! Oh, you ignorant sack o' soap—you turn a hoof in this yard again in your life an' I'll render you into lard an' get a dog just to feed your fucking bones to, you useless bag o' shit—"

Her heels hit the wet kitchen floor and she went down for the fourth time. "Oh, God," she moaned. "She's got to live through it. I ain't goin' to."

She felt as if she were back in that ethereal, odd-lit slant of space and time she had lived in for the week after her accident; she sought the picture of Jesus as Aidan panted and sweated and stifled her screams; that picture was all that had let her know the difference between nightmares and reality then, and as long as she could find it now, she knew this nightmare was reality. Doc arrived, grinning over where he had found James's horse until he realized how far progressed his patient was into her business, and how precarious a business it was going to be.

He only had to look at Joss for her to understand. She shook her head, a silent plea: don't say it aloud. Don't let her hear the word. Just let her do the work without fearing it.

It felt like quivering near-panic; it felt like helplessness and desperation and prayer, the kind of prayer sent with promises attached: God, please if you do this for me I swear I'll never, or I'll always—"

"Save the baby," Aidan panted. "Doc, save the baby. Let me go—"

He looked at Joss.

"She's all I've got," she whispered, Aidan between her legs, cradled against her belly; her hands felt broken and swollen. She could see tiny legs and the belly and cord, but the baby's head and arms were stubbornly unborn. "Jesus God, Doc, she's all I've got."

"Close your eyes," he said tightly. "I've got to help her, and you don't want to see it."

"Aidan."

Dimly, Joss heard him.

"Joss—"

She dragged her head up from Aidan's sweat-cold hair.

"She didn't cry, but she's breathing—she's fine," he said gently. "She's fine, Joss. All her fingers and toes and bald as an egg. She'll be as blonde and beautiful as her mama."

She shuddered against the limpness in her arms; Aidan hadn't moved since the afterbirth had come. "What price?" Her voice was thick in her throat. "At what price, Doc?"

He smiled. "Josie, she's but asleep. Lord, child, she's worked harder in the last twenty hours than you work in a month. She's all right, Joss. It's just your turn to take care of her. She'll need a long lying-in." He laid the tiny flannel-wrapped bundle on Aidan's belly. "Aidan, you have a daughter," he said softly.

Aidan's hand sought the baby, tracing over flannel until her fingers found the wrinkled little face. "A girl?" Her voice was barely a breath.

"A bit more than seven pounds of her, I'd say, almost twenty inches long, and perfect in every respect."

"Naomi," she whispered. "Naomi Ruth."

On the wall, Jesus and Ethan Bodett, flannel-shirted, sheepskin-vested, arms slung companionably around each other in a golden slice of late September sun, grinned out at them, beaming their approval.

273

Bella Books, Inc.

Women. Books. Even Better Together.

P.O. Box 10543
Tallahassee, FL 32302

Phone: 800-729-4992
www.bellabooks.com